Margaret Oliphant

The Makers of Florence

Dante, Giotto, Savonarola, and their city

Margaret Oliphant

The Makers of Florence
Dante, Giotto, Savonarola, and their city

ISBN/EAN: 9783337314958

Printed in Europe, USA, Canada, Australia, Japan

Cover: Foto ©Andreas Hilbeck / pixelio.de

More available books at **www.hansebooks.com**

THE MAKERS OF FLORENCE

DANTE, GIOTTO, SAVONAROLA

AND THEIR CITY

By MRS. OLIPHANT

Author of "THE MAKERS OF VENICE," "ROYAL
EDINBURGH," "ST. FRANCIS OF ASSISI," "THE
LIFE OF EDWARD IRVING," etc., etc. ❧ ❧ ❧

WITH ILLUSTRATIONS

" Aggi pietade de' miei gravi errosi
Pero ch' io sono debile ed infermo
Ed ho perduti tutti i miei vigosi."

A. L. BURT COMPANY, ❧ ❧ ❧ ❧ ❧
❧ ❧ ❧ ❧ PUBLISHERS, NEW YORK

INTRODUCTION.

THE history of Florence has been often written, and in many ways. In the life-like annals of the old chroniclers, who set down with vigorous simplicity, what they themselves did and heard and saw; and in the more philosophical narratives, compilations, and collections, made with elaborate care and judgment, which make the study of Italian history more grateful than most researches of the kind; the tale of her greatness and of her weakness has been told over and over again, from each man's different point of view. Some have occupied themselves with the art story of the city—an aspect of her life which is full of the deepest interest; others have devoted themselves to the varied strifes which have rent her in pieces—chronicling the casting out and taking back of her successive exiles, and her own often blind and foolish struggle against supposed tyrannical attempts, and confused misapprehension of her true safety and interest. Others, again, have treated Florence as but one actor in the great drama of Italian history. There is enough material for all; and even the fragmentary efforts contained in this volume—"short swallow flights" of biographical essay—do not, I hope, require apology, so rich is the ground in all directions, so tempting to the writer, so full of pleasant illustration of the life and meaning of the great past. I do not promise the reader that he will find any consecutive history of Florence in the following pages; for new histories are scarcely needed, nor is the present writer qualified to undertake such a task. The biographical chapters which follow, however, cannot but touch upon and indicate a certain portion of the greater story ; and involuntarily I have been obliged to trace the progress, to some extent, of the struggle which was always going on, surging and storming in the public palazzo and narrow streets around, and in the wider, but more passive country which was *fuori,* outside, the significant word employed to indicate everything that was not Florence—all Europe, and all that the world contained of good and lovely, being but a desert to those unhappy ones who were on the wrong side of the walls ; and at the same time to show how, in the midst of this struggle, in every interval, and even through the conflict of arms, the din of internal fighting over a fierce barricade, or the wild clamor with which one party after another was driven *fuori*—there still went on, in strange serenity, another life in the very heart of the warlike city. How the chippings of the mason's chisel, and the finer tools of the wood-carver, and the noiseless craft of brush and pigment, could keep going on through all the din, is as curious a problem of Florentine life as any the imagination can grasp. Yet they did so. One of the most costly, splendid, and elaborate structures in the world—at that time the most elaborate and costly —got itself built and garnished while still the tocsins of immemorial strife were sounding all about, the fierce old bell pealing out its periodical summons from the airy heights of the Palazzo Vecchio, and armed men, fierce and furious, swarming about the streets. Giotto, tranquil and silent in the heart of Florence, was working out the plans for his campanile with pencil and compasses, while Dante, in all the bitter wrath of exile, roamed to and fro outside, cailing upon heaven and earth to avenge his wrongs, and appealing alike to emperors and *condottieri* to fall upon Florence and open the gates to him—most wonderful and instructive contrast. And Fra Angelico, on his knees in his cell, was painting those heavenly angels who got him his name, while the struggle had begun with the Medici, which made them, after much resistance, masters of the city. Did those painters, those builders, those busy craftsmen, powdered with the marble dust of the rising Duomo, take no notice of the fighting? or did not, rather, the strokes of the chisel fall fast and furious in the early morning to let the bold mason off, his day's bread earned, to cut off some other craftsmen's living in the afternoon, when " the old cow," the big hoarse *Vacca* of the city bell, lowed out her summons? In this strange way the peaceful work and the strife went on side by side, all the convulsions of the city offering little or no hindrance to the adornment of the city in which the antagonists were equally interested ; nor, more strangely still, to the growing wealth of Florence, where trade flourished and bankers multiplied, notwithstanding that every other year there was a revolution. We do not pretend to explain how this could be ; but that it was so is very apparent. The sight of Florence as she still is, is proof enough of the prosperity which accompanied her struggles ; for none of all those glorious churches and decorations with which she is adorned like a bride, and few of the pictures that fill her galleries, have come into being during the years of deadly quiet in which she has languished under native and foreign masters, fighting no longer. Did not Michael Angelo, with whom her glory came to a culmination, build rough walls of defense, trenches, and battlements, with the same masterful hand which carved the lovely anguish of the Dawn and the half-accomplished passion of the Day in San Lorenzo? And after that last conjunction of War and Peace, the apotheosis of the great art-workman, who wrought so fiercely at his forlorn hope on the slope of San Miniato, and made the record of his despair so glorious in the sacristy sacred to the Medici, what has Florence done more in art? Ben-

venuto Cellini, with the Pegasus of his genius put in toy
harness and yoked to toy chariots of gold and silver; and
a school of painters who died slowly out after the great
Buonarotti ; but except effete dukes and Renaissance Cu-
pids entangled in chains of roses, and a people without
life and hope—nothing more.

We do not pretend, however, to follow out, even by
secondary means, all the lines of the story which is concentrated into epic force and distinctness by the limited
space in which it is enacted. But the great figure of the
poet which stands near the beginning of the most articu-
late and important period of Florentine history, and the
equally remarkable preacher, who holds a similar position
toward its end, gives a certain historical and epical form
to the narrative ; and it is scarcely possible to indicate
them distinctly without embracing much of the general
tenor of the larger tale. In both lives the central interest
is in the struggle which we find going on violently in
Dante's time, and which, greatly changed, yet the same,
reaches a kind of climax in Savonarola's—a struggle
which kept on raging with more or less force through the
two intervening centuries, never wholly extinguished,
changing in form, but scarcely in character, from one
generation to another. It is not within our range to
search into the very beginnings of the city for the beginning of the quarrel. It is enough to find it in full force,
in absolute height of unreason, in the end of the thirteenth
century; a quarrel which we have not even the satisfaction
of being able to regard as a struggle between good and
evil, the natural conflict of opposing principles. There
is no doubt a certain formal meaning attached by the historian to the titles Guelf and Ghibelline, words which
have wearied the mind of the world ever since, as they
distracted it in the day of their power; and we suppose
there can be no doubt that the feudal party, the nobles

who would fain have held rich Florence in bondage, maintained a vague allegiance to the alien ruler, the German
emperor, under the shield of whose distant power they
might oppress and overrun their neighbors ; and that the
burghers, who had gradually pushed off their yoke and
risen into freedom of trade and prosperity, felt themselves
better able to hold their own with the support and patronage of the great popes, who were the arbitrators and
judges of Christendom, than in their isolated position as
an independent city. Thus a vague general meaning was
in the party names which rent Florence asunder while
yet it was the straightest of walled cities within its *cerchia
antica ;* but hundreds suffered for their cause on both
sides, to whom that cause meant nothing more than a dear
and cherished hostility against their neighbors over the
way—a true civic grudge, deep and bitter with constant
encounter, and a hundred daily pricks of insult or injury ;
and to the majority of the factions, which apparently bore
exile and misery for their political creed, that creed represented only the well-known but never exhausted principle
that every Bianco had a right to hate every Nero—to kill
or banish him, and rob his house or burn the goods he
left behind. We cannot even make sure that the reign of
the Guelf faction, though under its sway Florence began
to put on her glorious apparel and to make herself notable
and renowned over all the earth, was any better than that
of the Ghibellines, or bore any rich fruit of national happiness and prosperity which might not have been attained
under their rivals ; for the balance of good sways throughout the story like Fortune herself, sometimes remaining
with one party, sometimes with the other, and having
little or nothing to say to the continuance of the perennial
struggle which raged between one citizen and another, one
family and another, one side of a street against the dwell-
ers opposite, without rhyme or reason, or thought of any

loftier meaning. It is difficult to say which side, when in power, ruled best. Both sides had a certain dogged regard for the city, and desire to enrich and adorn and make her great; but neither would seem to have had that moral pre-eminence which satisfies the looker-on, or warrants him in giving his adherence to one of two contending parties. Naturally the wish of the reader who does not pretend to know much about it would be to take Dante's side in a question with which the poet was so greatly involved; but even that strong inducement to partisanship fails us, and we find it impossible to be altogether on Dante's side —the other, in its time of ascendency, being more patriotic, more truly Florentine than Dante, as he himself was intensely patriotic and Florentine when in power. Thus the struggle surges on through centuries, always confused, gloomy and hopeless in its destitution of any great principle or leading idea; a warfare taken up by one family after another, the Donati against the Cerchi, the Medici against the Albizzi; a vague, endless, bitter personal quarrel, which having no real or worthy motive in its beginning, might have gone on, as long as mean motives and personal hostilities lasted, to the end of time.

The struggle changed, however, when it entered into the wise heads of those Medici who were the last on the field, and who overcame all resistance in the end, to frame a determined scheme of conquest, and apply themselves to the setting up of a hereditary despotism in the free and turbulent city. Such a design had been imputed before to almost every party leader, but never before had Florence met with any but a momentary master, or felt herself cowed, and unable by a sudden rising to snatch the reins out of the usurper's hands. When, however, Cosimo had founded, and Lorenzo confirmed, this complete though unacknowledged supremacy, there arose to dignify the struggle the moral principle which all this time it had wanted. When the question became one between Florence and the Medici, between a nascent tyranny and the free institutions of the city, the principal of resistance changed from the mere enmity of faction into the old zeal of jealous patriotism, which is the highest of classic virtues. Curiously enough it was no classic Brutus, no citizen Rienzi, no indignant and outraged Florentine, who took the leader's part in this renewed and nobler warfare, but a monk, a stranger, a man of another city, Girolamo Savonarola, of the preachers, whose championship added at once another element to the struggle, and made it one, not only of civic freedom and law against tyranny and absolute personal rule, but also of Christianity against paganism, of moral purity against vice. We would fain have done more justice than space has permitted to what we may be permitted to call the devil's side in the quarrel as thus developed ; for the wise Cosimo, the brilliant and magnificent Lorenzo, and such a strange and mysterious genius as that of Machiavelli, are well worthy of consideration. But the limits of time and space have balked intention so far as these eminent personages are concerned. Lorenzo de' Medici has had full justice in the world of letters ; his qualities are such as to make him a favorite figure with all to whom love of the arts, a magnificent disposition, a heart not without noble and generous impulses, and a touch of genius, are greater recommendations than such less brilliant qualities as truth, mercy, and patriotism. And in the whole course of Florentine story there is perhaps no individual more intellectually interesting than Machiavelli, the clearest and coolest of observers, curious, unimpassioned spectator of the conflicts and abuses around him, perhaps not even ironical at all in his profound seriousness, yet conscious of the grave and deep irony involved, and as capable of discriminating between good and evil as he was

of tracing out with tremendous impartiality the best way
to be politically wicked. The workings of such a mind
are so full of interest that it is diffiult, however, to realize
how small an immediate share this great intelligence had
in the guidance of his age; smaller than that of many a
much inferior mind, less important for the moment than
such a bold citizen, for example, as Piero Capponi—brave
Capon crowing lustily over all the shrill trumpeting of the
Gallic cocks, as Machiavelli himself said. This side of the
subject, however, we must leave with regret, under pres-
sure of necessity; the best that we can hope to do, is to
indicate, in a fragmentary way, to the reader who loves
Florence how the great city fought her special battle,
sowing the wind and reaping the whirlwind, wearing her
soul out by factious struggles, yet at last making one great
stand for life and freedom, and losing the cast, but not
without honor. Long and deep has been her slumber,
brooding over the recollection of her greatness, or bitterly
expounding her own beauty for the advantage of the
stranger. Now let us hope a greater career is again before
Florence—a life renewed and strengthened by steadfast law
and solid freedom.

CONTENTS.

THE POET:—DANTE.

xii   *CONTENTS.*

LIST OF ILLUSTRATIONS.

THE MAKERS OF FLORENCE

THE POET :---DANTE.

CHAPTER I.

HIS YOUTH.

IT IS a peculiarity of the great cities of Italy, that none of them are capitals in the ordinary sense of the word—types and representatives of the country, such as Paris is of France, or London of England. The great centers of old Italian life, Rome and Venice and Florence, are all as distinct as individuals, incapable on the spur of the moment —as has been demonstrated by recent experience—of being trimmed into any breadth of nationality, or made to represent more than themselves—the one strongly-marked and individual phase of character which their municipal separateness and independent history have impressed upon them. The action of time may fit Rome—once the mistress, and still accustomed to feel herself in one sense the capital, of the world—for becoming the capital of Italy; but it is scarcely possible to conceive a combination of circumstances which could have detached Florence from her grandiose and austere personality and made of her a national center. So long as her dark palaces cut their stern outline against the sky, and her warlike tower lifts itself high over the housetops, and the hills stand round her in embattled lines, must the great city remain herself

—the city of Dante and Michael Angelo, sternest of poets
and of painters—a grave, serious, almost solemn presence,
full of passion too profound and thought too vast to be
capable of light utterance, amid all the sunshine and the
songs, the gayety and levity of the south. The distinctness of her character could scarcely show itself more
completely than by the close unity which exists between
her and her great poet. Even to those who have never
been personally impressed by the lofty, almost melancholy,
seriousness of her aspect, the two images are one. Dante
is the very embodiment, the living soul of Florence, living
and full of the most vivid reality, though six centuries
have passed since his eyes beheld "*lo dolce lome*"—the
sweet light of mortal day. Genius has never proved its
potency so mightily as by the way in which so many petty
tumults and factionaries of the thirteenth century, so many
trifling incidents and local circumstances, passed out of all
human importance for the last six hundred years, have been
held suspended in a fierce light of life and reality, unable
to perish and get themselves safe into oblivion up to this
very day, in consequence of their connection with this one
man. Even now critics discuss them hotly, and students
rake into the dust of old histories for further particulars
of those street riots and rough jests, six hundred years
old, which led to so much blood and mischief; not that
they were of themselves more important than other local
mediæval tumults, but because the hand of the poet has
touched them, or his shadow somewhere fixed them forever on the common recollection, as daylight now fixes so
many vulgar portraits. The men who injured Florence,
and those who tried to save her in that day, were of themselves no more interesting than the generations of succeeding plotters and local heroes who came after them in a
perpetual succession of struggles, down to the time when
anarchy and the ceaseless changes of an unsettled govern-

ment found their natural quietus in the calm of absolute
tyranny. But the names of the older generations are writ
in brass on the glowing walls of the " Inferno," or in softer
lines across the hopeful glades of the " Purgatorio; " while
toiling historians have but succeeded in inscribing a record
of the others in the undisturbed dust of here and there a
library shelf.

This is what the poet has done for his generation; and
it is more than Shakespeare has done for his—a difference
which it is not difficult, however, to account for by the
different characters of the men and the scenes in which
they lived. To one poet his England was the world, full
of every possible type of humanity, affording him suggestions for his Moor, his Jew, his Venetian, as well as for his
Falstaff and his Prince Hal. But to the Florentine
Florence in all her straightness, shut in by the walls of that
Seconda Cerchia which antiquaries can still trace for us,
was the actual universe. No Othello, no Shylock, strange
to the soil, ever dawned upon his intense concentrated
vision; but he saw with tremendous vividness and reality
the people around him, the greatness of them and the
pettiness of their sycophants—Filippo Argenti in the
mud, as well as Brunetto Latini on those burning sands
where fall like snow the " dilated " flakes of fire. Dante
was born, lived, loved, and struggled for all the momentous
part of his life not only in that small old Florence, but in
a corner of it, knowing from his childhood every individual
of the *vicini*, and loving and hating them as only people
so closely shut up together could love and hate; while
Shakespeare had the freedom of the country to range
through—a little youthful vagabondism at merry Stratford
—a taste of the great life of his noble patrons, and of the
Bohemian life of his players, and of everything that was
going in the fresh island air crisped by the sea. The circumstances are as different as the minds of the two poets,

if anything tangible can ever be so different as the genius of Dante from that of Shakespeare. Accordingly the Italian has lifted his entire generation with him into the skies, and by so doing has not only secured for us an acquaintance with the time which is unparalled in minuteness and vivid force, but has hampered us with a literature of commentary which we suppose no other writer of the modern world has ever called forth. We will not attempt to follow the crowd of learned Italians who live and breathe and have their being in Dante through the many convolutions of history, which sometimes bid fair to strangle, like the Laocoon, the poet himself and his great poem in their multiplied and intricate folds. Indeed we think the time has come when, in as far as the "Divina Commedia," is concerned, a reverse treatment would be advantageous, and those parts of the poem which belong to humanity, and are everywhere comprehensible, might be separated from those which are woven into the tangled web of Tuscan history. However, our present occupation is with the man rather than the poem, so far as the great, impassioned, intense spirit who wrote it can ever be detached from that memorable record of himself and his age, in which all the lofty but fierce passions, all the exquisite softenings of feeling, all the strange exalted thoughts, rigid opinions, antiquated learning, and profound humanity of the man are and continue as if he still lived among us. What Dante is in the "Divine Comedy," we know—how Dante grew to be what he is, and among what surroundings, he himself has left us the means of finding out, aided by a band of patriotic biographers, such as do honor to the unswerving faithfulness of Italian enthusiasm for the greatest poet of the race.

The little Florence in which Dante was born was very much unlike the noble and beautiful Florence which is now, like Jerusalem, a joy of the whole earth, and whose splendor and serious beauty seem to justify the wonderful adoration of her which her children have always shown, and which this her greatest son made into a kind of worship. The high houses that rose in narrow lines closely approaching each other, with a continual menace, across the straight thread of street, had not yet attained to the characteristic individuality of Tuscan architecture. The beautiful cathedral, which so many a traveler, thoughtless of dates, has contemplated from the Sasso di Dante, with a dim notion that Dante himself must have sat there many a summer evening watching the glorious walls rise and the great noble fabric come into being, had not, even in the lower altitude given to it by Arnolfo, begun to be when the poet was born. The old Bargello and the Palazzo Vecchio were still in process of building. Santa Croce, Santa Maria Novella, and Giotto's lovely Campanile were all in the future with all their riches. The ancient Badia, or abbey of Florence, still struck the hour, as the poet records, to all the listening city ; and though the bridges, curiously enough, had all been built, there was scarcely as yet any Oltr' Arno, only a very small scrap of that side of the river being inclosed within the second circle of walls, which extended from the Ponte della Grazie, or Rubaconte, newly built, to the Ponte alla Carraja, also new, and so round by San Lorenzo and the square of the cathedral, then cumbered by houses and occupied only by the ancient little church of Santa Reparata, facing the baptistery, the only one of the great group which existed in Dante's day. Very different then must have been that double square. The baptistery had not even got its coating of marbles, but was still in flint, gray and homely, when the child of the Alighieri was christened there ; and little Santa Reparata, with its grave-yard round it, lay deep down as in a well in the heart of the tall houses. The baptistery, too, was surrounded by graves, its square being filled up by

sarcophagi of a still older date, in which—a curious fancy
—many of the greater families of Florence buried their
dead. The tower of one of the great houses in the square
was called *Guarda-morte,* "watcher of the dead," so closely
round that little center of the buried clustered the houses
of the living. But to the old church of the Baptist, the
"bel San Giovanni" of the poet, every child of Florence
was carried, then, as now, to be made a Christian. That
great solemn interior, still and cool and calm amid the
blazing sunshine, remains alone unchanged amid all the
alterations around. The graves have been cleared away,
the great Duomo has been built, the tower of Giotto, airy
fabric of genius, defying all its tons of marble to make it
less like a lily born of dew and sunshine, has sprung up
into the heavens ; but San Giovanni is still the same, and
still the new Florentines are carried into its serene
solemnity of gloom to be enrolled at once in the church
and in the world by names which may be heard of hereafter—as was the infant Durante, Dante, prince of poets
and everlasting ruler of Florence, in the year 1265, in that
month of May which, under Tuscan skies, is the true May
after which in our nothern latitudes we sigh in vain.

Only five years before, Florence herself, with all her
fame and promise unfulfilled, was as near destruction as
ever city was—not by her enemies, but by her own sons
born in her bosom. The ceaseless and sickening struggles
of the Guelfs and Ghibellines had begun some time before,
and once all the Guelfs and once all the Ghibellines had
been banished from the city, when the victory of Montaperti made the Ghibellines masters for the second time of
the town. It seems incredible, after all we have heard and
said of the intense devotion of Italian citizens of those
times to their city, that there actually was a discussion
between the victors whether or not they should destroy
altogether the home out of which, as the most dreadful of

punishments, each faction in its turn drove its opponents ;
but such was the case. After this victory of Montaperti,
a general meeting of the Ghibelline party was held at
Empoli, where this proposal was made, and, supported
warmly by the delegates of all other Ghibelline cities,

PORTRAIT OF FARINATA UBERTI.

would certainly have been carried out, save for the resistance of Farinata degli Uberti, a member of a family so
thoroughly detested in Florence that their palace had been
quite recently destroyed, as Jericho was, under penalties
against any one who should attempt to rebuild it. Farinata
was the sole Florentine bold enough to stand up for the

city in which his paternal home had been razed to the
ground. The reader of the "Inferno" will remember the fine
passage in which his great deed has been made immortal.
It is one of the most remarkable in the whole poem. The
great Ghibelline, raising himself from the sepulchre in
which he is imprisoned, lifting up breast and brow "as if
he held hell in scorn," and the old Cavalcanti beside him,
who, hearing the name of the mortal visitor, immediately
rises too, to look if his Guido, Dante's friend, is with him,
are among the most impressive figures in all that gloomy
landscape. "I was not alone," says Farinata, "in the
deeds which moved the wrath of Florence against my
race; but alone I stood when all around me would have
destroyed Florence, and defended her with open face." *

---

* Those to whom this beautiful passage is familiar will bear us no
malice for repeating it here, and those who have forgotten it will, we
trust, be pleased to have it recalled to them. Dante has penetrated
into the city of Dis, and, traversing the ring of burning sepulchres
which surround the walls, talking with Virgil, is suddenly addressed
by one of the sufferers.

> " ' O Tuscan, thus with open mortal speech,
> That by the burning city living goes,
> Please you to pause a while when here you reach ;
> To me the language of your utterance shows
>   That from that noble land you take your birth
>   To which perchance I brought too many woes,
> Suddenly came this voice, that issued forth
>   From out a tomb : at which I faltering drew
>   A little closer to my leader's worth.
> He said to me : ' Turn ; know you what you do !
> 'Tis Farinata who, thus raised upright,
> From brow to girdle shows herself to you.'
> I had already fixed on him my sight.
>   Proudly his brow and breast upward he swayed,
>   As one who held his hell in high despite.
> With eager hand and quick my leader made
>   Between him and the sepulchre a way,

This extraordinary risk, from which the city, rising into so much importance, escaped only by the patriotism of one of those party leaders who were her ruin, is as notable as anything in the exciting record of her tumultous history. -

When Dante, however, grew old enough to mark the world about him the days of Ghibelline triumph were over, and the Guelfs had again got the upper hand. They, too, had banished and confiscated, right and left, as soon as their turn came, as indeed all parties continued to do in Florence, whatever they called themselves—the Guelfs and the Ghibellines to-day, the Neri and the Bianchi to-morrow; after a while, the Albizzi and the Medici, the Arrabiati and

---

And thrust me there. 'Thy time is brief,' he said,
When to the tomb's foot I had made my way,
He looked at me; then, with a half-disdain,
Questioned me thus: 'Thy fathers? who were they?'
To do his will eager I was and fain,
And all recounted to him, hiding nought,
A little rose his eyebrows proud: again
He spoke: 'Fiercely adverse were they, in thought
And deed, to me, my party, and my race:
So were they twice to flight and exile brought.'
'If they were exiled, driven from place to place,'
Quickly I said 'yet home they found their way;
Your faction never learned that happy grace.'
Then rose there suddenly from where it lay
Unseen, another shade, the face alone
O'er the tomb's edge raised, as one kneeling may,
And round me looked, gazing, as if for one
Who might perchance be following after me;
When it was clearly seen that there was none:
Weeping—'If these blind prisons thus you see,'
He said, ' and thread by loftiness of mind,
Where is my son? why is he not with thee?'
I said: ' Not by myself my way I find,
And unto him who leads and makes it plain
Thy Guido's soul perchance was ne'er inclined.'
Thus by his words and manner of his pain

the Piagnoni: the name mattered little, the thing existed through century after century. When it was not two parties which contended for the mastery, it was two families, a still worse kind of faction. The reader will not expect, nor we trust desire, a recapitulation and description for the hundredth time of the political faith of the Guelfs and the Ghibellines. Probably at their beginning, as we have already said, the former were supposed to be on the side of the church as the grand arbitrator of all national concerns in Europe, and the latter to look to the emperor as holding

Guided I was to answer full and right,
  So clear I read his meaning and his name.
'How saidst thou?—*was?* Ah, lives he then no more?
  Strikes his dear eyes no more the blessed light?'
  When he perceived me pause, and I forebore
Unto this question any quick reply,
  Prostrate he dropped, and thence appeared no more.
  But that heroic shade whose prison I
Had first approached and by whom still remained,
  Unchanged in aspect and in gesture high,
  Moved not, but the first argument maintained.
'If,' said he, ' they have badly learned that art,
  By that, more than this bed, my soul is pained.
  But ere the queen who rules this gloomy part
Shall fifty times uplift her gleaming face,
  That lesson, hard to learn, shall crush thy heart,
  If in the sweet world thou wouldst e'er find grace,
Tell me why thus 'gainst all who bear my name
  The people rage, and hard laws curse and chase.'
  I answered him: 'The bitter strife and shame
That dyed the flowing Arbia crimson-red
  Has in our temple raised such height of blame.'
  Sighing, he said and, shook his mournful head:
'In these things was not I alone, nor could,
  Without grave reason, be by others led
  But I stood sole, when all consenting would
Have swept off Florence from the earth; alone
  And openly in her defense I stood.'"

that supreme position; but it would be rash to conclude from this that either church or empire had much share in the thoughts of these pugnacious Florentines, whose personal feuds and hatreds, one neighbor against another, were infinitely more real and vivid than anything so far off as

DOORWAY OF DANTE'S HOUSE.

pope or emperor. Between the two central points of the city—the great public square surrounding the Pallazzo Vecchio, the seat of government so to speak, where all public business was transacted, and the other square in which now rises the cathedral—lies an obscure little open-

ing among the thronging houses, in which the little old
homely church of San Martino still stands, and where in
the thirteenth century the houses of the Alighieri stood.
An old doorway opposite, almost the only remnant of the
original house, which is still used for homely, every day
purposes, shows where the "Divino Poeta" was born.
Between this church and the old walls of the second circle
was the scene of his life—not Florence, but his street and
quarter of Florence, among the neighbors who, closely
packed together, made part of each other's lives as only in
the tiniest and most primitive of villages, neighbors can
do nowadays.   Each family held together in its cluster of
houses, building on new stories, thrusting forth new
chambers as the branches of the tree grew, and the name
increased in number and strength.   The Portinari, the
Donati, the Cerchi, inhabited each their palace-colony,
their homely fortress, side by side with the Alighieri.
They were neighbors in the most absolute form of the
word.   Impossible to know each other more closely, to be
more completely aware of each others' defects and weaknesses, of each others' virtues and good qualities, than
were the generations which succeded each other in the
same hates and friendships as in the same names and
houses.   Thus the boy Durante, Alighieri's son, no doubt
knew from his cradle not only Folco Portinari's little
Beatrice, but also the young Donati, Forese, and Piccarda,
and probably that Gemma of whom he leaves no record
though she was his wife.   That little corner of the closely-
inhabited mediæval city was in itself an *imperium in
imberio*.   "In war," says Balbo, "every *sestiere* formed a
distinct company with its own officers and ensigns; in
peace, they assembled together for the elections. . . . . All
this drew close the private relations between the inhabitants.   The festivities of any one house were for all the
neighborhood, like that which was made in the Casa Por-

tinari in May; and among the neighbors were those meetings, those talks seated at the door of the house, and all those details of social life which we find in Boccaccio." This kind of familiar, homely, common life has fallen nowadays to the poorer classes alone. No noble matron, no cavalier bearing arms and authority, can now be found seated at the *uscio di casa* in kindly talk with the passing neighbors, as they cross the street in the cool of the evening from vespers at San Martino, or, fresh from politics and business, from the palace of the priors: such close and friendly intercourse exists no longer. But the very sight of the narrow old streets conjures up the scene. The evening so cool and sweet after the hot day: the heavy cornices of the old houses marking out that strip of intense celestial blue above; here and there over a garden wall the early summer betraying itself in breath of abundant roses, in the scarlet glow of a pomegranate blossom; the high tower of the Badia pealing the hour, no nobler belfry yet existing in the city; somewhere from the end of a street a glimpse visible beyond the walls of the terraced cone of Fiesole, with the darker hills behind; and low down at the doorways, on the projecting stairs in the cortile, upon which in dangerous times gates of defense can close, what talk of the advance of trade, of the glorious buildings about to be begun which will make the world wonder, of those drivelling Ghibellines, crushed in every foolish town about which had thought to rival Florence! or perhaps, in lower tones, Madonna Bella, Alighieri's young wife, half happy, half afraid, whispering to some young mother of the Portinari that dream she had before her child was born. Cheerful, narrow, yet kindly burgher life; narrow, knowing no friendship out of the *vicinato*, yet broader by the very limits of that *vicinato* than our shut-up evenings indoors; and how they could hate each other, those neighbors, when occasion served, more passionately still than they could love!

One day in Folco Portinari's great house round the corner there was a friendly gathering. It was in the year 1275, just six centuries ago, and all the neighbors were invited, as was natural and seemly, parents and children. It was to celebrate the coming of May. The sweet delusion of the May—to which, deceived by our poets, themselves led into the error by southern troubadors, we cling with a fond and foolish faith which is always disappointed but never shaken even in these colder regions—is no delusion in Italy. The Tuscan May is something like, we should suppose, what weather is in heaven ; and, frankly, given that exemption from grief and evil which is the first condition of heaven, it is scarcely possible to fancy that any one could desire more for simple blessedness. The Florentines had the habit in those early days of going about the streets in bands, the *vicinato* now assembled by one neighbor, now by another, " with dancing and delight "— *di festeggiar l' entrante primavera.* Upon this special May that good and rich Folco who afterward built the great hospital gave the feast to his neighbors. The story of it is told by two rare historians—Dante himself in the curious exaltation of his " Vita Nuova," and " Boccaccio." We will let the old story-teller, unrivalled in his craft, give his less impassioned description first :

" It happened that Folco Portinari, a man of great honor in those times among the citizens, had assembled the neighbors in his house to entertain them (*festeggiare*), among whom was the young man called Alighieri, whom (since little children, especially in places of merry-making, are accustomed to go with their parents) Dante, not having yet completed his ninth year, had accompanied. And it happened that, with the others of his age, of whom both boys and girls there were many in the house, after he had served at the first tables as much as his tender age permitted, childishly with the others he began to play. There was among this crowd of children a daughter of the above-named Folco, whose name was Bice (though he always named her Bea trice her formal name), who was about eight years old, gay and beautiful in her childish fashion, and in her behavior very gentle and agreeable ; with habits and language more serious and modest than her age warranted ; and besides this with features so delicate and so beautifully formed, and full, besides mere beauty, of so much candid loveliness, that many thought her almost an angel. This girl then, such as I describe her, and perhaps even more beautiful, appeared at the *festa*—not I suppose for the first time, but for the first time in power to create love—before the eyes of Dante, who, though still a child, received her image into his heart with so much affection that from that day henceforward, as long as he lived, it never again departed from him."

The " Vita Nuova " of Dante, is the story told, in detail, of the love which thus began—a love which has been perhaps more questioned, criticised, and commented upon than any other which the world has known of since then. It is difficult to give any just description of this book to those who are unacquainted with it without something which may look to his adorers like irreverence toward the great poet. The student of the " Divine Comedy " can scarcely fail to experience a slight shock when he leaves the great and serious Florentine, most solemn of all travelers between life and death, and finds himself suddenly transplanted into the unreal and dazzling dimness of that curious fantastical world of mediæval youth, with its one sentiment upon which are rung perpetual changes, its elaborate and sophistical refinements yet childlike simpleness—a picture most artificial yet most real—fantastic as a dream, yet penetrated, by the intense verity of the dreamer, with a life which is beyond question. When, however, the strange atmosphere has become a little more familiar to the eye, the reader begins to find again, by help of this intensity, the same vivid and extraordinary individual whom under another guise he has accompanied in all his different moods —stern, tender, indignant, always himself—through the shadows and torments of the "Inferno." The strange youthful figure of the poet, so *bizarre* yet so true, possessed by a love so intense and passionate, which yet is expressed with all the artificial cadences and elaborate harp-twanging of a troubador, is one of the most wonderful things in literature : only youth could be at once so real and so unreal, so occupied by the manner of expressing its emotions and yet so genuine in feeling the emotion itself. The form of the strange romance is fictitious to the last degree. The elaborate sonnet put forth avowedly to a little quaint, old-world company of answering sonneteers, the fantastic explanations of every bit of verse, analysis and *résumé* done by rigidest rule of those impassioned utterances of love, the sole reason, and excuse for which is their spontaneous outburst straight from the heart—are all strangely out of harmony with what seems to us nowadays the straightforwardness of passion. And whether it was the passion of love, commonly so-called, which moved Dante toward Beatrice is a question now never to be solved by the most curious inquiry. It would seem at least to have been not only one of those "loves which never knew an earthly close," but never to have looked for or even dreamed of one—rather a passion of sublimated admiration, that high worship of chivalry for the supremely fair and distant which elevated and inspired the worshiper without suggesting any meaner desires than that more hot and fleshly passion which generally bears the name. To look at Dante, highest prophet and poet of his country, and already full of all the awakening thoughts and blossom of his greatness, thus wandering through the old-world fields, in which flowers do not grow but are embroidered in quaint over-richness and imitation of the natural growth ; in which there is no stir of common life or purpose, but only one overpowering sentiment which fills all hearts ; in which only the "*Donne che hanno intelletto d'amore,*" and fair sympathizing youths, each with a love like his own, live, and wander with him through a magical radiance of

light which is neither of the night nor of the day ; himself
clad in quaintly imagined garments of the troubadour,
passing the hours in song, occupied with nothing but
Beatrice, except (and with this perhaps even more than
with Beatrice) how to set the young lovely verses in which
he celebrates her—is the strangest sight. This moonstruck
mystical young lover, is this he who out of the confusion
and dark problems of life could find no nearer way than
that tremendous round he made through hell and heaven?
He had leisure enough in those *" beaux jours quand il était
si malheureux ;"* leisure to weep his young eyes dim, and
fill his listening world with echoes of his lady's name, or
rather of her sweetness and beauty and excellence above all
praise ; how to look at her made a man good and pure, how
shame and evil fled before her mild eyes, how her gesture
of salutation was enough to transport a soul to paradise,
and how heaven and earth grew dim with sympathy
when she shed a tear. Not Laura herself was worshiped
in such superlative sort, for Petrarch was not young, nor
had he that superb simplicity of self-consciousness, that
intense individuality, which could thus make itself the
center of a whole world, coloring and shaping it into
accord with his ruling mood.

The whole phantasmagoria is at the same time so true
that Florence herself, in that ancient form she then wore,
rises before us, not like any city the world ever saw, yet
with a dream-reality which no one can doubt ; and we
become spectators at those strange assemblies where
Beatrice's lover went to have sight of her, and seeing her
afar off, amid the circle of ladies round, was rapt into a
mystic heaven of delight, or even swooned with longing to
approach her or fear of her displeasure, yet never ventured
upon a word to her so far as he dares say ; or stand with
him by the doors, and hear the ladies speak who come and
go from visiting her in her sorrow, till our hearts are wrung

like his by the thought that even peerless Beatrice, like
others, must sometimes weep. Yet this intense truth of
feeling, and the strange reality of the picture at once so
dim and so dazzling, never make us forget the fantastic
unreality of the whole, and the strange artificial framework
of it, conventional to the fullest limits of mediæval con-
ventionality though so fiery-true. The sonnets, with their
explanations, throw the most curious light upon the whole
mental existence of the time. How elaborate they are,
made a solemn business of in all the fantastical sublimation
of their sentiments ; mapped out line by line, lest any one
should miss the meaning, with transparent pretenses at
obscurity, which give the young poet an excuse for lingering over and interpreting and caressing his own verse.
This was his " Vita Nuova " the new sweet life which love
revealed to him apart from the common existence which
he had by nature. No doubt the dream-world in which
Beatrice was queen, and through which moved very softly
with sympathetic looks and low-voiced questions, the
" ladies who have intelligence in love," was jostled by a
rude enough real world, a life which looked old and stale
and common in the young man's glowing eyes. He ig-
nores that life which to later spectators appears the best
and most important ; puts out of sight his studies, his
preparations for the public service, his sharp taste of the
excitement of war at Campaldino and elsewhere, and all
the trade and wealth, the broils and commotions that were
going on in Florence. Historians would have preferred
that existence of fact ; and a great many even who are not
historians would rather have known how Guido Cavalcanti
got drawn to the side of the Cerchi, and whether Forese
Donati and the gentle Piccarda were ashamed of that arrogant brother Corso, whom popular wit called Baron Do-me-
harm. But no—it is the " Vita Nuova " that entrances
the young poet into its charmed circle. There the ladies

stand about in groups, and talk of him and his devotion,
and speak softly to him, turning gentle eyes upon the love-
sick youth ; and his friends answer him in sympathetic
sonnets, and all the world breathes a melancholy melodious
echo of the names of Love and Beatrice. Not a harsh
thought, not an evil impulse, not a stir of jealousy nor
look of envy—nothing that is not as pure and sweet as it
is visionary, is in the fantastic-delicious record. Every
woman in it, and women are its chief inhabitants, is a
gentil donna, stately and spotless and pitiful ; every man
is chivalrous and pure. It is all of love ; but the love is of
angelic purity, elevated above all alloy of fleshly passion.
It is fantastic as a novel of Boccaccio, but spotless as a
dream of heaven.*

And now to return to the story. Here is Dante's own
description of the first meeting with Beatrice recorded
above :

" Her dress on that day was of a most noble color, a subdued and
goodly crimson, girdled and adorned in such sort as best suited with
her very tender age. At that moment I say most truly that the spirit
of life, which hath its dwelling in the secretest chamber of the heart
began to tremble so violently that the least pulses of my body shook
therewith ; and in trembling it said these words : '*Ecce Deus fortoir
me, qui veniens dominabitur mihi.*' . . . From that time Love ruled
my soul, which was so early espoused to him, and began to take such
security of sway over me by the strength which was given to him
by my imagination that it was necessary for me to do completely all
his pleasure. He commanded me often that I should endeavor to
see this so youthful angel, and I saw in her such noble and praiseworthy deportment that truly of her might be said these words of the
poet Homer—' She appeared to be born not of mortal man but of
God.' "

---

* The English reader who does not know Italian enough to read
this wonderful book in the original, will find a very good translation
by Mr. Dante Rossetti in the volume entitled " The Circle of
Dante."

After nine years (which mystic number, magical combination of threes, has much to do with the pathetical-fantastic narrative) the boy-lover once more saw that youngest of angels. It is not to be supposed that they had not met many a time between, at kirk and market, or that he had not watched her from that corner long called the *Nicchia,* or niche of Dante, in some massive angle of the thick walls of the Portinari's house, flitting across the courtyard, or through the narrow street. But it suits the romancer to leap over this mystical interval of nine years, during which it would appear no words but only looks had passed between the lad and his goddess; and the next point in the tale is that miraculous moment in which she first spoke to him. The description of *"questa gentilissima"* has here as always the same mingling of intense reality and dreamlike, glorified dimness, the minutely recorded circumstances aiding somehow to perfect the shadowy character of the vision.

"When so many days had passed that nine years were exactly fulfilled . . this wonderful creature appeared to me, in white robes, between two gentle ladies who were older than she; and passing by the street, she turned her eyes toward that place where I stood very timidly, and in her ineffable courtesy saluted me so graciously that I seemed then to see the heights of all blessedness. And because this was the first time that her words came to my ears, it was so sweet to me that, like one intoxicated, I left all my companions, and, retiring to the solitary refuge of my chamber, I set myself to think of that most courteous one (*questa cortesissima*), and thinking of her there fell upon me a sweet sleep, in which a marvelous vision appeared to me."

The dream which he had is thus described: he saw Love, carrying in one arm a sleeping lady, in the other hand a burning heart, with which when he had wakened the sleeper he fed her, notwithstanding her terror—then vanished so weeping that the dreamer too woke. The lady

was Beatrice, the flaming heart was that of Dante. When
the youth woke, what should he do but put the vision into
verse, a manner of speech which already his glowing soul
had learned? This was irresistible; but the manner in
which he did it was of his time and not of ours; it belongs
to the age of the troubadours, to that early singing time of
new-born poetry, when there went on a sweet commerce
and rivalry between the professors of the young art,
most delicious of all the inventions of man. Here is
how Dante himself describes his next step in the new
life:

"Thinking of this which had appeared to me, I proposed to make
it known to many who were famous *trovatori* in that time; and because it happened that I had already found out for myself the art of
telling my meaning in verse, I proposed to make a sonnet, in which I
should salute all the faithful followers of love, and praying them to
give their opinion of my vision, write to them an account of that
which in my sleep I had seen. . . . . This sonnet was answered by
many, and in different ways, among whom one replied whom I call
the first of my friends, in a sonnet which begins ' *Vedeste al mio
parere ogni valore.*' And this was the beginning of the friendship
between him and me when he knew that it was I who had sent that
first sonnet to him."

The other troubadour, who answered the boy's sonnet
and became the first of Dante's friends, was Guido
Cavalcanti, of whom mention has already been made, and
whose name is associated with that beautiful passage in the
"Inferno" which we have quoted. He was one of the best
endowed of those singers who preceded Dante, and to the
son of the burgher Alighieri, who belonged at best to the
petite noblesse, and besides was but a boy eighteen years
old, the notice and friendship of this splendid cavalier,
knight, and minstrel, a mature man and recognized poet,
must have been very important, as well as very sweet and
flattering. They were friends henceforward as long as

Guido's life lasted—friends so close and intimate that the poet felt himself entitled to make old Cavalcanti start from his burning tomb at the sound of his name, looking for the inseparable companion who on that great journey was not with him. It is but little more that we know of this noble Guido. He appears in the traditions and histories of his time always in an interesting and attractive light, but with few details. He was "a gentle, · courteous, and ardent youth," says Dino Compagni, "but disdainful (*sdegnoso*) and solitary, and intent on study." "Besides this, he was one of the best lawyers in the world," adds Boccaccio, "and an excellent natural philosopher; he was lively and gracious, and loved to talk (*parlante huomo*); and everything that he wished to do which was becoming to a gentleman he could do better than any other man; and besides this he was very rich . . . . . But because Guido sometimes in his speculations became very abstracted among men, and because he to some degree held the doctrines of the Epicureans, it was said by the vulgar that his speculations were all made with the hope of finding that there was no God. Whether this reproach was true or not cannot now be decided; but the *animo sdegnoso* appears in some of the stories told of him, and specially in that one of Boccaccio's novels where he is represented as leaping scornfully over one of the sarcophagi which surrounded San Giovanni, in order to escape from a band of revelers who pursued him with their importunities, entreating him to join them; whom he answered by telling them that they in their uselessness and folly were at home there among the dead, while he 'solitary and intent on study,' belonged to the living." Guido was married to the daughter of Farinata degli Uberti, the great Ghibelline chief, whom Dante associates with the elder Cavalcanti in the "Inferno"—one of those marriages so continually recurring in mediæval times by which wisdom labored, for the most part ineffectually, to make an end of, or at least soften, the virulency of faction. Either for this reason, or because his "disdainful" mind got weary of unswerving adherence to the party in which he had been born, Guido, Guelf by origin, joined that party of Bianchi who inclined toward the almost extinct doctrines of Ghibellinism, and drew Dante with him into it—a very momentous result of their friendship. Perhaps also because of this state-marriage the gallant Guido seems to have been somewhat light of love, the names of two ladies, Giovanna and Mandetta, being associated with his, neither of them, it is to be supposed, his Ghibelline wife. Giovanna, however, at least must have been a *gentil donna,* and object of pure and chivalrous adoration, since we find her in the society of the spotless Beatrice in those lovely visionary groups of the "Vita Nuova," which was composed especially, as the poet afterward informs us, for the ear of Guido, the first of his friends.

Others of the best known *trovatori* of the time—those poets whose songs were sung about the streets when all Florence danced and sung the sweet May in, and nothing but delights were heard of—replied to the young Alighieri's verses, some of them in lighter mood, laughing at him and his vision; but from this period it is evident the popular knowledge of him as a poet began. We can trace him only through a few of the transports, now joyful, now melancholy, of his love-life. One scene, all thrilling with sensations ineffable, love-agonies and languishments beyond the reach of words, shows the young poet to us, faint and trembling, leaning against a painting which went round the walls of the house, so confused by the sudden sight of his lady among the other *gentili donne* present that he had no longer any strength in him. He had been brought to this assembly, whatever its purpose was—a **marriage feast** apparently—by one of his friends. "To what end are we come among these ladies?" he had said. "To the end that they may be worthily served," said the other, Guido perhaps, for the words are full of chivalrous grace. It is supposed by many commentators that this was one of the feastings which celebrated the marriage of Beatrice herself, and that this fact accounts for Dante's extraordinary emotion, his confusion of mind, and the tears which he was unable to conceal. But if it is so it is the only reference in the whole mystical record to that event which, had his love been an ordinary love, would have involved the very bitterness of death to so true a lover. But while this is passed over, the fact that Beatrice, hearing, it is supposed, evil tales of him, withdrew from her habit of recognizing Dante when she met him, as fully recorded, with all the grievous solemnity which befits such an event. Here is a curious little scene displaying the disconsolate lover among his sympathizers, which is full of the characteristic atmosphere of the story:

"As by the mere sight of me many persons had understood my secret, certain ladies who were in the habit of meeting, in consequence of the great delight they took in each other's society, knew well my heart, for some of them had been present at my misfortunes. And I, musing near them (for so fortune arranged it), was called by one of these gentle ladies. The lady who called me was very animated in conversation; so that when I came to this group and perceived that my own most gentle lady was not among them, I was emboldened, and, saluting her, asked, ' What is your pleasure?' There were many ladies present, and some of them laughed among themselves; but others looked at me, waiting for what I should say, and others again talked with each other. Then one, turning her eyes toward me, called me by name and said these words: ' To what end lovest thou this thy lady, since thou canst not endure her presence ? for certainly the end of such a love must be a great novelty.' And when she had said this, not only she but all the others began to look at me, waiting for my answer. Then I said, ' Madonna, the end of my love was heretofore the greeting of that lady, perhaps, of whom you speak; and in this was all my happiness, the object of all my good desires. But since it pleases her to deny me this greeting, my lord Love, in his mercy, has placed all my happiness in that which cannot be taken from me.' Then these ladies began to talk together among themselves; and as one sees rain falling mingled with beautiful snow, thus I seem to see their words mingled with sighs. And when they had thus talked among themselves, the lady who first spoke to me said these words: 'We pray thee tell us in what thy happiness now stands?' And I replied, 'In the words that praise my lady;' to which she replied, 'If thou sayest what is true, thou shouldst have acted differently.' And I, musing on these words, abashed went away from them, saying to myself, 'Since there is so much blessedness in the words which celebrate my lady, why should other talk be mine?' And thus I made up my mind to take for the subject of my words always that which should be to the praise of this very gentle one."

The image of the "rain mingled with beautiful snow," which he compares to the words and sighs of these *gentili donne*, is thoroughly Dantesque, and will remind the reader of many a similar similitude. He went away with his heart full, and breathed forth his address to the "*Donne ch' avete intelletto d' amore*"—after his fashion. He has always a cluster of these gentle ladies (a phrase which, however, does not express all the sweetness of the *gentil donna*) about him in the soft radiance of this strange love-tale.

We may pause here, however, and turn a little to the ruder life outside of the "Vita Nuova," yet going on all the same, without interruption, though without any such mystic record. Young Dante, though he would fain make us believe it, did not spend all his days singing nothing but the praises of Beatrice, speaking to none but those who had understanding in love, breaking his heart over the thought that his lady no longer recognized him when they met. Other incidents were in his life, rapt as it would seem, in that sad ecstatic vision. While Beatrice was still living, at the very time perhaps when his heart was wrung to see her pass without sign or word, there

occurred the battle of Campaldino, in which he was one of
the *feditori* or wounders, *i.e.*, one of the band of volunteers
who, according to the fashion of warfare common in Italy,
made the assault upon the enemy, thus turning every
battle into a kind of deadly tournament, where the
knights fought out the quarrel in presence of the humbler
army which backed them on either side, but perhaps was
not personally engaged at all. The fight in this case was
between Arezzo and the combination of Ghibelline forces
which had possession of that city, and Florence with her
allies from all the Guelfic cities near. In this battle,
where young Dante, at twenty-four, appears in the crowd
only, we find all at once in full disclosure the two heads
of the parties, not yet formed in Florence, which were to
affect so fatally the poet's life—Vieri dei Cerchi, the
future leader of the Bianchi, and Corso Donati, hereafter
at the head of the Neri. At this moment, while neither
Bianchi nor Neri yet existed, these two were both strenuously Guelf, like all their city. Donati was a hot and
arrogant noble, Cerchi a man of the people, risen into
wealth and greatness, and making a house and name for
his descendants. They were neighbors in that *sestiere*,
near St. Martin's little church, near the house of the
Alighieri, where Dante had grown under their shadow.
They were great people, distinguished, one for nobility, the
other for wealth, towering in public importance and grandeur far above the youth who roamed through the neighboring streets thinking of Beatrice; but how entirely
they owe their recollection now to such entanglement as
good fortune permitted them, with the poet's name! The
feditori were selected by the captains of each district from
the volunteers who presented themselves. Vieri dei Cerchi
was captain of his *sesto*, and had hurt his leg, and had
therefore a complete excuse for exemption; but, instead of
taking advantage of this, he at once placed himself, his

son and his nephews at the head of the list, which gained
him great reputation, "*grande pregio,*" says the old chronicler. He was at the head of the assailing knights on the
Florentine side, and with his son made great proof of
valor. His rival, Corso Donati, who was at the time
podestà of Pistoia, was at the head of the reserve, under
orders to hold apart and refrain from fighting at the peril
of their heads. "But," says old Villani, more moved by
the valor than by the disobedience to orders, "when he
saw the battle begin, he said, like a valiant knight, 'If we
lose, I will die in the fight with my fellow-citizens; and
if we win, whosoever would condemn me, let him come to
Pistoia and do it;' and frankly set himself in motion with
his band, and fell upon the enemy's flank, and was greatly
the occasion of their rout." Dante was too young and
too unimportant as yet to take any leading part where all
were brave, but he has left a record of the fight not less
graphic. "At the battle of Campaldino," he says, "when
the Ghibelline party were almost all killed and destroyed,
I was present, not a novice in arms; and there had much
fear, and afterward very great delight in the various occurrences of the battle." A man who confesses to having had
temenza molto did his part like a man, we may be sure,
among the *feditori* under the leadership of Messer Vieri,
the advanced guard and first rank in the fight. Dante
was also present, as he proves by using it as an illustration
of his great poem, at the siege of Caprona, the only other
incident in this brief campaign.

The world outside the "Vita Nuova" was indeed a troublous world, out of which a young lover might well be fain
to take refuge among the *gentili donne* and the *trovatores*
of mystical romance. In this same year when Beatrice's
sad adorer proved his manhood, and felt at once both fear
and the fierce delight of battle at Campaldino, the key was
turned in the door of that "horrible tower" at Pisa, where

Count Ugolino and his children perished so miserably. The story was in all men's mouths, and no doubt inspired the arms of the conquering Guelfs against the Ghibellines who had done it, when, a month or two afterward, Florence met Arezzo in the field. Another tragedy, with which politics had nothing to do, the pitiful story of Francesca of Rimini, came to its conclusion a little later. Thus the wildest of passions were raging, the most terrible events happening. But there is no trace of them in the dreamworld to which the young poet returned after these scenes of blood and fierce excitement. Not a sign of Campaldino, or of the previous events which had left him "not a novice in arms," appears in the record of his other existence. There no factions or fightings enter, but Love is lord of all, and Beatrice exercises a gentle sway which even the people in the streets acknowledge. "This most gentle lady was in so great favor with all, that when she passed in the streets every one ran to see her. And when she approached any one, so much was his heart touched that he did not dare to raise his eyes nor to answer her greeting. And she, crowned and clothed with humility, went on her way, showing no pride in that which she saw and heard. And many said when she had passed, 'This is not a woman, but one of the most beautiful angels of heaven.'" The air is still as in a vision; the common mortals stand and gaze with bated breath while stately stepping through the old-world streets that most gentle one, *questa gentilissima,* "crowned and clothed with humility," goes upon her way. Strange haven of poetic rest among the fierce contentions of the time, magical heart-existence, abstract and wonderful, in the midst of the tumultuous and cruel day!

But, alas! ere now it had come into the poet's mind, amid deepest thoughts of life's burdens and miseries, that one time or other even the *gentilissima* Beatrice must die.

He had even written in a sonnet, with more than usual trembling of heart, how the angels had asked God for her, but how the Almighty had pitifully left her for a little "there, where one is who expects to lose her." The anticipated blow fell in the summer of the year 1290, the year after Campaldino. Suddenly the lingering record of the "Vita Nouva" interrupts itself. There is a pause—a broken line; and then comes a sudden change of style and language. The poet, at an end of all his sonnets, finds in an older tribulation than his own the sublime words that fit best his sudden desolation:

"How doth the city sit solitary, that was full of people! How is she become as a widow, she that was great among the nations!"

It is thus that he heads the later part of the record after the death of Beatrice. He heard of the event in the middle of one of those tender compositions which were all in her honor. "I was still in the making of this canzone, and had completed only the above verse, when the Lord of that most gentle one, the Lord of justice, called that noble lady to be glorified under the banner of that blessed queen the Virgin Mary, whose name was ever held in the highest reverence by this blessed Beatrice." Strength and words fail him to add anything to this sad statement. The sudden tottering of reason which is natural to a man dazed and bewildered by such a calamity seems to come over him, and he falls to babbling, yet with all the intensity of his ardent soul, about the number nine which regulated that lovely concluded life—the perfect number, conjunct of threes, which signified "that at her birth all the nine heavens were at perfect unity with each other." In their ninth year the two had met, nine years after, they had spoken; she died on the ninth day of the month, and the ninetieth year of the century. "This number was her own self, that is to say, by similitude." Most strange mix-

ture of the truest genuine sentiment with the passing follies of an artificial age ; and yet the one as characteristic
of the great poet as was the other—a truly human jumble,
pathetic in its foolishness as in its woe.

The " Vita Nouva " all but ends here, but does not quite
end, for there is a curious little postscriptal episode describing how near he was to finding consolation in the sweet
sympathetic looks of *"una gentil donna, giovane e molto
bella,"* who looked at him from her window, and gave him
unconscious comfort. This was two years and a half after
Beatrice's death, but he blames himself for having permitted those sweet looks to become too dear to him, and
has much discussion with himself on the subject, which
ends, however, in a dream, in which Beatrice appears to
him calling back to herself all his thoughts. Then he
seeks consolation in philosophy and religion, and finally
the record ends as follows :

"Then there appeared to me a wonderful vision ; in which I saw
things which made me resolve not to speak more of this blessed one,
until the time should come when I could speak of her more worthily.
And to arrive at this I study as much as I can, as she truly knows; so
that if it pleaseth Him by whom all things live that my life should
continue for a time, I hope to say of her that which has not yet
been spoken of any one. And after, may it please Him, who is the
Lord of courtesy that my soul may see the glory of my lady, that
blessed Beatrice, who gloriously beholds His face *qui est per omnia
sæcula benedictus. Laus Deo.*'

This is the conclusion of the most wonderful picture of
a young man's love and dreamy experience of youth which
the world has ever seen. We do not know where to lay
our hand upon anything at all resembling it. Shakespeare's
sonnets have no such unity of meaning, even could the
critics manage to settle at all what their meaning is ; and
there is nothing in them but poetical beauty which suggests
the comparison. Dante stands by himself in the passionate

elaborate tale, so subtle in transparent artifices, so full of
the self-preoccupation of youth, so taken up with that
pose of passion of which the young *trovatore* was proud,
yet at the same time so full of genuine devotion and fantastical visionary love. If there is some alloy in the adoration of Beatrice consequent on the elevation thereby of
Beatrice's lover, it is at least alloy of a noble kind, the
pride that soars with its goddess, not that which essays to
pluck her down. And with all his mediæval affectations—
those affectations so threaded through with the intense reality
of the man that they look more genuine than the deepest
sincerity of many another—the " Vita Nuova " will always
be dear to those who love Dante, and interesting far above
the interest of many a more reliable production to the
students of literature and of his time.

Many commentators have benevolently hoped, perhaps
on slender grounds, that the *gentil donna* whom he saw at
her window, and whose pitiful looks so consoled him, was
Gemma Donati whom he married. There is no evidence
for this, nor any evidence against it, so that the reader if
he pleases may indulge in the thought. For as the other
life outside had gone on roughly all the time, through
boyish studies and youthful dissipations, and gay company
and sharp fighting, alongside of the mystic poetic existence of the " Vita Nuova," so it continued when that sweet
chapter was closed ; and some time in 1293, about the time
when the record ends with his resolution to abandon all
thoughts of the *gentil donna consolatrice*, and to give himself up to the memory of Beatrice and to the " wondrous
vision " in which he should speak of her, as no one else had
ever been spoken of—he was married to poor Gemma,
whom no one has ever celebrated, but who seems to have
been a faithful wife to him, in the little church of St. Martin
opposite. At the very time of the marriage his mind must
have been already full of those first cantos of his great

poem in which Beatrice is the inspiring center, the more than goddess; and it is to be hoped, for her own sake, that Madonna Gemma—if it was she who looked at him so tenderly from her window and almost charmed away his grief—was one of those simple souls so absorbed in unselfish affection as to make no attempt to judge its object or inquire into the return he makes. She has had the usual share of posthumous abuse which is the common fate of a great man's silent wife, and is quite gratuitously classed with that Xantippe who probably was as innocent as she. No contemporary historian says a word either for or against her; and the instinctive impulse to blame the wife for much that happens to the man is so strong, that we are bound in fairness to conclude that there was nothing to say. Boccaccio objects to marriage at all for such a man. "Let philosophers leave marriage to rich fools, to noblemen, and to laborers," says the old novel-writer, "and let them delight themselves with philosophy, who is a much better bride than any other;" but he says not a word against the voiceless Gemma. She was of a family much more elevated than Dante's, and one which he was evidently proud to be connected with; and two of her near relations figure in his great poem; one of them, Forese, is in the "Purgatory," where he is expiating his love of good cheer—an innocent vice among so many worse—and the other, Piccarda, is found in the "Paradise" itself. "*Oh dolce frate,*" Forese says to Dante, "what wouldst thou that I should tell thee?"—therefore it is evident that this could not be the Forese Donati resurrected and torn above ground by some of the darkling moles who are forever at work upon Dante, as an enemy of the poet, the author of some halting and virulent verses addressed to him. We are not even told what was the relationship between Gemma and these two, but probably it was not distant; and as all the members of a family lived together in and about the central palace of the head of the house, there can be little doubt that the young Donati had known the poet from his cradle, neighbors as they were. Very likely they were all together at that May-day feast in Folco Portinari's house, when the child Dante first loved the child Beatrice, and had known her also, and been aware of that wonderful innocent Platonic and poetic devotion of his. If Gemma was the lady of the window, no doubt her soft eyes had followed him, in the fanciful, tender sympathy of youth, while still Beatrice lived, and the glory of the young *trovatore's* exalted passion filled all the *vicinato*, where the old people would smile at him, but all the young understand and envy and revere. Perhaps even, being younger, she too shared in his adoration for their beautiful neighbor with that enthusiasm of girlish worship which is so often bestowed first upon an elder woman before it becomes love and finds its natural end. When we hear that one of Gemma's children was called Beatrice, we find this hypothesis doubly probable. She had seven children—poor soul—in the seven years of her marriage ; and after that saw her illustrious exile no more. Such is the little record of Gemma, for whom nobody had a word to say until all personal recollection of her had departed from the world— when, and not till then, wanton biographists assailed her with those unprovoked and unfounded slanders which so often are the fate of faithful women. There is no evidence whatever that she deserved any one of them. To Dante probably she was but the useful housewife, for whom quite a secondary tame affection suffices ; but even this cannot be affirmed, since if she was the *gentil donna* of the " Vita Nuova," there are as beautiful things said of her, of her sweet looks and tender pity, as any woman could desire. But the dream-world was at an end when the young Alighieri led his bride across the stony street from little St. Martin opposite, and no more knowledge of his love, save

in the sanctified, celestial way of poetry, is given to us.
His spiritual life was to stray henceforward through regions
more wondrous than those dazzling dream-streets of the old
city; and the stronger life, with its deeper problems, surged
in and swallowed up the delicate strain which had made
the charm of his youth.

CHAPTER II.

HIS PUBLIC LIFE.

IN THE year of Dante's marriage a very strange political event took place in Florence. The Guelf party was absolute in the city, so much so that no basis of familiar enmity, no good cry for a faction fight, was to be had on that argument. History does not inform us whether any special manifestation of oppressive predominance on the part of the nobles—a predominance always jealously resisted by the mass of Florentine citizens, who regarded with perpetual suspicion everything that could be construed into an attempt upon their liberties—had preceded this curious outbreak of rampant democracy. The tendency of the Guelf party had always been more or less democratical, and it was a necessity of existence to the great towns, as they struggled into independence, to subdue, and indeed crush, if possible, the feudal power of the great nobles near them, who ruled as princes within their little territories, and were the natural enemies of trade and municipal freedom. The same strong impulse, at once of prejudice and policy, had, through acting in a less open manner, virtually closed to the noble families residing within Florence the highest rank among the rulers of the state. In the year 1282 this position at the head of the civic hierarchy had been appropriated to the Priors, or heads of the different crafts and arts, workers in wool and silk, traders in money, etc., among whom a noble could gain admittance only by enrolling himself in the trade and

winning for himself the position of its head.   This law,
however, could not take from the nobles the natural power
which rank always retains to some extent, especially when

PORTRAIT OF DANTE.

supported by wealth ; and to expect from them an absolute self-restraint and abstinence from all reprisals would
have been, we fear, to expect more than humanity has
ever shown itself capable of.   " Oppressed in public " they

were " oppressors in private," as was but too natural ; and in the year 1293 there was a great rising against them, under the leadership of Giano della Bella, who himself had noble blood in his veins. What special wrongs the people had to avenge it is difficult to find out, except indeed the insolence of patrician manners, and those petty insults which often give a sharper sting than more serious injuries. The revenge taken, however, was tremendous. It was no less than the complete disfranchisement of the Florentine nobility. Already shut out from the highest offices in the state, they were now deprived even of the humbler privilege of a vote, and condemned, great and small to political annihilation. This harsh and extreme measure was not confined to the greater families, who might have abused their power, but extended to every race which counted a knight among its ancestors. No despot, no oligarchy, could have enacted a law more tyrannical and unjust. No doubt it carried its punishment within it, as all such oppressive legislation does ; and Machiavelli attributes to it the failure of Florence in arms and her incapacity for conquest, even indeed for self-defense : the classes who naturally bear arms, and whose spirit and training qualify them best for the arts of war, being thus deprived of their just share of power, which was left entirely in the hands of those whose excellence was in the arts of peace—a short-sighted policy at the best.

There was, however, still a sideway left by which those members of the aristocratic party who love their country better than their caste, or who preferred active life and power to the sullen seclusion of the opposed, could still seize upon the birthright thus unjustly taken from them. They were permitted to enroll themselves in any guild or art, without more than a nominal adoption of the craft in question, by way of retaining their political rights, and by this means the *petite noblesse* at least found a way out of

the difficulty. Corso Donati and such great persons held
apart as a matter of course, and confined themselves to
conspiracy and an eager watch for every opportunity of
troubling the public peace, and perhaps procuring another
revolution, the results of which might be more favorable;
but Vilani informs us that "Many houses, of those who
were neither tyrants nor very powerful, withdrew themselves from the ranks of the nobles and joined those of
the people."

Such was the state of affairs when Dante emerged out of
the dreamy beginning of his life, out of the "Vita Nuova,"
and the lingering sorrow that followed it. His fitful
studies, and the various fancies that passed through his
mind in that disturbed interval, have already been indicated. There is even some reason to suppose that, in his
despair, he entered the Franciscan Order, then in all the
freshness of its beginning, as a novice. Various myteri-
ous references to a cord in his great poem strengthen this
conjecture, and it was a likely enough step for him to
take in his great despondency. But he was not of the
stuff of which monks were made even in the thirteenth
century. He was too vehement in life, too independent
in mind, to bear the coercion of such vows, and, impatient and restless, must soon have rushed into the world
again, feeling the excitement of the Piazza and the stir of
politics to be, after all, necessary to the mature existence,
which could no longer be fed, as in youth, with love alone.
He was twenty-eight at the time of his marriage, in the
very prime and force of early manhood, and of a spirit
very little likely to accept any disability. That he was
deeply and bitterly sensible of the injustice and tyranny
of the popular movement, no reader of his great poem can
doubt; but the indignation which he expressed so warmly
was not inconsistent with a determination not to permit
himself to be shelved and put aside. Neither was his

house great enough to bind him inalienably to the aristocratic party. He belonged evidently to one of those families *che non erano tiranni nè di gran potere*, with no traditions of splendor or dignity to prevent him from taking advantage of the expedient provided. His name is found in a register of the art or profession of doctors and apothecaries—one of the great guilds of Florence, and that which, later, produced its rulers, the Medici—about the year 1297. " *Dante d' Aldighiero degli Aldighieri, poeta fiorentino,*" is the entry. It is not at all likely that it meant anything more than conformity to a rule which required every citizen professing the franchise to be a member of a trade.

This was Dante's entry into public life. Boccaccio, without troubling himself about the details of how it came about, thus describes, with whimsical peevishness, this further step away from poetry and philosophy of his hero :

"The care of a family drew Dante to that of the republic, in which he was so soon enveloped by the vain honors which are conjoined with public office, that, without perceiving whence he came or whither he went, he abandoned himself almost entirely to the occupations of government. And in this fortune so favored him that no embassy was heard or answered, no law was framed or abrogated, neither peace nor war made—and in short no discussion of any importance took place, in which he had not a part."

The condition of Florence, notwithstanding the revolutionary proceedings which had just taken place in it, seems to have been extremely prosperous at this period. Everything was going well with the proud republic, which, after all, was indebted to its guilds and arts, its bankers and burghers, not its nobility, for its wealth and greatness. The revolution by which all nobles were placed under a ban occurred in the year 1293. In 1294 the foundation was laid of the great church of Santa Croce, that magnificent temple of fame which still exists, enshrining the greatest names of Italy. In the same year, "the city of Florence being in good and tranquil condition, the Florentines permitted themselves the pleasure of renewing the chief church of Florence, which was then of rude form, and small in comparison with such a city, and ordained that it should be increased and extended, and made all in marble, with sculptured figures. And it was founded with great solemnity, on the day of Santa Maria, in September, by the cardinal legate of the pope, with many bishops and prelates, and called Santa Maria del Fiore." Two years later "the commune and people of Florence began to found the Palazzo of the Priors," the noble palace and tower which is now known as the Palazzo Vecchio. Again, in 1299, "the new and third walls of the city were founded in the Prato of Ogni-santi, the bishops of Florence, Fiesole, and Pistoia giving their benediction to the first stone." When the reader recollects that this *new* wall is, or rather was a dozen years ago, the existing wall of the city, he will be able to form some idea of the wonderful thrill of new life and prosperity which must have moved the narrow mediæval city to such an outburst of great works.

It was during this high tide of prosperity that Dante began to take the active part indicated by Boccaccio in the government of the city. His first great occupation in the public service seems to have been that of ambassador. Filelfo, one of his biographers, gives details of these missions which are quite uncontradicted at least, if there is not much confirmatory evidence. He was sent, according to this authority (a century later in date than Dante, but with all the public documents and traditions to guide him), to the various cities about, to arrange various grounds of quarrel, to the Venetian republic, the alliance of which was so valuable to all the independent cities of Italy; to

Naples, to King Charles of Anjou, and to his son, Carlo
Martello of Hungary, between whom and Dante there had
sprung up a sudden but warm friendship on the occasion
of that prince's visit to Florence ; and also to the pope,
more than once ; and to King Phillippe le Bel of France,
from whence, says Filelfo, he brought back, "an everlasting
chain of friendship, which continues till the present day ;
for he spoke not without grace (*savore*) in the French language, and it is said even wrote something in that tongue."
With these embassies so quickly succeeding each other,
the days of the poet must have been full of business ;
his life spent in journeys, his faculties taxed sometimes
perhaps to make the worse appear the better cause, and to
promote in every way the prosperity of his city.

In the meantime, while Dante himself was kept out of
mischief by his much occupation, trouble was brewing in
that turbulent town. The feud of populace against nobility had recommenced the old round of warfare, and now
the two great families, near neighbors to each other, who
had long indulged a private quarrel, began to exceed those
decent limits of neighborly hostility which are everywhere
allowed. The rich and vulgar Cerchi had grown too great
for the taste of the very noble but not very rich Donati,
who with fierce displeasure watched their plebeian splendor and strength growing. Corso Donati, the head of
that house, was a type of all that was worst and finest in
the mediæval noble. He was handsome, of a commanding
person, eloquent, splendid, and wicked. It was he who
abducted by violence his own sister, Piccarda, from her
convent, in order to marry the shrinking nun to one of his
friends and *consorti*. He was so proud in his deportment
that he was called the baron by his admirers and followers
—the Baron Malefammi, or Do-me-harm, by the populace; and he had some justification for his bitter wit and
intense enmity to his more popular neighbor, in the fact

that he was one of the chief of those utterly silenced and
set aside by the last change of law; for Corso was too great
a noble to give up his own side as Dante had done, and become a tradesman in order to be a ruler. Vieri of the
Cerchi, on the other hand, though good and brave, was
heavy and unmannerly, with no command of speech nor of
ideas.   When his neighbor called him the Ass of the Gate,
he could find nothing malicious to say in reply, save to
echo the Malefammi, which was Corso's nickname among
the populace.   No encounter of wits was possible to him,
but only sharp blows from stalwart young Cerchi, in reply
to the cutting gibes of the other party.   The existence of
these two families so near each other—one on the popular
side, yet feeling their inferiority to the noble race all the
more on that account, the other inheriting the old potency
of a great house, but embittered by present helplessness and
want of power—was in itself a standing menace to the
peace of the city.   Why it was that Guido Cavalcanti,
himself among the noblest in Florence, should have been
on the side of the Cerchi, we have no means of knowing.
Possibly enough it may have been because of some private
feud with the haughty Donati.   Anyhow, this noble
trovatore, the first of friends to Dante, belonged to the
party headed by the honest but heavy man of the people.
Guido was a thinker as well as a troubadour—a philosopher
in his way, possibly a free-thinker, epicurean, contemner
of authority; and it is likely enough that his contempt for
the useless young gallants who roamed about the city in
search of gayety, quarrels, or mischief, extended theoretically to all those possessors of hereditary authority who
were great without any virtue of her own, and believed
themselves better than their neighbors without doing anything to deserve that distinction.   It would not seem that
he drew Dante with him further than friendly sympathy
required; **for** throughout all this quarrel and tumult the

poet keeps his independent position—an arbitrator, not a combatant; but the step he had himself taken in enrolling his name on the popular side, and accepting employment from the revolutionary state, must have separated him from the noble party and from the family to which his wife belonged, to whom, like enough, this descent in the social scale, even though it brought public distinction, was little agreeable.

While the feud thus smoldered, ever ready to break out, an event happened which gave the pretense of a public quarrel to the hostile neighbors. A large and powerful family of Pistoia called Cancellieri—divided by its descent from two wives of its founder, one of whom bore the name of Bianca—had lately carried its intestine tumults so far that Florence had stepped in as suzerain of the lesser city, and sentenced both parties to banishment. They obeyed, but only by carrying their feud into Florence itself, where the two smoldering animosities already existing leaped with delight at this good occasion of declared and open strife. The Cerchi adopted the cause of the Bianchi, the Donati of the Neri. It was but another chapter of the conflict between the noble and the plebeian, the Guelfs and Ghibellines. To say what was the question between the original Bianchi and Neri is beyond our power, as we have already said it is difficult to decide what at any given period was the precise question between the Guelfs and Ghibellines; but whatever the pretense might be, the real occasion of the continually renewed and varying quarrel was that overwhelming impulse of the mediæval mind to warfare which took advantage of every chance of conflict. One party got the upper hand, and banished with fierce jubilee its opponents ; then the balance swung round, and the victors became exiles in their turn, accepting the inevitable vicissitude : thus the story goes on. Churches had been founded and walls built and trade had flourished, and

the proud city had begun to adorn herself during her short
period of peace. But what was trade and wealth, or even
the splendor of their Florence, to the Donati and Cerchi,
thirsting from the opposite sides of the street to be at each
other's throats, and drawing their swords upon each other
in the very heart of the *festa*, amid the rejoicing of the
crowd ? We may quote one incident which shows how
suddenly a brawl might rise. The time was early in May,
when Florence was full of wandering bands, dancing and
singing in every square in honor of the spring; the scene
occurred in the Piazza Santa Trinità, the little square close
to the bridge of the same name, which every one knows
who has seen Florence. That corner of the old town is
probably but little changed since then. The merry-makers
were dancing on the rough pavement as best they might,
in the shadow of the tall houses, a lightsome crowd, with
garlands and greenery, with songs of *trovatori* and *im-
provisatori* while the people stood by looking on, not bewildered as we should be by so strange a spectacle. Florence
was used to them. "In those times the Florentines
abounded in delights and pleasures, ever feasting together ;
for every year at the calends of May almost the whole city
went about in bands and companies of men and women,
with dances and many delights." So says the historian
Villani : and this was what they were doing in the Piazza
Santa Trinita on that May-day in the year 1300, as their
neighbors had done in Folco Portinari's *vicinato* twenty-
five years before.

"While the unusual amusements were going on, with merry
dances of men and of women in the Piazza, a number of the young
gallants of the Cerchi party arrived on horseback, being armed because of the Donati, and going about Florence to see all that was going on. And as they stood by looking on, there appeared also a party
of the Donati, who, either not recognizing the Cerchi, or perhaps because they recognized them, spurred on them with their horses.

Then the Cerchi turned round, and a tumult arose and swords were drawn and several persons were wounded, among whom were Ricoverino di Messer Ricovero de' Cerchi, wounded in the nose, no one knew by whom, the Cerchi themselves saying little about it, in order to have more secure revenge."

This brawl, adds an ancient historian, was preceded by a public misadventure quite enough to account for it. "The year before this the Palace of the Commune was built, which began at the foot of the Ponte Vecchio over Arno, toward the castle Altafronte; and in order to build this, a pillar was made at the foot of the Ponte Vecchio, and the statue of Mars was removed there; and whereas first it looked toward the east, it was turned toward the north, upon which, according to an ancient prophecy, the people said, "Please God that there be not great changes in our city."

Other events, however, which were of greater individual importance in the poet's life occurred in the same spring, which so threatened the peace of Florence. By this time he was one of the best known among the poets of his time—known by the sonnets and *canzoni* of the "Vita Nuova," and most likely by many fugitive compositions which have not lasted to our day; but he was not as yet the poet of heaven and hell, the greatest singer of Italy. The popular knowledge of his productions is shown by various quaint stories still preserved in the records of Boccaccio and Sacchetti. The following taken from Sacchetti gives us a glimpse of the poet's impatient temper as well as his popular fame:

"When Dante had dined he went out, and passing by the Porta San Pietro heard a blacksmith beating iron upon the anvil and singing some of his verses like a song, jumbling the lines together, mutilating and confusing them, so that it seemed to Dante that he was receiving a great injury. He said nothing, but going into the blacksmith's shop, where there were many articles made in iron, he took up his hammer and pincers and scales, and many other things, and threw them out into the road. The blacksmith, turning round upon him, cried out, 'What the devil are you doing? are you mad?' 'What are you doing?' said Dante. 'I am working at my proper business,' said the blacksmith, 'and you are spoiling my work, throwing it out into the road.' Said Dante: 'If you do not like me to spoil your things, do not spoil mine.' 'What thing of yours am I spoiling?' said the man. And Dante replied: 'You are singing something of mine, but not as I made it. I have no other trade but this, and you spoil it for me.' The blacksmith, too proud to acknowledge his fault, but not knowing how to reply, gathered up his things and returned to his work ; and when he sang again, sang Tristram and Launcelot, and left Dante alone."

It is odd to think of Dante's delicate canzones, even of *smozzicato* and *tramestato*, in the mouth of the rude worker in iron, keeping time to the beating of the hammer. Another anecdote of the same kind follows, in Sacchetti's simple record :

"This story moves me to tell another of the same poet, which is short and very good. As Dante was going one day about his own affairs in the city of Florence, wearing armor as was the custom, he met an ass-driver, who walked behind his asses, which were laden with the refuse and sweepings of the streets, singing as he went out of Dante's book; and when he had sung a verse he struck his ass and cried '*Arrhi!*' When Dante heard this he gave the fellow a blow on the shoulder with his gauntlet, and said, 'I did not put in that *Arrhi.*' The man, not knowing who Dante was, nor what this meant, when he was out of reach put out his tongue at him, with other rude gestures, saying, 'Take that !' 'I would not give one of mine for a hundred of thine,' said the poet. Oh gentle words full of philosophy ! Many would have pursued the fellow and made an end of him, others would have thrown stones at him; but the wise poet confounded the wretch, and had praise of all who heard these wise words."

The old story-teller's enthusiasm here may seem a little misplaced, but yet the poet's quaint reprisals show a certain genial sense of humor scarcely to be expected from the man. Another curious trait, less amiable but still more striking, is linked by Sacchetti to his story of the blacksmith. Dante was on his way, when he heard the grimy artisan singing at his work, to speak a good word to the "Esecutore" of the district for a certain young cavalier of the Adimari, his neighbors, who had got into trouble for unruly behavior, and who was awaiting the sentence which his friends hoped might be lightened by the intercession of so important a public man as the poet-ambassador. Dante, having dined with the Adimari, set out on his mission with goodwill enough, it would appear; but as he went he began to think :

" As he approached the house of the Esecutore, he reflected that this cavalier was a haughty young man, ungracious and proud, who when he went about the city, especially when on horseback, so spread himself over the street, which was not wide (*andava si con le gambe aperte*), that the toes of his boots rubbed against the passers-by ; and such behavior was very displeasing to Dante, who observed everything. Accordingly he said to the Esecutore, ' You have before your court a certain cavalier, for such and such offenses. I recommend him to you; his behavior is such that he deserves great punishment; for I think that to usurp the rights of the commonwealth is one of the greatest of offenses.' Dante did not say this to deaf ears. The Escutore asked what rights of the commonwealth were those which he usurped. Dante answered, 'When he rides about the city he rides in such a manner that those who meet him have to turn back and cannot pass upon their way.' ' Does this seem a joke to you ?' said the Esecutore ; 'it is a greater fault than that with which he is charged.' ' *Ecco !* ' said Dante. ' I am his neighbor. I recommend him to you.'"

This curious mode of intercession was, as may be supposed, little appreciated by the Adimari, though it affords us a very curious picture of the man, more just than pitiful, himself so arrogant, yet remorseless to the arrogance of others, waking up from his abstraction after he had undertaken to plead the young man's cause, finding him unworthy, and winding up his description of the young braggart's public sins by the fine irony of that recommendation "as a neighbor." No wonder the Adimari did not like it. It was "the principal reason," Sacchetti tells us, of Dante's exile. And no doubt so keen a personal injury would not be forgotten.

These glimpses of him are very valuable through the dimness of the time. How he appeared in his greater occupations as ambassador and as one of the magnificent signoria, an honor to which he came shortly after, we cannot tell; but he is very clear to us making his way about the streets in his gorget and gauntlets, "observing everything" —the arrogant young horseman with his toes stuck out to make the narrow path impassable, the blacksmith at his work, the dustman putting in his rude "Gee up!" as a refrain to those exquisite sonnets which were dearest to the poet. We have other passing glimpses of him of a similar kind to those already recorded, for which, however, we can scarcely find room here. But there is one which we must not leave out, which shows another aspect of the poet who observed everything. This took place away from home, in the streets of Sienna, where, having received a book which had been promised to him, he fell to reading it on the bench outside the door of an apothecary, leaning his breast against the bench with his back to the street, and there he stood all day, from early mass to vespers, unconscious of the great *festa* which was going on behind him. There were "dances of pretty maidens," Boccaccio tells us, and "games of well-disposed and gallant youths," and various instruments, and applauses, which made *grandissimi romori.* "How could you keep yourself from looking at so fine a *festa?*" some one asked the poet, who lifted wondering eyes from his book, and declared, "I heard nothing." This is how Dante appears to us in his early manhood, when every glimpse of him about the streets is precious, short as was to be his sojourn there. For, alas, we have no longer a "Vita Nuova" to guide us; to show us how the thoughts arose in his mind, and where he went, and how his musings shaped themselves into immortal verse.

Failing all clearer indications, however, the theory of his biographer, Balbo, as to the immediate beginning of the "Divina Commedia" is interesting, and possesses much appearance of reality. The opening pages of this great work point, as the reader will recollect, to a distinct crisis —a moment when suddenly arrested in his progress "half way upon the road of life," he finds himself to have lost the right path. Such a discovery might indeed have been made in the stillness of his chamber in the midst of his ordinary existence; but the period indicated corresponds entirely with a great public event, of a character most likely to awaken serious thoughts, and bring back past resolutions and purposes to the mind of the poet. It was the tradition of the church that the last year of each century should be made the occasion of special religious solemnities, bearing, but on a greater scale, the character which all churches have thought suitable to the end of a year, or any marked and noteworthy period. The jubilee was no farce or empty ceremonial at a time when faith was absolute and heresy almost unknown. Accordingly in the Easter of that year, 1300, all the world thronged to the center of Christendom. Rome was so crowded by pilgrims, earning the indulgence proclaimed by Pope Boniface by fifteen days of devotion at the shrines of St. Peter and Paul, that the old bridge of St. Angelo was divided by a barrier, so that the throng which went toward St. Peter's should not interfere with the other crowd who were on their way to St. Paul's outside the gates, the ancient Byzantine temple which still existed in comparatively recent days. Dante proves to us his own presence at the jubilee in the most characteristic way by quoting this example to show how the throngs of tortured sinners came and went across the *ponticelli* into Malebolge in his "Inferno." And the poet was no skeptical bystander looking on at the devout crowds, hot and eager and weary, but a pious Catholic of the middle ages, no doubt thankful enough for the indulgence which gave him a tremulous sense of forgiveness and amnesty for all his errors, and humbly earning the same by the fifteen days of devotion prescribed, making his weary way from San Pietro across the bridge to San Paolo on the other side of the river. Many thoughts were in his mind, no doubt, among his Aves and Paternosters, as he made the daily pilgrimage. His fellow-pilgrim, Giovanni Villani, was so touched and stimulated by the unusual scene, finding himself "in that blessed pilgrimage, in that holy city of Rome, seeing all the great and ancient things, and reading the histories and great deeds of the Romans," that he made up his mind to begin his history of Florence "the daughter and creation of Rome," as soon as he returned home. The poet's thoughts might well have received a similar yet still higher impulse. A great purpose had risen in his mind years before when the world had been made dim to him by the loss of Beatrice, and he had vowed in a passion of love and grief, "to say of her that which never yet was said of any woman." What had become of this high hope and resolution? Years had passed since then, and the commoner life had seized upon Dante, and his force of manhood and vitality had carried him into many busy scenes, and passions far removed from that sacred circle in which Beatrice dwelt. He had lived in a vulgar, every-day region far out of the "Vita Nuova;" he had fought, argued, ruled, contended with, and persuaded his fellow-creatures, and had found solace and enjoyment in the *ringhiera* and the council chamber and before foreign kings and potentates, and he had loved—perhaps coarsely, vulgarly—tasting those grosser sweetnesses which are as apples of Gomorrah, full of ashes and bitterness. Storming through this mid-career of his life, the vehement,

ardent, impassioned man had done perhaps—who has not?
—things which filled him with bitter shame when he
turned toward the pure and lofty ideal of his youth; but
what time was there for thought or consideration amid the
journeys, the high audiences, the discussions and debates
of which a politician and ambassador's life was full in those
stirring days? But now at last a moment had come for
thought, a religious pause in the common affairs of life. It
is natural at such moments that everything that is purest
and loftiest in the past should be recalled to the touched
and softened soul; and what so likely to return to him as
the exaltation of that great visionary love and grief which
had been the inspiration of his youth? How far he had
strayed from the purity, the high thoughts, the holy and
lofty sorrow of those days? He had lost his way in the
midday of his life, now waking up suddenly to a sense of
all the time he had squandered and all the energies he had
employed in less worthy ways, where was it that he found
himself?

> "Mi ritrovai per una selva oscura
> Che la diritta via era smarrita."

This is the hypothesis of Balbo, and it seems, in the
absence of other evidence, a reasonable suggestion. Anyhow, whether at Rome during these pilgrimages or at
home in some moment of quiet, it is apparent that about
this time Dante did arrest himself in his career, and finding himself astray from the *verace via*, set out boldly to
find it again on that marvelous round through hell and
heaven.

For the moment, however, we hear nothing of the
"Divina Commedia." The tumults of life which swallowed
up the poet on his return from Rome were too noisy and
crowded to leave room for the lower and sweeter notes of
poetry. It becomes apparent afterward that the work

was begun in Latin, which all the world then supposed to be the only language worthy of a great subject ; and that in the intervals of his state labors, and while he and his colleagues in office were struggling with the Neri and Bianchi and doing their best to keep peace in the disturbed city, Dante employed his moments of leisure in the composition of those first cantos which will always remain the most interesting part of the great poem to most readers. All the lofty poetry of that beginning—the heavenly lady roused out of her celestial seat by the pity of human love, the poet-guide chosen for the wandering poet, high paradise resplendent with power and universal oversight, dim Limbo in its wistful calm, obedient and dutiful, though without hope—glimmered before his eyes as he trod the often riotous streets between San Martino and the Piazza, where the other anxious Magnificos, not knowing how to hold the balance straight between Messer Corso and Messer Vieri and all their habitual following, took counsel with him and with each other, not without a leaning in their disturbed bosoms to Vieri and the Bianchi, though, so far as good behavior went, there was not much to choose. In the month of June of this same year 1300, Dante became one of the priors, or signoria, of Florence, and it is believed to have been during his term of office that the feuds of the two parties becoming insupportable, the signoria took the bold step of banishing the heads of both factions. So decisive a measure does credit to the impartiality of the authorities, a virtue very rare and hard to cultivate in such an age, and it may be easily supposed that its exercise cost the poet no small struggle with himself, since his beloved friend Guido Cavalcanti was one of the exiled leaders. It was apparently almost the first attempt ever made in Florence at an impartial punishment of both sides and honest endeavor to secure the public advantage solely. How far Dante deserves the credit of this attempt to put down the rising feuds of the city it is impossible to tell, but as there can be little doubt of his leaning toward the Bianchi party, and none of his warm devotion to Cavalcanti, the effort at public virtue was worthy of the highest praise. Unfortunately it did not last so long as might have been desired ; the fortitude of the rulers of Florence, not used to such impartiality, wavered after a time. " Envy and evil speaking grew," says Leonardo Aretino in his biography of the poet, " because those of the citizens who were banished to Serazzana (the White party) soon returned to Florence, while the others remained in exile." Dante, however, defends himself from this accusation in a letter now lost, asserting that the return of the Bianchi was after the conclusion of his priorship. Its immediate cause was the sickness of Guido Cavalcanti, who had fallen ill in his banishment, and who died not long after his return to Florence, in the beginning of the ensuing year. No one will doubt that a friend so warm and vehement as the poet must have exerted all his influence to procure the recall of the exiles as soon as he knew that his beloved Guido was suffering and in danger, and their return while their rivals remained in banishment no doubt impairs the splendor of this first attempt at impartial justice ; but at the same time it was an effort in the right way, and the poet merits his full share of the credit, imperfect as it was.

Dante's *priorato* lasted, as was usual, only two months, but during the ensuing year his influence and power were great. Buccaccio's testimony on this point is very strong.

" In him all public trust, all hope, all excellence, human and divine seemed to be concentrated. But Fortune, the enemy of all wisdom and destroyer of all human well-being, as she had held him gloriously at the top of her wheel for some years, now turned it to other purpose. In his day the citizens of Florence were furiously divided into two factions. Dante applied all his genius and every act and thought to bring back unity to the republic, demonstrating to the wiser citizens how even the great are destroyed by discord, while the small grow and increase infinitely when at peace. But seeing that all his trouble was in vain, and knowing the souls of his hearers to be obstinate (fearing the judgment of God), he at first proposed to give up all public office and return to private life ; but afterward, drawn by the sweetness of glory and of vain popular favor, and also by the persuasions of the greatest citizens, and believing beside that he might in time to come be better able to serve the city if he was known in public business than if he remained in private life . . . he continued to follow the fading honors and vain pomp of public office, and perceiving that of himself he could not establish a third party, which should overthrow the injustice of the other two and turn the city to unity, he united himself to those who according to his judgment had most justice and reason on their side, and continually used his influence for that which he knew to be best for his country and for his fellow-citizens."

This very high character, however, had its darker side, which is given as follows:

" He had a great opinion of himself, nor did he ever underrate his own public importance, as appears very notably in this incident among others. When he and his party were at the head of the republic, those who were on the losing side made an appeal to Pope Boniface to send a brother or cousin of King Philip of France whose name was Charles, to regulate the state of the city. In order to consider this, a council was called of the chief members of the ruling party and Dante with them. And, among other things, they resolved to send an embassy to the pope to oppose the coming of the said Charles or to arrange that he should come with a friendly meaning toward their party. And when they came to deliberate who should be the head of this embassy, it was proposed by all that it should be Dante. When he heard this, Dante, almost beside himself, said : ' If I go who will stay ?—if I stay who will go ?' As if he alone were the man of worth among them who gave weight to the others. These words were heard and remembered."

The reader will scarcely be surprised that a saying such

as this should rankle in the mind of the proud Florentines
and work disastrous consequences to the speaker. The
embassy was sent, with Dante at its head, bent upon opposing the mission of the Frenchman, Charles of Valois,
whose intervention had been called for by the other party.
This was in the autumn of the year 1301. The pope received the ambassadors graciously, and sent back two of
them to persuade the city to yield to the *paciero*, keeping
the others with him. Among those who remained was
Dante, for what reason no one seems to know. Perhaps
the pope felt that so strong a personality was safer kept
out of the way ; perhaps—for no force seems to have been
exercised, and Bonifazio appears to have acted in good
faith—Dante himself had become disgusted with the
tumults and the struggle, or had seen by the aspect of his
companions that his influence was waning. But whatever
was the cause the poet did not take advantage of the opportunity to return along with his colleagues. He stayed
behind in Rome, abandoning suddenly the public
duties which he had fulfilled with so much fervor. He
allowed events to take their course in Florence, though he
had so lately said, "If I go, who will stay?" and suffered
Charles of Valois to enter the city, with all the overturns
and commotions that followed, without attempting to go
back to the help of his struggling fellow-citizens or his
forsaken family. This strange proceeding on Dante's part
is not explained by any of his biographers. Perhaps he
felt that the tide had turned beyond his power to arrest it,
and that his wife and children were safer without him, as
she was a Donati, and had a right to the protection of her
family and of Messer Corso, now once more the most
powerful man in Florence. Anyhow the poet let a year
pass over amid all kinds of revolutions and disturbances ;
he suffered the Bianchi and his moderate and patriotic
friends to go to the wall, and the enemies of order and of

his party to come in triumphant, and all that he had done to be overturned ; he let anarchy, misery, killings, and burnings, and destruction resume their sway in the city, without rushing to its aid. A contrast more striking than that which is suggested by this strange inaction, and his previous overweening opinion of his own importance, could scarcely be found. This makes it less wonderful, perhaps, and less cruel that the revolution banished him, and that, as it happened, he never in the many years of life that yet remained to him entered Florence again.

In this strange way ends the first part of the poet's great career. Out of the soft poetic vapors, lovely extravagances, foolishness, and reality of the "Vita Nuova," the young man burst forth splendid into full potency of life, a power among his fellows, a princely ambassador to princes, a patriot ruler among his own people, aiming with genuine force and truth at something better than the past, at generous and honest public service distinct from party. Then of a sudden, midway in the path of life, something arrested the vehement and splendid traveler. He who was going, to all appearance, so straight and true on his way to honor, stopped short. Some unseen hand caught at him, some voice unheard by others called him in the midst of the crowd. He found himself in a bewildering wood, where he had lost the true way. This was the great spiritual event which happened to him before fate came in to arrest his steps in earnest. Ere ever Guido Cavalcanti sickened in Serezzana, this sudden pause had occurred in his existence. Another "Vita Nuova," but this time a life *aspra e forte,* had begun. The sudden revolution in Florence was but a formal carrying out by circumstances of the separation already effected in his heart, the divorce between him and fortune, between him and power, and his reawakening to that deeper and grander inspiration that had hovered over him for years, before absolute misfortune marked his path. Beatrice had already moved from her place in heaven, where she sat by the side of the ancient Rachel, and had roused out of dim Limbo, where those great souls dwell who live without hope, in desire of God and goodness—the courteous Mantuan spirit, with his ornate words, who was the most suitable guide for her wandered but faithful lover. The gates of Florence, when they were shut against him, did no more than formalize that sentence of banishment which had already been pronounced in his own breast. His city cast him away, to her everlasting shame: but already he had ceased to be Dante the magnificent signore, the ambassador of an arrogant republic, the representative of a crowd of turbulent burghers. He had turned back to the life to which he vowed himself in his dreaming youth; he had taken his first steps on that mystic *giro* through hell and heaven; and become the Dante of all Italy and of all poetry, representative of his age and of his race—the Dante of the world.

CHAPTER III.

IN EXILE.

THE FEELINGS with which Dante in Rome, awaiting the news of all that was passing in Florence, heard of the ruin and exile of his party and the complete victory and ascendancy of its enemies, it is needless to attempt to realize. The state of feeling altogether, the habits and modes of thinking of the time, are too different from our own to make such an effort easily practicable. Did we not know how rapidly rumor leaps over hills and plains, and flies, especially in Italy, without any apparent means of communication, on some kind of spiritual telegraph invented long before the other, we might suppose that information of such a change in the city got but slowly and in a fragmentary way to the ears of the belated ambassador, thus superseded in his office while in the very act of exercising it. But the first hint of what had happened no doubt presented at once a suggestion of the last detail of the overturn to the citizen envoy, who knew exactly what happened at such a crisis. No need of daily or hourly telegrams to tell him how the familiar revolution was going on. The ringing of the great bell, the thronging of armed men through the streets, the agitated meetings of the threatened faction in San Giovanni or elsewhere, swearing to stand by each other and guard the city; the boisterous bands, elated with the knowledge that the tide had turned in their favor, who began suddenly to appear on the other side; all these steps in the drama were as well known to Dante as are the steps by which one ministry succeeds another to ourselves. The known is less exciting, or at least less disturbing in its excitement, than the unknown ; and the poet, whose grandfather at furthest had borne the same fate, and who had himself helped to mete it out to others, could have been in no doubt as to the fact of his own banishment and all its consequences. He had left Madonna Gemma and her seven small children in the house behind San Martino ; and all his possessions besides, including, to our eyes, the most precious of all, a certain *abozzo ébauche*, scrawl so to speak, of seven cantos of a poem, often interrupted by public business, and which perhaps he had begun to think was but badly done in stilted Latin. If a sigh for this rose in his mind, there is no record of it. No doubt he took its loss for granted, as a natural consequence among so many others of his banishment. His wife and children would be safe, thanks to the Donati ; but his goods were lost beyond redemption. Of this there could be no doubt in the mind of any Florentine who knew his city and his time.

In the meantime, however, Madonna Gemma—a sensible woman, it is evident, whether or not a much-beloved wife —had taken her precautions. When she saw how things were turning, and that the Bianchi had ceased to be masters of the city, and confiscation and fire might be expected any day, she put the household valuables together, packing them in the strongest chests she possessed, and had them at once removed to the houses of neutral friends, or other safe places, as possibly the women of Florence, used to keeping their wits about them, were in the habit of doing when emergencies arose. And thus the *abozzo* was kept safe, though probably in bad Latin, through fire and tumult and all the anarchy, of the transition. Evidently the seven little frightened Florentines behind their barred windows, of whom she was left the sole protector, got through that interval of danger in safety too.

The state of Italy at this time, and indeed not only at this time but for centuries after, was very peculiar and characteristic. The country was studded with great independent cities, within which, masterful and imperious, reigned the dominant party for the time being, safe within their walls, and in command of all the wealth and forces of their respective towns; while without those walls, in the nameless country, possessing otherwise no individuality of its own, and peopled in its own right only by peaceful peasants, cultivating their fields under the sway of here and there a feudal lord—were bands of exiles—*fuor-usciti*, the issued-forth or turned-out, of the cities—every party of them, and every man of them, thinking of nothing else but how, by hook or crook, to be "in" again, and turn out the others in their turn. One of the strangest peculiarities in this strange surging sea of conspiracy and plot "outside," was that the *fuor-usciti* of different cities thus inevitably shaken together, were by no means necessarily of the same party. The exiles from Florence might be Ghibelline, but the exiles from Arezzo were Guelf; and from the jumbling up of various factions, united in the same personal wrong, arose alliances of the most extraordinary kind, the White of one town coalescing with the Black of another town in order to get the better of the Black of their own, and giving their aid in return to abolish the White sway over their neighbors. What could these turned out ones do but conspire? Their living, their homes, their associations, and their hopes for the future were all within the walls of the town from which they were *fuor-usciti*. Every other town had its ranks filled, and citizens enough of its own to provide for; therefore to plot, to scheme, to stir up old enemies or make new alliances against the city they loved most in the world—to take advantage of all grudges against it, of all foreign cupidities, of every alien sentiment—was the natural occu-

pation of the exiles. Let Florence perish, so long as they
got back to Florence ; let her streets run with blood, her
treasures be exhausted, her foes victorious until the *fuor-
usciti* were once within the walls again ; when they turned
to bay on the instant, and repaid the allies who had helped
them back with defiance, as no longer their allies, but the
enemies of their city.

Such was the natural course of events. It brought with
it naturally many modifications of sentiment, especially in
the minds of reasonable men, who perhaps never in their
lives before had been brought in contact with the opposite
party except in the arena of a faction-fight. This, no
doubt, was one of the ways in which Dante's mind was
worked upon, and his feelings changed. He was by birth
a Guelf, and the son of fathers exiled in their day for their
party ; but these hereditary politics had been softened in
him by his own clear judgment we may hope, as well as
by his friendship with the moderate Bianchi with whom
he had become identified during his last years in Florence.
At his exile he was naturally thrown not only into the arms
of the Bianchi party, exiled along with him, but into the
next circle of opinion, that of the moderate Neri on the
other side, which fraternized with the mild Bianchi, as
the Right-Center sympathizes with the Left-Center—one
set of moderate men drawing closer to each other in a forlorn attempt to compass something like unity and peace.
Then, in the jumble and excitement of exile, what more
natural than that, with a soul too ardent for moderation of
any kind, the fiery and indignant poet should come to find
something congenial to himself in other sublimated and
fiery souls, who were not moderate, but of the fullest blood
of the Ghibellines ? and that some of their political doctrines took hold of him perhaps almost without his knowledge, twisting themselves into the other strain of Guelfic
belief with that eclecticism which comes natural to the

thoughtful mind? This complication of influences no
doubt worked secretly, molding him in private to changed
thoughts ; but he was not without other and more strenuous reasons for his political change. The primary article
of the Guelf tradition was adherence to the pope in distinction to the emperor ; *i. e.* to what was in reality a certain theory of Italian unity, vaguely conceived—an arbitrator on Italian soil of all the differences that might arise
between Italians. Pope Bonifazio, however—he who had
detained Dante in Rome while his ruin was accomplished
—had but poorly carried out this great idea. It is true
that he had sent from time to time certain ineffectual
pacieri to Florence, men who had made processions and
negotiations, but never peace. But it was Bonifazio also
who had sent the stranger, Charles of Anjou, to Florence,
as completely an alien as any German emperor, to turn
everything into confusion. The employment of this ignorant and insolent Frenchman was against all the traditions
of the Guelf party, though its more exaggerated faction
took advantage of him to gain the upper hand, as it was
the fashion in Italy to take advantage of anything which
would give a chance of getting hold of the reins of government. To the exile, however, the employment of this
foreign emissary added a new bitterness to downfall. Better an emperor with a great name and great responsibili-
ties, and that Divine Right which as yet no rebel had
thrown any doubt upon, than a lay emissary from the pope,
not clothed with any sacred responsibility of office, though
intrusted by the natural arbitrator of Italian quarrels, with
power over Italians. When the pope had thus deserted
one of the leading ideas of the Guelf party, what so natural
as that a sufferer from this desertion should be moved in
his turn to desert the party altogether, and try what the
new rallying point of the emperor, possibly a noble and
impartial monarch, great enough to act upon ideal prin-

ciples and ignore self-interest, might do? And this sharp
revulsion of feeling, from a mere political point of view,
no doubt was strongly enforced by the new associations
into which the *fuor-usciti* was suddenly thrown.

These new associations procured for Dante various
friendships which lasted all his life. Not only with the
noble brothers Scaligeri of Verona, but with other leaders
of the Ghibelline party, he formed ties which, sometimes
relaxed and sometimes dropped, yet were never quite
thrown aside. We are not exactly informed when he left
Rome; probably the sting of his own public condemnation
and outlawry roused him into activity and drove him back
to his party; but one of his first places of refuge after
leaving Rome, when it was known for certain that the
gates of Florence were shut against him, was Arezzo, a
city steadfastly Ghibelline, and against which he had
fought on the field of Campaldino. The Podestà for
the moment was Uguccione della Faggiola, a man
whose *membra vastissime* and *straordinari robostezza del
corpo* seem to have made a great impression on the chroniclers, and to whom the poet became bound in such warm
alliance of affection, that the first part of the "Divina Commedia" was, on its completion, dedicated to this gigantic
soldier of fortune. The chronology of the first three years
of the poet's exile is vague, but not the general scope of
them. Like all the exiles, his companions in misery, he
seems to have roamed up and down the world in a passion
of wild endeavor—to get allies, to get help, to get back
again to Florence, the one aim to which all others were
given up. Like children shut out of their father's house,
restlessly promenading up and down within sight of the
windows, trying every mode of entrance, every side door
and postern, every passing servant who might be cajoled
into opening, every intercessor who might work for them
within, this hapless band of grave and desperate men seem

to have haunted the neighborhood of their city, neglecting all other objects in life, plotting, conspiring, fighting, catching at every hope, hanging on to every possible enterprise, however hostile to Florence, which could by force or fraud, or any how, push open an unguarded door. It is strange and pitiful, and at the same time repulsive, to note the passion and unscrupulousness of their struggle, their carelessness as to who or what it was that should carry them back. Love and longing, and a strange bitter patriotism, extraordinary as the word sounds in such a connection, were at the bottom of it all; but the patriotism carried them into alliance with their country's enemies, and the love prompted reprisals of wrong and cruelty which it is difficult for the calm spectator, so many generations off, to forgive. Dante's first piece of apparent work after the conclusion of his ambassadorship for Florence, was an embassy of a very different description, across the hills to Verona, to persuade Bartolommeo della Scala to send a little army against Florence, four thousand foot-soldiers and seven hundred cavalry, who came from the banks of the Adige to help the *fuor-usciti* to ravage the Mugello, but not to get back to their city. Another armed attempt of the same kind was made a little later, in a still less justifiable way. Pope Bonifazio died, and was succeeded by Pope Benedetto who, after making the usual ineffectual attempt to pacify the factions by means of a cardinal-legate, called Corso Donati and his friends before him to try what his personal intercession could do for the new set of exiles. While the good pope was arguing at Perugia with the Florentine leaders, thus taking them out of the way, the exiles attempted to break into Florence, as thieves break into a house from which the master is absent. But, like all other attempts of these conspirators, this too failed, and though they actually got within the gates, they were driven back again, partly by their own folly, partly

by the inactivity of the members of their party still left in
Florence. This was their second attempt by arms, within
three years, to get themselves back to their city; and these
armed failures were preceded by how many missions, conspiracies, combinations of all kinds, and fiery labors on
the part of their leaders, among whom Dante was still
foremost. Everything else—poetry and useful work, and
everything that is good for man—was postponed to this
one object. The time came when the poet asked indignantly
whether he could not see the sweet stars and ponder upon
heavenly truth elsewhere than in Florence ; but no such
enlightenment had come to him in the earlier part of his
exile. To get back, was to him, as to the rest, the one
aim and passion of a stormy and wasted life.

This tempestuous period, which in itself is too painful
for detailed description even were that practicable, offers
few incidents to attract the attention of any but the
sternest of historical students. Nevertheless on the eve of
that last attempt upon Florence, the wife of one of the
exiled assailants brought into the world, in that blazing
July weather, when " the heat was so great that the very
air seemed to burn," a child, born on the 19th or 20th of
the month, in the year 1304, who was afterward known
to the world as Petrarch. And we have one glimpse into
the city itself which is very curious if not very attractive.
Pope Benedetto's messenger, the cardinal-*paciero*, entered
Florence in the spring of 1304 to do what he could for the
exiled Bianchi, as his predecessor not long before had tried
his best for the exiled Neri. He was received with the most
gracious welcome, with the waving of olive-branches, sym-
bolic decorations, and every appearance of probable success; and among the other entertainments provided for his
eminence was one in which we seem to see a reflection out
of the very soul of the *fuor-uscito*, then wistfully from a
tower in the Apennines gazing toward Florence, waiting

for the news of deliverance. It was May once more, the
festive time of Florence, when all kinds of out-door revels
were common, and the city was roused by the announce-
ment of a new and remarkable spectacle. " The Borgo
San Friano " (San Frediano, the old suburb, still bearing
the same name, with its gaunt church on the other side of
Arno) " sent out messengers to say that whosoever would
have news of the other world was to go on the calends of
May to the Ponte alla Carraja and to the banks of the river.
And upon Arno they placed boats and rafts of wood, and
showed upon them the similitude and figures of the infer-
nal regions, with fires and tortures, misshapen men and
demons horrible to see, and others which had the appearance of naked souls; and put them to divers torments with
great cries and groaning which were terrible to hear and
to see. This new play drew many citizens to see it ; and
the bridge, which was then made of wood, being full and
thronged with people, fell by their weight, so that many
were drowned and died in Arno, and many were injured ;
so that the comedy was turned into truth, and, according
to the invitation, many by dying acquired news of the other
world, with great weeping and dolor to all the city."

Was this strange scene an unconscious reflection from
Dante's *abozzo* then reposing somewhere in darkness and
secrecy in one of Madonna Gemma's strong boxes? or is it
merely an indication how the mind of the time was turning, occupying itself with such dramatic guesses at the
darker side of the future existence as grew into a vivid revelation under the poet's touch? Between the blue skies of
May and the glimmering Arno, overshadowed by its bridges,
what strange phantasmagoria it was which bewildered the
crowded spectators on the banks! the red gleams of the
fires floating on the dark river, the cries of the fictitious
victims, the shouts of the demon-actors, the smoke and
burning that figured hell; and then all at once a real hell

of terror and suffering—the crash, the plunge, the wild dismay, the fantastic horror come true. Must not the exile, straining his eager ears outside, have heard some echo of the great outcry? and felt with characteristic pride and scorn that nothing less than some unconscious reverberation from the visionary world which he alone had revealed could have conjured up this extraordinary scene?

Pope Benedetto and his *paciero* failed, as all popes and peacemakers had failed before them; and so did every other effort made by the exiles. For three years from the date of his banishment Dante struggled with and for his party in the attempt to get back again to his home, in vain; but he was not the man to fall hopelessly into that miserable rôle of conspirator, which is the very curse of political exile; and by this time it is evident he had begun to feel the disgust of a higher nature for the crowd of common factionists with whom he found himself mixed up. He had already learned by experience how difficult was the art of getting back from banishment—*"quanto quest' artepesa,"* as Farinata had warned him in the *"Inferno"*— and now his mind seems to have been brought to the point indicated in the indignant outburst which he puts by way of prophecy into the mouth of his own ancestor Cacciaguida:

> " That which shall hardest weigh upon thy mind
>   Shall be the hateful company and vile
>   With which confounded thou thyself shalt find.
> Which all, ungrateful, empty, vain, with guile,
>   Shall turn against thee, though not thou but they
>   Ruined their ark of refuge; rude and vile
> The actions of their baseness shall convey
>   Proof to thy mind, that of thyself to make
>   Thy only party is the better way."

It was after the failure of the first three attempts, by

warlike and by peaceful means, to return to Florence, that this disgust seems to have seized upon him. The squabbles, the vanities, the jealousies and grudgings, of his exiled companions, revolted his loftier and more impetuous soul. He had done what was in him to secure success to their efforts, and for the third time they had failed miserably from their own weakness and infirmity of purpose. Perhaps the turning against him of his party described above had to do with some reluctance on the part of the Scaligeri, his friends, to renew the aid which they had formerly sent; but anyhow after this last failure the party of *fuor-usciti;* seems to have tumbled to pieces, and Dante, indignant and wounded, forsook them and politics together, and turned back to the pursuits which he had abandoned for that thankless path of public life. He went to Bologna, no doubt with much despiteful melancholy mingling in his nobler desire for a practicable life, and resumed his long interrupted studies, giving himself over to philosophy, and such comfort as she could bestow. He would seem to have spent about two years in the learned city. His eldest child, Pietro, a boy now about thirteen, came to him from Florence, probably beginning his studies when his grave father recommenced his; but we know nothing of the poet's intercourse with his children, nor can we guess what share this little Florentine, fresh from his mother's care, had in the life or the thoughts of the imperious and melancholy exile, embittered by the privations of his life and the contradictions of men, who thus turned back to his books in his moment of need, spurning, one cannot but feel, with something of the scorn of wounded pride, the world and the party which had not done justice to him. During the following years of tranquillity and solitude, Dante wrote the "Convito" and his Essay on Eloquence, two works more valuable for the indications of himself to be found in them than for their own excellence. The latter work, the

"Volgare Eloquio," was, though composed in Latin, specially designed to prove and illustrate the fitness of the *lingua volgare,* the vulgar tongue, to be adopted as the medium of literature—a curiously appropriate preface to his own suspended work, the *abozzo* which he supposed to be lost, and with which in its first disguise of clumsy Latin he may well have grown disgusted, but which was yet to rise out of its ashes like the phœnix, new-made and transformed, creating and forming the very language of modern Italy, as well as the greatest literary work she has ever produced.

No doubt the quiet interval thus spent at Bologna served its purpose in collecting and concentrating the powers of his mind, which had been distracted by the cares and labors of public life, and the plottings and conspirings of his exiled condition. Even his temper seems to have softened in this moment of retirement, when with only the hills between him and his home, and his child beside him quickening all his longings, he grew humble in his anxiety, "and endeavored by good works and good demeanor to gain the grace of a recall to Florence by the spontaneous revocation of his banishment by those who ruled the city. And for this he labored much, writing letters not only to the principal citizens but also to the people; and among others a long letter beginning ' *Populo mi quid fui tibi?* ' " Here is his own description of himself, poor, wistful, and homeless, with, for the moment, all his haughty pretensions subdued, and his heart more sad than angry in the sense of wrong:

"Since it pleased the most beautiful and most famous daughter of Rome, Fiorenza, to cast me forth from her sweetest bosom (in which I was nourished till I reached the highest point of life, and in which peacefully I desired, with all my heart, to rest my weary soul and end the days allotted to me), through almost all the regions where this language is spoken, I have gone, a pilgrim, almost a beggar, striving against wrong, with the wounds of fortune, which are often unjustly imputed as faults to the person wounded. Truly I have been a bark without sail and without helm, blown about to different ports and coasts by the dry wind which miserable poverty breathes forth: and I have appeared vile to the eyes of many who perhaps had imagined to see me in another form; in whose sight not only am I degraded by fortune, but of smaller value is made every work I have done, as well as that which I am now about to make."

The time of quiet, however, did not last long. Nothing is more remarkable in the history of that age than the constant changes and modifications which took place in one after another of these fierce and powerful municipalities. Bologna, which had been White and friendly for two years, giving a grateful refuge to the exile, changed her political creed and her rulers in 1307, and became no longer a safe resting-place for the Florentine *fuor-usciti*; and Dante was driven away from his studies into the wilds of Lunigiana, where he found refuge with a nobleman of the Malespina family. The story of the *abozzo* here comes in, making a picturesque break in the somber tale. Changes, too, had taken place in Florence. Messer Corso, the haughty head of the Donati, had formed an alliance with big Uguccione of Arezzo, the moderate Ghibelline who was Dante's friend; and this fact, which was hopeful for her husband, perhaps encouraged Madonna Gemma to shake off her terrors, and cautiously to gather together again her own and her husband's property which she had so prudently locked up and hid away in friends' houses at the time of his banishment. For this end she called to her aid a certain Andrea Poggi, a nephew of her husband, and marvelously like him in form and figure, according to the evidence of Boccaccio; and giving him the keys of the strong boxes sent him with a procurator to search for the title-deeds and other papers which were necessary for the recovery of her possessions. While the procurator looked

for these documents, Andrea, no doubt young and fond
of such trifles, seeing in the great chest other writings
of his uncle's, examined them, and found many sonnets
and *canzoni,* and along with these something more
valuable still, of which Boccaccio thus continues his narrative:

" But among the rest that which pleased him most was a *quadernetto,* in which were written, in Dante's own hand, the first seven
cantos ; and therefore taking it he carried it away with him, and reading it again and again, though he understood but little of it, yet it
appeared to him a very beautiful thing, and therefore he decided to
take it, in order to know what it was, to an excellent person of our
city, who in those times was a very famous writer (*dicitore*) in rhyme,
whose name was Dino, of Messer Lambertuccio Frescobaldi. The
which Dino being marvelously delighted, had copies of it made for
some of his friends, and seeing th it the work was rather begun than
complete, concluded that he ought to send it to Dante, and to pray
of him that. as he had begun, he would finish it ; and having found
that Dante was in those days in Lunigiana with a nobleman of the
Malaspini, called the Marchese Moroello, who was a man of understanding and very much his friend, he decided not to send it to Dante
but to the marchese ; and this he did, praying the marchese to persuade
Dante as much as he could to continue the undertaking and bring it
to completion. The seven cantos thus came to the hand of the marchese, who, being marvelously delighted with them, showed them to
Dante, and having heard from him that the work was his, prayed
him to continue it. To whom Dante replied : ' I certainly supposed
that this, along with all my other things and a quantity of writings,
had been lost when my house was sacked, and therefore I felt my
mind and my thoughts lightened of all care for it. But since it has
pleased God that it should not be lost but sent back to me, I will do
my best to follow up the work according to my first intention.' And
thus, turning back into his old thoughts and resuming the interrupted
work, he began the eighth canto with these words—*I' dico segui-
tando.*"

How picturesque is the sudden entry thus afforded us
into the old narrow streets, so jealously shut against the
exile ; to prudent Gemma drawing the family fortunes

together again, getting back quietly this and that bit of
property which friends had claimed as their own to screen
it from confiscation, looking out her papers, her marriage
contract, and the deeds that established her rights, but
perhaps not so careful of the other papers in the *cassone*,
which she had bundled in, in hot haste, "in the fury of
the revolution," along with them! And as the lawyer
rummaged for these important documents through all that
mass of celestial rubbish, unprized by procurators, young
Andrea, perhaps himself something of a *trovatore*, catching
sight of those irregular scribblings that made his eyes
shine, grasping at the sonnets and the songs, but finding a
larger something embarrassing his handful! What was it?
Latin, not the vulgar tongue, for which, over the hills in
Bologna, the exile had been writing himself into enthusiasm. Curious, and reverential and excited, how the
young Florentine must have pored over it, making out,
for all so little as he could understand, that here was
something worth the trouble, a *bellissima cosa*, something
of which perhaps all the Alighieri might be proud. Little
cared the procurator, hunting after his parchments ; and
not much, it is to be supposed, Madonna Gemma, who had
seen enough of this sort of thing, *scrittura assai*, and so
long as her deeds were found, left Andrea free to what
he liked with the *quadernetto*. This young Andrea was
the son of Dante's sister—"*il quale maravigliosamente
nelle lineature del viso somigliò Dante ed ancora nella stature
della persona.*" It is pleasant to think that it was he, so
like the poet and so near him in blood, who found the lost
treasure.

This was in the opening of the year 1307, five years after
Dante's banishment; and another grateful pause ensues
forthwith in the exile's life. Rumor, indeed, points to him as
serving as secretary to the general who led another Ghibelline army against Florence, but of this there is no authentic

evidence; and it seems much more probable that, ardent
and eager as he was in every pursuit, he shut himself up in
that friendly castle of Malaspina with the recovered cantos
which had been brought back to him as by a miracle, and
plunging into the splendid task—into that gloomy world of
the "Inferno," where it was his, like a god, to award everlasting praise to his friends and infamy to his enemies—
gave himself up to the perfection and completion of the
work. Certain it is that he disappears from public view
for a time, reappearing authentic and visible only in the
end of the year 1308, and then with the "Inferno" complete
and finished in his hand. In the meantime, however,
before we show to the reader the great wayfarer who
knocked at the convent gate of Santa Croce, when Fra
Ilario was prior, another change had happened in Florence,
which it seems likely destroyed a dawning hope of better
fortunes for the poet. Once more he was to prove by sad
experience how difficult for an exile was the act of returning to the city which had cast him forth.

Messer Corso, the head of the Donati, had been no friend
to Dante. Indeed it had been his victory and that of his
party which had driven the poet into exile; but in the
course of years Corso too, like all the rest, began to change
his alliances and modify his views. He had formed ties,
as we have said, with Uguccione della Faggiola, the captain
of Arezzo, and probably Dante saw in this alliance between
his wife's relation and his own personal friend a promise of
happier days for himself. The jealous Florentines, however, did not like the new-found connection, and all
the old suspicions and dislikes which Corso's haughty behavior had long ago raised in the popular mind came to the
surface again. "It was said that Messer Corso meant to
make himself lord of the city," and the actual rulers were
seized with panic, "knowing his great spirit and power
and following . . . . and that he had made a league with

Uguccione." The result shows very clearly the summary progress of events in those wild times:

" Upon this great jealousy was awakened in the city, and a tumult arose, and the priors rang the bells, and the whole city rushed to arms, on foot and on horseback, along with the party of Catalans who were under the orders of the government. And immediately an in- quisition was appointed before the Podestà against the said Messer Corso, accusing him of the intention of betraying the people and overthrowing the government of the city by bringing in Uguccione with the Ghibellines and enemies of Florence. And as soon as the demand was made and heard, he was condemned in less than an hour, without any more formal trial, as a rebel and traitor to his commune; and incontinently the priors, the Gonfalonier of Justice, with the Podestà, the captain, the executioners and their followers, and the populace armed, bearing the banners of their companies, and with a battalion of cavalry, set out, with shouts and tumult, to the house of Messer Corso, close by San Piero Maggiore. Messer Corso, hearing of the prosecution against him, had barricaded himself in the Borgo of San Piero . . . and in the road of San Brocolo, with strong barricades, and a great force of friends and allies shut up within, and with bowmen at his service; and it was said that he had fortified himself so to await Uguccione and his people, who had already arrived at Remolo. The people began to attack the barri- cades, and Messer Corso and his followers to defend them; and the struggle lasted for most of the day, and raged so hotly that, notwith- standing the strength of the people, if the reinforcements of Uguc- cione and the other friends expected by Messer Corso had arrived, the people of Florence would have had enough to do on that day. For though their numbers were great, they were badly ordered and little in accord. When the followers of Uguccione, however, heard that Messer Corso was attacked by the people they fell back, and those who defended the barricades began to withdraw, so that Corso remained with but a small following. At this point some of the people made a breach in the wall of the garden opposite the Stinche, upon which Messer Corso and his party, seeing that the help of Uguccione had failed them, abandoned the houses and fled toward the country, and the said houses were immediately robbed and de- stroyed by the people, and Messer Corso was pursued by various citizens on horseback, and by the Catalans who were sent to take him . . . . Messer Corso, escaping all alone, was overtaken and secured above the villa called Ravazzano, by certain Catalans on horseback; and as they led him back to Florence, when they were passing San Salvi he implored them to let him go, offering them great sums of money. And as they would not listen to him, but were faithful to their duty, Messer Corso, fearing to fall into the hands of his enemies and to be murdered by the people, having his hands and feet tied, let himself from his horse. The said Catalans seeing him on the ground, one of them gave him a mortal blow in the throat with his lance, and leaving him there for dead, the monks of San Salvi carried him into the monastery, and some said that before he died he found repentance by their means, but others said that he was dead when they found him; and the next morning he was buried with little ceremony in the monastery, few people being present for fear of the people. This Messer Corso was the best instructed, the most worthy cavalier, and the finest orator, and of better deportment and higher reputation than, in his time, was any other in Italy."

This strange sudden tumult, fierce street fighting, and hot personal vengeance; the bristling barricades, over which those fiery neighbors confronted one another; the houses robbed and wrecked in the war; the solitary fugitive taken in his despair—he who had been almost lord in Florence, and left to die there on the dusty road, the last offices tremblingly done for him by the poor monks—makes a curious pendant to the peaceful vignette of mediæval burgher-life which came before, and which showed us how the families of the fallen lifted their heads, and the robbed houses recovered the guise of life, and the alienated property stole back again by friendly aid into the lawful owners' hands. But if there had been hope in the house of Madonna Gemma that the father might come back to it, and life begin anew, and the prosperous days return, here was an end of that hope. The powerful Donati, however, their opinions might modify, were now, for a time at least, powerful no longer, nor like to be of efficient service to any banished man.

It is after this event that Dante suddenly appears again in the full light of a graphic personal narrative, upon one

of the hills which overlook the lovely bay of Spezia, knocking, as we have said, at the gates of the convent of Santa
Croce del Corvo. The story comes to us in the form of a
letter from Fra Ilario, prior of the monastery, addressed
to Uguccione della Faggiola, and beginning with quaint
monkish moralities and scriptural quotations about the
good things which a good man brings out of his heart, and
about the necessity of shunning idleness and making a
good use of all gifts. " This which is here said of the
profitable employment of the inner treasure," says the
Frate, "seems to have been so well observed from childhood upward by no Italian as by the man whose work,
with the exposition of it made by my own hand, I hereby
send to you; who (as I have heard from others to my great
wonder) from his youth up has said such things as man
never heard before; and (more wonderful still) those things
which the greatest can with difficulty explain in Latin, he
has essayed to make clear in the vulgar tongue—in the
vulgar, I say, and not rudely expressed, but musical."
With this curious and artless preamble the monk proceeds
to tell the story of his visitor. Upon the sunny hills overlooking the eastern Riviera stood at least one castle of that
Malaspina who was Dante's protector; and the poet was
probably at this moment on his way to the northern side of
the Alps, to Paris, and the alien world far from Italy. No
doubt his meaning was to leave his work in safety before
he wended his way into those strange and barbarous countries whither he went in exile and poverty and something
like despair.

"His intention" (resumes Fra Ilario) "being to travel into ultra-
montane regions, he passed through the diocese of Luni, and, either
in devotion to the place or from some other cause, came to this monastery. As he was unknown to me and my brethren, I asked when I
saw him, ' What would you?' And he, answering not a word but
gazing at the building, I asked him again what he sought. He then,

looking round upon me and my brethern, answered 'Peace.' From which there began to kindle in me a knowledge of what manner of man he was ; and leading him aside, apart from the others, and talking with him, I came to know him ; for although I had never seen him until that day, his fame had reached me a long time before. When, then, he perceived that I gave him my entire attention, and saw that I was well affected to hear all he said, he drew from his bosom in a familiar manner and freely showed to me, a little book. ' Here,' said he, ' is one part of my work which perhaps you have not seen. I will leave you this memorial that it may give you a more lasting recollection of me.' And as he gave me the little book, I received it gratefully in my lap, opened it, and in his presence fixed my eyes upon it with eagerness. And seeing that it was written in the vulgar tongue, and showing in my looks that I was astonished he asked me the reason of my surprise ; to whom I replied that I was astonished at the language in which it was written ; that it appeared to me not only difficult but unimaginable that he could embody in the vulgar tongue so arduous a work, and that it scarcely appeared to me seemly to array so much knowledge in a popular garment. ' Your ideas are according to reason,' he replied, ' and when at the beginning (moved perhaps from heaven) the seed of this undertaking began to germinate, I chose for it its legitimate language, and not only chose it, but thus in the usual mode I began to rhyme (*poetando*) :

> " Ultima regna canam fluido contermina mundo
> Spiritibus quæ lata patent, quæ prœmia solvunt
> Pro meritis cuicumque suis."

But when I considered the condition of the present age, I saw that the songs of the most illustrious poets were neglected of all, and for this reason high-minded men who in better times wrote on such themes, now left (oh, pity !) the liberal arts to the crowd. For this I laid down the pure lyre with which I was provided, and prepared for myself another more adapted to the understanding of the moderns ; for it is vain to give to sucklings solid food.'

" Saying these things, he added, very affectionately, that if I permitted myself to take trouble about such matters, I was to supply certain notes to the work, and send it, accompanied by those remarks, to you. And if I have not entirely elucidated all that is hidden in his words, yet have I done what I could faithfully and with a free mind ; and as that most friendly man enjoined upon me,

I destined the work for you.   In the which if anything seems am-
biguous, impute it wholly to my insufficiency; for the text itself
ought without doubt to be held as perfect in every way."

This vivid and touching glimpse of the wandering poet,
already so well known that the eager monk could see at
once what manner of man he was, and recognized him as
soon as he had talked to him, disperses the shadows for one
brief moment and lights up the gloom in which the
wanderer was almost lost to us.   Who could it have been
but Dante? straying abstracted by the convent walls,
looking at the building while the curious friars surrounded
him with their questions, saying out of his deep, weary,
melancholy soul the one word "Peace," when they asked
him what he wanted.   Alas! that was the thing he was
. not to have any more than the rest of the world.   He had
done away with the Latin of the *abozzo,* and set forth the
great landscape of that hell, secure, so that neither revolution nor confiscation, nor danger of any sort, could
touch it; and having thus deposited it—probably the
corrected copy especially prepared by his own care (for
other copies were already floating about the world)—in the
safe hands of Fra Ilario, who no doubt must have had some
reputation in his day to warrant the choice thus made, the
poet felt himself ready to go forth, having, as it were, made
provision for the better part of him—the thing which
neither he nor Italy, hard though Italy had been upon
him, would willingly let die.

Only for a moment, however, is such a glimpse of the
great wayfarer permitted to us.   Very soon he has to resume his journey, leaving the sheltering convent, where
the kind prior admired and wondered over his great work,
solitary and sad, yet noting with glowing, abstracted eyes
every natural feature of the way, transplanting the "wild
and broken paths" between Lerice and Turbia into his
purgatory, and receiving into his heart the music of the

sea and the winds. Gazing wistfully from those heights over that loveliest of sea-lines, perhaps hearing the tinkle behind him, as he went forth into the unknown, of Fra Ilario's peaceful convent bells, what softening moisture must have stolen into the poet's eyes as the magical momentary Italian twilight grew dim over the shining water between night and day, and into his soul breathed the music of these words—*volgare,* yet as exquisite as any words could be :

> " Era gia l'ora che volge il disio
> Ai naviganti, e intenerisce il core
> Lo dí che han detto a' dolce amici addio ;
> E che lo novo peregrin d'amore
> Punge, se ode squilla di lontano
> Che paia il giorno pianger che si more."

Not on so peaceful a sea as the Mediterranean was Dante's voyage ; but as he gazed over the resplendent waters and listened to the distant bell, and saw the soft day die before him, drawing a sudden veil over her sunset glories, what a touch of tender sadness was that which made him think of the *naviganti,* the parting sailors who that day had bidden sweet friends farewell. He, too, was saying farewell to sweet friends, to dear hopes, to Italy— while yet one of the fairest of her landscapes held him, and the soft dying cadence of the religious bell pursued him like a recalling voice. How love pricked at the heart of the new pilgrim ; yet with a resolute melancholy in that lofty face of his, still beautiful as in Giotto's portrait, but growing stern with years and disappointments, he turned toward the north, toward the country of the stranger. Upon such a picture, sad as it is, the imagination loves to linger—loving Dante better in his wandering and poverty than in the person of the soured and bitter *fuor-uscito* in which he reappears only too soon.

The poet would seem to have passed about two years in

Paris, another moment of quiet in his life, when, as
Boccaccio tells us, "he gave himself to the study of theology and philosophy," discussing questions in the schools
and distinguishing himself greatly among the learned there,
but not without great "inconvenience in the things necessary to life." "Ah," he cries in the " Paradiso," "if the
world but knew the heart of him who goes from trouble to
trouble, begging his life." These *impedementi*, things in-
convenient—sharp poverty and want—look very sordid and
miserable to the sufferer ; yet there are many things in a
life more painful to look back upon, both to himself and
his friends, than those moments of need and of care.
Dante, poor and worn, maintaining his thesis against all
comers, seated on his student's sheaf of straw, wandering
about the narrow streets of that ghostly old Paris, or perhaps—who knows ? getting as far as England, has nothing but our sympathy.   But his next aspect is not so noble.
While he was still occupying his mind and his time with
scholastic questions of theology or metaphysics, a new
emperor, Henry of Luxemburg, was elected in Germany :
and with this new monarch the exile's hopes sprang back
into new vigor, vigor unfortunately marked and stained
with the growing bitterness of spirit which had been quies-
cent or hidden from us during those years of quiet.   When
he heard that at last the emperor was about to make a
descent on Italy, and set everything right that was wrong,
and redress all injuries, the long-restrained impetuous
current of his impatience burst forth.   He would seem to
have rushed back at once to some corner of Tuscany,
where we see him watching, eager and chafing at its delays, the emperor's progress, and thundering from some
refuge among the hills " near the springs of Arno," against
Florence, appealing against her to Henry and to heaven.
The emperor had come to Italy with the best intentions,
such as indeed seem to be the patrimony of German em-

perors, however carried out. He invaded Italy for her good, to pacificate and set her right, calming the rebellious independence of her cities into dutiful subjection, restoring her exiles and mending her feuds—whether with or without her will, what did it matter? It seems very strange to us that even the *fuor-usciti* whom it was Henry's object to restore to their homes—here Guelfs, there Ghibellines, with imperial impartiality—did not perceive what a tremendous blow was struck at the cherished independence of their cities by this dictation; but years of exile and suffering do not tend to make the judgment clear, and abstract principles of right and wrong were perhaps less fully perceived in the beginning of the fourteenth century than those personal rights and wrongs which a conquered party are always so deeply conscious of. However this may be, it is evident that Dante at least had no objection to owe his recall to the mandate of the emperor. He had loved and guarded the liberties of Florence when they were in his hands; but something still more near and pressing than the liberties of Florence came now between him and them. His own restoration, and her punishment who had used him so cruelly, were the first things of which he thought; and to see the emperor, upon whom he had set his hopes, wasting his time in Lombardy among cities like Brescia, and Pavia, whose quarrels were unworthy his notice, and leaving Florence uncared for, filled his mind with impatience and dismay.

"Signore!" he writes, addressing the emperor in the name of his fellow-exiles, "you who are the most excellent prince of princes, you cannot perceive from your height of greatness where the wolf has hid herself from the hunters. In truth, that deceiver does not drink of the flowing Po or of your Tiber. It is the water of Arno that is made into poison by her guile. That cruel death is called Florence. This is the viper that rends her mother's womb;

this is the diseased sheep that infects the flock of the
Lord." Such was the bitter tone of his outcry, against
the city which was as heaven to him, loved and longed for
with a love which by this time had grown sharp and fierce
as hatred. When Dante thus appealed to him, the Teuton
emperor was doing what he could—with that curious indifference to all human probabilities and experience which
seems to distinguish his race—to carry out his mission:
stamping out momentarily the fires of domestic feud in
one small belligerent municipality after another, with
solemn disregard to the certainty that these flames would
burst forth again the moment his back was turned. If he
lingered on his way it was with this object; the pacification
of Lombardy in the first place, and restoration of peace on
earth, on that side of the Apennines at least. But what
was Lombardy or the exiles of insignificant Brescia to the
hungry and eager Florentines, who felt their own woe of
exile to be so much greater than any other woe? Henry
did not pause to take any active steps against Florence on
his way to Rome, where he was going for his coronation,
but stopped the mouths of the *fuor-usciti* for the moment
by an imperial mandate ordering her to pacificate herself
on pain of more strenuous measures when he should come
back. Florence was no doubt encouraged in her resistance
to this mandate by the re-bursting forth of a great proportion of the pacificated cities behind him which, while he
was still scarcely out of hearing, packed about their business the exiles whom Henry had restored, and in many
cases his own imperial *vicario* after them—a violent and
unmistakable protestation of their independence and determination not to submit to foreign sway. Even the
exiles themselves, one would have supposed, must have
sympathized in this resistance to the foreigner; but it is
difficult to enter into the strangely-mingled feeling which
could make a patriotic Italian of the middle ages—vehe-

ment in defense of his country's liberties while in that country—invite with the very violence of passion any and every hostile intervention which would restore him to the place which he had lost.

The aspect of Florence, however, at this moment was as valiant as that of the exiles was unnatural. Strong in the very essence of her Guelf creed, the maintenance of individual independence and civic freedom, the city set herself from the first to resist the arbitrary settlement of her affairs and reconcilement of her difficulties which the emperor would have made by force had his powers equaled his intention. It was unjust and cruel, no doubt, to banish so many of her sons from her bosom, but having for a supposed good reason banished them, it would have been little to her credit to have suffered them to be forced back upon her at the will of a stranger. Florence set her face like a flint against the invader. To the first mandate of the emperor she made proud answer that "never to any lord would Florence bow her head." By and by, however, so much prudential regard for her safety moved her, that of her own accord she recalled a certain number of the banished ; but maintained her independence and vindicated her pride even while doing so, by making formal exception from this amnesty of a certain number, "four hundred and twenty-nine persons," among whom Dante is specially named. Henry took no positive steps against the rebellious city until August, 1312, when, on his return from his coronation at Rome, he besieged her ineffectually for three months. Dante, it is hoped and believed, though he had instigated and encouraged the assault, was not actually present in arms against his city on this or any other occasion. And Florence, firm and self-collected within her walls, resisting alike his overtures and his siege, baffled the emperor, with all his forces. Henry withdrew in the beginning of 1313 and retired to Pisa, where he left Uguccione della Faggiola as imperial *vicario* and captain. Then making his way toward the sea across the Maremma, the emperor, weakened no doubt by all his fatigues and the discouragement of non-success, fell a victim to the bad air of that unwholesome country, and died, by the wayside as it were, a pitiful fate, while yet the imperial crown was scarcely warm upon his brows. So ended the would-be pacification of Italy, with which great aim the Teutonic emperor had begun his career; a noble enterprise enough, had the intention only been taken into account. That it should have been hailed with feverish enthusiasm as a godlike mission by such a spectator as Dante, is, however, the best that can be said for it. The turbulent cities which kept life at the boiling point of energy in Italy, with their perpetual squabbles, overturns, revolutions, and casting forth now of one faction, now of another, had much in them that might have been mended ; but still it is impossible not to sympathize with their universal determination to resist the dictation of the stranger.

Dante withdrew after this last failure of his hopes to Pisa or Lucca, both of which were under the sway of Uguccione, and there solaced the smart of disappointment by a strange, wild essay upon monarchy ; that is, upon the universal monarchy which was the dream of the Ghibelline party—as wild a fiction of fancy as perhaps was ever formed in any mind crazed by political wrongs. His universal monarch, who was—by divine right of the Roman people, the race elected to have rule in the world by the ordinance of God—to be always the Roman emperor, was an ideal and poetical despot reigning only to make evil into good, to be the unfailing referee in all questions of national right and wrong, to redress all grievances and punish all offenders, and do infallible justice over all the world ; but without interfering with

individual laws or government, without encroaching upon
any privileges or lessening the force of any municipal rule.
A wilder dream, or a more fantastic, could not have been.
Just such another disinterested and splendid arbitrator,
defender of the weak, redeemer of all wrongs, champion
of every one who was injured, was the Papa Angelico, the
possible pope, emblem and impersonation of all the virtues,
of whom, on their side, the Guelf party dreamed, and of
whom, too, Dante, had seen visions in his day. But neither
heroic universal monarch nor Papa Angelico was to come
to the waiting age, eager for ideal means of escape from
the imbroglio itself had made. Human life then, as now,
had to tread its common way, reaping what it had sown,
the whirlwind more often than any more substantial
harvest. But it was so much in favor of the earlier
centuries that, too young in existence to be convinced by
hard experiment, as we are, of the hopelessness of all such
splendid expedients to make chaos into order, they still
could dream of and look for some great impossible man,
some divine hero or god out of the machinery, who should
step forth suddenly from the skies and make every wrong
into right.

Here, too—a wiser and better undertaking than his speculations upon monarchy—the poet wrote his " Purgatorio "
Another tranquil interval of two years, the measure apparently of time during which he could remain at rest, he
seems to have been occupied thus peacefully, living in Pisa
or in Lucca, both of which were under the sway of his
friend and patron Uguccione. This warrior-giant was one
of the soldiers of fortune of whose sudden successes and
reverses the history of the middle ages is full. He was at
this time at the very climax of his prosperity. Lord of
Pisa by right of election, and of Lucca by conquest, holding the appointment of imperial vicar or deputy from the
late emperor and with a thousand German cavaliers of

Henry's dispersed army in his pay, there was no more powerful potentate in Tuscany or Umbria. He was strong
enough even to wage war with and defeat, at the battle of
Monte Catino, the whole force of the Florentines and their
allies, commanded by a brother of King Robert of Sicily;
a victory, however, of which nothing seems to have come
except a further exasperation of the Florentines (not without some appearance of excuse) against Dante, who was
known to be one of Uguccione's chief friends and counselors; and who, after his public letters to the emperor,
could not be supposed guiltless of inciting assaults against
his native city. Uguccione's power, however, was short-
lived. In the height of his greatness some foolish proceedings taken by his son, who was his deputy in Lucca,
against a popular citizen, raised that city against their sway.
Uguccione, immediately on hearing of this, set forth to re-
duce the rebellious town, but had no sooner got out of sight,
midway between the two, than Pisa also revolted, and shut
her gates against him—a whimsical kind of overthrow.
The nominal ruler of both cities was thus left on the road
between them with his band of mercenaries, rejected by
both, and no longer ruler of anything except those rude
German free-lances, ever ready to sell themselves to the
highest bidder. He took refuge, it is said, in a friendly
stronghold of the Malaspini, who had also been protectors
and friends of Dante, and to one of whom the "Purgatorio" was dedicated, as the "Inferno" was to Uguccione;
but finally found shelter in Verona; where, descending
altogether from his lofty estate, the soldier of fortune
resumed his original place, and entered the service of Can
Grande, the ruler of Verona, as captain of his forces, along
with his strong band of Germans, no contemptible addition
to the army of any Italian city.

What happened to Dante in this sudden revolt against
his friend there is no evidence, but it would appear that he

very soon followed him to Verona, where already the poet
had more than once found a temporary refuge. Indeed
that beautiful city is more closely associated with the exile
in the reminiscences of history than any other of his
many refuges. The three brothers Scaligeri had reigned
over it in succession during the time of Dante's banishment. With the first, Bartolommeo, he had found a gracious reception in its very beginning, and aid had been
sent to the Florentine *fuor-usciti* by this prince, at Dante's
request. The second, Alboino, finds no place among the
list of the poet's friends ; but he, too, had died and given
place to the youngest brother, Cane della Scala, who seems
to have received Dante with all the enthusiasm of youth.
Can Grande, Cane the Great, was a splendid young prince
in those days, the very ideal of a poet's patron, loving letters and art and everything magnificent, as Italian princes
were so apt to do. He had already held supreme authority
for years, though he was but twenty-five, and was as popular as he was splendid and powerful, surrounded by the very
enthusiasm and glory of youthful success. With this magnificent young prince Dante seems to have formed one of
those hot and sudden friendships which men of passionate
temperament rush into, often to their cost. But indeed it
is perhaps scarcely just to the poet to say this, for no doubt
he had known Can della Scala as a boy at his brother's
court ten years before, and had watched his progress up to
this full bloom of princely excellence with that indulgent
admiration which it is the privilege of all promising young
creatures, but of none so much as of princes, to excite.
Can Grande received the stranger with enthusiasm, and it is
evident that Dante, with the poet's glamour always in his
eyes, and probably with the partiality of mature age for the
youth whose promise he had watched into full development in his mind, was seized with an equally enthusiastic
appreciation of his young host. So great was his opinion

of him that, according to Boccaccio, " it was his custom,
when he had written seven or eight cantos, before any one
else had seen them, wherever he was, to send them to Messer Cane della Scala, whom he held in respect above every
other, and after they had been seen by him copies were
made for others, and in this manner he did with all except
the last thirteen cantos." Indeed Dante himself leaves us
in no doubt as to his sentiments. The following extract
from the letter of dedication by which he presents to Cane
the " Paradiso " which was inscribed to him, gives full
expression to his admiration and gratitude. It is addressed
to the " Magnificent and victorious Signore, the Signore
Cane Grande della Scala, *vicario* of the most sacred and
serene prince in Verona and Vicenza :"

" The praise of your magnificence, spread by vigilant and flying
report, makes so much impression upon different minds that in some
it increases hope and puts others in fear. . . . Not to remain in
long uncertainty, like that eastern queen who came to Jerusalem,
and as Palladius came to Helicon, so came I to Verona to judge faithfully with my proper eyes. Then I saw your magnificence which I
had already heard of from every quarter. I saw and proved your
kindness. And as at first I feared that what was said exceeded the
facts, so now I know that the facts go beyond the report. From
which it came that as by simple hearing I had been moved toward
you in a softening of the spirit, so at first sight I became your devoted friend. Nor do I think by assuming the name of friend that
I am presumptuous, as many may suppose ; for the sacred chain of
friendship links together those who are unequal in rank as well as
those who are each other's peers, and between the former may be
seen delightful and useful friendships."

This epistle shows the mutual warmth of personal intercourse between the poet and his magnificent young
patron ; though even already there are signs that Dante
had begun to feel the humiliations of exile. " The narrowness of my opportunities," he says (*stre tezza di mie
facoltà*), "compels me to give up this (the ' Divine Comedy')

and other things useful for the public weal, but I hope by
your magnificence soon to have very different means of
useful occupation." The *strettezza di mie facoltà* have
been explained to bear reference to the humble office of
magistrate which Dante seems to have held in Verona, and
which, much inferior to his claims and character, filled
him with painful humiliation and that sense of downcome
which is perhaps, of all other sensations of poverty, the
most hard to bear. The various anecdotes which have
come to us of this period seem to indicate a court full of
flatterers, parasites, and rival wits, not of a very refined
character (and indeed the wit of the middle ages was seldom
either brilliant or refined), all concurring in the one aim
to please and amuse the prince who was the center of all
their hopes ; an object which Dante, loftily extending his
friendship to the young Magnifico, was very little likely to
strain after. Here is a story reported by Petrarch, and
marked by the well known unfriendliness of that poet
toward his greater predecessor, which nevertheless has
about it the stamp of truth ·

"Dante Alighieri, my townsman, was a very enlightened man for
compositions in the vulgar tongue.* but in his habits and speech, by
perversity, more independent than was agreeable to delicate and nice
ears and to the eyes of the princes of our age. Who being an exile
from his country, and dwelling with Can Grande, then the universal
refuge and consolation of the afflicted, was at first held by him in
great honor, but little by little fell back, and from day to day became
less agreeable to the prince. There were in the same court actors

---

* The reader will note with amusement a certain condescension
in all the contemporary writers toward Dante's production in that
sermone volgare which they could only wonder over and tolerate,
speaking of the great poem which formed the Italian language, as
Milton notes, with lofty yet condescending admiration, how

"Sweetest Shakespeare, fancy's child.
Warbles his native wood-notes wild."

and parasites of every description, one of whom in particular by his
amusing words and gestures, gained much importance and favor with
all. And Cane being in a disagreeable mood, which Dante endured
badly, the prince called this man before him and praised him greatly
to the poet. ' I wonder,' he said ' that a foolish man like this should
know how to please everybody and to make himself beloved by everybody, which you cannot do who are called a wise man.' To which
Dante replied: ' You would not wonder at this if you knew that the
real foundation of friendship is in the resemblance of habits and the
equality of minds.' "

This curious and bitter commentary upon the words still
warm on his lips, in which the poet, in lofty superiority to
poor limitations of rank, had protested that there might
well be *dilettevoli ed utili amicizie* between persons of unequal station, is but too distant a proof of the growing
discord—the

> "little rift within the lute
> That by and by should make the music mute."

Still more distant is another and coarser story—the kind
of practical joke which might still be paralleled perhaps at
some rude cottage table where an unwelcome guest had
seated himself, but which then does not seem to have been
considered an unprincely jest, notwithstanding the fierce
retort it called forth :

"At the table, too largely hospitable, where Dante was placed by the
side of jesters and parasites. . . . a boy who had hidden himself one
day under the table-cloth to gather the bones thrown down, according to the fashion of the time, by the guests, made a little
heap of these bones at Dante's feet. And when the company rose
and this heap became visible, the prince put on an air of wonder,
'Certainly,' he said, ' Dante is a great devourer of meat.' To whom
Dante made instant reply:' Messere,' he said, ' you would not see so
many bones if I were a dog '" (*voi non vedreste tant' ossa, se cane io
fossi*).

The bitter ferocity of this allusion to Cane's name shows

how far the rupture had gone between the proud exile and
his careless patron. Another allusion of the same sore and
painful kind is in the words put into the mouth of
Cacciaguida in the "Paradiso:"

> "Tu proverai sì come sa di sale
> Lo pane altrui, e com'e duro calle
> Lo scender e'l salir per l'altrui *scale*."

These lines the reader of Dante will recollect appear in
one of the "thirteen last cantos," which as Boccaccio sig-
nificantly says, were not sent like the others for Cane's inspection before they appeared to the world. Before they
were written the proud Florentine had left the court where
he met with such unworthy treatment, and, with his unfinished poem and his burning heart, had wandered forth
again into the world ; still indeed to eat the bread and to
go and come by the stairs of strangers, yet to find a more
honorable and tender reception in lesser palaces than that
of the great and foolish Scaligeri, who, "Grande" in those
days, has left no memorial behind him so lasting as the
cruel levity of these probably unconsidered jests. The poet
may be but little powerful in his day, but what tremendous
vengeance he can take.

The other incident in the Ravenna streets, narrated by
Boccaccio, though almost too well known to require repetition, comes in naturally here; and the scene is very picturesque, revealing to us, as in a picture, the shady deep
Italian street, low down between its high houses, the
women seated at the doors, cool and still out of the rays
of the sun, grouped upon those bits of outer stair which
even in our northern climate make the old streets picturesque, but which the hand of vulgar regularity sweeps
heartlessly away.

"Our poet was of middle height and stooped when he walked, being now of mature years; his aspect was grave and quiet, and his

dress seemly and serious as became his age. His face was long, his
nose aquiline, his eyes rather large than little, his nostrils large, and
the underlip a little prominent; his complexion was dark, his hair and
beard thick, black, and curling, and his countenance always melancholy and thoughtful. And thus it happened one day in Verona (the
fame of his work being already known to all, and especially that part
of the "Commedia" which is called the "Inferno," and himself
known to many, both men and women), that as he passed before a
door where several women were seated, one of them said softly, but
not too low to be heard by him and those who were with him, 'Do
you see him who goes to hell and comes back again when he pleases,
and brings back news of those who are down below?' To which
another of the women answered simply, 'Certainly you speak the
truth. See how scorched his beard is, and how dark he is from the
heat and smoke!' When Dante heard this talk behind him, and saw
that the women believed entirely what they said, he was pleased—
and content that they should have this opinion of him, went on his
way with a smile."

Thus the popular honor and wonder healed a little the
sharp wounds made by court buffoons and contemptuous
patrons. With that simplicity as of a child in the greatness of his genius, which it is always so touching to see,
the great sad poet was pleased with the matter-of-fact belief in him thus ingeniously expressed. "He went on
smiling;" liking in his loneliness the homely looks of awe
and wonder.

This is the last perfectly authentic and distinct appearance in the outer world. From Verona he strayed, it is
supposed, back toward his own country, to Umbria, to the
monastery of Fonte Avellana, in that lovely land of hills
and woods which St. Francis had recently filled with
associations and recollections. There is some floating
gossamer-thread of tradition which says it was the poet
who composed and invented the pictures with which his
friend Giotto filled the great new sanctuary, dedicated in
San Francesco's honor. He is also reported to have passed
some part of this uncertain time with a noble of Gubbio,

Bosone dei Raffaelli; and again traditions of him are found
in Udine, where the peasants still give the name of *Sedia
di Dante* to a rock overlooking the river Tolmino. It was
most probably when he was lingering upon those Umbrian
hills, gazing wistfully where the horizon closed over
Florence, that a last attempt was made to open a way for
him back into his old home; but such a way as it would
have ill become the greatest of Florentines to tread. "It
was an ancient custom," says Balbo, "that on the festival
of Saint John certain criminals should receive their pardon
in Florence, offering themselves to the saint, candle in
hand, and paying a fine." On one of these occasions, in
the year, 1320 or 1321, this somewhat humiliating favor
was offered to political offenders, and a nephew of Dante
(let us hope it was not Andrea, who was so like him, and
who found the papers in the great chest), and some of his
friends made a strenuous attempt to induce him to accept
this way of ending his exile. The Piazza of the baptistery
has seen many strange sights, but to see among the other
fuor-usciti that stooping yet proud figure, that melancholy
and thoughtful countenance, brown and scorched with the
smoke and flames through which he had passed scathless,
in penitential robes, with candle in his hand and words of
submission in his mouth, was not to be within its long list
of memories. When the proposal was made to Dante, he
burst out to the well-meaning, but foolish priest who had
conducted the negotiation in indignant eloquence. "Is
this the glorious revocation of an unjust sentence by which
Dante Alighieri is to be recalled to his country after suffering almost three lusters of exile?" he cries. "Is this
what patriotism is worth? Is this the recompense of continued labor and study? Far from a man familiar with
philosophy be such a cowardly and earthly baseness of
heart, that he could allow himself to be thus offered up,
almost bound, like Ciolo or some other infamous fellow!

Far be it from a man claiming justice to count out, after having endured injustice, his own money to those who did it. Oh, my father, this is not how an exile comes back. Another way might surely be found by yourselves or by others which should not derogate from the fame, from the honor of Dante. Such a way would I accept and that not with slow steps. But if by this way only I can return to Florence, Florence shall never again be entered by me. And what then? Should not I still see the sun and the stars, wherever I may be, and still ponder the sweet truth, somewhere under heaven, without first giving myself, naked of glory, almost in ignominy, to the Florentine people? Bread has not yet failed me." The indignation of the refusal is hot with all the lofty passion of his nature excited by a last and crowning insult. The very anguish of righteous anger is in it, along with a simple grandeur of consciousness, which is no longer arrogance. It was not only Dante but Genius whom that miserable Guelfish rabble insulted in the person of the poet whose home-bringing should have been a triumph. Had he lingered there among the chestnut woods in Umbria, in that convent high upon the hill, with his eyes gazing always where Florence lay, for this? And is it wonderful that after this lines more and more bitter should start even into the song of that celestial " Paradiso," which, by himself, among the woody glens and on the sunny far-seeing hill-tops, he was pondering day by day?

His last refuge of all was, as all the world knows, at Ravenna, where he was the guest, and a guest deeply honored, of Guido da Polenta, the nephew of that Francesca of Rimini whom likewise all the world knows, and for whom, from Dante's day till now, gentle eyes have shed salt tears. Another of the same house had fought by Dante's side in his youth on the field of Campaldino, so that the friendship was evidently an old one. After his

many solitary wanderings, the hard life of a stranger
which he led here and there, in all kinds of temporary
interrupted sojournings, learning how hard it was to get
back when once driven out, and how salt was the bread of
others, and how steep the *scale* of a stranger's bounty, he
came at last to a safe refuge, where all the world was
tender of the poet. Withdrawn altogether from all nearness and sight of Florence, from all possibility of straining
his exiled eyes for a sight of her, or wearing out his exile-
heard with fallacious sickness of deferred hope, he sank
into the melancholy old city, with its great mournful-eyed
mosaics, old even in Dante's day, and its pines, through
which the wind swept with that mournful cadence which
is dear to all sad and musing souls. Guido of the Polen-
tini used his great guest better than splendid Cane of the
Scaligeri had done. He did not set him among buffoons
and jesters, or leave him to the poor office of a *giudice*, but
honored him at his own table and sent him upon princely
embassies, which no doubt recalled to the exile the day of
his early prosperity and statesmanship. One of these
missions took him to Venice, where he wrote certain lines
beneath an image of the Virgin, which are still preserved.
He is said also to have written a letter concerning the
condition and manners of the Venetians which would be
extremely severe and unfriendly if it were not almost
universally denounced as spurious. His son Pietro, the
eldest of his family, whom we have already seen in at-
tendance on him, and also the second, Jacopo, both joined
their father here, and he seems to have had many friendships and correspondences which were pleasant to him.
By one of his correspondents, for instance, he was entreated to come to Bologna to receive there the crown of
poetry, an invitation which Dante seems to have evaded,
still dreaming, it would appear, of some sweeter acknowledgment of his genius, some triumph which yet might be.

If he were to be crowned at all, it should be, he says, within the solemn walls of San Giovanni itself, that "bel San Giovanni" which he had never ceased to love, and where it had been suggested to him, wronged and guiltless, that he should offer himself as a penitent. "Thy Guido," this correspondent wrote, "would take no harm though thou didst leave Ravenna and that fair Pineta which girdles her on the Adriatic." In similar strain Dante replies—"Sweet would it be to decorate my head with the crown of laurel in Bologna, but sweeter still in my own country, if ever I return there, hiding my white hairs beneath the leaves;" all this in Latin verse not too melodious, not like the immortal *terza rima* which was *volgare*, too poor a medium for poets to interchange civilities in. To find the poet, so near the end of his career, still indulging in such a vision, is a singular and touching evidence of the pertinacity of the imagination and hope; or was it perhaps that Dante only evaded the solemn foolery of a poetical coronation by this half-satirical, half-sad, postponement of it until so unlikely a moment? This, however is not probable, for the age had not found out any folly in such ceremonials; and Boccaccio even, with quaint solemnity and shallowness, attributes Dante's preference of poetry over philosophy to the fact that the "glorious and unusual honor of the coronation with laurel" belonged to the art of song alone!—strangest misinterpretation, perhaps, of the mode of expression most congenial to genius which ever sympathetic bystander gave.

The poet's life in Ravenna has altogether a softened, calmed religious twilight about it. He had wandered far and wide—solitary, finding no rest for his feet—by great cities and by lonely places; now embracing, now proudly turning his back upon some capricious protector; now knocking at a convent gate far away among the silent hills;

now drawing wondering looks after him in the narrow
mediæval streets ; always alone, always with his lofty head
in the clouds, and a shadowy crowd moving about with
him ; yet with those glowing eyes so quick to see, that here
and there at the highest of his dreaming a sudden gleam
of the landscape about him would break into paradise
itself, or light a gloomy circle of the "Inferno" with the
reflection of some mortal scene. And he had been but an
imperfect man ; not always so high in heart and meaning as in genius, fiercely serving the purposes of hatred or
vengeance when that angry humor took him ; revenging his
wrongs or the wrongs of his country with sudden fiery
stroke, as by some indignant angel, and dropping the
enemy into hopeless hell, to writhe there henceforward forever—let commentators do what they will to clear him.
Nor was Dante always so spotless as became Beatrice's
lover ; an impassioned soul, never satisfied, sometimes desperate, torn out of his true place in life, storming and toiling to regain it, unconquerable in passion, in power, in
energy—how was he to keep himself spotless in all those
wearinesses and wanderings, those indignations and
wrongs ? But the *animo sdegnoso* had at last come to a
moment of rest ; when his great work was completed, he
took to "vulgarizing" those psalms in which the Christian soul has always loved to breathe its penitence, and the
Credo, and Paternoster, and others of the chief utterances
of Divine truth.

> " Aggi pietade de' miei gravi errori
> Però ch' io sono debile ed infermo
> Ed ho perduti tutti i miei vigori."

These are not the mighty verses of the " Divine Comedy ;"
but in the evening quiet, in the stillness, with faint echoes
of the alien sea breathing through the Pineta, and great
Florence and greater life growing dim in the far distance,
how touching are they, like the sound of that distant bell,

"seeming to weep the day as it dies," which brings tears
to the traveler's eyes. Dante's day was ending in premature night; and yet not premature ; for how long he had
lived in that half-century, a *vita nouva* all love and youth,
and after that how many lifetimes more !

He died at Ravenna in the month of September in the
year 1321, in his fifty-sixth year; dying in autumn with
everything that is lovely, as he had been born with everything that was beautiful in May. "There he rendered his
weary spirit to God," says Boccaccio, "not without great
sorrow, *grandissimo dolore,* of Guido and generally of all
the citizens. And there can be no doubt," adds the sympathetic historian, "that he was received into the arms of
his most noble Beatrice, with whom in the presence of
Him who is the chief good, leaving all miseries of the
present life, they now most lightsomely live in that happiness to which there comes no end."

Thus ended the mortal existence of the poet. Florence,
sdegnosa like himself, folded her arms and averted her
head, making no signs even of a tardy penitence. "It is
usual that hatred ends with the death of the person hated,"
says good Boccaccio, "but this did not happen at the death
of Dante. The obstinate ill-will of his fellow citizens continued as rigid as ever; no sympathy was shown by any
one, no tears were given him by the city, no public
solemnity for his funeral. By which pertinacity it is evident that the Florentines were so destitute of knowledge
that among them no distinction was made between a vile
cobbler and an exalted poet." But if it was any comfort
to Dante's survivors, his gracious patron Guido, after
burying him reverentially, returned to his house, and there
made, in praise of the poet and for the consolation of his
children and friends, "*uno esquisito e lungo sermone.*"
This kind and liberal friend intended besides to build a
splendid tomb, *egregia e notabile sepultura* for the poet, but

was balked by the common Italian reason, a sudden revolution, which took from him the lordship of Ravenna; and by death which followed soon after. But Dante had plenty of Latin verses and *ornamente poetici* for his funeral —flowers, we fear, of not much more savor than the dry and manufactured *immortelles*, which are not unlike them; and after awhile a tomb was built for him, though not *egregia e notabile*. And in the course of time, though centuries later, Florence woke to her shame and glory and made him that enormous catafalque in marble which is to be seen in Santa Croce, and tried hard to recover in its dust and decay the exiled body which once was Dante. But in this the proud city has never been successful. Dante, cast out from her bosom with contumely—once offered, almost a worse indignity, the chance of returning in shame and penitence as a criminal—is still an exile, and returns to the land of his fierce love and hatred no more. But the shame of her treatment of him has faded by this time out of the very memory of Florence: she remembers now only the glory, which is one of her richest possessions.

Respecting the end of the "Divina Commedia," those thirteen last cantos which were not sent to Can Grande, Boccaccio tells us a quaint and touching story, upon the marvelous part of which doubt is naturally thrown by later and more-matter-of-fact historians, and in which it is possible there may be only such a reflection and reconstruction of the finding of the original seven cantos in Madonna Gemma's strong chest as is not unusual in personal history. But such repetitions do doubtless occur in fact sometimes as well as in art, and anyhow the postscript seems a not unfitting one to the wandering, uncertain life of the poet, and the curious fragmentary and much interrupted composition of his great work. The concluding cantos, according to Boccaccio, were missing at Dante's

death, and as soon as the shock of that event was over, his
friends began anxiously to question his two sons, Pietro
and Jacopo, whom he had left behind him in Ravenna,
about the end of the great poem. The young men, however, could give no information, and apparently did not
even know whether their father had finished the work or
not. When, however, after many searches they found
nothing, the two lads, both of them *dicitori*—as who should
say poetasters—began to be tempted—moved by their own
ambition perhaps (for why should not the son be able to
do what the father has done—and more?), or by that long-
standing excuse, the desire of friends, "*degli amici pre-
gati,*" says Boccaccio—to put their hands to the work and
make the conclusion themselves, a bold undertaking.
The world and young Pietro and Jacopo were, however,
saved from this experiment in the following remarkable
way:

"But a wonderful vision appeared to Jacopo, who was the most
fervent in this idea, not only releasing him and his brother from this
foolish presumption, but showing where the thirteen cantos were to
be found. It is told by a worthy gentleman of Ravenna, by name
Piero Gardino, long a disciple of Dante, a man of serious mind and
worthy of belief, that after his master had been dead for eight months,
Jacopo di Dante came to his house in the middle of the night, and told
him that on the same night he had seen in a dream his father Dante,
clad in very white raiment, his face shining with unaccustomed light,
whom he asked if he was living, and heard from him the reply, 'Yes;
but in the true life, not yours.' Then it occurred to Jacopo to ask if
he had finished his work before he passed to the true life, and, if he
had completed it, where the conclusion was, which they had not been
able to find? To which question a similar answer was given. 'Yes,
I completed it:' and then it appeared to Jacopo that his father took
him by the hand and led him to the room in which he had lived during
his lifetime here, and touching a panel said, 'That which you seek
is here;' and having said these words Dante disappeared, and along
with him his son's sleep. Upon which he, Piero Gardino, affirmed
that Jacopo not being able to rest without coming to tell what he had

seen, the two went together to examine the place indicated, which the
dreamer had exactly noted, in order to see if it had been pointed out
by a true spirit or a false delusion. And so, though it was still night,
they went together to the house in which Dante had died, and calling
him who then lived there, were admitted by him, and going to the
place found a wooden panel fitted into the wall, such as they had always been accustomed to see; and removing this they found in the
wall a little window, which none of them had ever seen nor knew
that it was there, and in this they found many writings, molded by
the damp of the wall, and which would have been destroyed altogether had they been left longer there; and when they had carefully
cleared them from the mold, they found, in continuous order, according to the numbers, the thirteen missing cantos. And in great joy
they copied them, and, according to the custom of the author, first
sent them to Messer Cane, and then added them to the imperfect poem;
and in this way the work which had been carried on through so many
years was at last finished."

If it was, as some biographers suppose, a direct consequence of Dante's quarrel with Can Grande that these last
cantos had not been sent to him, what a wonderful message
of peace and forgiveness, as from the grave, must have
been the arrival of this precious packet, the last and loftiest crown of the great work! And nothing can be more
touching than the suggestion conveyed in the concealment
of these last cantos: the grieved and wounded affection in
the breast of the poet, the pride which prevented him,
after the breach between them, from sending his new work
to his estranged friend, yet the love which would not produce that work to the world without the old tender preface and formula. To throw aside on the ledge of the
hidden *finestrella*, the little window in the deep old wall,
shut up from common gaze, this last magnificent effusion
of his genius, in pathetic despite because he could not
bring himself to send it to the favorite who had wounded
him, was an action quite consistent with all we know of
the poet; and it is the kind of personal revelation which
goes straight to the heart. Women do such things some-

times, and so does youth; but how few men over fifty have
ever borne such a curious and angry testimony to the force
of the love in them! This pathetic gleam throws just such
a light on Dante as his lovers will love to leave him in.
Still and always an *animo sdegnoso,* indignant—wounded,
and hurt by the evils round him as most men are hurt only
in their bodies, not in their souls; but with how much
tender, remorseful love behind! His friend had made his
heart bleed—how could he make the first advance, and
send that celestial messenger to him? But if not for Cane
the great work, then for no one. Let it lie, and the mold
gather on it in the *finestrella,* until heaven had calmed and
cleared those burning eyes and wiped the last tears out of
them, and left nothing but pure sweet grace and tender
charity for Cane and all the world!

And it is pleasant to know that when kind Guido in his
turn, after that long and exquisite discourse of his over
the poet's grave, was *cacciato,* after the manner of Italian
princes, from Ravenna—the young Alighieri, Pietro and
Jacopo, went back to Verona, and once more, under Messer
Cane's protection, established themselves there, and
became citizens of that city. So that Can Grande, too,
must have felt the power of that message from the dead.

THE CATHEDRAL BUILDERS.

CHAPTER IV.

GROUP I.—ARNOLFO—GIOTTO.

IT IS curious to step out of the disturbed and turbulent city life, in which nobles and commons, poets, historians, and philosophers, were revolving in a continual turmoil, now up, now down, falling and rising and falling again, with all the bitter hopes and fears natural and vicissitudes so painful, into the artist world, where no such ups or downs seem to have existed, but where work went on placidly whatever happened. In later days, indeed, such a fiery soul as Michael Angelo might storm or struggle with his country, but the burly peasant Giotto would seem to have taken little thought what or who his employers were, or what was happening in the city where he went about the streets busy and humorous, always some joke on his lips, always some beautiful thought in his heart. Dante might toss himself like a caged bird against the stone walls and closely-barred gates which neither fear nor entreaty would open to him ; Dino Compagni, citizen and chronicler, might first create the history which "Io, Dino" afterward recorded ; but the painters took no such prominent place in the world. Enough for them that it was all to be theirs afterward, and that when the factions and the families had done their worst and torn each other in pieces, and all the magnificoes had had their day, they were to pass every one of them, and leave the silent painter, the patient worker in stone, omnipotent in the city which has come to belong to them—to be its princes and potentates for ever and ever.

And the sky lightens, the air grows softer when we thus change the scene. There is a lively coming and going, a pleasant stir of life ; but no more note of any warfare than if all had been heavenly quiet in Florence. The Florence of Vasari and his successors is not the Florence of the historians, that riotous town of which Compagni and Villani wrote, and in which so many murderous encounters, so many fierce dramas, were always going on. No painter, so far as we can remember, was ever among the *fuor-usciti.* There is something in the mingling of quiet material labor with all the sentiment of art which seems to calm the spirit and subdue the passions. Giotto wandered about over the world as much as Dante did, but how different were his wanderings ! He strayed about Italy from town to town, among the feastings and the fighting, here leaving a mild-eyed madonna, there a group of saints in glory or sinners in pain ; jogging cheerfully along for pleasure and profit, everybody's friend, unarmed, unattended, ever received with honor, pursuing his peaceful way with a merry word and a jest, the ready homely wit that was country born ; and betraying his course wherever he went by something beautiful, some bit of rude common wall blossomed into an immortal thing. To all the cities round about—Arezzo, Bologna, Pisa, even as far as old Padua near the other line of the sea, on the eastern side of the Italian boot, and Verona—how the painter went wandering ! Some of the towns were hostile to Florence, but none of them were hostile to Giotto. He painted something for Robert of Naples, who made much of him, and something for Dante's friend and enemy Can Grande—two men who would have flown at each other's throats, but who both· were

courteous to the painter. Wherever he went with his
art, peace went with him, her white banner all flowered
over with loveliest images ; no complaint, nor bitter prayer,
nor indignant protestation, came from his lips ; to no
emperor or deliverer does he ever require to appeal ; to
Florence and to the stranger he was ever alike welcome. This
is one of the most wonderful triumphs of the peaceful
pictorial art, subduing the painter first, and in him tran-
quilizing all other warlike things. Neither science, nor
philosophy, nor poetry, nor even religion, has been so
entirely received and welcomed as friendly and catholic,
belonging never to a faction but to all men. The monk,
indeed, was the universal negotiator and bearer of missions
from one foe to another, but whenever he ascended to the
higher eminences of the church, he too became, in his turn,
a factionary and political leader ; and neither poetry nor
philosophy defended their votaries from fierce and obstinate
political passion. But he whose study is among the shadows
and lights of nature, whom a sudden effect of sunshine or
cloud can seize upon and carry away in the midst of whatsoever business, whose mind is fully occupied by those
subtle secrets of form and color which only the patient
laborer can fathom—he has a peaceful armor, an unsuspected coat of mail, defending him among all the turmoil.
He moves about amidst it, taking no thought of it, never
suspected, never feared. Except Michael Angelo, whose
personality was so great as to surmount and overbear his
art, we know no warlike painter of sufficient note to be
worthy mention. All other crafts are either of the soul
alone or of the body alone, and thus leave the other half
of the man open to all the temptations about him ; but the
painter's art is at once ethereal and material. Unfortunately it cannot be said that all temptations are shut out
by it ; but peace is indispensable to the laborious preparations which are necessary for art, and war is her enemy

most to be feared, who can in an hour destroy the work of
centuries. Reasons even so powerful, however, do not
always succeed in taming down the natural impulses which
lead a man to take one side or another in popular strife,
and perhaps the fact that few members of the ruling class
have been artists may tell for something in the matter.
Cimabue was of noble race like Michael Angelo, who stands
at the other end of the succession, summing up the great
story of Florentine art as his fellow-gentleman began it;
but between the two there is more genius than blood to be
found, and perhaps no such stir and pride of ambition and
rivalry as might exist in the veins of a well-known race
stirred those of the peasant or homely burgher, called fresh
out of the heart of the lower people, to whom fighting
means little more than fighting, and who bear the penalties without sharing the rewards of the strife. Anyhow,
let the reason be what it may, the result is evident. The
painters moved about safely and peacefully when everything was in disorder, and all the rest of the world in free
fight around them ; and sang at their work when the factions were in fiercest conflict, and studied pigments and
flesh-tints while their next-door neighbors were fighting
across barricades, coloring the streets with unlovely red.
Only thus could such great edifices as the Florentine Duomo
have come into being—a marvel not only of majestic construction, but of patient, painful, tedious labor, to the
wonder of all after time.

Only a very few years before Dante was finally banished
from Florence was the work of the cathedral begun. Of
all the beautiful group which we now see in the center of
the city, her great poet knew only the quaint octagon of
the baptistry, to our eyes externally so much the least noble of the three, but to him " *il mio bel San Giovanni,*" the
heart of his town, the center of the world. Let us be
thankful that the tombs had been cleared away from about

GIULIANO DE' MEDICI, CALLED " IL PENSIERO: " MICHAEL ANGELO.   107

it, the walls adorned with marbles, the solemn interior
paved and made orderly; and that when the poet, still
young and doubtless with a long and splendid future, as he
thought, before him, sat in the glowing summer nights
and watched the last red of the sunset dying away over the
high housetops, leaving nothing but soft coolness and
grateful shade upon San Giovanni—the first courses of the
new walls had begun to rise, and a new cathedral, more
beautiful than ever was realized by man, appeared in visions to the proud Florentine.   We may be sure that had
he seen it completed, even the great Duomo, all glistening
in sheen of marble and rich with carven work, would not
have fully come up to the visionary great dream cathedral
of the poet's thoughts.

Arnolfo, sometimes called di Cambio and sometimes di
Lapi, was the first of the group of cathedral builders in
Florence.   Nothing can be more strange than the confusion of names which seems to have existed in Italy in the
humbler classes, at least during the Middle Ages, a confusion which Baldinucci remarks and comments upon, and
which must strike every foreign reader.   Whether there
were any family names at all in these early times among
the workmen and poorer burghers it seems difficult to tell.
The primitive custom, so universally diffused, which recog-
nizes John as the son of William, the first of all hereditary
distinctions, seems to have still survived in those democratic
cities, yet not without many exceptions to the rule, since
sometimes it is the name of the master instead of the father
which is adopted, or some accidental appellation dependent
upon the locality or trade.   Even in the present day the
Italians make use of the Christian name in a manner quite
unknown among us, and neither Arnolfo, nor his successor
in the great "opera" of the cathedral, Giotto, seems to
have found much occasion for a second name.   Who Arnolfo was seems to be scarcely known, though few archi-

tects after him have left greater works or more evidence of
power.   His first authentic appearance in history is among
the band of workmen engaged upon the pulpit in the
Duomo at Sienna, as pupil or journeyman of Niccolo Pi-
sano, the great reviver of the art of sculpture—when he
becomes visible in company with a certain Lapo, who is
sometimes called his father (as by Vasari) and sometimes
his instructor, but who appears actually to have been nothing more than his fellow-workman and associate.   The
same band of workmen, under the same master, Niccolo,
worked also in Niccolo's native town, at the great and
beautiful group of buildings in which is still concentrated
so much of the interest of fading and silent Pisa, and had
other engagements in hand at Perugia, Cortona, Orvieto,
Bologna, Florence, and Rome.   Cathedrals were being
built then as railways are made now, by one great firm all
over the world, though each individual workman in the
earlier undertaking was a man of note, perhaps a man of
genius, and the works they have left continue still the wonder and admiration of mankind.   How rich the country
must have been in which, within a very limited circle of
territory, three such cathedrals as those of Pisa, Sienna,
and Florence were being executed at almost the same time,
one generation of artists working at all of them with perpetual emulation and eager rivalry !   Florence, perhaps
because of her distracted condition, was a little behind her
sister (but bitterly hostile) cities, and it is not wonderful
that when once roused to this humiliating fact, she should
have flamed forth with such a magniloquent proclamation
as the following, making up with additional arrogance and
pomp of bearing for the soreness of inferiority which must
have rankled in her breast :

"The Florentine republic, soaring ever above the conception of
the most competent judges, desires that an edifice should be con-

structed so magnificent in its height and beauty that it shall surpass
everything of the kind produced in the time of their greatest power
by the Greeks and Romans."

This breathes the true spirit of the proud city, impatient

PALAZZO PUBBLICO, OR DELLA SIGNORIA; WITH THE
TOWER OF THE VACCA.

of any rival, and how much more to be out-done or fore-
stalled by a neighbor. The sudden ardor with which she
awoke to a sense of her shortcoming at this particular
epoch is very startling. The cathedral, the Palazzo Pub-

blico, the two great churches of Santa Croce and Santa
Maria Novella, all leaped into being within a few years,
almost simultaneously. The Duomo was founded, as some
say, in 1294, the same year in which Santa Croce was
begun, or, according to others, in 1298; and between these
two dates, in 1296, the palace of the signoria, the seat of
the commonwealth, the center of all public life, had its
commencement. All these great buildings Arnolfo designed
and began, and his genius requires no other evidence. The
stern strength of the Palazzo, upright and strong like a
knight in mail, and the large and noble lines of the cathedral, ample and liberal and majestic in ornate robes and
wealthy ornaments, show how well he knew how to vary
and adapt his art to the different requirements of municipal and religious life and to the necessities of the age.

The position of the Palazzo is of itself an example of
those distracted times. It was built at the side, and not,
as the architect wished, in the center of the square over
which it still presides, for the strange reason that upon
part of the square the palace of the Uberti family had once
stood, and, fiercely fanatical in party feeling, the Guelf
rulers would not touch even with the foundation of their
public buildings the accursed soil upon which that race of
Ghibellines had once flourished! Well might Farinata, in
the " Inferno," ask and wonder why his townsmen so hated
his family and name. Peaceful Arnolfo, who had been
working out in the world for Guelf and Ghibelline alike,
had to yield to this passionate enmity, and shrugged his
shoulders no doubt, and changed his plan, knocking down
a few other old houses and part of a church to make room
in the corner for his palace, where it still stands, slightly
askew, an everlasting monument of that superstition of
faction and hatred which is worse than any other superstition. He had to please his masters of the signoria at the
same time by building into his new erection a certain

tower called the Tower of the Vacca. or cow, in which the
great bell of Florence, so long in fierce wit and fondness
called by this name, was placed. To "accomodate" this
tower in the center of the building was a troublesome
business, Vasari tells us; but it was so skillfully accomplished by "filling up the tower with good material, that
it was easy for other masters to add the lofty campanile
which we now see." Who these *altri maestri* were who
actually completed the beautiful tower of the Palazzo in
which the great bell has hung for centuries, we are not
informed, nor who they were who carried out the design
of the Duomo. Arnolfo only lived to see a portion of this
his greatest work, completed—"the three principal tribunes
which were under the cupola," and which Vasari tells us
were so solid and strongly built as to be able to bear the
full weight of Brunelleschi's dome, which was much larger
and heavier than the one the original architect had himself
designed. The cathedral, as Arnolfo planned it, may be
seen in Simone Memmi's great picture in the Spanish
chapel at Santa Maria Novella, where its marble walls and
round red cupola form the background to a line of popes,
cardinals and emperors, less interesting figures than the
group of attendants, which comprises several contemporary
portraits—Cimabue, fine and dainty, Petrarch, Arnolfo
himself, our architect, and Giotto; and that fair Laura
whom the poet made famous, and by whose worship in
return he won for himself the laurel. Simone was the
friend of Petrarch, and knew Madonna Laura as we know
our next-door neighbors: and no doubt such a group might
have met any day, the poet and the painters—and even a
greater poet with them, and a lady still more devoutly worshiped—lightly, as we meet our acquaintance; though the
picture of them gathered in a group is one of the things
we go half across the world to see.

Arnolfo died, as we have said—when he had built his

Palazzo in rugged strength, as it still stands with walls
like living rock and heavy Tuscan cornices, though it was
reserved to the *altri maestri* to put upon it the wonderful
crown of its appropriate tower—and just as the round apse
of the cathedral approached completion; a hard fate for
a great builder to leave such noble work behind him half
done, yet the most common of all fates. He died, so far
as there is any certainty in dates, in 1300, during the brief
period of Dante's power in Florence, when the poet was
one of the priors and much engaged in public business; and
the same eventful year concluded the existence of Cimabue,
the first of the great school of Florentine painters—he
whose picture was carried home to the church in which it
was to dwell for all the intervening centuries with such
pride and acclamation that the Borgo Allegri is said to
have taken its name from this wonderful rejoicing. What
if there might in reality be other reasons for naming the
suburban street outside the walls "Allegri?" The very
suggestion that this could have been its origin shows the
interest and excitement of the community over the first
great picture which had been made in Florence, gift of
heaven and work of genius for the glory and delight of the
city, a something which neither Pisa nor Sienna could
boast of, though it might be that their cathedrals were
further advanced.

> " Credette Cimabue nella pittura
> Tenir lo campo,"

says the poet; and so he did, until a greater than he arose.
He was the first in whom the pictorial art had resurrection
after the thraldom of Byzantine tradition and the long
reign of mosaic; and in this respect will keep the field forever, notwithstanding that he was surpassed, as nature ordained, by his own pupil, who in his turn yielded to the
next greater. Cimabue, however, kept to his painting more

exclusively than most of his brethren in art, and except
that he was associated with Arnolfo, perhaps only nominally and as a matter of compliment in the great "opera"
of the cathedral, seems to have had little or no share in the
mass of architectural work which was then getting itself
done on all sides with such wonderful energy and zeal.
He seems to have been a proud man, arrogant and assuming, perhaps thinking it beneath his nobility to keep up a
bottega and enter into the full exercise of his craft, and
has left little knowledge of himself in the world except by
his pictures, which are more valuable as landmarks in art
and indications of the approaching moment when true
beauty and grace were to vanquish the conventional and
untrue, than beautiful in themselves. Whether he did
anything at all in the cathedral we do not know. By the
time of Arnolfo's death Cimabue too was near his end, and
ora ha Giotto il grido. A new monarch had arisen in
Art and Florence, a man of greater genius and kinder
soul.

For just about the same date, before Dante had left the
city on that disastrous mission to Pope Benedict from
which he never returned, and Cimabue and Arnolfo, dim
figures in their decay, were fading out of the world, a new
painter, the apprentice and pupil of the old, who had been
painting in the new church in Assisi and had already made
himself famous, got his first great public commission,
which was to paint a Paradiso over the altar in the chapel
of the Podestà in the old stern Bargello palace, where that
officer lived. What more natural than that Giotto, peacefully painting the saints of his Paradise, should introduce
the portraits of his friends among them, and above all
that especial friend whose notice of the young painter was
so flattering, and whose acquaintance at once as statesman,
ambassador, and poet, it was a pride to possess? Swung
high up upon his scaffold upon the lofty wall, unaware of

the speedy severance from home and friends which awaited
the young magnifico, in pleasant ease of friendship and
familiar compliment, and with a painter's admiration for
the beautiful countenance yet unworn with anything worse
than the sweet sorrows of a visionary love, Giotto set

THE BARGELLO, ANCIENT PALACE OF THE PODESTA.

Dante in the front of his group, and thus preserved to us
forever such a softened representation of the poet's face,
and along with it of his character, as has been most gratefully received by all lovers of Dante. Giotto was about
ten years younger than the poet, who had scarcely then

reached the *mezzo del cammino di nostra vita*—a young man
about twenty-four, taking his first important independent
step in life; and it was a happy inspiration, as well as a
very natural one, which led him to leave us this noble
legacy, so long lost under the whitewash, and so imperfect
yet so precious. Everybody knows the beautiful head, so
soon to contract and sharpen with the storms of exile, but
here caught at its noblest moment in full maturity yet
youth—the face so thoughtful, so tranquil, yet touched
with a half disdain, an indication even now of the *animo
sdegnoso*, who, like his own Farinata, held *in gran dispetto*
the vulgar things and men about him. Dante and the two
figures behind him have been revealed to us out of the dim
mass around with only too much zeal of repainting and
elucidation; but there is something curiously symbolical,
like a parable, in the misty distinctness of the poet, partially dragging out of oblivion the two faces for which nobody cares much whether they happen to be Corso Donati
and Brunetto Latini or not. We confess that to ourselves the
conjunction seems to be an unlikely one, though all the
critics, usually so willing to doubt Vasari, take his opinion
unhesitatingly on this point. The youthfulness of the
countenance and devout attitude do not seem much like
the turbulent Corso, who was a much older man than the
poet, and not so linked with him by any bond of friendship
that they should stand thus side by side forever and ever.
Might it not more probably be Corso's younger brother
Forese, whom the poet met in purgatory, and for whom
he had so much friendship? But this is a digression, and
has nothing to do with our subject, which is the painter
and not Dante, fascinating though every mention of him
always is.

Giotto, the second name in the history of art in Florence
as also in the building of Santa Maria del Fiore, is a much
more recognizable man than his predecessors either in

painting or architecture. Cimabue and Arnolfo are for
the most part abstractions to us, and the manner of them,
what kind of men they were, is unknown to posterity,

STAIRCASE IN THE CORTILE OF BARGELLO.

their works alone living after them. But no more notable
or distinct figure than Giotto is in all the history of Florence. He was born a peasant, in the village of Vespignano
in the Mugello, the same district which afterward gave

birth to Fra Angelico. His father was a countryman
called Bondone, a *naturale persone*, as Vasari describes him
no way superior to the other peasants about. Fortunately
the critics have found nothing to say against the pretty
story which tells how Cimabue, fine painter-cavalier,
making some chance expedition into the country, encoun-
tered in his way a flock of sheep grazing about the wilds,
in the charge of a brown peasant boy of ten, with buskined
legs, no doubt, and unkempt locks, like those still to be
met with by all the rural ways of Italy. The child, intent
upon his occupation, was drawing, or trying to draw with
no instruction but that of nature, with a pointed stone
upon a piece of slate, a picture of one of his sheep.
Cimabue, captivated by the adventure, and seeing in the
childish outline that something of aptitude and possibility
which an artist's eye is so quick to see, asked if the boy
would go with him to be taught, and Bondone, hastily
called from his fields and overawed no doubt by the appearance of so fine a gentleman, consented, "because he
was very poor," Vasari says ; but he could not have been
so very poor, since we find that he left land to his son in
the Mugello, though he had no claim to gentility, and was
only a "natural person," an Italian clown, like all the other
villagers and plowmen about. After this pretty introduction to him, we hear no more of the lad till we find him
at Assisi, doing work of a wonderfully advanced character
for the age, already with more beauty in it than that of
his master, and distinctly different and individual. Even
at so early a period he was himself and not merely
Cimabue's pupil ; Vasari remarking in the after record
upon a series of drawings which were said to be "*invenzione
di Dante,*" suggests that even in the much-praised designs
of Assisi the young painter had been aided by the poet.
In most cases this is as foolish a suggestion as it is derog-
atory, for few people have either leisure or inclination thus

to spend their strength for others, even were it not equally
certain that most people prefer their own ideas to those of
anybody else, and are as little disposed to be aided as the
others are to aid. But the possible conjunction of Dante
with Giotto is so full of interest that we cannot but hope
there was some truth in it. Dante has himself described
the sad abstraction in which, after the death of Beatrice,
he sat "drawing an angel," too much engrossed to see the
fine people who visited him ; and if in the fervor of poetic
talk, in the midst of some lengthened *ragionamento,* we
could believe that the poet took up the painter's tool, and
fired by enthusiasm for all things beautiful, dashed upon
the paper the rude outline of some quick-springing fancy
or plan struck out by the conversation, a new interest would
be thrown upon those great frescoes which are now being,
so much as remains of them, laboriously and painfully preserved. Anything more than this could not be possible,
and this of course is pure conjecture, though it opens to
the imagination the possibility of a pleasant picture, a
friendly conjunction agreeable to think of. Were they
held, these *ragionamenti,* in the depths of Cimabue's *bottega* while his pupil worked, among all the unfinished can-
vases and great bare crucifixes waiting to be painted, the
architectural plans, and chippings in marble, which denoted
the young painter's universal study in all branches of his
art ? or was the country lad, perhaps, in all the homeliness
of his simplicity, invited to go in at leisure moments to
that old house behind San Martino where the noble magnifico lived, one of the first men of the city, and at the
head, for the moment, of all public affairs? The scene is
one upon which the imagination loves to dwell. The bare
room, with little in it but the table on which stood the old
classic lamp which still exists in Italy, throwing its light
upon those two eager faces—the big *cassone* by the wall,
rudely painted, in which Madonna Gemma brought home

her plenishing when she married, and the heavy stools
upon which the talkers sat. Petrarch, whose time was a
little later and who was never driven into exile, possessed
a picture of Giotto's to leave behind him and bequeath by
will with the solemnity which such a possession warranted;
but Dante does not seem to have had any such wealth,
though all the world no doubt seemed before him while he
talked, advising his friend about Assisi and other
matters, with no foresight of coming troubles in his
mind.

The period in which we find these two men together, and
in which no doubt the Bargello portrait was painted, was
not more peaceful than those which preceded it, yet it
seems so in comparison with what was to come; and both
painter and poet were in the fullness of their strength, and
the city was still gay, as it has always been in every interval of calm. We are tempted to introduce here, though
a little out of date, a sketch given by Villani of one of
those halcyon intervals. It is earlier than the time of
which we are speaking; but the historian began his history
in that fruitful year, the last of the old century, when
most likely Giotto, high upon his scaffolding, was painting his picture, so that there is a certain connection
between them, though Villani's sketch carries us back for
nearly twenty years :

"In the year of Christ 1283, in the month of June, on the Feast of
St. John, the city of Florence being in a good and peaceful condition,
very tranquil and useful for the merchants and artisans, and especially for those of the Guelf party, who were in power, there
were assembled in the suburb of Santo Felicita, on the other side of
Arno, where dwelt the Rossi and their allies, a noble and rich company, dressed all in white, with a leader who was called Love. And
in this party nothing was thought of but games and pleasures, dances
of ladies and of cavaliers and other honorable people, going about the
city with trumpets and other instruments, in great joy and gladness
and with many guests assembled to dinner and to supper. This

lasted nearly two months, and was the most noble and worthy to be named that ever had been made in Florence or Tuscany. And to this assembly came, from many different places and cities, many noble persons, who were all honorably received and provided for. And note that the city of Florence and her citizens were more great than they had ever been in this time, which lasted till the year of Christ 1289, until the division of took place between the people and the nobles, and afterward between the Bianchi and the Neri. And in those days there were three hundred cavaliers in Florence, and many bands of cavaliers and of damsels, who spread rich tables morning and evening, and gave away many things in honor of Easter; and from Lombardy and all Italy they brought jesters and players and courtiers to Florence, and everything was done lightsomely; and no stranger of renown, worthy to be honored, passed through Florence who was not invited by these companions and detained as long as possible, and, accompanied on foot or on horseback as he liked, passed through the city or the surrounding country according to his pleasure."

Whether these popular delights were ever intermitted except in the hottest moments of intestine warfare we cannot tell; but it is a popular error to suppose that they were novel when they came to light again in the gay days of Lorenzo de' Medici, as if that prodigal potentate and his renaissance had invented them. In reality they date far back into the Middle Ages, and were in all likelihood an inheritance of classical times. Thus, Folco Portinari led his guests home to dinner, the little Alighieri trotting after his father, nine years old and all unwitting what fate awaited him, on the day when he first saw Beatrice. Two hundred years later Lorenzo had nothing but the last and newest canzone of his own or his satellites to give character to the long-established festival, at which canzones of better poets, Dante himself among the number, had been already sung time out of mind.

Giotto, who drew his first breath on the fertile fields of the Mugello, and had at least part of his professional training in the great cathedral at Assisi built over the

bones of St. Francis, was one of those homely, vigorous
souls, "a natural person," like his father, whom neither
the lapse of centuries nor the neighborhood of much
greater and more striking persons about them, can deprive
of their naïve and genuine individuality.   The art of the
Middle Ages has so many learned expositors that we may
be excused if we prefer to dwell upon the man whose
character is in many respects so unlike that of the ideal
artist.   Burly, homely, characteristic, he carries our

PORTRAIT OF GIOTTO.

attention always with him, alike on the silent road, or in
the king's palace, or his own simple *bottega*.   Wherever he
is, he is always the same, shrewd, humorous, plain-spoken,
seeing through all pretenses, yet never ill-natured in doing
so—a character not very lofty or elevated, and to which
the racy ugliness of a strong, uncultivated race seems
natural—but who under that homely nature carried
appreciations and conceptions of beauty such as few even

of the finest minds possess. High above himself in his strongly-marked peasant-Florentine personality are the visions that come to him unawares, like the visions of the prophets, and which he puts forth, as the prophets did, dimly aware of the divinity in them, and that here was something more than the day's work he had bargained to give, yet never so clear in his mind as to intend or fathom all that his inspired hand executed. The glory confused him though it was his, and he seems always glad to escape from the heights to which genius carried him, and drop down with good-humored yet cutting jest upon those who gaped below, laughing perhaps at himself too, who was so little better than they were, though able to do so much which they could not do. "If I were you," said the condescending king, who visited him at his work in sunny Naples on a blazing day of summer, making a kingly show of condescending equality, "I would not work when the weather was so hot." "Neither would I," says the painter, looking up at King Robert with that twinkle of humor and insight in his eyes, seeing through and through him, "if I were you." All the sayings which are preserved have the same character of shrewd and homely wit, biting but goodnatured. When he and the other ugly citizen, Forese di Rebatta, were riding along upon their mules from an inspection of their respective *podere*, their cornfields and vineyards in Mugello, how graphic is the description of them in Boccaccio's detailed and simple story :

"Messer Forese was of short stature and deformed ; his face and nose were flat ; yet he was so perfectly versed in the study of the law that he was considered by many as a well of knowledge. Giotto was a man of such genius that nothing was ever created that he did not reproduce with the stile, the pen, or the pencil, so as not merely to imitate but to appear nature itself. . . . . They joined company, and were both caught in a shower which drove them for shelter into the house of a farmer. The rain, however, seemed disinclined to stop, and the travelers, being both anxious to return the same day to Flor-

ence, borrowed from the farmer two old cloaks and hats and pro-
ceeded on their way. In this guise they rode, drowned in wet and
covered with splashes, until the weather began to clear, when Forese,
after listening for some time to Giotto, who could always tell a good
story, began to look at him from head to foot, and, not heeding his
own condition, burst into a fit of laughter and said, 'Do you think
that any stranger who should meet you now for the first time would
believe that you are the best painter in the world?' 'Yes,' said
Giotto promptly, 'if he could believe that you knew your A B C.'"

Here there is a mixture of friendly flattery and com-
placency in the merry remark. The quaint absurdities of
outward seeming, so often contemplated with bitterness
and painful sarcasm, are here pleasantly laughable, ministering to a certain pleased self-consciousness in both the
splashed and ugly but witty wayfarers. A touch of quaint
tenderness is in another incident, which shows at the same
time how the streets of wealthy and cultivated Florence
were kept in the thirteenth century. On his way to or from
San Gallo, on a monthly pilgrimage common to the citizens, Giotto, always talkative and friendly, had stopped,
as is the habit of Italians, to give with more effect the
point of some story, when a pig, hurrying by upon more
urgent affairs, ran between his legs and deranged his periods by knocking him over. The painter picked himself
up with a laugh and characteristic comment—the pig had
the best right to the way. "Have not I earned thousands
. of scudi by the help of his bristles? and yet I have never
given to one of his family a cup of minestra!" said the
genial soul. Another curious and amusing story, related,
like the last, by Sacchetti, is worthy of being quoted entire.
The reader will see that through all these anecdotes of
Giotto's humor there runs a subtle thread of unity, the
same amused perception of the difference between what is
and what seems to be—intensified in the following instance
into good-humored reproof, by contact with vulgar pride
and pretension :

"Everybody has heard of Giotto, and that he was a great painter above all others. A common person who had heard of his fame, and had occasion, perhaps because of some official place he had to fill in his village, to have his shield painted, went to Giotto's shop one day with a man behind him carrying the shield in question. When he had found Giotto, 'God save thee, master,' he said. 'I want you to paint my arms upon this shield.' Giotto, looking at the kind of man and his manners, answered nothing except, ' When do you want it ?' and when he had heard this said, ' Leave it to me.' When the painter was alone, he asked himself what was the meaning of this. Had some one sent this fellow to him for a joke ? No one has ever asked me to paint a shield before (he said to himself), and this man is an absurd simpleton who tells me to paint his arms as if he were one of the princes of France ! Certainly he shall have arms, and something more. And thus musing to himself he took the shield, and making the design according to his fancy, told one of his pupils to paint it. There was then painted upon it a helmet, a gorget, a pair of armlets, a pair of gauntlets, two cuirasses a pair of greaves or leg pieces, a sword, a dagger, and a lance. When the worthy man came back to fetch it, he said, 'Master, is the shield painted ?' 'Certainly,' said Giotto ; 'let them bring it down.' And when it arrived, this officially made gentleman (*gentiluomo per procuratore*) looked at it and said, 'Oh, what rubbish is this you have painted on it ?' 'It seems to you rubbish when you have to pay for it,' said Giotto. 'I would not give four farthings for it,' said the other. 'What did you tell me to paint on it ?' asked Giotto. 'My arms,' was the answer. 'Well ! are not they all there ? is any one wanting ?' said the painter. 'You must be a fool indeed. You scarcely know who you are yourself should any one ask you : yet you come here and say to me, paint my arms. If you had been one of the Bardi, perhaps that might have been enough. What arms do you bear ? from whence came you ? who were your ancestors ? Are you not ashamed of yourself ? Go into the world a little, before you talk of arms as if you were Dusman of Bavaria. I have armed you to the teeth on your shield : if there is still another to add tell me, and I will paint it.' 'You abuse me,' said the other, 'and you have spoiled my shield for me.' And going out he went direct to the courts and had Giotto summoned. Giotto appeared, and brought a counter charge against him, claiming two florins for his work. When the judges heard the case, and saw that Giotto spoke the best, they gave their verdict that the man should take his shield, painted as it was, and give Giotto six lire for the painting. Thus he who measured not himself was measured."

This quaint meditative humor and consciousness of all the pretensions and false seemings natural to humanity is the very heart of Giotto's far off mediæval wit, which by right of this quality remains fresh and comprehensible, not by any means a common thing with the *burle*, which so often lose savor and meaning in the recital. The mixture of that elevated and poetic art, in the development and expansion of which out of the old rigid types Giotto took so great and eminent a part, with this homely humorous character, so racy, fresh, and original, is very curious. Except in these moods of humorous observation, we have very few details of his life. The monthly pilgrimage to San Gallo was perhaps no great evidence of piety, but it shows at least that the painter followed the religious use and wont of his time ; and the incidental glimpse we have of him in his workshop, amused yet wondering at the commonplace piece of work brought to him to do, the shield to be painted, which was occupation for a humbler hand, is the clearest view afforded to us of Giotto at home. But outside of Florence the homely, solid figure is visible enough. His peaceable, industrious life, with its strange mingling of the wonderful and the common, carries us along through all the feuds and strifes of history in placid indifference or unconsciousness. On he jogs, quiet and friendly with his jokes and his workmen, filling Italy with pictures more glorious than as yet eye of man had ever seen, and earning good solid silver florins with which to add field to field in Mugello, and portion his plain children, ugly like himself. One is at a loss to know whether the pictures or the florins were most in his mind as he went about from place to place, working like a man inspired, yet living the homeliest, merry life, undisturbed by all the commotions around him. How strangely, with those humorous yet penetrating eyes, must he have looked at that other Florentine, driven here and

there by fierce winds of strife, poor, proud, embittered and
solitary, whom chance or friendship brought across his
path once again in the course of the years! It was at
Padua that he again met the exiled Dante, and by this
time their positions were strangely reversed. Giotto, it
would appear by a repartee of his in answer to his friend's
remark upon the plainness of his children, had his family
with him, and was settled in his own hired house, with a
noble and profitable piece of work in hand, and all his
troop of assistants, pupils, and journeymen round him, a
true master craftsman, leisurely executing the princely
commission of the Paduan noble, when his old friend
came to his door—no longer the magnifico whose beautiful
commanding face he had painted on the Podestà's chapel-
wall, but an anxious and threadbare envoy, hunting every
forlorn hope of emperor or *condottiere* who might get him
back to Florence. How strange must that second meeting
among the clouds and glooms of angry fortune have
seemed to the poet who had in his day encouraged and
helped on the humble young painter! Giotto took Dante
in, and entertained him no doubt with news of the home for
which he pined; and again there followed many a *ragionamento*, and once more perhaps the poet, lavish of ideas,
schemed out upon some scrap of paper that sequence of
Apocalyptic scenes, painted afterward in Naples, which
Vasari calls *invenzione di Dante*, and which, executed after
his death, were, as another story says, suggested by him
out of the unseen world to his painter in a dream. Vasari,
rejecting this hypothesis, thinks it very natural that the
two might have talked over the subject, "as happens often
between two friends;" and indeed nothing could be more
probable, for both, one would think, must have been glad
to escape into abstract subjects from the force of the contrast between this and their previous meetings. Even
Dante's remark, unkind as it seems at the first glance,

about the plainness of little Francesca and Niccolo and Beatrice, might it not spring from some sudden acute pang of remembrance of those fairer faces that had been about his own board when Giotto was his visitor and he the patron and superior, elevated worlds above the peasant *protégé* of Cimabue, the unknown, struggling painter? Such encounters, though they give its highest and noblest tone to faithful friendship surviving all vicissitudes, yet how much is in them that wrings the heart!

It is almost a relief, after this touching and melancholy meeting (though even this is most clearly revealed to us by the sudden gleam of the painter's witty sayings) to find Giotto again at home in tranquil occupation, always humorous, and this time half satirical, though never with any sting in him. The story is well known. The reigning pope, Boniface VIII. or Benedict XI. (most likely the latter, but what does it matter which?), concocting in his thoughts some great scheme of art-decoration which should make him famous, sent a special messenger into Tuscany to collect from the rising schools of art in Florence and Sienna the best specimens procurable from each master, in order that he might select an artist to his taste. Giotto, working in his shop one morning, quite unexcited and undisturbed by the prospect, was visited by this envoy, who explained to him his errand, no doubt with all the pomp that became a messenger from a pope.

"Giotto, who was very polite, took a piece of paper and putting his arm close to his side to make it like a compass, drew with a brush full of red color, with a turn of his hand, a circle so round and perfect in outline that it was a marvel to see. This done he said to the courtier, 'Here is the drawing.' 'Am I to have nothing but this?' said the other stupefied. 'That is enough, and too much,' said Giotto; 'send it with the others, and we shall see if it will be understood.'"

Was there a certain pride in this, or only the half-disdainful test of a humorist of the patron's knowledge who took it upon him to put genius to the proof? Giotto's reply was, as who should say, if he is capable to judge, he will recognize me through this symbol as well as through the most elaborate performance. Probably the daring half-jest, half-defiance, took the pope's fancy, for it was an age in which artists were independent, and there was but one Giotto in the world. But the reader will enter into the feelings of the poor courtier-envoy, with his portfolio of sketches, not sure whether this peasant-painter fellow was making fun of him, or what his holiness might say. The incident has given rise to a proverb, as everybody knows, and the dull and stupid are still characterized in lively Italian talk as "round as the O of Giotto." The O proved sufficient for the purpose, as he had foreseen, and he went, Vasari says, to Rome, where he made some pictures, now destroyed, in St. Peter's; but other critics, more severe and searching, find the termination of this story in a mere engagement to go to Avignon, never carried out. But he went to Padua, as we have seen, and thence to Verona, where, probably by means of Dante as a mutual friend, he painted various subjects for Can Grande, none of which have survived, and also visited Ferrara and Ravenna, in which latter city the traces of him may still be found. Thus the painter traveled in these distant days with his little band of workmen, his brushes and pigments, working sometimes for love, but usually for the solid recompense which nobody grudged, and leaving every corner of Italy which he passed by the richer and the prouder for his visit. In this, as in other things, he has an immense advantage over the poet. Tradition can only point to the name which clings to a certain locality, or an image which seems to be drawn from it, to give a vague and shadowy proof that Dante had once gone that way; but Giotto betrays himself by footsteps more apparent,

and, if time and the chances of war would let him, might
write his itinerary, like a giant, upon the very stones of
his country, leaving his mark here and there in touches
too precious to be allowed to fade. It was after this that
he went to Naples, from the midst of the Ghibellines
straight into the strongest of Guelf strongholds, evidently
with undisturbed composure. This was in 1330. *"Magis-
ter Joctus, de Florentia, pictor familiaris et fidelis noster,"*
was received by King Robert with all honor and kindness, and worked and jested as we have already noted.
Here too a practical joke of his, no less incisive and distinct than his sayings, is recorded. The king had asked
the painter, "faithful and familiar," whom he petted, to
draw him a miniature picture of the kingdom of Naples.
The temptation was strong, even with a non-politician like
Giotto. He drew an ass, saddled and harnessed, snuffing
at another saddle which lay at its feet. The king, whose
capriccio was thus oddly satisfied, did not understand, or
made a pretense of not understanding; and the bold
painter explained undauntedly, that "such were his subjects, and such the kingdom, in which day by day a new
master was wished for." This record of sharp wit is the
only evidence that Giotto cared anything at all about
public matters; perhaps a burst of burgher arrogance—
the sense of being a better man as a free Florentine than
even the insecure master of "Il Regno," the half-mocking
name by which Naples has gone for centuries among all
the republics of Italy—was in his mind, too independent
to care for the effect his pleasantry might produce.

Then he left the south and came back northward again
to his home at Florence, where he appears once more in the
year 1334, beginning at the age of fifty-eight, one of his
most important works. Of all the beautiful things with
which Giotto adorned his city, not one speaks so powerfully
to the foreign visitor—the *forestiere* whom he and his

fellows never took into account, though we occupy so large a space among the admirers of his genius nowadays—as the lovely Campanile which stands by the great cathedral like the white royal lily beside the Mary of the Annunciation, slender and strong and everlasting in its delicate grace. . It is not often that a man takes up a new trade when he is approaching sixty, or even goes into a new path out of his familiar routine. But Giotto seems to have turned without a moment's hesitation from his paints and panels to the less easily-wrought materials of the builder and sculptor, without either faltering from the great enterprise or doubting his own power to do it. His frescoes and altarpieces and crucifixes, the work he had been so long accustomed to, and which he could execute pleasantly in his own workshop or on the cool new walls of church or convent, with his trained school of younger artists round to aid him, were as different as possible from the elaborate calculations and measurements by which alone the lofty tower, straight and lightsome as a lily, could have sprung so high and stood so lightly against that Italian sky. No longer mere pencil or brush, but compasses and quaint mathematical tools, figures not of art but arithmetic, elaborate weighing of proportions and calculations of quantity and balance, must have changed the character of those preliminary studies in which every artist must engage before he begins a great work. Like the poet or the romancist when he turns from the flowery ways of fiction and invention, where he is unincumbered by any restrictions save those of artistic keeping and personal will, to the grave and beaten path of history—the painter must have felt when he too turned from the freedom and poetry of art to this first scientific undertaking. The cathedral was so far finished by this time, its front not scarred and bare as at present, but adorned with statues according to old Arnolfo's plan, who was dead more than thirty years before; but there was no belfry, no companion

peal of peace and sweeetnss to balance the hoarse old *vacca*
with its voice of iron.   Giotto seems to have thrown himself into the work not only without reluctance but with
enthusiasm.   The foundation-stone of the building was
laid in July of that year, with all the greatness of Florence
looking on; and the painter entered upon his work at once,
working out the most poetic effort of his life in marble and
stone, among the masons' chippings and the dust and blaze
of the public street.   At the same time he designed, though
it does not seem sure whether he lived long enough to execute, a new façade for the cathedral, replacing Arnolfo's
old statues by something better, and raising over the doorway the delicate tabernacle work which we see in Pocetti's
picture of St. Antonino's consecration as bishop in St.
Mark's.   It would be pleasant to believe that while the
foundations of the Campanile were being laid and the ruder
mason-work progressing, the painter began immediately
upon the more congenial labor, and made the face of
the Duomo fair with carvings, with soft shades of those
toned marbles which fit so tenderly into each other, and
elaborate canopies as delicate as foam; but of this there
seems no certainty.   Of the Campanile itself it is difficult
to speak in ordinary words.   The enrichments of the
surface, which is covered by beautiful groups set in a
graceful framework of marble, with scarcely a flat or un-
adorned spot from top to bottom, have been ever since the
admiration of artists and of the world.   But we confess,
for our own part, that it is the structure itself that affords
us that soft ecstasy of contemplation, sense of a perfection
before which the mind stops short, silenced and filled with
the completeness of beauty unbroken, which art so seldom
gives, though nature often attains it by the simplest means,
through the exquisite perfection of a flower or a stretch of
summer sky.   Just as we have looked at a sunset we look
at Giotto's tower, poised far above in the blue air, in all

the wonderful dawns and moonlights of Italy, swift darkness shadowing its white glory at the tinkle of the Ave
Mary, and a golden glow of sunbeams accompanying the
midday Angelus. Between the solemn antiquity of the

CATHEDRAL AND CAMPANILE FROM THE PALAZZO PITTI.

old baptistery and the historical gloom of the great
cathedral, it stands like the lily—if not, rather, like the
great angel himself hailing her who was blessed among
women, and keeping up that lovely salutation, musical and

sweet as its own beauty, for century after century, day after day.

Giotto made not only the design, but even Vasari assures us, worked at the groups and *bassi-relievi* of these "stories in marble, in which are depicted the beginning of all the arts." Not very long ago one of the most distinguished of living critics, Mr. Ruskin, exhibited to the boys in the greatest of English schools the photograph of a dog taken from one of these minute groups, a picture which in its absolute simplicity and truth drew a shout of applause from the lads, and brought perhaps some soft moisture to older eyes. Here, with a sentiment which all could understand—scarcely humor even, but the sympathetic genial fun which is its lower phase—were set forth before us, the wise-foolish, innocent looks of a mediæval puppy, transmitted straight over six centuries from the hand of the old artist, who doubtless himself had some soft recollection of such a baby-companion of his own childish sheep-minding, guiding his hand as he worked. Perhaps he felt himself once more on the roadside where Cimabue found him making his first picture, with his doggish comrade wisely looking on, when at the height of his greatness he put on paper and on stone this tender little image. We are not sure that it does not draw the heart of the distant beholder to Giotto as much as the most beautiful angel countenance he ever drew.

Thus the three great buildings got together into a perfect group which are the pride of Florence. The *altri maestri*, employed more or less upon one or other of the three, furnish us with little more than a list of names to which we can attach neither individuality nor distinct examples of work. Yet there are various quaint stories in existence, brought us by the hands of Boccaccio or Sacchetti, which throw a curious light of antique mirth, uproarious and primitive, upon the dark old town, and the crowded workshops, and all the beautiful painter work which went on, as if it had been tailoring, in the most matter-of-fact way, the higher enthusiasms working themselves out upon the canvas, and only the vigorous Tuscan life, rough, sturdy, joyous, and sometimes half grotesque, showing in words or outward appearance. The painter who made the great Christ in mosaic which glimmers in uncertain light from the solemn vault of the baptistery, Andrea Tafi, who was no genius, but a stubborn, honest art-workman, was one of the very first of the group, working inside with his enamels while Arnolfo, outside, applied his marbles, and cleared away the encumbering sarcophagi which filled up the piazza. In Andrea's workshop there was a certain apprentice, a merry, lazy lad, Buonamico, a kindly name—afterward known as the painter Buffalmacco, a somewhat shadowy and mythical personage in art, though more important in the "Novelle" than many a better painter. Like most apprentices, he had other homely work to do besides learning his trade, which was in those days like any other trade, notwithstanding the pride which all the city took in its triumphs. Tafi, who was more a mosaicist than a painter, had a habit of getting up very early in the dark winter mornings to his work, which did not please his sleepy 'prentice, who forthwith set his young wits to work to find some way of escaping those dark and chilly labors. It is clear that Buonamico was a thoroughly idle apprentice, neglecting his sweeping as well as his art, from the quaint narrative that follows:

" Having found in an unswept corner thirty great beetles, he stuck upon the back of each with a short pin a small taper, and when the hour was come at which Andrea usually got up, he introduced them one by one into his room by a crevice in the door, lighting the candle upon each as he did so; and when Andrea awoke to call Buffalmacco he suddenly saw these little lights, and, full of fear, began to tremble; and being an old man and timid, recommended himself under his

breath to God, and began to say his prayers and psalms, and finally
burying his head under the clothes did not call Buffalmacco at all, but
remained there trembling till it was broad day. In the morning, when
he got up, he asked Buffalmacco if he had seen, like himself, more
than a thousand devils. To whom Buffalmacco answered no; that he
had kept his eyes shut, and was surprised that he had not been called
to work. 'To work!' called Tafi; 'I have had other things to think
of than painting, and I am determined to change into another house.'
The next night, though Buonamico put three beetles only into the
chamber of Andrea, he nevertheless, through the fear of the former
night and the few devils whom he now saw, could not sleep; and it
was no sooner day than he left the house with the intention of never
going back, and strong arguments were necessary to make him change
his opinion. However, Buonamico fetched the parish priest, who did
his best to console him. After this, as Tafi and Buonamico discussed
the matter, the latter said, 'I have always heard that the worst
enemies of God were the demons, and consequently they ought to be
very great enemies of painters, because besides that we represent them
always as very hideous, our whole business is to make saints, both
male and female, on all the walls and panels, and by that means, in
despite of the devils, to make men more devout and religious. For
which reason, the demons being very angry with us, and having more
power during the night than in the day, they come to plague us with
their games, and no doubt will go on from bad to worse if this habit
of getting up in the middle of the night is not given up by all.'
With these and many other words (strengthened by what the priest
said) Buffalmacco accomplished his purpose so well that Tafi left off his
habit of rising in the dark, and the devils ceased to carry lights about
the house. But when, not many months after, Tafi, drawn by the love
of gain and forgetting his fright, began again to get up in the dark
and to call Buonamico, the beetles immediately recommenced their
wanderings, and the master was forced by terror to give up this
custom entirely, to which also he was advised by the priest. And
the thing having become known in the city was the reason why for a
time neither Tafi nor any other painter did any more work by
night."

The curious primitive state of society in which such a
rumor could affect a whole craft and stop their work, and
consequently diminish their gain, is remarkable enough,
though the malicious lad, hiding his delight under, no

doubt, an aspect of portentous gravity while he discussed the ways of the demons, and getting up delighted in the middle of the night to frighten his master with his beetles, though he disliked getting up to work, is a very recognizable picture which could be paralleled in all ages. This whimsical story lights up, like one of the tapers on the backs of the poor beetles, the quaint dark chamber of the frightened old painter, the grinning lad outside, the solemn priest with his grave discourse of demons, and even the temporary panic of all the shops in which *santi e sante* were being painted by glimmering lamplight in the winter mornings, as with a Rembrandtish gleam among the shadows. Little as those big, gaunt mosaics, with their melancholy almond eyes, have to do with humanity, such a grotesque story links them oddly to us. There is a great deal more about this wicked apprentice in the tales of Boccaccio and Sacchetti, from which perhaps—were they not so penetrated by the matter-of-fact and brutal licentiousness which, alas! belonged to the age as well as its love of beauty—a better idea is to be acquired of those early times than in any other way.

Altogether it is very evident that Dante's generation could laugh as well as labor, and that the Florentine public of the time which sang the great poet's canzones about the streets, and had his wonderful tale to occupy their graver moments, by no means despised the quaint buffoonery peculiar to their race. Giotto himself affords us an admirable example of the commoner level of individual character among those stout and independent burghers, of whom Dante gives the higher impassioned type. The painter's steady industry, which made genius a reason for work, not an excuse for brilliant idleness; his union of common sense with the highest appreciation of beauty; his devout and poetic art, always nobly ideal and spiritual amid the defects of practical knowledge; and his homely,

quaint, incisive wit and humorous ins'ght, round out
before our eyes the outlines of one of the most real figures
of all that vigorous age. He was not too fine for his time,
nor too advanced, notwithstanding the decided step he had
taken before all who preceded him in the history of art.
With all his keen perception of that vanity of appearances
which affords to such a mind a standing wonder and
amusement, half melancholy or half cynical according to
its temperament, he was too reasonable, and natural to
make any wild disruption of life from those common veils
and disguises which he saw through. Broad, solid, tem-
perate, tolerant, and honorable, he stands before us, among
all the ravings and riot of so warlike a time, with a smile
in his eyes; one of those rare men who see through
humanity without despising it, conscious of their own
share in all its weaknesses, and not unconscious of its
loftier aspects, more like Shakespeare than Dante; an
observer, with no gift of speech except within the concise
limits of a passing jest, and with no possibility of putting
even upon his canvas any other result of his observation
than that which belongs to the outer aspect of things, or
the higher emotions which suited his ideal subjects. What
social pictures he might have left us had art leaned to
this side! But he did better. He worked as a poet, which
it was also in him to do, and pushed forward the whole
system of art, enlarging her horizons and keeping them
pure from any noisome shadow; and stands; thus fronting
us, his ideal labors done, a merry man and an honest,
noting with pitiless good-humor any false pretense, smiling
undeceived at the fine vanities and make-believes about
him, yet never cruel in his wit—kind and content and
friendly through change of fortune and lapse of years.

CHAPTER V.

GROUP II.—GHIBERTI, DONATELLO, BRUNELLESCHI.

A LAPSE of a hundred years is not much in the story of such a city as Florence, and there is no less than the interval of a century between the completion, so far as it ever was completed, of the old structure of Santa Maria del Fiore and the new beginning which brought it to its present splendor, crowning old Arnolfo's exquisite walls with the great dome of Brunelleschi. During the interval, the noble group of buildings which form ecclesiastically the center of Florence, had been in the hands of a succession of artists, including Giotto, his pupil and godson Taddeo Gaddi, and Andrea Orcagna, under whose care the cathedral was maintained in order and beauty, with the addition of an ornamental embellishment here and there, though no one seems to have ventured to complete the cupola which was in Arnolfo's original design. The next energetic art-impulse seems to have begun in the very beginning of the fifteenth century, when the competition for the gates of the baptistery reveals to us at once a new group of young artists—Ghiberti, Brunelleschi, and Donatello. The first of these in success, if not in fame, was Lorenzo Ghiberti, the pupil and stepson of a certain Bartoluccio, one of those art-workmen working indifferently in gold or in iron, casting bronzes or setting jewels, who belonged especially to that wealthy age. The youth, not then much over twenty, had left Florence on a ramble not unlike the *Wanderjahre* of the German workman, moved by a desire to see and to hear, to raise himself from the paternal profession into higher fields of sculpture, and at the same time to escape the plague which raged in the year 1406, and was followed by tumults and troubles not favorable to art. Wandering through the Romagna and the Marches, painting here and there a *salone* in a palace, casting with "much grace" little figures in bronze, exercising his faculty even in wax and stucco when no better was to be had, the lad had come to Pesaro, and was working there, when he got a letter from his stepfather Bartoluccio, informing him that the signoria and the trades had determined at last to make the other two gates to San Giovanni, and that all the best masters in Italy were summoned to the competition, to furnish a "story in bronze" as a specimen of what they could do. Bartoluccio wrote that here was an occasion for Lorenzo to show his genius, and that if he could but succeed in this, with his stepfather's aid, neither the one nor the other need trouble themselves any more with carvings. Young Lorenzo's mind was so excited by this, that "it seemed to him a thousand years before he could reach Florence:" where he set to work at once, with all the advantages of Bartoluccio's practical experience and anxious personal aid.

Filippo Brunelleschi, a young man about Lorenzo's own age, was one of the other competitors, and so, Vasari says, was Donatello; but this seems very unlikely, as Donato was still but a boy. Naturally the competition made a great noise in Florence, and was a very anxious business for the signoria and the operai—the commissioners of works so to speak—who had to decide upon them, and who called to their aid many grave burghers, and even *forestieri* from regions beyond Florence, painters, sculptors, and art authorities of all kinds. Among all these potent and reverend signors were two self-appointed judges, the lads above mentioned, who, not without a pang of disappointment, made up their minds at once who was to win. Filippo, with his boy friend and fellow-student Donato (Donatello—as who should say little Donato, favorite of the workshop, *bon enfant* and sympathetic comrade), went wandering through and through the show, eager, comparing, criticising, with beating hearts. Jacopo dalla Quercia had done well but wanted refinement, Francesco de Valdambrina showed fine heads but a confused composition, Niccolò d'Arezzo was out of drawing ; but, as for Lorenzo Ghiberti, the friends paused upon his group, weighing and comparing it with that of Filippo no doubt, and afterward with a chill of disappointment, yet with generous artist appreciation, went into a corner and said to each other that it was the best, and that he ought to win. The story comes before us like a picture ; and how easy it is to realize the swift, half-unwilling, magnanimous verdict of the two lads, forestalling, with quick artist perception and quicker spring of youth, the slowly formed decision of the great people who took no note of them in their course ! The two artists thus brought before us, the successful and the unsuccessful competitor, were both under four-and-twenty and Donatello was but seventeen ; and among them they were to make the great Duomo glorious and inaugurate a new period in art.

The signoria and the operai and all their advisers ended by being of the same opinion as Filippo and Donato—and Lorenzo was chosen to do the baptistery gates. He was thus in a moment lifted up from a wandering sculptor-journeyman, no more distinguished than any other young artisan, to be at the head of a great *bottega* of art and one of the notable men of his time. Let us hope that old Bartoluccio, thus delivered at a stroke from the trinkets which evidently had plagued his soul, found himself happier in the great undertaking into which he had piloted his boy. The work was indeed work for a lifetime, and advanced it

would seem very slowly, the first door taking twenty years
to complete and the second as much longer, so that altogether they were forty years in hand ; which did not,
however, hinder the master from executing many other
works and filling various appointments at the same time.
Whether there were difficulties in the casting, or the delay
belonged to the naturally slow progress of original art,
every man employed in which was more or less an artist,
we cannot tell, but at all events there was not much delay
about the beginning.   Baldinucci quotes a public notice of
the date of 7th January, 1407, by which a very picturesque
indication is afforded of this commencement. It is thereby
announced to the public and all concerned, that Lorenzo
and his workmen, whose names follow, "all working at the
doors of San Giovanni," are licensed "to go about Florence
at all hours of the night, but always carrying lamps
lighted and visible." This curious reminder of the dark
and deserted streets, haunted only by lawless and dangerous persons, through the long, cold nights of winter,
affords us another glimpse, as clear as any picture, into the
old Florence of five hundred years ago. With perhaps now
and then a band of wild *condottieri* about, or the young
gallants of the dominant house, whatever that might be,
hangers-on of the Medici ready to rush at the throat of any
Albizzi—in the deep dark streets, between those two tall
rows of houses, how pleasant must have been the glimmer
of the lamp carried by the peaceable artist on his way to
see after his furnaces, or the stout art-workman, brown as
his own metal, marching with honest resounding steps,
bold in right of his license, holding the crown of the
causeway, and not afraid of the very signoria themselves
should he meet one of those magnificoes on his way to the
great workshop of Santa Maria Novella! There was not
the difference between master and man in those days that
there is now, and probably in Lorenzo's workshop there

were none whose names, at least in their own generation, were unknown to fame. The foundry, if we may so call it, where the gates were cast, was in a little street opposite Santa Maria Novella, which Vasari recollected to have seen still existing in his youth. The silver shrine of San Zenobia in the cathedral, and many other works which we need not specify, show that Lorenzo by no means confined himself to one undertaking however important. Besides, his supposed and fictitious share in the great architectural work of the dome, which the reader will presently see, his real help in the decoration of the cathedral was considerable, and shows the faculty to turn a hand to anything which is so characteristic of early artists. He seems, for instance, to have taken in hand and superintended the putting in of those windows which still glimmer rich and dim, giving a glow of color to the solemn twilight under Brunelleschi's dome. For this purpose he brought from distant Lubeck on the northern seas "the most singular master who, in this art, was known in the world," and himself arranged the sequence of the pictures, and composed the three *occhi* over the three doors of the cathedral. And the reader does not need to be reminded that when the gates of the baptistery were finally set up after these long years, to the wonder and delight of a succeeding generation, another young artist, Michael of the Buonarotti, with that fine mouthing speech of his, magniloquent and generous, declared them fit to be the gates of heaven.

This great work was followed in Florentine art-history by another still greater, the construction of the great cupola of the cathedral. Filippo of Ser. Brunellescho of the Lapi, which is, according to Florentine use, his somewhat cumbrous name, or Brunelleschi *tout court*, as custom permitted him to be called, was the son of a notary, who, as notaries use, hoped and expected his boy to follow in his steps and succeed to his practice. But, like other sons doomed their fathers' soul to cross, Filippo took to those *figuretti* in bronze which were so captivating to the taste of the time, and preferred rather to be a goldsmith, to hang upon the skirts of art, than to work in the paternal

INTERIOR OF CATHEDRAL.

bottega. He was, as Vasari insinuates, small, puny, and ugly, but full of dauntless and daring energy as well as genius. From his gold and silver work, the "carvings" which old Bartoluccio had been so glad to escape from, and from his *figuretti*, the ambitious lad took to architectural

drawing, of which, according to Vasari, he was one of the
first amateurs, making "portraits" of the cathedral and
baptistery, of the Palazzo Pubblico, and the other chief
buildings of the city. He was, as we have said, one of the
competitors for the gates, but at once, on seeing Lorenzo's
group, ceded to him as the more worthy. He was so
eloquent a talker that a worthy citizen declared of him
that he seemed "a new St. Paul;" and in his thoughts he
was continually busy planning or imagining something
skillful and difficult. The story of his early victory over
Donatello, his beloved companion, is well known. They
were men of very different natures—or rather lads, for the
incident seems to have occurred early in their career.
Vasari has so little to say of Donato's birth, not even his
father's name, that it is evident the simple, eager, kindly
artist must have been nobody—a genial, noisy, liberal soul,
with a certain simple self-confidence and admiration of his
own works, which was combined with the true artist's
ready perception of greater excellence. When Donato
(called Donatello, if not "for short," at least for love, as is
the gentle use and wont of the Italian tongue) had made
his first great crucifix, which still stands in Santa Croce, he
showed it to Filippo "*suo amicissimo,*" says Vasari, with
the tenderest use of that superlative, "his most friend-
liest," if it will bear translation. "Filippo, who by
Donato's description had expected something much better,"
said nothing, which was not very friendly, but smiled.
Donatello, disappointed, entreated him, by the friendship
between them, to express his opinion, which Filippo, who
was *liberalissimo* in such matters, more strong-minded and
less sorry to wound than his simple friend, at last did,
telling him that it was a *contadino* and not Christ whom
he had put upon the cross—a reproach which might indeed
be made to most painters who have attempted that sublime
figure. Poor Donatello, wounded and angry, answered

impatiently. "If it is so easy as you think, take wood and make one yourself"—a most natural reply, from which the Italians have taken, it is said, their proverb, *"Piglia un legno e fanne uno tu."** Filippo, who could keep his own counsel, took the advice, and going home began a similar crucifix, over which he took great pains in order to justify his criticism of the other. When it was finished, after several months' private work, he invited, with somewhat cold-blooded malice, his friend to dine with him one day. As they went together to Filippo's lodging, the two young artists, passing the Mercato Vecchio, bought the materials for their simple feast, eggs, bread, and fruit with which simple Donatello charged himself, carrying the honest, homely fare in his apron, for *"in quel tempo i pittori non facevano il cavaliere."* Never was a better example of low living and high thinking, for the simple young fellow with the eggs in his apron had his head full of the freshest poetry of art ; and one's heart aches for him going through the Mercato so pleasantly to the friendly meal, without any notion of what was coming. Filippo, somewhat cruel, one cannot but feel, bade his friend go in and wait for him under some pretense of business. Then Donatello, entering without suspicion, found himself suddenly in presence of the new crucifix, set forth in a good light. He was so startled by this vision, and so stupefied by the superiority of his friend's work, that, raising his hands in wonder, he let his apron fall, and eggs and cheese and apples all dashed upon the floor together. When he had got over the first surprise, Filippo, *malizioso*, came in laughing, and crying out, "What do you mean, Donatello ? How shall we dine, now that you have spoiled everything?" "As for me,"

---

* The same remark was made, we believe, by the late Augustus Welby Pugin, when suffering under the criticisms of Mr. Ruskin, then a young critic *liberalissimo*, like Brunelleschi, of censure. "Let the fellow build a church," said the architect scornfully.

cried poor Donato, "I have had my share for this morning; if you want any dinner, take it. But no," the good fellow added, with a burst of magnanimous admiration, "to thee it is given to make the Christ, to me only the *contadini!*" The reader who does not feel that good Donatello had the best of it after this, notwithstanding that his heart was wrung and his pride wounded and all his eggs broken, will be of a different mind from most of the many generations who have heard the story ; and it is very much to be doubted whether the triumphant Filippo, though he could make the better crucifix, could have made such a speech. It gives the generous soul a higher claim upon our sympathies than if he had made the best statue in Florence.

However, the thing which Filippo really had to make was greater and more difficult than any statue. The idea of completing the cathedral by adding to it a cupola worthy of its magnificent size and proportions seems to have been in the young man's head before the signoria or the city took any action in the matter. Arnolfo's designs are said to have been lost, and all the young Filippo could do was to study the picture in the Spanish chapel of Santa Maria Novella, where the cathedral was depicted according to Arnolfo's intention ; and this proof of the usefulness of architectural backgrounds, no doubt, moved him to those pictures of buildings which he was fond of making. After his failure in the competition with Ghiberti for the baptistery gates, Filippo went to Rome, accompanied by Donato. Here the two friends lived and studied together for some time, one giving himself to sculpture, the other to architecture. Brunelleschi, according to Vasari, made this a period of very severe study. He examined all the remains of ancient buildings with the keenest care ; studying the foundations and the strength of the walls, and the way in which such a prodigious load as the great dome, which already he saw in his mind's eye, could best be supported. So profound were his researches that he was called the *Treasure-hunter* by those who saw him coming and going through the streets of Rome, a title so far justified that he is said in one instance to have actually found an ancient earthenware jar full of old coins. While engaged in these studies, his money failing him, he worked for a jeweler according to the robust practice of the time, and after making ornaments and setting gems all day, set to work on his buildings, round and square, octagons, basilicas, arches, colosseums, and amphitheaters. perfecting himself in the principles of his art. In 1407 he returned to Florence, and then there began a series of negotiations between the artist and the city, to which there seemed at first as if no end could come. They met, and met again, assemblies of architects, of city authorities, of competitors less hopeful and less eager than himself. His whole heart, it is evident, was set upon the business. Hearing Donatello at one of these assemblies mention the cathedral of Orvieto, which he had visited on his way from Rome, Filippo, having his mantle and his hood on, without saying a word to any one, set straight off from the Piazza on foot, and got as far as Cortona, from whence he returned with various pen-and-ink drawings before Donato or any one else had found out that he was away. Thus the small, keen, determined, ugly artist, swift and sudden as lightning, struck through all the hesitations, the consultations, the maunderings, the doubts, and the delays of the two authorities who had the matter in hand, the signoria and the operai, as who should say the working committee, who made a hundred difficulties and shook their wise heads, and considered one foolish and futile plan after another with true burgher hesitation and wariness.

At last, in 1420, an assembly of competitors was held

in Florence, and a great many plans put forth, one of
which was to support the proposed vault by a great
central pillar, while another advised that the space to be
covered should be filled with soil mixed with money, upon
which the dome might be built, and which the people
would gladly remove without expense afterward for the
sake of the *quattrini!*—an expedient most droll in its
simplicity.   Brunelleschi, impatient of so much folly,
went off to Rome, it is said, in the middle of these discussions, disgusted by the absurd ignorance which was
thus put in competition with his careful study and long
labor. Finally the appointment was conceded to him,
but even then in a grudging and unpleasant way, Lorenzo
Ghiberti, who was high in favor with the Florentines,
being associated with him, though entirely incapable of
the work. So annoyed was Filippo by this conjunction,
that it was all his friends could do to keep him from
burning his models and drawings and leaving Florence.
Donatello and Luca della Robbia, however, "comforted"
him, and so did the committee of the operai, who
smoothed him down by assurances "that the inventor and
author of the fabric was he alone ; but, notwithstanding,
they gave Lorenzo the same salary as Filippo." The consequence was that the artist began his work languidly enough,
knowing that he would have all the trouble, and then
would have to divide the honor and fame with Lorenzo.
This being the case, Filippo set his active mind to work
to get rid of his undesired partner, and the struggle forms
an amusing episode in the more solemn and solid history
of the cathedral. For a long time the thousand expedients of Filippo to show the ignorance of his companion
seem to have fallen harmless against the quiet and passive
resistance of the other, who would not perceive himself to
be in the way ; and the manner in which he was at last
ousted, and the contrast and conflict of character between

the choleric, keen, indignant, yet *rusé* artist, and the
steady man of business, calmly considerate of his salary,
and holding to his place, is one of the most amusing
passages in Vasari. After various unsuccessful attempts
Brunelleschi at last tried the plan of falling ill and
leaving the burden of the work on his partner's
shoulders :

"One morning, Filippo, instead of appearing at work, stayed in
bed, and, calling for hot applications and fomentations, pretended to
have a severe pain in his side. When the master workmen heard of
this, while they waited to know what they were to do that day, they
asked Lorenzo what was the next thing? He answered that it was
Filippo who arranged all that, and that they must wait for him. 'But
do not you know his mind?' they cried. 'Yes,' said Lorenzo, 'but I
will do nothing without him.' And this he said to cover himself ;
for not having seen the model of Filippo, and having never asked of
him how he meant to conduct the work for fear of appearing ignorant,
he was now obliged to remain inactive, making doubtful answers, for
he knew that he held his appointment against the will of Filippo.
This lasted two days, and the workmen at last betook themselves to
the commissioners who provided their materials, asking what they
were to do. 'You have Lorenzo ; let him exert himself a little,' was
the reply, and much talk and blame arose on the subject when this
was known. Some said that Filippo's sickness arose from the failure
of his power to carry out the work, which he repented to have undertaken ; while his friends defended him, saying that it was disgust to
have Lorenzo forced upon him, and that his illness arose from over-
work. Thus a great disturbance arose, and the workmen who were
kept idle murmured and grumbled against Lorenzo, saying, 'Basta,
he is very good at drawing his salary, but not at arranging our work.
If Filippo is long ill what can he do? Is it his fault if he is ill?' The
Operai, ashamed of all this commotion, went to see Filippo, and having condoled with him in his illness, told him in what disorder the
work was, and what harm his absence was doing. Filippo, divided
between his feigned illness and his love of the work, answered them
with passionate words. 'Is not Lorenzo there?' he cried. 'Why
does not he do something!' The Operai answered, 'He does not wish
to do anything without you.' 'I could do very well without him,'
said Filippo. Upon which his visitors left him, perceiving that he

was ill of desire to be alone in his work. They then sent friends to persuade him to get up, holding out hopes that Lorenzo would be removed. But when Filippo returned to the work and saw how great was the feeling in favor of Lorenzo, who drew the salary without taking any trouble, he tried another way of getting rid of him and of showing how little he really knew about it, and thus addressed the building committee, Lorenzo being present : 'Signori Operai, if the time which is lent to us to live in was at our command, there is no doubt that many things which are begun would be finished instead of remaining imperfect. The sickness which has now passed, might have taken away my life and stopped this work, therefore if it ever happened that I got ill again, or Lorenzo, whom God preserve, it would be better that the one or the other should continue his work ; therefore I have concluded that as your excellencies have divided the salary it would be well also to divide the labor, that each of us being thus stimulated to show how much he knows, may be honorable and useful to the republic. There are two difficult things to be done—the bridges upon which the mason must stand to build . . . . and the chain . . . . which is to bind together the eight sides of the cupola. . . . . Let Lorenzo take one of them, the one he thinks he can best carry out, and I will take the other, that no more time may be lost.'"

This practical proof of his inferiority made an end of Lorenzo. He took in hand the construction of the chain, and, failing lamentably, was at last removed from the works, leaving Filippo supreme.

The greatest difficulty with which he had to contend after this was a strike of his workmen, of whom, however, there being no trades' unions in those days, the imperious *maestro* made short work. And thus, day by day, the great dome swelled out over the shining marble walls and rose against the beautiful Italian sky. Nothing like it had been seen before by living eyes. The solemn grandeur of the Pantheon at Rome was indeed known to many, and San Giovanni was in some sort an imitation of that ; but the immense structure of the cupola, so justly poised, springing with such majestic grace from the familiar walls to which it gave new dignity, flattered the pride of the Florentines as something unique, besides delighting the eyes

and imagination of so beauty-loving a race. With that
veiled and subtle pride which takes the shape of pious fear,
some even pretended to tremble, lest it should be supposed to be too near an emulation of the blue vault above,
and that Florence was competing with heaven; others,
with the delightful magniloquence of the time, declared
that the hills around the city were scarcely higher than the
beautiful Duomo; and Vasari himself has a doubt that
the heavens were envious, so persistent were the storms
amid which the cupola arose. Yet there it stands to this
day, firm and splendid, uninjured by celestial envy, more
harmonious than the *sorella grande* of St. Peter's, the
crown of the beautiful city. Its measurements and size
and the secrets of its formation we do not pretend to set
forth : the reader will find them in every guide-book. But
the keen, impetuous, rapid figure of the architect, impatient, and justly impatient, of all rivalry, the murmurs
and comments of the workmen; the troubled minds of the
city authorities, not knowing how to hold their ground
between that gnome of majestic genius who had fathomed
all the secrets of construction and built a hundred Duomos
in his mind while they were pottering over the preliminaries of one; and the steady, respectable, salary-loving
Lorenzo; have all the interest of life for us. Probably
Lorenzo was not so convinced of his own incapacity as
Filippo was, and felt his youthful success a guarantee of
universal power, as so many, both of artists and laymen,
are apt to do. Brunelleschi, sitting now in stone opposite
to his work, as he does these many years, contemplating it
night and day out of solemn marble eyes, conveys to the
spectator a very different idea from the living and breathing one which we find in Vasari's delightful pages. The
past in its dead stillness and stony completion is always a
poor substitute for the present, and we prefer to see him
fighting over his work—like Dante, an *animo sdegnoso,*

swift, sudden, capable, impatient of all stupidity and inde-
cision ; his head held high and his nostrils expanding, as
in Vasari's picture, like a horse that scents the battle.
" Nature," says the old biographer, " has created many,
small in person and external power, whose souls are so
great and whose hearts are full of such immeasurable force

THE CENTER OF FLORENCE.

(*smisurata terribilità*), that if they do not begin great and
almost impossible undertakings, and carry them out to the
wonder of all beholders, they have no peace in their lives."
Such was Filippo Brunelleschi. Though unshapely in person, as was the witty Forese di Ribatta, and ugly as the
great Giotto, this "unmeasured terribility" of soul carried him through all difficulties. Through the calm
fields of art he goes like a whirlwind, keen, certain, unfailing in his aim, unsparing in means,
carried forward by such an impulse of will and self-confi-

dence that nothing can withstand him. Sure of his own powers as he was when he carved in secret the crucifix which was to cover poor Donatello with confusion, he saw before him, over his carvings, as he worked for the Roman goldsmith, the floating vision of the great dome he was to build—and so built it, all opposition notwithstanding, clearing out of his way with the almost contemptuous impatience of that knowledge which has no doubt of itself, the competing architects, the uncomprehending Lorenzo. This certainty and confidence does not always, by any means, accompany genius, but, when it does, what force on earth can stand before these two united powers?

Donatello is a totally different man. Without the humor of Giotto, and without the higher religious feeling which gave refinement to the painter, it is again the frank and simple peasant with whom we find ourselves face to face. He too is self-confident, but in a very different and much more winning way than his friend Filippo. It is not in him to prepare a triumph over friend or foe by the energy of secret labor and long-concealed plan ; but simply, good soul, he thinks his crucifix, the first he has made, a *rarissima cosa*, and talks so of it with open-hearted candor and satisfaction as to give the critic, when taken to see this great work, occasion to smile. Nor does he grow wiser as life goes on. As he was making the statue called the "Zuccone," for the decoration of Giotto's campanile, he struck the marble, it is said, in an agony of pleasure and content, bidding it "Speak!" and his favorite oath after its erection in its place was "By my faith in my Zuccone," (*Alla fe ch' io porto al mio Zuccone!*) This ingenuous and artless vanity is rather prepossessing than repellent; its frank utterance suggests a touching trust in the bystander's sympathy, and hard-hearted must the spectator be who can quite close his heart against the appeal. Notwithstanding this delightful self-applause, we have already seen how ready he was to acknowledge the superiority of his friend to whom "*e conceduto fare i Christi*"—one of the finest testimonials ever given by one artist to another, and given with such generosity, at a moment when his heart must have been sore with the sudden revelation of this unsuspected, long-premeditated rivalship, that the acknowledgment is almost sublime. At a later period of Donatello's life he went to Padua to execute some works there, which were found so excellent and wonderful that the spectators stood *maravigliati* and *stupiti*, dumb with admiration before compositions so surpassing. Oddly enough, however, this excessive applause wearied the simpleminded artist, notwithstanding his own *naïve* appreciation of his own productions. Finding himself considered a miracle, and praised for every kind of intelligence, he declared that he must go back to Florence, for the whimsical reason that if he stayed there where he was praised by everybody he would soon forget all he knew, whereas at home he was notoriously abused and found fault with, and thus kept up to the mark : "the constant blame forcing him to study and consequently to greater glory." It would be very desirable that all artists should take criticism in this exemplary way.

Beside the Zuccone, which was a portrait statue, and of which the sculptor himself thought so highly, the fine image of St. George at the Or San Michele, to which Michael Angelo, copying the artist himself in genial exaggeration, said " *Cammina!* " " March! " as his sole criticism, will occur to all lovers of art in connection with Donatello's name. In front of the same church is another statue, that of St. Mark, of which a curious story is told. It was done for the trade of linen-workers, and though admirably adapted to the position in which it was to be placed, alarmed and dissatisfied the officers of the guild when it was exhibited to them placed on a lower level—these good men

being unprepared to take into account the difference
between their point of vision and that from which their
St. Mark on his pedestal would be regarded. Donatello
took their strictures with the calm of superior knowledge
without losing his temper, and promised that when they
saw the figure in its place, so carefully would he adopt all
their suggestions that they would not know it to be the
same. Accordingly before the next inspection he had it

HEAD OF ANGEL: AFTER DONATELLO.

placed on its proper pedestal in the place for which
it had been made. When the worshipful linen-officials saw
it again they agreed that it was indeed quite a different
thing, and that their suggestions had been taken to great
purpose. It was, however, precisely the same statue, untouched by intrusive chisel, simply put into the place for
which it was made. This excellence of proportion is sometimes attributed to his warm and close relationship with
Brunelleschi. The artist, however, was not always so
reasonable or gentle as when with secret smiles he confuted

the strictures of the linen masters. On another occasion we are told that a rich merchant of Genoa had commissioned from Donatello a colossal head. When, however, the model was finished, the Genoese began to object to the price required, and, with an ignorance not unusual in rich patrons, declared that Donatello had been only a month in making it, and that the sum he was asking was equal to half a florin a day! "Donatello, turning round angrily exclaimed, that it was possible in the hundreth part of an hour to spoil the work of a year; and with a sudden push threw the head to the ground, where it fell and broke into a hundred pieces." It was clear, he added scornfully, that his patron had been used to cheapen vegetables and not statues; and no argument or entreaty, not even those of Cosimo de' Medici, his patron, could induce him to make the bust over again.

But yet with this fiery mixture of pride and candor and ingenuous vanity, the hasty sculptor was open-handed and open-hearted as the day. "He was a man of cheerful mind, modest and disinterested," says Baldinucci, "thinking much more of the advantage of others than of his own." "Liberal, lovable, and courteous," says Vasari, "better to his friends than to himself; neither did he care at all for money, but kept it in a basket hung to a beam, where all his workmen and friends might help themselves without a word of explanation." Naturally a man of such habits never grew rich, but private patronage did for Donatello what the absence of all thrift or care prevented him from doing for himself. "He lived through his old age gayly," says Vasari; and adds a story how Cosimo, dying, had recommended the old artist to Piero, his son, who on his side bestowed upon Donatello, to keep him in comfort when he became unable to work, a *podere* or farm, the resources of which were so considerable that he could live comfortably upon them. But, with characteristic inaptitude for the

cares of a well-regulated existence, the old sculptor before
a year had passed, came back to his patron, begging for
permission to give back the property. It took away all the
quiet of his life, he declared, to be obliged to give an ear
to the complaints of the countrymen who cultivated it for
him, and who destroyed his peace of mind by coming to
him every three days with the news that the wind had un-
roofed the pigeon-house, or that the commissioner had
seized the cattle for the taxes, or that a storm had spoiled
the fruit; which things were so much trouble and care to
him that he would rather die of hunger than have the
weight of them upon his mind. Piero, laughing at his
trouble, nevertheless took back the farm, and allowed the
painter a certain weekly pension instead, " which contented
him mightily, so that he lived gayly and without care all
the rest of his life, a servant and friend of the house of
Medici," says Vasari, who himself was among the partisans
of that liberal and princely family. He died in the Via
del Cocomero on the way to the cathedral about which he
had labored so long, where his beloved Zuccone stood, and
still stands, on the west side of the campanile, looking
toward the spot where the sculptor died, at the age of
eighty-three. He was buried in San Lorenzo, which his
friend Brunelleschi had helped to build, near the tomb of
his old patron Cosimo. The artists of that age were long-
lived. Notwithstanding their enormous labors, travels, and
unfailing industry, or perhaps in consequence of the health-
ful effect of such constant occupation of mind and body, it
was not unusual for them to reach even such an advanced
age as Donatello's. And homely as it was from the time
when he spilled and broke the eggs out of his apron in consternation and admiring wonder over his friend's work,
until the day when, *allegro* still though old and feeble, he
threw up his landed property and took his little pension
instead, the busy artist life was no doubt a happy one to

the simple-minded, vehement sculptor. When he was dying some of his relations sought him out for apparently the first time in their lives, for he had another little *podere* of his own somewhere to bequeath, which was worth looking after. But the generous old craftsman was not a fool. He told them that a single visit paid to a relation in so many years was a poor price for a piece of property, and that the *figuerolo* who had labored the soil for years had done much more to deserve it than they had; then "courteously dismissing them," he left the land to his laborer who had done the work of it—a piece of even-handed justice entirely in Donatello's way.

The architect, whose works were of a more imposing kind than those of his friend, came to high fortune in Florence. Brunelleschi was not the kind of man who would hang up his fortune in a basket for every comrade to take his will of. He was drawn for the *magistratura*, and held office, the highest honor of citizenship, although indeed the time was come, or nearly so, when the great offices of the state became the easy possession of the party of the Medici. Filippo, like most other artists, was for Cosimo, and was consulted and employed continually by that cunning and liberal patron of the arts, for whom he worked at San Lorenzo and other places, making many designs, which, however, were only partially carried out. Among others Brunelleschi, "putting aside every other thought," employed himself in designing "a most beautiful and great model for a palace," which it was the desire of the wealthy Medici to build. "And while he worked at this model it was Filippo's wont to give thanks to fate for giving him the occasion of building a house, which he had for years desired to do, and for one who had both the means and the will to carry out his design." The architect, however, in this reckoned without his patron, for the design into which he threw himself with such enthusiasm appeared to Cosimo

too sumptuous and splendid, "not for the cost but for the
envy it would excite." When this unexpected disappointment befell him, Filippo showed no more philosophy than
his friend. "When he heard Cosimo's resolution not to
carry out the work, he tore the design, indignantly, into a
thousand pieces." That Cosimo himself was very sorry
afterward was perhaps but small consolation to the
master; but the able old statesman held the great builder
in his high esteem, and was in the habit of saying that he
had never talked with any man of more intelligence or a
greater soul than Messer Filippo. Indirectly, however, he
did prepare a house for the Medici and their descendants
in the Palazzo Pitti, afterward the residence of the
reigning dukes, which he designed and partially built.
Nor were Filippo's labors of a peaceful character alone.
The fortifications which he built at Mantua and at Pisa
were of such a character as to justify the complimentary
assertion, that "if every state had a man like Filippo they
might consider themselves safe without arms." And with
all these varied accomplishments he was a man of a keen
and bitter wit, full of resource and readiness. One only
joke of his, Vasari chronicles, and it is more sharp than
pleasant. His old rival, Ghiberti, had a little property
called Lepriono, which had been much the reverse of profitable to him, and which he had at last got rid of. Some
innocent person, probably unaware of the enmity between
them, asked the architect what was the best thing that
Lorenzo had done. "The sale of Lepriono," said the sharp-
witted artist. He died first of the three who were so
closely connected in the work of the cathedral in the year
1446, before Lorenzo's great gates were finished, and twenty
years before Donato ended his light-hearted days. No
record of his domestic circumstances, his family, or descendants has come down to us, one of his pupils alone
being mentioned as his heir. Donatello, who has not even

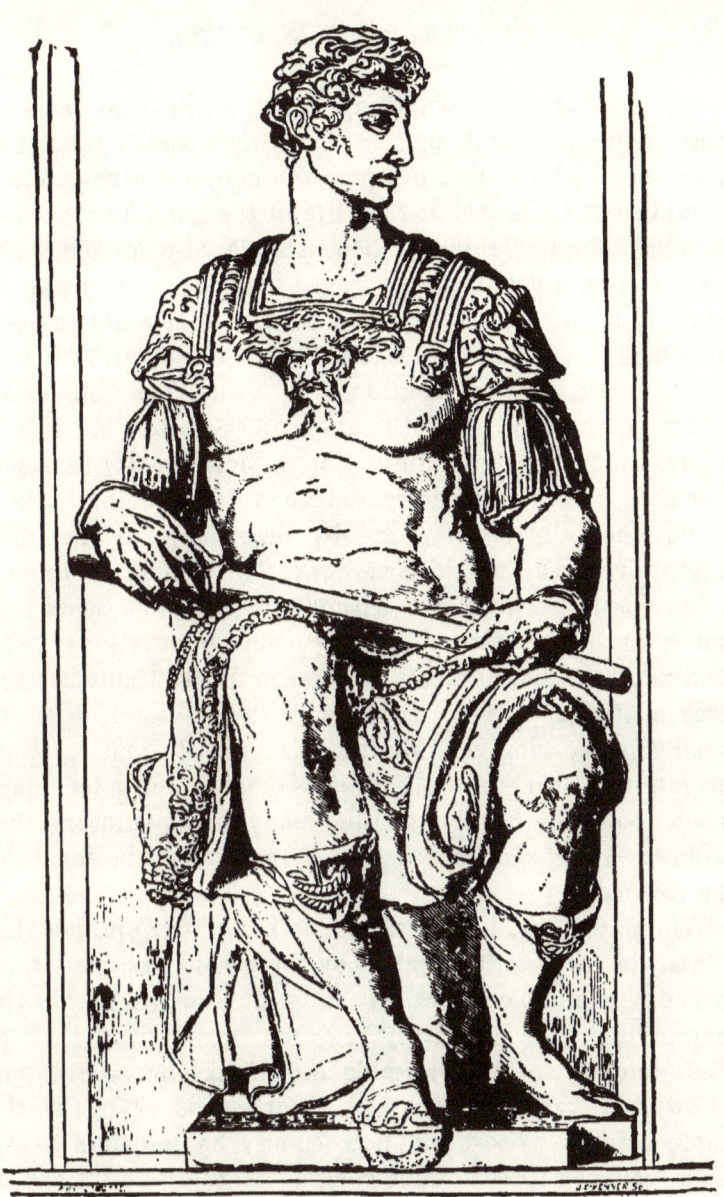

LORENZO DE MEDICI: MICHEL ANGELO.   161

a name to brag of—nothing but the Christian name at
least, which, in that age, was the safest—was clearly un-
married ; and his more prosperous and dignified companion
would seem to have ended his life in the same way, leaving
no one behind. Ghiberti died in 1455, also an old man,
with sons and grandsons to guard his good name ; and in
the end of his life even wrote a book with the same object,
in which Vasari says he refers indeed to the great artists
of the past, "those mentioned by Pliny," as well as the
more recent glories of Cimabue and Giotto; but this is
done, the biographer thinks, "with more brevity than was
becoming, for no other reason than that he might thus
handsomely introduce himself, describing, as he does
minutely, one by one, his own works.' " There are those,"
adds Vasari, perhaps not without an agreeable sense that
he himself was safe from any such imputation, "who
can paint, chisel, and cast in bronze better than they can
weave stories." The reader who loves Vasari, as every
reader must do who studies his quaint and graphic
pages, will feel the unkindness of the reminder made
in a foot-note by one of his many commentators, that
Messer Giorgio unfortunately wove stories better than
he painted.

We may pause, however, here to record our opinion that
Vasari is very hardly treated by those said commentators,
every one of whom has his fling at him, although the
comparison, for example, of such a work as that of
Baldinucci with his admirable and lifelike narratives, will
show how very little that is important is added by the
more critical writer, and how calmly he transfers to his
own pages, without acknowledgment, the descriptions of
his predecessor. In the matter of dates indeed our biographer is evidently fallible, but is it not a kind of
necessity in historical work that the first workman should
guess, and stumble in this particular, if only to leave room

for the after-exertions of others? The three men whom he
thus places before us are drawn in the distinctest outlines,
from that earliest chapter in their history when young
Lorenzo's group gains the prize and sets him afloat at once
in life, while the other two look on, admiring, with a
generous consent to his elevation and acknowledgment of
his right to it, which is all the finer that posterity now
has it in its power to judge how little, if at all, superior
Lorenzo's design was to Filippo's. Then how graphic is
the after-story! The two sworn brothers in friendship and
art, buying their homely provisions as they pass through
the market, discussing their fine visions, their high hopes,
the great things they were to do; and frank Donatello's
humiliation and keen Filippo's half-unkind triumph—only
half-unkind, for perhaps in hot impulse of youth and
eagerness he had not thought of the sting he was inflicting
—and it did not, it is evident, disturb their friendship.
And when we leave them in the last chapter of their
existence, how true is still the picture to human nature
and character—Lorenzo's last aged glorification of *io stesso*,
and Donatello's unteachable indifference to worldly affairs
and contempt of the property which was a burden to him!
As for Filippo, whose soul was all in his work, and whose
entire object from youth to age had been to carry out his
much-studied enterprises even if left unremembered in the
doing of them, how characteristic is the one lament over
him which his kind biographer makes: "In some things
Filippo was very unfortunate; for besides having always
some one to struggle with, many of his buildings were
never completed, either during his lifetime or after." How
fine a touch of human sympathy and comprehension is in
these words! for Vasari felt how doubly hard upon
Brunelleschi was this commonest fate of the great artist—
the one unspeakably grievous to his keen and eager soul.

We cannot leave the great cathedral of Florence, thus

finally delivered to posterity in all its solemn gloom and
greatness by this last group of workmen, without a word
concerning another whose productions are so individual, so
fine, and so completely Florentine, that though the greater
part of his work in its decoration has been removed from
the Duomo, his presence is necessary here to complete the
band.   No one who has seen them can forget the lovely
groups of singing boys, so fresh in natural life, grace, and

FIGURES FROM ORGAN-SCREEN.   LUCA DELLA ROBBIA.

vivacity, with which Luca della Robbia once adorned the
organ-loft, to use a homely English title, in Santa Maria
del Fiore.   Probably they are better placed for the enjoyment of the spectator now, where they stand in the
museum of the Bargello, than if hung high in the twilight
of that vast interior, the place for which they were made,
and where, our good Vasari complains, they were too
highly finished to have their full effect, though he cannot
refrain from an expression of true artist delight in their
perfection.   "Though raised seventeen *braccia* from the
ground," he tells us, "you can see the dilation of the

throat in him who sings, the measured beating of him who conducts the music, over the shoulder of the smaller figure, and the other diverse expressions of playing, singing, dancing, and all those charming movements which form the delights of music." Nevertheless the corresponding groups of Donatello were done with "more judgment and discretion" than those of Luca, "because his work was done roughly (in *bozza,* as in a sketch) and not care-

FIGURES FROM ORGAN-SCREEN. LUCA DELLA ROBBIA.

fully finished, and therefore it has a better appearance at a distance . . . from which," says Vasari, "the artist ought to learn ; for experience shows that things which are to be seen at a distance, whether pictures, sculpture, or anything else, have more effect and force in a bold sketch [*una bella bozza ;* the word sketch seems quite inapplicable to sculpture, but we know no other English word to use] than when finished ; and not only does distance produce this effect, but often, in all circumstances, subjects boldly dashed in, produced in a moment of inspiration (*dal furore dell' arte*) express the idea in a few strokes." We do not

think, however, that the comparison will hold, now that
both works are brought close to the eye, in favor of Donatello, vigorous and fine as his corresponding groups are, or
that the lover of art would willingly consent to part with
one line of those lovely living creatures, living and laughing all over in every dimple, or standing up with the
gravity of childhood, with open mouths and eyes intent,
to chant forth their responses. The robust and lavish
strength of an age which had come with fresh delight to
the study of life, and of that simplicity of mind which
found nothing inappropriate to the use of religion in the
innocent jollity of childhood, are in every curve. Whatever reflection of Greek there may be in it, it is yet all
Tuscan, racy of the soil, with a delightful natural large-
ness and roundness and rustic vigor added to that
variety of expression which demands all the refinements of
art.

These glorious groups, however, are not in the special
branch of art which has associated itself with the name of
Luca della Robbia. It is one of the most striking evidences
of an age of great activity and warmth of intellectual impulse, that genius, getting impatient of universal repetition strikes out for itself new paths on every side, not so
great indeed as the old broad highways of everlasting art,
yet always interesting so long as genius continues to tread
them, and they are not left to that feeble imitation which
sooner or later succeeds to every original work. Luca was
not one of those great men who dominate art and leave
upon it an impression which lasts for generations. He had
not the vigor and force of his contemporary, Donatello, to
take possession of and give a new, bold impulse to the
highest branch of sculpture ; but it would seem that he was
impatient of the meaner fate of toiling after another's
footsteps and taking a secondary place in the profession he
loved. Perhaps even the inferior effect, when carried to

their place, of his own carefully finished groups in comparison with Donatello's dashing *bozza*, may have stimulated the artist to seek for a way of his own, in which his
special qualities might tell at their best. Like so many
others, Luca had been bred to the trade of goldsmith, and
that finer and more delicate work would seem to have been
congenial to him. "Feeling," Vasari says, "that he had
advanced but little with very great labor" in that larger

FIGURES FROM ORGAN-SCREEN. LUCA DELLA ROBBIA.

field of art where there were so many competitors, "he
resolved to leave marble and bronze and to see if he could
find better fruit elsewhere. Therefore considering that
clay was easily worked with little labor, if a method could
only be found to make it adhere and to defend it from the
action of time," he betook himself to scientific experiments to find an *invetriamento* glassing or glaze, which
"should make works in clay almost eternal." It is not
within our range to discuss whether Luca was really the
sole and first inventer of this method ; but at least he was
the first great artist who worked in majolica, and his

beautiful groups in this material are the chief things that
will occur to any reader in connection with his name.
Nothing more lovely, pure, and tender than his white
visionary Madonnas and divine children can well be conceived ; the spotless material and the delicate art lend
themselves to each other and to this oft-renewed and
always delightful subject with a touching appropriateness.
They are like an embodied dream, ethereal and pure and
colorless, a thing made of heavenly mist or cloud. His
first efforts in this new art were consecrated, as his great
essay in marble had been, to the Duomo, and represented
the Resurrection and Ascension of Christ. They were admired as a *cosa veramente rara*, Vasari tells us, when put
in their place over the doors of the sacristy, and henceforward Luca devoted himself to the use and perfection of
his invention, which gave both to himself and his family
thereafter a special vocation and career.

Luca della Robbia was the son of a Florentine citizen,
and brought up in the most approved way (*allevato costu-
matamente*); that is to say, as soon as he could read and
write and count, he was apprenticed to a goldsmith, out of
whose workshop he very soon progressed into higher work,
"abandoning altogether the trade of jeweler and giving
himself to sculpture." He threw himself into his art
with so much zeal that often, standing drawing in the long
nights, his feet were almost frozen, and he had to warm
them by fires made of shavings. "Nor do I wonder at
this," says Vasari, pausing for one of his frequent good
and simple reflections, "for no one ever became excellent
in any exercise whatever who did not from a child learn to
put up with heat and cold, hunger and thirst." So well
did this industry succeed, that when he was no more than
fifteen he began his independent work by some bas-reliefs
in Rimini, and from thence was summoned to join in the
labors of the " Opera " of Santa Maria del Fiore, the

greatest compliment that could be paid to a Florentine artist, and the most proud duty. We may thus conclude that the delightful fire and vigor of a youth not very far removed from the childhood which he represented in his lovely groups, was in his first great effort. They were all young, the busy masters of that great "Opera," not like old Arnolfo and old Giotto, crowning their fame by the dedication of powers at the ripest to the beloved work, but throwing themselves into it with all the fervor of first love, and that enthuiasm for glory, fame, and triumph which belongs especially to the young. With the versatility of the time, Luca, his marble friezes finished, began to work in bronze the sacristy doors; then crowned them with his newly discovered art, with the white, visionary groups which ever since have been connected with his name. The special use of this new invention, as not only beautiful in itself but affording a means of ornamentation for places *dove sono acque*, where pictures cannot be placed in consequence of the damp, is much insisted upon by Vasari. Even the damp corners demanded ornament in those wealthy days when artists abounded, and imagition could not picture to itself the humblest sanctuary or the most common house without some attempt at beauty as well as use. Luca's attempts to get color into his porcelain were, in our own opinion, less happy than the original invention; but he "went, thinking," we are told, about all his busy labors, trying hard to work out this problem and enrich his material. Old Cosimo's son, Piero de' Medici, was the first who gave him a commission in the colored work. The invention altogether binds together the craft of the workman with the genius of the artist in the most attractive way. Nothing can be more poetical than those white foam-groups, glancing out of dark corners, over doorways, always with a delightful surprise to the spectator which is almost like a natural effect; for there is nothing that more piques and pleases the fancy than the adaptation of a thing so common to uses so beautiful. The soft sympathetic angels, the round limbs of the lovely children, the serious, sweet Madonnas, glimmering in a light which proceeds from themselves, or seems to do so, are always delightful to behold; in convent cloisters, over the doors of hospitals, here and there, hung on a bit of dark wall in some aisle chapel, they make a mild radiance about them, a softened homely illumination, not great, but sweet, and full of ethereal and visionary grace.

And at the same time what a busy *bottega* the new invention made! Luca had to call his brothers from their nameless marble works—for they too were sculptors though unknown to fame—to help him as orders came in. All the princes and the trades sent their commissions to the master. "The fame of his works flew not only through Italy but over all Europe, and so many wished to have them that the Florentine merchants kept Luca continually at work." The brothers and the brothers' sons made a school of themselves, keeping the secret among them with all the precautions natural to a family treasure. One at least of the nephews, Andrea, became famous like his uncle, and the race did not last long enough to fall into much bad work, but came to an end in the third generation, carrying with it the invention and the secret. Perhaps it was well so, both for the fame of the Della Robbia work and for the taste of posterity. So easy a material could scarcely have avoided debasement and degradation in times of less originality and power.

And it seems ungrateful to leave the cathedral of Florence without a word about the good Vasari, who is, after all, the most sure as well as the most delightful guide that posterity has produced. Excellent Messer Giorgio! though perhaps it would on the whole be kinder not to say

that he painted the cupola with the aid of Zucchero, to
the great affliction of his generation, which only consoled
itself with the hope of whitewash.   He was not a great
painter, and sometimes he is mistaken in his dates, and
makes one man paint a picture for another who was not
born, and a third murder his fellow-workman,   notwithstanding the fact that the supposed victim outlived the
supposed murderer.   These are trifles upon which it is un-

FIGURES FROM ORGAN-SCREEN.   LUCA DELLA ROBBIA.

necessary to dwell; and notwithstanding all the holes that
can be picked in his coat, Giorgio Vasari remains the foun-
tain-head of knowledge in everything that concerns the
history of art, or rather of artists, up to his time.   He
has a hand in the Duomo, not so much to his credit perhaps
as might be desired ; but what uncertain guesses, what
dead facts, dates, and unrememberable bones of history
should we have had about the Duomo without his lively
friendly guidance ?   The tale of Filippo's long struggle,
and how he ousted his duller persistent rival, and had his
way and enjoyed it, is of far more importance to us than

a picture in the cupola. Brunelleschi himself, grateful unwittingly for the coming benefit, has furnished a soft twilight, an indulgent darkness in the majestic vault, which makes it less important that his biographer should have plastered and daubed its roof, with some help from Lorenzo, though he has less reason to be grateful, and from that "singular master" of Lubeck who painted the jeweled windows, and made the gloom harmonious.

The reader whom Vasari has instructed and charmed may well be content to leave in that half-light the im. perfect picture which is his least worthy work of art.

CHAPTER VI.

A PEACEFUL CITIZEN.

WE HAVE said that it is very difficult to understand how ordinary existence could go on, and fortunes be made, and families founded, and art cultivated, among all the turbulence and agitation of such a life as that of Florence. Internal conflicts, which showed not only in the public square and public palace, but which convulsed every petty alley and made a fortress of every street corner; and external assault by neighboring cities, by marauding emperors, by now one now another, league of belligerent towns, backed up by bands of mercenaries, kept up such a continual commotion that the existence of the shop, the manufactory, or the studio behind, seems almost incredible. Yet that background of calm to all these fierce contentions seems to have appeared entirely natural to the Florentines. Trade flourished among them, not only as it does among ourselves, underneath the brilliant surface on which the great and wealthy and non-laboring keep up a princely show, but in the hands of the very men who formed the surface of Florentine life; the same men who negotiated with princes, and led armies, and had a share in all the imperial affairs of Europe, yet return to their banking-houses or their woolen manufactories unchanged, talking of the *bottega*, the business which gave them their standing, with the most perfect satisfaction and content in that source of their fortune. The life and prosperity of the simple citizen in these circumstances is almost more extraordinary than that of the artist, for the latter knew that his art was a passport with men of all factions, and that whatever party was uppermost in Florence, that progress of the cathedral or its decoration would always be of the first importance. But the good man in his shop, who throve and prospered and held his own opinions without ever going so far perhaps as to be sent packing *fuori* when the other side got the upper hand, how did he manage ? how did he increase and prosper, and add scudo to scudo, and get himself a peaceful villa in the neighborhood, and live as Agnolo Pandolfini lived in the year of grace 1400 and the following years ? This is a question which it is very difficult to answer ; but we can at least communicate to the reader the directions left behind him by the said Agnolo as to the ruling of a family, which will show in what a peaceful and prosperous way it was possible to live, even when you were liable at any moment to be sent by your city on an embassy to a besieging king or other potent assailer. The good citizen who has left us so full an account of what it became a good citizen to do, preserves in this picturesque Florentine mediæval garb so strong a natural resemblance to the amiable and excellent city man of all times, that his very tone strikes us as perfectly familiar, and we forget that his old Italian, with a few obsolete words cropping up into it here and there, is not quaint English. He is the very type and emblem of the good burgher, or rather perhaps the good *bourgeois*, a word which 'more forcibly conveys the meaning, a citizen citizenish in every aspect, somewhat pompous in his kindness and wisdom, with the most perfect satisfaction in all he has himself done and appreciation of his own excellence. The old Italian shopkeeper, who had in his days played with credit the part of an ambassador, seated in his advanced age among his sons, who, gathered round him in his autobiographical narrative,

receive all he says with plaudits and echo the gratification
and contentment with which he reviews his long and well-
spent life, is as interesting a figure as can be found in the
byways of history. That it has been a well-spent life
Carlo and Gianozzo are proud to acknowledge—a model of
everything that life ought to be in Florence; and with
those exclamations of delight and praise, that appreciation
of old jokes and admiration for the paternal cleverness
which perhaps in our days daughters are more apt to show
than sons, and neither so much as they ought, the little
monologue runs on. How one ought to save and spare,
how one ought to mind one's business, how one ought to
choose one's house, and, above all, how one ought to
govern and regulate one's wife, are the subjects treated in
detail; though there is scarcely a word about the public
life which must have filled so large a part in the citizen's
career, but which this citizen rather recommends his sons
to avoid, notwithstanding that both they and he filled
important offices in the commonwealth. A greater contrast could scarcely be than the revelation given in this
book of the background and peaceful undercurrent of
Florentine existence, while the turbulent tide of faction
and revolution ran so high above.

Agnolo, son of Filippo, son of Ser Giovanni Pandolfini
(so described by his biographer) and ancestor of the important family still existing in Florence, was not the off-
spring of a time of peace, though he won for himself the
worthy distinction of peacemaker, and, in sign of this,
added to his arms, with the complacent yet amiable self-
consciousness amply recorded in his book, a serpent surmounted by a cross. His peacemaking, however, was
chiefly out of doors. Within, the Albizzi and the Medici
were having that last struggle for supremacy which ended
in the downfall and rising again of crafty Cosimo, the first
real despot of Florence. Agnolo gave his vote against the

banishment of Cosimo, but ineffectually. He succeeded better, however, in his conciliatory undertakings with enemies outside, one of whom, King Lancislaus, consented by his meditation to deliver over to Florence, in payment of some claims of hers, the rich city of Cortona, a compensation which the republic accepted joyfully, with that delightful indifference to the independence of other cities which was characteristic in those days of the very fiercest and proudest maintainers of their own. Besides this and other splendid missions—to the Emperor Sigismund, whom he coaxed into peace, to Pope Martin and others—Agnolo was three times Gonfaloniere della Giusitzia, and sat over and over again in the signory. He was " learned in the Latin tongue, and especially in philosophy, both moral and natural ;" and a friend of Lionardo Aretino, a manuscript of whose life of Dante was found in the same bundle of parchment in which Agnolo's treatise, " Del Governo della Famiglia," had lain dusty but not unknown in the Pandolfini Palace for nearly four hundred years. His wisdom kept him apart from rash and new steps in policy, his biographer tells us. " Neither in this novelty nor in any other would he be of the Eight, or in the position of counselor to the other citizens," though he warned Rinaldo, the head of the Albizzi, against the banishment of Cosimo, as a step which would bring ruin both to himself and the city. In his latter days (he lived to be eighty-six) he retired to his villa at Signa where he lived a patriarchal life and wrote his treatise to the admiration of sons and grandsons. Here is a description of the patriarchal state he held and the genial hospitality he dispensed in these latter days :

" Here he had a most worthy house, full of everything necessary to the condition of a man of gentle blood—dogs, hawks, and every kind of nets both for fishing and birding. In this house all guests were received honorably. He was very liberal, and there being no other house near Florence of such quality and so well regulated, all the great personages who came were lodged there. There he received Pope Eugenius, King Rinieri, Duke Francesco, often the Marchese Niccolo, and many other great people; and the house was always so well provided that nothing was wanting. When it happened that on a *festa* or other day his children came from Florence to visit him without bringing other guests, he complained and reproved them. This house was a habitation of well-doing. And Agnolo was in his time another Lucullus, having his dwelling furnished with every kind of poultry and provision for guests, to do honor to those who came. When it happened that there were no visitors in the house after a great hawking, he sent to the road to see if any one passed that way, and gave orders to bring in all wayfarers to dinner. When they reached the house, water was given them to wash their hands, and dinner was served; after which, when they had eaten, he thanked them, and said that they were free to go—that he did not wish to hinder their journey. The exercises followed here were those of gentlemen, hawking with falcons and with dogs; and he never went out after the birds with less than fifteen or twenty companions on horseback, besides those that went on foot with the dogs."

This liberal and almost splendid existence, with its seignorial amusements of hunting and hawking, sounds more like the life of a great noble in his castle than of a *bourgeois* in his villa; but Agnolo's book, which was written in the genial retirement thus described and amid all its generous expenditure, is full of the maxims of economy and good management—*masserizia*, the art of careful stewardship, wasting nothing and putting everything to careful use. *La masserizia* is indeed the text on which he preaches throughout his treatise, carefully separating it from avarice and parsimony, as will be seen from the following definition of the word :

" Economy does not consist only in saving and sparing, but also in using everything when there is need for it. Have you ever noticed that poor little widow-woman! She gathers her apples and her other fruit, shuts them up, saves them, and never eats them till they are spoiled and rotting; the result is that three parts of them have to be thrown out of window; so she saves them to throw them away. Would it not be better, silly old woman, to throw away a few at first, and to use the good for thy table or else give them to others? I do not call this saving but wasting. The same thing may be seen when it begins to rain a little in hay-making. The miser waits for to-morrow and the day after, not wishing to spoil anything ; again it rains; and at the last his hay rots and is destroyed, and that which might have cost him one soldo now costs him more than ten. And thus it is made apparent that it is a bad thing not to know how to use and spend according to the seasons and necessity, and that to spare and to spend with prudence is of greater value than prosperity, industry or gain. Having thus seen that economy means both saving and use, let us see what things we have to use and to save ; not the goods of others, which would be violence, arrogance, and injustice, but those which are our own."

Another definition, very clear and fine in its way, of the things which we may call our own, follows this. Not houses nor lands, not even wife and children, says the old citizen, for these can be taken away from us and are not always ours. The things which can be called our own are three in number—our bodies, our souls, and our time ; and he proceeds to instruct his sons as to the right use of these primary possessions of humanity.

First as to the soul—no doubt Agnolo was a good Catholic enough, for the days of heresy were not as yet—but very simple are the maxims of his religion. "How," ask Carlo, Giannozzo, Pandolfo, and the rest, " how do you preserve the soul to God?"

"AGNOLO. I do this in two ways. One is to keep as much as I can my heart light, nor ever disturb it with anger, hate or any covetousness ; because the pure and simple soul is always pleasing to God. The other method is to keep myself as much as I can from ever doing anything upon which I have a doubt whether it is good or evil, or which I may repent of having done.

"CARLO, GIANNOZZO. And you think this is enough?

"AGNOLO. I believe that it is enough ; since I have always understood that those things which are good and true are also clear and comprehensible in themselves, and therefore ought to be done, but those things which are not good are always found to be entangled in perplexity and ambiguity by some pleasure or desire, by some corrupt intention, and therefore ought not to be done but avoided. Follow the light, flee from the darkness. The light of our actions is in their truth and goodness, which extend and grow with our well-doing, with our good reputation, with our good name. Nothing is more dark in the life of man than ill-doing, fear, error, infamy ; nothing so gracious as virtue, goodness, and bounty."

This very mild material rule of goodness, which can scarcely be called Christian, has yet a certain spirituality in it, a lofty kind of heathen innocence and rectitude, little adapted we fear for ordinary mortals, but not out of place in the admirable old citizen with whom everything has prospered so well, and who has found himself able to conduct his life to such good and comfortable purpose in honor and wealth and reputation, by the aid of this strange light, somehow innate in things good and true, which has lighted his steps he knows not how. Curiously enough through all the book there is scarcely a mention of a priest or a religious service. Neither praise nor blame goes to the church ; it is simply ignored and out of the question altogether. Such an excellent heathen, one would have supposed, might at least have grumbled at the interference of the priestly element, but he never once mentions it, which is a very strange fact. It was the very lowest and darkest period of the church, when she was more than usually subject to animadversion, and the early impulse of the Renaissance, just then beginning to influence the world, had already sent forth smatterings of classical philosophy, to supply as they best could the place of religious faith and principle. Agnolo, however, though his entire profession of religion is contained in the words we have just quoted, does not even launch a passing arrow at the priesthood, a proof either that he believed more than he professes, or that his habitual prudence kept him from defying or even touching with the lightest shaft an influential class. His rule for the body is equally simple, regulated by the same rule of *masserizia* which he has already insisted upon—the

use without abuse of every faculty ; prodigality and
narrowness being equally discountenanced in this as in the
rules which concern money and property. Work, exercise
and cleanliness, are the chief points which he impresses
upon his sons. He bids them keep themselves "clean and
civil" with admirable conciseness and exactitude ; and
dwells upon the advantages of abundant and pure air, a
wholesome house, and personal activity with an enlightenment worthy of an age more deeply interested in sanitary
science than the fifteenth century is supposed to have been.
"Exercise," he says, "preserves life, kindles the natural
warmth and vigor, carries off superfluities and evil
humors, fortifies the body and the nerves, is necessary to
youth, useful to the aged. He who takes no exercise can
never live a cheerful and healthy life." We need not
linger upon the excellent advice he gives about the use of
time, advice which is more admirable than original, and in
which his favorite economy is largely dwelt upon. After
these fundamental rules of *masserizia* the excellent citizen,
whose first thought is for his family, begins to furnish his
children with rules for the management of theirs. His
audience, called by the general name of *Nipoti*, consisted of
his sons and grandsons, not nephews according to our use
of the word, the elders of whom were already no doubt
adepts under his training in all the necessary organizations
of a family. He gives them his advice first about the
house, in which the domestic center of all interests is to
be made. "I chose a house," he says, taking his own
experience as the example, "in a good neighborhood and
well-known street, where honest citizens lived of whom I -
could without danger make friends, while my wife found
good company among their wives. And I informed myself
who had lived in it in times past, and inquired whether
they had been healthy and fortunate. There are certain
houses in which, it would seem, no one can live happily."

But of all houses he prefers the country house, the villa, in which everything is at once more secure and more abundant than in the town. " There are," he says, " near Florence, many places in the purest air, in a pleasant country, with beautiful views, rare clouds, no bad winds, and good water, everything wholesome, pure, and good, in which houses may be found like palaces. . . . Try to get possession of one of these." And with this text he forthwith falls into such a rapture of enthusiasm for his villa, as perhaps the prosperous city man, thriving and satisfied and feeling all the associations of his country residence to be happy, is more apt than any other to feel. Clearly the very poetry of the good merchant's life, its idyllic part, dearer than gain or civic honors, more delightful than power or wealth, was in his home outside the walls, with all the stores of kindly nature ripening round it, vines and fruits and golden corn, objects of that genial husbandry and stewardship, the *masserizia* which is above all others, his favorite theme.

" A great and pure usefulness is always found in the villa. All other occupations are full of labor, danger, suspicion, harm, repentance, and fear. In buying there is care, in guiding fear, in saving danger, in selling anxiety, in credit suspicion, in drawing back trouble, in commuting debt deceit, and from every business transaction comes much annoyance and agony of mind. But the country is gracious, trustworthy, true ; * if you give yourself up to it patiently and lovingly it never seems to be satisfied with what it does for you, but continually adds reward after reward. In spring the river gives thee continual delight ; foliage, flowers, odors, songs of birds, and in every way makes thee gay and joyful—all smiles upon thee and promises a good ingathering ; fills thee with every good hope, delight, and pleasure. How courteous is the country ! She sends you

---

* " Whatsoever is lovely, whatsoever is honest . . . . if there be any virtue, if there be any praise." St. Paul's words are loftier, and perhaps an echo of them was in good Agnolo's ears, caught in passing from the epistle in a mass, though he does not acknowledge it.

now one fruit, now another, never leaving the house empty of some
of her gifts.   In the autumn she pays thee back for all thy trouble—
fruit out of all measure to thy labors, reward and thanks.   And how
willingly and with what abundance.   Twelve for one : for a little
sweat many bottles of wine ; and that which gets stale by keeping
the country gives in its season, fresh and good.   She fills the house
all the winter through with grapes fresh and dry, with plums, nuts,
figs, pears, apples, almonds, pomegranates, and other fruits wholesome and fragrant and delightful, and from day to day the later

PONTE VECCHIO.

fruits.   Even in winter she does not forget to be liberal ; she sends
you wood, oil, branches of laurel and juniper, drawn from the snow
to make a fragrant and cheerful flame , and if you continue to live
there, the villa will comfort you with splendid sunshine, and will
give you the hare, the wild goat, the boar, the partridge, the pheas-
ant, and many other kinds of birds, and the wide country in which
you can follow them at your leisure ; she will give you fowls, milk,
kids, junket, and other delicacies which you can preserve the whole
year through, so that through all the year your house may want for

nothing; and will take pains that in your heart there should be no sorrow or trouble, but that you should be full of pleasure, and usefulness. . . . . Among citizens are injuries, fightings, pride, and other dishonest things terrible to tell ; but in the villa nothing can displease you ; there all talk to you with pleasure, you are listened to and understood by everything. . . . At the villa we enjoy days airy and clear and open ; we have the gladsome and joyful sight of fruitful slopes, of sweet plains, of those fountains and streams that leaping forth hide themselves under tufts of herbage. And what is still more delightful, we escape from the noise, the tumults, and the turmoil of the city, the piazza, and palace. . . . How blessed it is to live in the country, an unappreciated happiness ! "

When, however, after this outburst, his sons press him as to whether it is best to bring up a family in the town or country, Agnolo reluctantly decides in favor of the city, for the curious reason that there the young learn to know what vice is, and to avoid it. " For no one," he says, " can judge what vices are who does not know them, as no one can judge of a sound who has not heard that sound, nor can criticise either the instrument or the player." Therefore he concludes it is best that youth should be brought up in town, that " they may be warned by many examples to flee from vice, and that they may see how great a thing honor is, and fame and good reputation, and how excellent is the glory of virtue, how sweet is true praise, and to be esteemed and entitled virtuous." These are the only motives which he seems to think worth consideration. The ideas upon work and occupation which this splendid old burgher, in his beautiful villa where he had lodged kings and popes, communicated to his sons, who, like himself, had reigned in Florence and gone upon imperial embassies, are very curious to read, and contrast as sharply with what would be the opinions of such a man now, as his desire that youth should know what vice is in order to avoid it, would clash with all the

theories of education popular in the present day. "What
occupation would you take up?" inquire Carlo and the
rest. "An honest occupation," he replies, "and the most
useful I could see."

"CARLO, GIANOZZO. Perhaps it would be the occupation of a
merchant?

"AGNOLO. Perhaps; but for greater ease of mind I would rather
choose something more secure; working in wool or silk, or some such
trade, which are occupations requiring much labor; and most willingly would I give myself to that in which many hands would be
employed, and the gain divided among many persons, and a means of
help afforded to many in need.

"CARLO, GIANOZZO. This is a pious office, to be useful to
many.

"AGNOLO. That is beyond doubt. I would have many workmen
and boys, and would not put my own hand to anything, further than
to command, provide, and regulate, so that each one did his duty;
and often I would say to them. 'Be honest and just, reasonable and
friendly, not less with strangers than with friends; with every one
be truthful, and take good care that no one goes out of the shop deceived or discontented by your cunning or hard dealings, for this
would be to lose instead of gaining, and instead of getting money by
it, you would lose liking and goodwill. A pleasing seller will
always have plenty of customers, and among artisans good fame and
competition do more than wealth. I should command them to sell
nothing too dear, and with whatsoever debtor or creditor they made
engagements, the contract should always be distinct and clearly expressed; that they should never be importunate, proud, or evil-speak-
ing, not quarrelsome but agreeable, and above all anxious and diligent in writing and in regard to what has been written. In this way
I should hope in God that he would prosper me, and I should hope
for many customers and much favor for my shop; by which things
with the grace of God first, and with a good name among men,
my gains would increase every day."

There is a certain magnanimity and grandeur in the
selection of a trade "which would employ many hands
and be useful to many in need," which throws a glimmer
of romance and the ideal life upon the old Florentine shop

into which we are thus permitted a glimpse. Shops in our own days fulfill Agnolo's requirements frequently enough, and give employment to many; but we have ceased to think this a "pious office," or anything more honorable than a way of making money. Nothing can be more odd than the preference expressed by so important a personage for the superior security of the woolen or silk trade, the manufacture which perhaps he considered of more indispensable necessity than banking or large business transactions, though indeed he takes pains to tell us that he himself took no part of the manual labor, but reserved himself for the congenial occupation of setting everybody right, indicating to each man his duties and informing their minds on all possible points. Thus he sums up his rule of external life—a rule just, amiable, and true, with a certain fine self-consciousness in it, and self-approbation, as of a man who has nothing to regret or repent, but knows he has done well, and feels it his duty to hold up so good an example to the world. This mood of mind is essentially civic, belonging to that straitened atmosphere of the town in which every man is judged by his contemporaries, whose knowledge of him is indisputable and profound, and where he who has the good fortune to satisfy the commonplace ideal of virtue receives his canonization in his lifetime, and has every reason to believe in himself and his fellow-citizens believe in him. Agnolo consciously came up to his own estimate of what the best of citizens should be, and the old man's recognition of this is almost touching in its broad and frank simplicity.

Here is a little canon of citizen virtue, drawn by another hand than Agnolo's which we may add as condensing the duties of the Florentine merchant just as he elucidates and explains them. It is found in the beginning of a Merchant's Manual, compiled by a certain Pegolotti, in the beginning of the fourteenth century, and is headed

"What the true and upright merchant ought to have in himself."

> "Always, in all, with uprightness to dwell;
> And careful foresight shall become him well;
> And ne'er to fail of any promise plight;
> And nobly live if that he may aright
> With sanction both of reason and of trade;
> And largely sell, with little purchase made,

THE ARNO, LOOKING EAST FROM THE PONTE VECCHIO.

> But without blame, honored in good men's sight;
> The church to serve, and to God's service give;
> By one just rule of sale, good fame to win.
> Apart from gambling and from usury live,
> Casting them altogether hence as sin,
> And just accounts to keep, nor ever err therein."

It is, however, in his discussion of the most intimate relations of life that Agnolo becomes more graphic and animated. There is a glance at the servants, from which we can perceive that neither the *villani* in the country, who cultivated the fields round the villa, nor the *fattori* in the town, who managed the *bottega*, were altogether satisfactory any more than they are nowadays. They "are more apt to seek their own interests than those of their masters," Agnolo complains, which is, we fear, a well-established principle in human nature. But it is when he comes to the very center of the family life that he becomes lively and humorous, his sense of his own admirable management swelling at this point into a climax of satisfaction which quite lights up the narrative, and brings the whole quaint scene before us in the most vivid distinctness. He begins this portion of his book with that strut and crow of conscious superiority which is still and always so common among his class. "The mind of the man," he says, "is more robust, more firm, more constant to support every opposition of enemies and every accident, than that of the woman," therefore it ill becomes him to give his attention to foolish housewifish cares, which are beneath his notice and which come within the woman's region. "He who does not hate these little female affairs, shows that it would not annoy him to be called a woman. . . . . It is the duty of the father of a family not only to do all things worthy of a man, but to fly from every female art and thing." The simple conclusion he draws from this large statement, however, is, that the household matters should be left entirely to the wife who with thought and study should provide for them. "Every wife," he tells us, "should know how to cook and prepare the best dishes, and to teach them to the cooks." But with his usual grandeur of sentiment Agnolo gives a larger motive for this than any English writer on the subject would dare to venture on. It is not that she may please her husband's palate by her personal exertions, but that when strangers come upon visits, *quando vengono i forestieri,* who ought to be received

with pleasure, she may never be taken unawares, but may
always, at the shortest notice, be ready to greet and entertain them *lietamente*, setting before them the best of
everything. "Thus she will do honor to her husband,
and win for him much kindness and many friends." So
far he addresses himself to the question in general; he then
enters into his special mode of treatment of his own wife
which he expounds jauntily to his sons, without feeling at
all restrained apparently by the reflection that it was their
mother of whom he thus discoursed. "You have good
reason to speak on this subject," say the listeners, "for
your wife was virtuous more than others." "True she
was prudent," admits Agnolo, ever master, "but still by
my management."

" When my wife, your mother, had been a few days settled in the
house, and the love and ambition of housekeeping had begun to delight her, I took her by the hand and showed her all the house, and
instructed her where everything was kept, the other provisions
above, the wood and the wine below. . . . . Then I took her into the
bed-chamber, and locking the door, showed her all my precious
things, the silver, the tapestry, the dresses, the precious stones and
all our jewels, and the places in which they were kept.

"Carlo, Giannozzo, etc. Then all these precious things were
in your chamber? no doubt that they might be more safe and more
secret.

"Agnolo. Also, my children, that I might see them when I
chose without any one knowing of it. Between ourselves, my sons,
it is not wise that all your family should know everything that
belongs to you. That which few know of is easier to keep safely,
and find again if lost. And therefore it is less dangerous to keep
your precious things as much as you can hidden far from the eyes
and the hands of the multitude. . . . But it was not my desire to
keep any of my precious things hidden from my wife; all that I held
most dear I opened to her, and showed and explained them all ; only
my books and my writings, then and afterward, I kept secret and
shut up, that she might neither read them nor even see them. I
always kept my writings, not in the sleeves of my dress, but in a

case locked up and lodged in a good place in my study, almost like
something religious, into which place I never gave my wife permission to enter, neither with me nor by herself, and besides I recommended her, if ever she found anything written by me quickly to
bring it back to me.* . . . . When she understood how everything
ought to be arranged, I said to her, 'My wife, all this which is useful
and dear to me ought to be dear to you also, and all that is dangerous
to it disagreeble. . . . . All this will be profitable to you, to me, and
to our children after us. And therefore it is right that you should be
as careful of everything as I myself am.

"CARLO, GIANNOZZO. How did she answer you?

"AGNOLO. She answered that she had learned to obey her father
and mother, and that she had been commanded by them always to

---

* Here follows a long digression and denunciation of the fools who
hold women in high esteem, which will show the curious reader how
little the tone of criticism on this point has changed from the
fifteenth to the nineteenth century. Ser Agnolo warns his wife, as
women seeking too much knowledge have been warned in our own
day, not to read his books or even glance at his scribblings, "because
women who search too much into things which belong to men cannot
do so without raising a suspicion that they have men too much in
their mind." The reproach is the same, though perhaps few men
nowadays would go the length of forbidding to their wives the
enlightenment which must be conveyed by a perusal of their own
individual works. Agnolo has logic on his side in the very extreme
to which he goes; but, like most of his successors in this dangerous
line of remark, he loses his temper and begins to vituperate, though
his rage is not against the weaker being whom he frankly depises,
but against the men who do not despise her., "Those husbands en-
rage me," he cries, "who take counsel with their wives, and cannot keep any secret in their own bosoms. Fools who esteem the
female mind, or believe that prudence or good counsel is to be had
from a woman! Madmen who believe their wives will be more silent
in their affairs than they themselves are! Oh foolish husbands, when
you chatter with a woman, do you forget that a woman can do everything but hold her tongue? And therefore take care that no secret
of yours should ever come into the knowledge of the woman."
"Not," he adds after this outburst, "that I did not know my wife
to be loving and discreet, but always it seemed to me safer that she
should not be able to harm me if she would."

obey me, and was ready to do so.   Then I said to her, 'She who has been obedient to her father and mother, donna mia, will soon learn to obey her husband.   Do you know now what we ought to do ?   We should be like those who keep watch by night on the walls of their city.*   If one of them fall asleep, he does not take it amiss if his companion awakens him to do his duty to his country.   I, my wife, will take it as a favor, if seeing anything wanting in me you will tell me of it, which will show me that our honor and usefulness and the advantage of our children is much in your mind ; nor let it be displeasing to you if I in the same way waken you up and remind you to provide for all that is necessary ; and that in which I am wanting do you supply : for thus doing we will advance each other in love and prudence.   These possessions, this family, and the children born, or to be born, are ours—yours as well as mine ; and therefore it is our duty to think and to do all we can to preserve that which belongs to both of us.   And according, donna mia, as I labor outside to provide what is necessary, do you take care within that all is distributed and used well.' "

This admirable address is followed by warnings as to fidelity, *onestà*, of the very matter-of-fact and outspoken kind which suited the age, and indeed many subsequent ages ; to all of which the sons listen admiringly, with a curious *esprit de corps*, as men with wives of their own to manage, which obliterates apparently all sense of natural reverence for their mother.   We will quote only one other portion of the long process of wife-instruction which both Agnolo and his sons seem to relish more than any other part of the treatise.·   It narrates the means by which this excellent husband cured his wife of the bad habit of painting her face, of which he speaks as of a custom universal among the women of the time.   After a short general preamble as to the wickedness of the custom, he proceeds thus :

---

* " *Per la patria loro*," for their country, is the expression.   Both in Italian and French the word signifying "country" is still used for the smallest village in the same strict and limited sense.

" Listen, my sons, how I demonstrated this to her. There was in the church of San Procolo, near my house, a beautiful statue in silver ; the head, the hands, and the breast were of the whitest ivory. I said to her, ' Donna mia, if you took your powder and plasters and plastered the face of that image in the morning would it be of better color and whiter? Yes ! but if afterward the wind rose and blew away the powder, would not that beauty be destroyed? Certainly. And if you washed it in the evening, and the next day again plastered and re-washed it, tell me, having thus painted it for many days, would not all your money be wasted? . . . . For he who bought the image would care nothing for this plaster, which could be put on and removed at pleasure, but would prize only the beauty of the statue and the genius of the master, therefore your trouble and your expense would be lost ; and tell me, if you went on whitening and painting it for months or years would you make it more beautiful?' ' I do not think so,' she said. ' Then,' said I, ' you will spoil it, making the ivory rough and raw with your powder and livid and yellow in color ; and if this would be the effect upon a very hard thing like the ivory, which lasts forever, much more would it injure thy cheeks and forehead, my wife, which are tender and delicate, but with every painting would become more rough and ugly.' "

This argument is somewhat feeble, not worthy of Agnolo's powers, and perhaps he may have seen some trace of this even in the countenance of the poor little wife, newly married, who replies so softly, and whom he describes as " blushing and casting down her eyes " when he delivered to her his plain-spoken admonitions. Accordingly he follows up the weak logic of this first example by a much more effectual and telling evidence of the folly of face-painting:

" Also that she might believe me the more, I spoke to her about one of our neighbors who had few teeth, and those spoiled, her eyes sunken, her face dismal and flabby, and her skin as if sodden, pale and ugly, and her hair had lost its color and was almost white. I asked my wife if she would like to be gray, and like this neighbor. ' Oh me,' she said, ' no!' ' Why,' said I, ' does she seem to you so old? How old do you think she is?' She answered me abashed, that perhaps she might be mistaken, but that our neighbor seemed to her as old as her mother's old nurse. Then I swore to her what was the truth, that this lady was born but two years before myself, and was not yet thirty-two, but by the use of paint had become thus disfigured and old before her time."

"Did she obey you?" asked the sons eagerly, not sure about it, it would seem, though deeply impressed by this alarming example:

"AGNOLO. Sometimes at weddings, or when she was ashamed to find herself unrouged among the others who were all rouged, or when she was heated by dancing, she seemed to me painted more than usual, but never at home in my house except once, when our relations and their wives had been invited to spend the *festa* of St. John with us; then my wife, painted and powdered, met every woman with much gayety, and going about everywhere enjoyed herself greatly. I perceived it.

"CARLO, GIANNOZZO, FILIPPO, PANDOLFO, DOMINICO. Were you angry with her?

"AGNOLO. Why should I be angry with her? Neither of us meant any evil.

"CARLO, GIANNOZZO. But perhaps you might be disturbed that in this she did not obey you.

"AGNOLO. Yes, that is true enough; but, however, I did not show myself disturbed by it.

"CARLO, GIANNOZZO. Did not you reprove her?

"AGNOLO. Yes, but with precaution. It seems to me always, my children, that correction should begin gently, in order that the defect may be made visible and good-will be awakened. Learn this of me. Women are more easily mastered and corrected with courtesy and kindness than with severity. Servants may endure threats or blows, and it is no shame to scold them, but the wife should rather obey from love of you than from fear of you. And every free soul will be more ready to please you than to serve you. Therefore the errors of wives should be reproved with delicacy. I waited till I found her alone, then smiled and said, 'I am sorry to see that you have got your face plastered; have you struck it against some saucepan in the kitchen? Wash thyself, let no one else see thee thus. A woman who is the mistress of a family should always be clean and in good order, that the family may learn to be obedient.' She understood me, and wept. I left her to wash away her paint and her tears, and never had occasion to speak to her more on the subject."

" *Oh moglie costumata!* " cry the sons after this story. " Oh best behaved of wives!" Might not the whole narrative have come out of the last century, when the fresh country ladies had to be warned against spoiling their natural roses with paint, and good Dr. Primrose cunningly

THE ARNO, LOOKING WEST FROM THE PONTE VECCHIO.

upset his daughter's wash in the fire? So little can the world guard itself as it grows older from the recurrence of the same follies, the repetition of the same old wisdom: no wiser and no foolisher, yet not less wise or foolish; going round the old well-beaten circle, generation after generation, age after age.

One small piece of enlightment at least mankind has gained by the progress of time, and that is the final relinquishment of any public and authoritative attempt to put a stop to the *luxe effréné*, over which every generation in succession bemoans itself, but which we have at length learned cannot be stopped by law. Agnolo says nothing of his wife's tastes in this way, and it is evident that he himself was of a magnificent disposition, and no doubt liked his family to be handsomely arrayed, though he objected to the paint. It is a pity he did not tell us how the foolish yet docile young wife was dressed, who was so ready to hear reason and who accepted his reproofs with such soft tears and downcast looks as make the reader at once side with her, though she did plaster her face in accordance with the bad and silly fashion of her time. But there are various sumptuary laws of Florence in existence which show how the old burghers made a stand against the vanities of the toilette, though it is curious to see that only women are aimed at, although undoubtedly the coxcomb's costume of the time was as fantastical and over-decorated as any woman's. Dante himself has his fling at the chains and crosses, the sandaled feet and girdles more notable than the person who wears them: *Cintura, che fosse a veder più che la persona;* and mournfully recalls the earlier days when the good citizen girt himself with leather, and his wife * saw herself in her mirror with no paint on her face. A little later the following laws stamped the disapproval of the republic upon the forbidden indulgences of dress and ornament:

---

* " Fiorenza dentro dalla cerchia antica
　Ond'ella toglib ancora e terza e nona
　Si stava in pace sobria e pudica
Non avea catenella, non corona
　Non donne contigiate, non cintura
　Che fosse a veder pi che la persona
Bellincion Berti vid' io andar cinto
Di cuoio e d'osso, e venir dallo specchio
La donne sua senza il viso dipinto."

" No woman of any condition whatever may dare or presume in any way in the city, suburbs, or district of Florence, to wear pearls, mother-of-pearl, or precious stones, on the head or shoulders, or on any other part of the person, or on any dress which may be worn upon the person.

" Item. She may not dare or presume to wear any brocade of gold or silver, or stuff gilt or silvered, embroidered or trimmed with ribbons, neither on her shoulders nor on her head, nor on any garment as described above.

" Item. She may not dare or presume to wear more than one pound of silver in the shape of garlands and buttons, or in any other way, on the head or shoulders, or otherwise as has been said above; except that besides the said pound of silver she may wear a silver belt of fifteen ounces weight.

" Item. She may not dare or presume to wear any slashings (*intagli*) at any robe or dress, neither at the bosom nor at the sleeves, nor to cuffs or collars, larger than the seventh of a yard according to the measure of the yard of the wool-workers, and these slashings shall not be lined with skins either of wild or tame beasts, or with silk, but only with woolen or linen, nor must they be trimmed with fringe either of silk, silver, or gold, or gilt or silvered.

" Item. She must not wear on her fingers more than three rings in all, and the said rings can have no more than one pearl or precious stone in each, and the said rings must not exceed the weight of silver allowed above.

" Item. No person in the city, suburbs, or district of Florence shall permit himself or presume to give in any way to any woman, any kind of collar, or buckle, or garland, or brooch of pearls, or of gold, of silver, or of any other precious stone or similar thing, by whatever name it may be called.

" Item. No individual, tailor, dressmaker, or furrier, shall dare or presume to cut, arrange, or line any of the said scarves, dress, or sleeves, prohibited garments, nor make any of the things forbidden by the present law."

The learned author of the " Storia del Commercio e dei Banchieri di Firenze" places beside these laws a whimsical commentary upon them—a list of articles constituting the *trousseau* of a Florentine bride of the fourteenth century, in which the rich stuffs are calculated by the pound weight, and even the *perle grosse*—though a trace of the law is found in the restriction "gold ring with one large pearl" —are evidently dealt out with an unsparing hand.

We return however, to our Agnolo. There are many other matters in which he instructs his wife, which are too lengthy for quotation ; but the reader will at least be able to perceive with what genuine relish and self-satisfaction the old citizen goes through his account of how he managed and directed her, making of her, it is evident, a very silent and submissive spouse, dutiful and docile. She died young, poor soul! for perhaps to have a husband so very instructive is almost as dangerous to the feminine soul as a really bad one. Before, however, we let her drop into the quiet of her obscure life and home, we may quote the conclusion of the very first scene of all, and what the young man did to impress upon the spirit of his young wife that lientenancy, so to speak, and authority under him with which he had just endowed her.

" When I had thus consigned the house to my wife, shutting ourselves up in our room, she and I knelt down before the shrine of our Lady, and prayed to God to give us grace to use well all the good things of which His goodness had made us partakers; and we prayed with devotion that He would give us grace to live long together happily and in good accord, and to give us many male children ; that he would give to me wealth, friends and honor, and to her integrity and faithfulness and to be a good housekeeper. Then when we rose from our knees I said to her, ' Donna mia, it is not enough to ask these holy things from God if we ourselves are not diligent and in earnest. I, my wife, will use all my skill and labor to obtain that for which we have prayed God. Thou likewise, as well as thou knowest, with much humility and humanity must act so as to be heard and accepted by God in all those things for which thou hast prayed to Him. And understand that nothing is so necessary to thee, so acceptable to God, to me pleasant, and honorable to thy children, as thy purity—*onestà.* . . . Fly then every mark of an incontinent and impure mind, and hold in horror all those appearances with which immodest and improper women endeavor to please men, believing themselves to be when painted, plastered and whitened, and clothed in worldly and indecent dresses, more pleasing to men than when they show themselves endowed with pure simplicity and true modesty."

Thus with mediæval frankness Agnolo separates the two portions of humanity— allotting to one the " honor, love,

LANTERN. PALAZZO STROZZI.

obedience, troops of friends," of the poet, and to the other honesty, modesty, and the gift of being a good housekeeper, a most curious and significant distinction. Let us hope that the silent Florentine woman who received the lesson was not clever enough to perceive the unintentional irony which made her husband appropriate all the good external gifts to himself and seek for her what he would have himself acknowledged to be the better internal virtues. Thus the rich man prays for contentment and spiritual consolation to the poor man, the strong being always much and deeply convinced of the necessity and beauty of disinterestedness in the weak. Curiously over these four long centuries—almost five, for it was in the very beginning of the fourteen-hundreds that this scene took place—these two figures rise and reveal themselves, standing before the shrine of our Lady in the the merchant's bedchamber, with all his jewels and his wealth shut up in secret drawers in old cabinets, and his tapestries, and costly stuffs in the painted, big *cassoni*, great oaken chests that stood against the walls, with pictures on their lids for which connoisseurs nowadays would give their weight in gold. She was one of the Strozzi, poor soul! but no soft Christian name remains of her, nor anything but her official title as it were, the " Donna mia " of this severe yet simple record.

In the part of the book which concerns his wife and his training of her, Agnolo has so much delight in the subject that he comes quite clearly to the foreground of the picture, out of all abstractions. There are, however, many other interesting remarks besides, which we should be sorry to pass without notice. Here is one point on which his views are curiously different from our English and modern ideas on the subject. He has been doing all he can to prove that it is ever most seemly and expedient that the entire family should live under one roof, and this not only as a matter of economy but also of family honor: .

"The father of a family is always more thought of and better known when he is followed by many of his children than when he is alone. A family is honored according to the abundance of men in it. The head which is not sustained by all the members falls; a divided family is not only diminished, but loses the rank and position it had acquired. I speak rather as a practical man than as a man of letters, and will add reason conformable to my proposition. At two tables two table-cloths are required; two fires are made, and two fires consume two

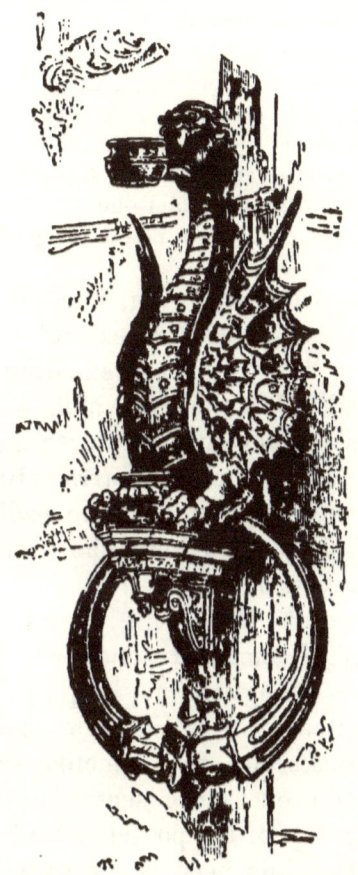

TORCH-HOLDER FOR EXTERNAL ILLUMINATIONS.

measures of wood; at two tables two servants are necessary, whereas one servant is enough at one table. . . . . If it was now dark and a torch was lighted in the midst of us, you, I, and all the others would have light enough to read and write, and do whatever was necessary. But if we separated, one going here and another there, I upstairs,

another below, a third in a different direction, do you think that the
same light would be enough for us, as if we were all together? And
if the weather was very cold and we had a great fire lighted, and
thou wouldst have thy part here, and another carry his there, should
we be better warmed or worse? Thus it happens in the family.
Many things are enough for many together which are little when
divided in little parts. . . . . I desire that all who belong to me
should dwell under one roof, and warm themselves at one fire, and
seat themselves at one table. . . . . A different aspect and different
favor will he have among his own people and among other citizens,
and a different reputation and authority will be his who is accompanied by those who belong to him—he will be feared and more
esteemed than he who has little or no following of his own."

The necessity of this following, this *compagnia de' suoi*,
brings us back out of the other peaceful details of Agnolo's
life to something like a real understanding of the kind of
age in which he lived, a time in which a strong backing
was of the utmost importance, and even the most venerated
patriarch who had no stalwart surrounding of sons and
grandsons and nephews, might fare badly in a popular
commotion. This gave no doubt the strongest of reasons
why all the members of the family should gather together
under one roof, each finding his place in the palazzo or
villa, the center of family existence, which it was everybody's interest to strengthen and keep up. And by way of
following the circle back again from the peaceful shops
and countinghouses and the homelike sweetness of the
villa, we may add one more sketch, to show what Ser
Agnolo's opinion was of the public and official life in which
he had notwithstanding been as successful as in his other
enterprises:

"I esteem nothing so little—nothing appears to me less worthy of
honor in a man than public office. . . . Every other life, every
other study, every other condition, seems to me more agreeable than
that of state officials, a life which ought to be displeasing to all ; a life
of abuse, of worry, of suspicious and unworthy thoughts ; full of use-

less trouble, inconvenience and slavery ; clouds of envy, mists of
hatred, thunder of hostility, from every point of the compass. . . .
Meeting together, advising, discussing, beseeching one, answering
the other, serving one, doing despite to another, coaxing, struggling,
abusing, bowing down, giving all one's time to such occupations without a single firm friendship, rather indeed with enmity. A life full
of lies, of fictions, ostentation, pomp and vanity, in which friendship
lasts just as long as your friend is useful to you, and in which no one
thinks it necessary to keep faith or promise. . . . Behold thee
seated in office, what use is it to thee? I will tell you. You can
then domineer, rob, and destroy with license, lightening your own
burdens. Oh iniquitous and cruel thing to wish to be rich by im-
poverishing others ! And how can you be enriched by the service of
the state if not by robbing the commonwealth and individuals, throwing off your own portion of the burden to put it upon others, and procuring your own advantage alone, caring nothing for public or private
misfortune ? To hear continued recriminations and complaints, and
unanswerable accusations and reproaches, and blame and tumult, and
to find always round you men who are avaricious, litigious, importunate, unjust, indiscreet, unquiet, insolent ; to fill thy ears with
suspicions, thy soul with covetousness, thy mind with doubt, fear,
hatred, and severity ; to give up thy shop and thy proper business to
follow the will and the ambition of others. Now to mend offices,
now laws ; to provide from the beginning for the expenses by new
burdens, for fear, for praise, for discord. . . . Oh foolishness of
men who esteem so greatly the privilege of going about with trumpets
blowing before them, that they give up their true repose and liberty !
They cannot suffer others to be their equals ; they will not live without coercing and domineering over the feeble and older among them,
and therefore they wish for the government ; and to have the government they favor those who are not good, and to submit to every
danger, and set fire to every evil licentiousness, and expose themselves
even to a violent death. . . . Certainly he who gives himself to
official life and public government with such a mind is the worst
of citizens. Nor can any such person have contentment or repose in
his mind if he is not cruel by nature ; since he has always to lend his
ear to complaints, weeping, and lamentation of people overcome by
calamity and misery, and who desire to raise themselves again by the
help of the commonwealth, or widows, or wards, or other ruined persons both out of the city and in the city. And what satisfaction can the
officer of state have who has to give his attention all day long to robbers,

fraudulent persons, spies, detractors, and men who give themselves to every kind of scandal and falsity in order that the *borsetto* (ballot-box) may be full ?   And what pleasure can he have to whom it is needful every day to tear away and do violence to the limbs of men, and to hear their cry for pity with wretched mouth, and to feel himself a murderer and a multilator of human members ? Thou then, humane and merciful man, thou seekest authority, thou seekest office ? You say yes, because you consider it praiseworthy to brave these troubles in order to punish the malefactors and favor the good.   But in punishing the malefactors you yourself become worse than they. . . . I do not blame him who honors his country by his good works and by his virtue, and bears its burdens as his own ; this I say to be true honor when those are prized by all citizens.   But to do as the most do, submit to this one, and bow to another, in order to be advanced over the most worthy, and to conspire and to make the state your shop and traffic, counting it as your private wealth and as a provision for your children, contending with one portion of the citizens and despising the other, this is a most pernicious thing for the city."

This description of the magisterial dignity in Florence is not attractive.   The speaker knew very well what it was of which he spoke, and so did his two sons, who in this instance listen without interrupting the monologue.   When good men shrink from and fear the offices of state and the cares of government, this too is, as Agnolo says, *cosa perniciosissima nella citta.*   But it is one natural and unfailing result, among many others, of a long series of misgovernments, especially of the democratic kind.   A tyranny has at least this one element of nobleness in it, that a bold and good man may take advantage of its very defects for the salvation of his country, or may, by overthrowing it, hope to build up a better constitution upon its ruins ; but in the bewildering round of revolutions made by the caprice of a supreme mob, what help is there but in despotism, a cure worse than the disease, from which all generous minds must shrink.   Yet notwithstanding the bad character thus given to the Florentine government, not only the Pandolfini were all members of it in their day, but some of the best men of every generation always found their way into it, and acted as salt at least, if they could not work any greater effect—a fact which kept it going through all the dangers of these turbulent centuries. But already even in Agnolo's death the factions were dying out, and the day of the Medici had come.

In this economy of substance, time, and health, with all these quaint peculiarities of custom, thinking highly of

FIGURES FROM ORGAN-SCREEN. LUCA DELLA ROBBIA.

himself and all his ways, yet not without reason ; peaceful, honorable, a little pompous, full of generosity and hospitality, with no narrowness in his self-esteem, but a certain splendor which partly justified it, this Florentine citizen lived to the age of eighty-six, having been for about twelve years retired in his villa, leaving the *bottega* and the state to his sons. Never was a fiercer conflict in Florence than that of the Albizzi and Medici which was going on while this calm and excellent *bourgeois* lectured his wife and set everything to rights in the little world around him. But the fightings and the banishments do

not seem to have disturbed either *bottega* or villa, the selling of the goods no more than the ripening of the grapes—
a curious and striking lesson. Ser Agnolo was buried in
his own fair marble tomb in the church of San Martino
near his villa, which tomb he had erected for himself and
adorned with his arms twenty-six years before, adding
with modest pride and the amiable self-consciousness
natural to him, the serpent and cross, which was the
emblem of the peacemaker, "*come autore della pubblica
pace,*" says one of his chroniclers. His funeral was followed *pomposmente* by the flags of the republic and his
trade, "and other usual honors," and by the greatest and
most illustrious citizens ; and there he still lies dignified
and self-content under his marble, as he stands equally
self-satisfied and dignified, setting everybody right, in the
book, much too homely for such a splendid citizen, which
was not published till the beginning of this century, and
from which we have quoted so largely: an example of how
honest men can thrive in the fiercest of times, and how
Florence lived and flourished and grew rich through
conflicts innumerable—fighting with one hand, it is true,
but working with the other, and building up more than
she destroyed.

THE MONKS OF SAN MARCO,

CHAPTER VII.

I.—THE ANGELICAL PAINTER.

Among all the many historical places, sacred by right of the feet that have trodden them, and the thoughts that have taken origin within them, which attract the spectator in the storied city of Florence, there is not one perhaps, more interesting or attractive than the convent of St. Mark, now, by a necessity of state which some approve and some condemn, emptied of its traditionary inhabitants. No black and white monk now bars smilingly to profane feminine feet the entrance to the sunny cloister: no brethren of Saint Dominic inhabit the hushed and empty cells. ·Chapter-house, refectory, library, all lie vacant and open, a museum for the state, a blank piece of public property, open to any chance comer. It would be churlish to complain of a freedom which makes so interesting a place known to the many ; but it is almost impossible not to regret the entire disappearance of the old possessors, the preachers of many a fervent age, the eloquent order which in this very cloister produced so great an example of the orator's undying power. Savonarola's convent, we cannot but feel, might have been one of the few spared by the exigencies of public poverty, that most strenuous of all reformers. On this point, however, whatever may be the stranger's regrets, Italy of course must be the final judge, as we have all been in our day ; and Italy has at

206 THE MAKERS OF FLORENCE.

least the grace of accepting her position as art-guardian
and custodian of the precious things of the past, a point in
which other nations of the world have been less careful.
San Marco is empty, swept, and garnished ; but at least it
is left in perfect good order, and watched over as becomes
its importance in the history of Florence and in that of
art. What stirring scenes, and what still ones, these old
walls have seen, disguising their antiquity as they do—but
as scarcely any building of their date could do in England
—by the harmony of everything around, the homogeneous
character of the town ! It would be affectation for any
observer brought up in the faith, and bred in the atmosphere of Gothic art, to pretend to any admiration of the
external aspect of the ordinary Italian basilica. There is
nothing in these buildings except their associations, and
sometimes the wealth and splendor of their decorations,
pictorial or otherwise, to charm or impress eyes accustomed
to Westminster and Notre Dame. The white convent
walls shutting in everything that is remarkable within, in
straight lines of blank inclosure, are scarcely less interesting outside than is the lofty gable-end which forms the
façade of most churches in Florence, whether clothed in
shining lines of marble or rugged coat of plaster. The
church of San Marco has not even the distinction of this
superficial splendor or squalor. It does not appeal to the
sympathy of the beholder, as so many Florentine churches
did a few years ago, and as the cathedral still does with its
stripped and unsightly façade ; but stands fast in respectable completeness, looking out upon the sunshiny square,
arranged into the smooth prettiness of a very ordinary
garden by the new spirit of good order which has
come upon Italy. It is difficult, in sight of the shrubs,
and flowers, and grass-plots, the peaceable ordinary houses
around, to realize that it was here that Savonarola preached
to excited crowds, filling up every morsel of standing-

ground ; and that these homely convent walls, white and blank in the sunshine, were once besieged by mad Florence wildly seeking the blood of the prophet who had not given it the miracle it sought. The place is as still now as monotonous peace and calm can make it. Some wrecks of faded pictures keep their places upon the walls, the priests chant their monotonous masses, the bad organ plays worse music—though this is melodious Italy, the country of song : and the only thing that touches the heart in the scene of so many great events is a sight that is common in every parish church throughout almost all Catholic countries, at least throughout all Italy—the sight of the handful of homely people who in the midst of their work come in to say their prayers, or having a little leisure, sit down and muse in the soft and consecrated silence. I think no gorgeous *funzione,* no Pontifical High Mass, is half so affecting. Their faces are toward the altar, but nothing is doing there. What are they about? Not recalling the associations of the place, thinking of Savonarola; as we are; but musing upon what is far more close and intimate their own daily trials and temptations, their difficulties, their anxieties. The coolness and dimness of the place, a refuge from the blazing sun without, now and then a monotonous chanting, or the little tinkle of the bell which rouses them from their thoughts for a moment, and bids every beholder bend a reverent knee in sympathy with what is going on somewhere behind those dim pillars— some Low Mass in an unseen chapel—all this forms a fit atmosphere around those musing souls. And that is the most interesting sight that is to be seen in San Marco, though the strangers who come from afar to visit Savonarola's church and dwelling-place stray about the side chapels and gaze at the pictures, and take little enough note of the unpicturesque devotion of to-day.

The history of the remarkable convent and church which

has thus fallen into the blank uses of a museum on the one hand, and the commonplace routine of a parish on the other, has long ceased to be great; all that was most notable in it indeed—its virtual foundation, or rebuilding, when transferred to the Dominican order, its decorations, its tragic climax of power and closely following downfall —were all summed up within the fifteenth century. But it is one of the great charms of the storied cities of Italy that they make the fifteenth century (not to speak of ages still more remote) as yesterday to the spectator, placing him with a loving sympathy in the very heart of the past. We need not enter into the story of the events which secured to the Dominican order the possession of San Marco, originally the property of an order of Silvestrini; but may sum them up in a few words. For various reasons, partly moral, partly political, a community of Dominicans had been banished to Fiesole, where they lived and longed for years, gazing at their Florence from among the olive gardens, and setting naught by all these rural riches, and by the lovely prospect that enchanted their eyes daily, in comparison with the happiness of getting back again to their beloved town. The vicissitudes of their exile, and the connection of the brotherhood with the special tumults of the time, may all be found in Padre Marchese's great work, "San Marco Illustrato," but are at once too detailed and too vague to be followed here. In process of time they were allowed to descend the hill to San Giorgio on the other side of the Arno, which was still a partial banishment; and at last regained popularity and influence so completely that the naughty Silvestrini were compelled to relinquish their larger house, and marched out of San Marco, aggrieved and reluctant, across the bridge, while the Reformed Dominicans, with joyful chanting of psalms, streamed across in procession to the new home, which was not only a commodious habitation, but a prize of virtue. Perhaps this kind of transfer was not exactly the way to make the brethren love each other; but history says nothing more of the Silvestrini. The Dominicans do not seem to have had, immediately at least, so pleasant a removing as they hoped, for their new convent was dilapidated, and scarcely inhabitable. Cosimo de' Medici, the first great chief of that ambitious family, the wily and wise founder of its fortunes, the Pater Patriæ, whom Florence had first banished with ignominy and then summoned back in almost despotical power, took the case of the monks in hand. He rebuilt their convent for them, while they encamped in huts and watched over the work. And when it was so far completed as to be habitable, princely Cosimo gave a commission to a certain monk among them, skilled in such work, to decorate with pictures the new walls. These decorations, and the gentle, simple, uneventful life of this monk and his brethren, furnish a soft prelude to the stormy strain of further story, of which San Marco was to be the subject. Its period of fame and greatness, destined to conclude in thunders of excommunication, in more tangible thunders of assault and siege, in popular violence, tragic anguish, and destruction, began thus with flutings of angels, with soft triumphs of art, with such serene, sweet, quiet and beautiful industry as may be exercised, who knows, in the outer courts of heaven itself. A stranger introduction to the passion and struggle of Savonarola's prophetic career could scarcely be, than that which is contained in this gentle chapter of conventual existence, at its fairest and brightest, which no one can ignore who steps across the storied threshold of San Marco, and is led to the grave silence of Prior Girolamo's cell between two lines of walls from which soft faces look at him like benedictions, fresh (or so it seems) from Angelico's tender hand.

The painter whom we know by this name, which is not

his name any more than it is the name of the Angelical doctor, St. Thomas Aquinas, or the Angelical father, Saint Francis, was born in the neighborhood of Florence, in the fertile and fair province of Mugello, the same district

FRA ANGELICO.

which, a hundred years earlier, produced Giotto—in the latter part of the fourteenth century. His name was Guido di Pietro—Guido, the son of Peter—evidently not with any further distinction of lineage. Where he studied his divine art, or by whom he was taught, is not known.

Vasari suggests that he was a pupil of Starnina, and Eyre and Cavalcaselle imagine it to be more likely that the Starnina traditions came to him through Masolino or Masaccio, and that he formed his style upon that of Orcagna. These, however, do not seem much more than conjectures, and the only facts known of his simple history are that in 1407, when he was twenty, his brother and he, taking the names of Benedetto and Giovanni, together entered the Dominican order in the convent at Fiesole. This community had a troubled life for some years, and the young disciples were sent to Cortona, where there are various pictures which testify to the fact that Fra Giovanni was already a painter of no mean power. All the dates, however, of this early part of his life are confused, and the story uncertain; for indeed it is probable no one knew that the young monk was to become the Angelical painter, the glory of his convent, and one of the wonders of his age. What is certain, however, is that he returned from Cortona, and lived for many years in the convent of San Domenica, half way up to Fiesole, upon the sunny slopes where nothing ventures to grow that does not bear fruit; where flowers are weeds, and roses form the hedges, and the lovely cloudy foliage of the olive affords both shade and wealth. There is not very much record of the painter in all those silent cloistered years. Books which he is said to have illuminated with exquisite grace and skill are doubtfully appropriated by critics to his brother or to humbler workers of their school, and the few pictures which seem to belong to this period have been injured in some cases, and in others destroyed. Fra Giovanni performed all his monastic duties with the devotion of the humblest brother; and lived little known, without troubling himself about fame, watching no doubt the nightly sunsets and moonrises over that glorious Val d'Arno which shone and slumbered at his feet, and noting silently how

the mountain watchers stood round about, and the little
Tuscan hills on a lower level stretched their vine garlands
like hands each to the other, and drew near, a wistful
friendly band, to see what Florence was doing. Florence,
heart and soul of all, lay under him, as he took his moon-

FLORENCE, FROM FIESOLE.

light meditative stroll on the terrace or gazed and mused
out of his narrow window. One can fancy that the composition of that lovely landscape stole into the painter's
heart and worked itself into his works, in almost all of
which some group of reverent spectators, Dominican
brethren with rapt faces, or saintly women, or angel
lookers-on more ethereal still, stand by and watch with
adoring awe the sacred mysteries transacted in their presence, with something of the same deep calm and hush
which breathes about the blue spectator-heights round the
City of Flowers. What Fra Giovanni saw was not what

we see. The noble dome which now crowns the cathedral was not then finished, and Giotto's Campanile, divinely tall, fair, and light as a lily stalk, had scarcely yet thrown up its highest crown into mid-air; nothing but the rugged grace of the old tower of the signoria—contrasting now in picturesque characteristic Tuscan humanity with the more heavenly creation that rivals it—raised up then its protecting standard from the lower level of ancient domes and lofty houses, soaring above the Bargello and the Badia, in the days of the Angelical painter. But there was enough in this, with all its summer hazes and wintry brightness, with the shadows that flit over the wide landscape like some divine breath, and the broad, dazzling, rejoicing glow of the Italian sun, and Arno glimmering through the midst like a silver thread, and white castellos shining further and further off in the blue distance, up to the very skirt of Apennine, to inspire his genius. In those days men said little about Nature, and did not even love her, the critics think—rather had to find out how to love her, when modern civilization came to teach them how. But if Fra Giovanni, pacing his solitary walk upon that mount of vision at San Domenico, evening after evening, year after year, did not note those lights and shades and atmospheric changes, and lay up in his still soul a hundred variations of sweet color, soft glooms, and heavenly shadows, then it is hard to think where he got his lore, and harder still that Heaven should be so prodigal of a training which was not put to use. Heaven is still prodigal, and Nature tints her palette with as many hues as ever; but there is no Angelical painter at the windows of San Domenico to take advantage of them now.

The Florence to which these monks were so eager to return, and where eventually they came, carrying their treasures, in procession, making the narrow hillside ways resound with psalms, and winding their long trains of black

and white through the streets of their regained home, was
at that time, amid all its other tumults and agitations (and
these were neither few nor light), in the full possession of
that art-culture which lasted as long as there was genius
to keep it up, and which has made the city now one of the
treasuries of the world.   The advent of a new painter was
still something to stir the minds of the people.   There is
little evidence, however, that Florence knew much of the
monk's work, who, as yet, was chiefly distinguished, it
would seem, as a miniaturist and painter of beautiful
manuscripts.   But Cosimo, the father of his country, could
have done few things more popular and likely to enhance
his reputation, than his liberality in thus encouraging and
developing another genius for the delight and credit of the
city.   Almost before the cloister was finished, historians
suppose, Fra Giovanni had got his hands on the smooth
white wall, so delightful to a painter's imagination.   We
do not pretend to determine the succession of his work,
and say where he began; but it is to be supposed that the
cloister and chapter-house, as first completed, would afford
him his first opportunity.   No doubt there were many
mingled motives in that noble and fine eagerness to
decorate and make beautiful their homes which possessed
the minds of the men of that gorgeous age, whether in the
world or the church.   For the glory of God, for the glory
of the convent and order, for the glory of Florence, which
every Florentine sought with almost more than patriotic
ardor—the passion of patriotism gaining, as it were, in
intensity when circumscribed in the extent of its object—
the monks of San Marco must have felt a glow of generous
pride in their growing gallery of unique and original
pictures.   The artist himself, however, worked with a
simple unity of motive little known either in that or any
other age.   He painted his pictures as he said his prayers,
out of pure devotion.   So far as we are informed, Fra

Giovanni, of the order of preachers, was no preacher, by word or doctrine. He had another way of edifying the holy and convincing the sinner. He could not argue or exhort, but he could set before them the sweetest heaven that ever appeared to poetic vision, the tenderest friendly angels, the gentlest and loveliest of virgin mothers. Neither profit nor glory came to the monk in his convent. He began his work on his knees, appealing to his God for the inspiration that so great an undertaking required, and —carrying with him the *défauts de ses qualités,* as all men of primitive virtue do—declined with gentle obstinacy to make any change or improvement after, in the works thus conceived under the influence of Heaven. While he was engaged in painting a crucifix, Vasari tells us, the tears would run down his cheeks, in his vivid realization of the Divine suffering therein expressed. Thus it was with the full fervor of a man who feels himself at last entered upon the true mission of his life, and able, once and for all, to preach in the most acceptable way the truth that had been dumb within him, that the Angelical painter began his work. The soft and heavenly inspiration in it has never been questioned, and the mind of the looker-on, after these long centuries, can scarcely help expanding with a thrill of human sympathy to realize the profound and tender satisfaction of that gentle soul, thus enabled to paint his best, to preach his best, in the way God had endowed him for, with the additional happiness and favor of high heaven, that his lovely visions, were to be the inheritance of his brethren and sons in the church, the only succession an ecclesiastic could hope for.

It would appear, however, that the interior of San Marco must have been so soon ready for Fra Giovanni's beautifying hand, that he had but little time to expend himself on the cloisters which are now bright with the works of inferior artists. It would be difficult to convey to any one

CRUCIFIXION: OUTER CLOISTER: SAN MARCO.

who has not stood within an Italian cloister, and felt the warm brightness of the pictured walls cheer his eyes and his heart, even when the painters have not been great or the works very remarkable—the special charm and sweetness of those frescoed decorations. The outer cloister

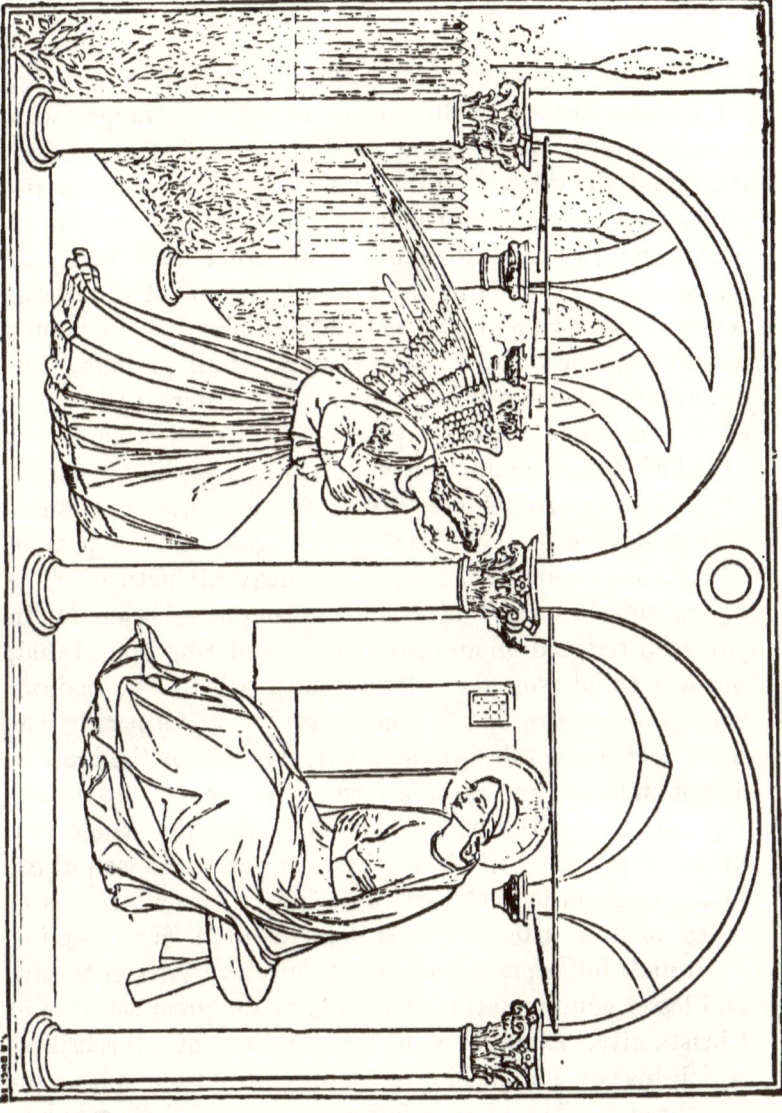

ANNUNCIATION: FRA ANGELICO, SAN MARCO.

217.

of San Marco glows with pictures—not very fine, perhaps,
yet with an interest of their own. There the stranger who
has time, or cares to look at the illustrations of a past age,
may read the story of Sant' Antonino, who was distinguished as a good archbishop of Florence, and canonized
accordingly, to the great glory of his order, and honor of
his convent. But Antonino himself was one of the brethren who stood by and watched and admired Fra Giovanni's
work on the new walls. Was the first of all, perhaps, that
crucifix which faces the spectator as he enters, at the end
of the cloister, double expression of devotion to Christ
crucified and Dominic His servant? It is the most
important of Angelico's works in this outer enclosure.
Our gentle painter could not paint agony or the passion
of suffering, which was alien to his heavenly nature. The
figure on the cross, here as elsewhere, is beautiful in
youthful resignation and patience, no suffering Son of God,
but a celestial symbol of depths into which the painter
could not penetrate; but the kneeling worshiper, in the
black and white robes of the order, who clasps the cross in
a rapt embrace, and raises a face of earnest and all-absorb-
ing faith to the Divine Sufferer, embodies the whole tradition of monastic life in its best aspect. No son of St.
Dominic could look at that rapt figure without a clearer
sense of the utter self-devotion required of himself as
Dominic's follower, the annihilation of every lesser motive
and lesser contemplation than that of the great sacrifice of
Christianity, example and consecration of all sacrifices
which his vow bound him to follow and muse upon, all his
life through. The picture fills something of the same place
as the blazon of a knightly house over its warlike gates is
meant to do. It is the tradition, the glory, the meaning
of the order all in one, as seen by Angelico's beauty-loving
eyes, as well as by those, stern, glowing eyes of Savonarola,
who was to come; and perhaps even in their dull, ferocious,

mistaken way by the Torquemados, who have brought
St. Dominic to evil fame. For Christ, and Christ alone,
counting no cost ; thinking of nothing but how to conquer
the world for Him ; conceiving of no advance but by the
spreading of His kingdom—yet, alas! with only every
individual's narrow human notion of what that kingdom
was, and what the way of spreading it. In Florence,
happily, at that moment, the reformed Dominicans, in the
warmth of their revival, could accept the blazon of their
order, thus set forth, with all their hearts. They had
renewed their dedication of themselves to that perpetual
preaching of Christ's sacrifice and imitation of His self-
renunciation which was the highest meaning of their vows;
and no doubt each obscure father, each musing humble
novice in his white gown, felt a glow of rapt enthusiasm
as he watched the new picture grow into life, and found
in the profound belief of the holy founder of his order at
once the inspiration and reflection of his own.

The other little pictures in this cloister which are pure
Angelico are entirely conventual, addressed to the brethren,
as was natural in this, the center of their common existence. Peter Martyr, one of their most distinguished
saints, stands over one doorway, finger on lip suggesting
the silence that befitted a grave community devoted to the
highest studies and reflections. Over another door are two
Dominican brethren, receiving (it is the guest-chamber of
the monastery) the Redeemer Himself, worn with travel,
to their hospitable shelter. Curiously enough, the beautiful,
gentle, young traveler, with his pilgrim's hat falling from
his golden curls, which is the best representation our gentle
Angelico could make—always angelical, like his name—of
the Lord of life, might almost have served as model for
that other beautiful, gentle, young peasant, Christ, whom
another great painter, late in this nineteenth century, has
given forth to us as all he knows of the central figure

of the world's history. To some has been given the power
to make Christ, to others contadini, as the two rival
sculptors said to each other. Angelico rarely advances
above this low ideal. His angels are lovely and beyond
description ; he understood the unity of a creature more
ethereal than flesh and blood, yet made up of soft submission, obedience, devotedness—beautiful human qualities;
but the conjunction of the human with the divine was
beyond him—as, indeed, might be said of most painters.
There can be little doubt that this difficulty of representing
anything that could satisfy the mind, as God in the aspect
of full-grown man, has helped, as much as any more
serious motive, to give to the group of the Mother and the
Child such universal acceptance in the realms of art—a
pictorial necessity thus lending its aid in the fixing of
dogma, and still more in the unanimous involuntary bias
given to devotion. The Christ-child has proved within
the powers of many painters : for, indeed, there is something of the infinite in every child—unfathomable possibilities, the boundless charm of the unrealized, in which
everything may be, while yet nothing certainly is. But
who has ever painted the Christ-man? unless we may take
the pathetic shadow of that sorrowful head in Leonardo's
ruined Cenaculo—the very imperfection of which helps
us to see a certain burdened divinity in its melancholy
lines—for success. Sorely burdened indeed, and sad to
death, is that countenance, which is the only one we
can think of which bears anything of the dignity of
Godhead in the looks of man ; but it is very different
from the beautiful, weak, fatigued young countryman
who is so often presented to us as the very effigy of Him
who is the King and Saviour of humanity, as well as the
Lamb of God.

Angelico never, or very rarely, got beyond this gentle
ideal of suffering innocence, enduring with unalterable

patience. Perhaps in his "Scourging" there may be a
gleam of higher meaning, or in that crowned figure which
crowns the humble mother; but the type is always the
same. It is curious to note how this incapacity works.

HOSPITALITY: FROM THE CLOISTER OF SAN MARCO.

In the great picture in the chapterhouse of San Marco,
which opens from this cloister, and is the most important
single work in the convent, the spectator merely glances at
the figure on the cross, which ought to be the center of the
picture. It really counts for nothing, except technically,
as a necessity of composition. The attendant saints are
wonderfully noble, and full of varied expression; but the
crucified form which attracts their gaze is little more than

a conventional emblem; the Virgin, it is true, swoons at
the foot of the cross, but the spectator sees no reason
except a historical one for her swoon ; for the cross itself
is faint and secondary, curiously below the level of
Ambrose, and Augustine, and Francis, who look up with
faces full of life at the mysterious abstraction. Underneath
that solemn assembly of fathers and founders—for almost
all are heads of orders, except the medical saints Cosimo
and Damian, who hold their place there in compliment to
the Medici—the monks of San Marco have deliberated
for four centuries. There, no doubt, Pope Eugenius sat,
with the pictured glory over him ; there Savonarola pre-
sided over his followers, and encouraged himself and them
with revelations and prophecy. The picture survives
everything—long ages of peace, brief storms of violence
in which moments count for years ; and again the silent
ages—quiet, tranquillity, monotony, tedium. Jerome and
Augustine, Francis and Dominic, with faces more real than
our own, have carried on a perpetual adoration ever since,
and never drooped or failed.

The new dormitory, which Cosimo and his architect,
Michelozzi, built for the monks, does not seem originally
to have been of the character which we assign to a convent.
It was one large room, like a ward in a hospital—like the
old "long chamber" in Eton College—with a row of small
arched windows on either side, each of which apparently
gave a little light and a limited span of space to the monk
whose bed flanked the window. To decorate this large,
bare room seems to have been the Angelical painter's next
grand piece of work. Other hands besides his were engaged
upon it. His brother, Fra Benedetto, took some of the
subjects in hand—subjects, alas, carelessly passed now by
the spectator, who takes but little interest in Benedetto's
renderings. How pleasant is the imagination thus conjured
up! The bustling pleased community settling itself in its

new house, arranging its homely crucifixes, its few books,
its tables for work, parchments and ink and colors for its
illuminated manuscripts, great branch of monkish industry;
here an active brother leaving a little breathing room in

SILENCE—ST. PETER MARTYR; IN THE CLOISTER OF SAN MARCO.

the beehive, going out upon the business of the convent,
aiding or watching the workmen outside; here a homely
Fra Predicatore meditating in his corner with what quiet
was possible, his sermon for next fast or festa; there,
bending over their work with fine brush and careful eye,
the illuminators, the writers, elaborating their perfect
manuscript; and all the while—tempting many a glance,
many a criticism, many a whispered communication—the

picture going on, in which one special brother or other
must have taken a lively, jealous interest, seeing it was his
special corner which was being thus illustrated! One
wonders if the monks were jealous on whose bit of wall
Benedetto worked, instead of Giovanni—or whether there
might be a party in the convent who considered Giovanni
an over-rated brother, and believed Benedetto to have quite
as good a right to the title of " Angelico." For their own
sakes let us hope it was so, and that good Fra Benedetto
painted for his own set ; while at the same time there can
be little doubt that the difference between him and his
brother would be much less strongly marked then than
now. Thus all together the community carried on its
existence. Perhaps a humorous recollection of the hum
which must have reached him as he stood painting on his
little scaffolding, induced the painter to plan that warning
figure of the martyred Peter over the doorway below,
serious, with finger on his lip ; for it could scarcely be in
human nature that all those friars with consciences void of
offense, approved of by pope and people : a new house just
built for them, warm with the light of princely favor and
the sunshine shining in though all those arched windows,
throwing patches of brightness over the new-laid tiles ;
and the Florentine air, gay with summer, making merry
like ethereal wine their Tuscan souls ; should have kept
silence like melancholy Trappists of a later degenerate
age. To be a monk in those days was to be a busy, well-
occupied, and useful man, in no way shut out from nature.
I should like to have stepped into that long room when
the bell called them all forth to chapel, and noted where
Angelico put down his brush, how the scribe paused in the
midst of a letter, and the illuminator in a gorgeous golden
drapery, and the preacher with a sentence half ended—and
nothing but the patches of sunshine and the idle tools held
possession of the place. No thought then of thunders

which should shake all Florence, of prophecies and prophets; nothing but gentle industry, calm work—that
calmest work which leaves the artist so much time for
gentle musing, for growth of skill, poetic thoughtfulness.
And when the scaffolding was removed, and another and
another picture fully disclosed in delicate sweet freshness
of color—soft fair faces looking out of the blank wall,
clothing them with good company, with solace and protection—what a flutter of pleasure must have stolen
through the brotherhood, what pleasant excitement, what
critical discussions, fine taste, enlightened and superior,
against simple enthusiasm! It is almost impossible not
to fear that there must have been some conflict of
feeling between the brother who had but a saintly Annunciation, too like the public and common property of that
picture called the "Capo di Scala," and him who was
blessed with the more striking subject of the "Scourging,"
so quaint and fine; or him who proudly felt himself the
possessor of that picturesque glimpse into the invisible—
the opened gates of Limbo, with the father of mankind
pressing to the Saviour's feet. Happy monks, busy and
peaceable! half of them no doubt at heart believed that
his own beautiful page, decked by many a gorgeous king
and golden saint, would last as long as the picture; and so
they have done, as you may see in the glass cases in the
library, where all those lovely chorales and books of prayer
are preserved: but not like Angelico. There is one glory
of the sun, and another of the stars.

It does not seem to be known at what time this large
dormitory was divided, as we see it now, in a manner
which still more closely recalls to us the boys' rooms in a
"house" in Eton, into separate cells. No doubt it is more
dignified, more conventual, more likely to have promoted
the serious quiet which ought to belong to monastic life;
but one cannot help feeling that here and there a friendly,

simple-minded brother must have regretted the change.
Each cell has its own little secluded window, deep in the
wall, its own patch of sunshine, its own picture. There is
no fireplace, or other means of warming the little chamber
between its thick walls; but no doubt then, as now, the
monks had their scaldinos full of wood embers, the poor
Italian's immemorial way of warming himself. And between the window and the wall, on the left side, is the
picture—dim—often but dimly seen, faded out of its past
glory—sometimes less like a picture at all than some
celestial shadow on the gray old wall, some sweet phantasmagoria of lovely things that have passed there, and cannot
be quite effaced from the very stones that once saw them.
For my own part, I turn from all Angelico's more perfect
efforts, from the "Madonna della Stella," glistening in
gold, which is so dear to the traveler, and all the well-pre-
served examples with their glittering backgrounds, to
those heavenly shadows in the empty cells—scratched,
defaced and faded as so many of them are—in which the
gentle old monk seems to come nearer to the modern
spectator, the pilgrim who has crossed hills and seas to see
all that is left of what was done in such a broad and
spontaneous flood of inspiration. Those saints, with their
devout looks, the musing virgin, the rapt Dominic; those
sweet spectator angels, so tenderly curious, sympathetic,
wistful, serviceable, that lovely soft embodiment of
womanly humbleness, yet exaltation, the celestial mother
bending to receive her crown. They are not pictures,
but visions painted on the dim conscious air not by
vulgar color and pencil, but by prayers and gentle
thoughts.

There are two separate cells in San Marco more important than these, yet closely connected with this same
early and peaceful chapter of the convent's story. We do
not speak of the line of little chambers, each blazoned with

a copy of that crucifix in the cloister, with the kneeling
St. Dominic, of which we have already spoken—which are
called the cells of the Gioviniti or Novices, and which
conclude in the sacred spot where Savonarola's great
existence was passed. These belong to a different period
in the history of the convent. But here is the cell where

Sant' Antonino lived as archbishop, and where still some
relics of him remain, glorious vestments of cloth of gold
beside the hair shirt, instrument of deepest mortification;
and the little chamber which it is reported Cosimo de'
Medici built for himself, and where he came when he
wished to discourse in quiet with the archbishop, whose
shrewd, acute, and somewhat humorous countenance looks

down upon us from the wall. This chamber is adorned
with one of Angelico's finest works, " The Adoration of
the Magi," a noble composition, and has besides in a niche
a pathetic Christ painted over a little altar sunk in the
deep wall. Here Cosimo came to consult with his archbishop (the best, they say, that Florence had ever had),
and, in earlier days, to talk to his Angelical painter as the
works went on, which the wise Medici was wise to see
would throw some gleam of fame upon himself as well as
on the convent. With all the monks together in the long
room where Angelico painted his frescoes it may well be
imagined that this place of retirement was essential ; and
when that long-headed and far-seeing father of his country
had been taken, no doubt with an admiring following of
monks, to see the last new picture, as one after another
was completed, and had given his opinion and the praise
which was expected of him, no doubt both painter and
prince were glad of the quiet retirement where they could
talk over what remained to do, and plan perhaps a greater
work here and there—the throned Madonna in the corridor,
with again the Medicien saints, holy physicians, Cosimo
and Damian at her feet—or discuss the hopeful pupils
whom Angelico was training, Benozzo Gozzoli, for instance,
thereafter known to fame.

All is peaceful, tranquil, softly melodious, in this beginning of the conventual existence. Pope Eugenius
himself came, at the instance of the Pater Patriæ, to
consecrate the new-built house, and lived in these very
rooms, to the glory and pride of the community. Thus
everything set out in an ideal circle of goodness and
graciousness ; a majestic pope, humble enough to dwell in
the very cloister with the Dominicans, blessing their home
for them ; a wise prince coming on frequent visits, half
living among them, with a cell called by his name where
he might talk with his monkish friends ; a great painter

working lowly and busy among the humblest of the brethren, taking no state upon him—though a great painter was a prince in art-loving Florence ; and when the time to give San Marco the highest of honors came, another brother taken from among them to be archbishop of the great city ; while all the time those pictures, for which princes would have striven, grew at each monk's bedhead, his dear especial property, gladdening his eyes and watching over his slumbers. Was there ever a more genial, peaceful beginning, a more prosperous pleasant home?

The way in which Antonino, according to the legend, came to be archbishop is very characteristic too. At the period of his visit, no doubt, Pope Eugenius learned to know Angelico, and to admire the works which he must have seen growing under the master's hand ; nor could he have failed to know the devotion of which those pictures were the expressive language, the intense celestial piety of the modest frate. Accordingly, when the pope went back to Rome he called the angelical painter to him to execute some work there, and with the primitive certainty of his age that excellence in one thing must mean excellence in all, offered to Fra Giovanni the vacant see of Florence. Modest Fra Giovanni knew that, though it was in him to paint, it was not in him to govern monks and men, to steer his way through politics and public questions, and rule a self-opinionated race like those hardheaded Tuscans. He told the head of the church that this was not his vocation, but that in his convent there was another frate whose shoulders were equal to the burden. The pope took his advice, as any calif in eastern story might have taken the recommendation of a newly chosen vizier ; such things were possible in primitive times ; and Antonino was forthwith called out of his cell, and from simple monk was made archbishop, his

character, there is little doubt, being well enough known
to give force to Angelico's representation in his favor.
This event would seem to have happened in the year 1445,
three years after the visit of Eugenius to San Marco, and
it seems doubtful whether Angelico ever returned to
Florence after his comrade's elevation to this dignity.
He stayed and painted in Rome till the death of Eugenius—then appeared a little while in Orvieto, where he
seems to have been accompanied by his pupil Benozzo, and
then returned to Rome to execute some commissions for
the new Pope Nicholas. San Marco had been finished
before this, with greater pomp and beauty than we have
attempted to tell ; for the great altarpiece has gone out of
the church, and other works have fallen into decay or
have been removed, and now dwell, dimmed by restoration
and cleaning, in the academy of the Belli Arti. At Rome
the gentle Angelico died, having painted to the end of his
life with all the freshness of youth. He was fifty when
he came down the slopes from Fiesole, singing among his
brethren, to make his new convent beautiful ; he was
sixty-eight when he died at Rome, but with no failing
strength or skill. The Angelical painter lies not in his
own San Marco, but in the church of Santa Maria sopra
Minerva in Rome ; but all the same he lives in Florence
within the walls he loved, in the cells he filled full of
beauty and pensive celestial grace, and which now are
dedicated to him, and hold his memory fresh as in a
shrine ; dedicated to him—and to one other memory as
different from his as morning is from evening. Few
people are equally interested in the two spirits which
dwell within the empty convent ; to some Angelico is all
its past contains—to some Savonarola ; but both are full
of the highest meaning, and the one does not interfere
with the other. The prophet-martyr holds a distinct
place from that of the painter-monk. The two stories are

separate, one sweet and soft as the "hidden brook" in the "leafy month of June," with the sound of which the poet consoles his breathless reader after straining his nerves to awe and terror. Like Handel's "Pastoral Symphony," piping under the moonlight, amid the dewy fields, full of heavenly subdued gladness and triumph, is the prelude which this gentle chapter of art and peace makes to the tragedy to follow. Angelico, with all his skill, prepared and made beautiful the house in which—with aims more splendid than his, and a mark more high, but not more devout or pure—another frate was to bring art and beauty to the tribunal of Christ and judge them, as Angelico himself, had his painter-heart permitted him, would have done as stoutly, rejecting the loveliness that was against God's ways and laws, no less than Savonarola. Their ways of serving were different, their inspiration the same.

The traditions of the Angelical painter's pious life which Vasari has collected for us are very beautiful. The simple old narrative of the first art-historian, always laudatory when it is possible to be so, bursts into a strain of almost musical eulogy in the description of the gentle frate.

"He was of simple and pious manners. He shunned the worldly in all things, and during his pure and simple life was such a friend to the poor that I think his soul must be now in heaven. He painted incessantly, but never would lay his hand to any subject not saintly. He might have had wealth, but he scorned it, and used to say that true riches are to be found in contentment. He might have ruled over many, but would not, saying that obedience was easier and less liable to error. He might have enjoyed dignities among his brethren and beyond them all ; but he disdained these honors, affirming that he sought for none other than might be consistent with a successful avoidance of hell and the attainment of paradise. Humane and sober he lived chastely, avoiding the errors of the world, and he was wont to say that the pursuit of art required rest and a life of holy thoughts;

that he who illustrates the acts of Christ should live with Christ. He was never known to indulge in anger with his brethren—a great, and to my opinion all but unattainable, quality; and he never admonished but with a smile. With wonderful kindness he would tell those who sought his work, that if they got the consent of the prior he should not fail. . . . . He never retouched or altered anything he had once finished, but left it as it had turned out, the will of God being that it should be so."

These details, vague though they are, bring before us the gentle painter—peaceable, modest, kind, yet endowed with a gentle obstinacy, and limited, as is natural to a monk, within the straight horizon of his community. It is told of him that when invited to breakfast with Pope Nicholas, the simple-minded brother was uneasy not to be able to ask his prior's permission to eat meat, the prior being for him a greater authority than the pope, in whose hand (Angelico forgot) was the primary power of all indulgences. There could not be a better instance of the soft submissive, almost domestic narrowness of the great painter like a child from home, to whom the license given by a king would have no such reassuring authority as the permission of father or mother. This beautiful narrow-mindedness—for in such a case it is permissible to unite the two words—told, however, on a more extended scale even on his genius. The Angelical monk was as incapable of understanding evil as a child. His atmosphere was innocence, holiness, and purity. To pure and holy persons he could give a noble and beautiful individuality; but absolute ugliness, grotesque and unreal, was all the notion he had of the wicked. To his cloistered soul the higher mystery of beautiful evil was unknown, and his simple nature ignored the many shades of that pathetic side of moral downfall in which an unsuccessful struggle has preceded destruction. He had no pity for, because he had no knowledge of, no more than a child, the agony of failure, or those faint tints of difference which sometimes separate the victors from the vanquished. While the fair circle of the saved glide, dancing in a ring, into the flowery gardens of paradise, a very " Decameron " group of holy joy, in his great " Last Judgment "—the lost fly hopeless to the depths of hell, ugly, distorted, without a redeeming feature. It was his primitive way of representing evil—hideous, repulsive, as to his mind it could not but appear. He loathed ugliness as he loathed vice, and what so natural as that they should go together? Fra Giovanni showed his impartiality by mingling among his groups of the lost, here and there, a mitred bishop and cowled monk, to show that even a profession of religion was not infallible : but he had not the higher impartiality of permitting to those huddled masses any comeliness or charm of sorrow, but damned them frankly as a child does, and in his innocence knew no ruth.

Thus ends the first chapter of the history of St. Mark's convent at Florence—a story without a discordant note in it, which has left nothing behind but melodious memories and relics full of beauty. It is of this the stranger must chiefly think as he strays through the silent, empty cells, peopled only by saints and angels ; until indeed he turns a corner of the dim corridor, and finds himself in presence of a mightier spirit. Let us leave the gentle preface in its holy calm. The historian may well pause before he begins the sterner but nobler strain.

CHAPTER VIII.

II.—THE GOOD ARCHBISHOP.

" WHAT is the use of the cloister in the midst of society," says Padre Marchese (himself a Frate Predicatore of San Marco), " if it is not a focus and center of morality and religion, diffusing and planting deeply in the hearts of the people ideas of honesty, justice, and virtue, in order to temper and hold in balance the brutal force of the passions which threaten continually to absorb all the thoughts and affections of men?   In this brief description of the monastic life is summed up the life of Sant' Antonino and of his disciples.   The saintly Costanzo da Fabriano, and Fathers Santi Schialtesi and Girolamo Lapaccini, with a chosen band of students, went through the cities, towns, and villages of Tuscany, or wherever necessity called them, extinguishing party strife, instructing the people, and bringing back the lost into the path of virtue.   Sant' Antonino used his ability and wonderful charity in encouraging the best studies, aiding in the reform of the clergy, and giving a helping hand to all the charitable works which were rendered necessary by the distresses of those unhappy times.   And since the people of Florence took great delight in the arts, and were in the habit of drawing comfort and pleasure from them, the blessed Giovanni Angelico undertook the noble office of making those very arts ministers of religious and moral perfection ; educating a school of painters, pure, heavenly-minded, and toned to that high sublime which raises man from the mud of this world and

makes him in love with heaven." Such is the affectionate description given by a son of San Marco of the first
Dominican community which inhabited the convent. And
his praise scarcely seems too liberal, either of the pure

SANT' ANTONINO, ARCHBISHOP OF FLORENCE.

minded and gentle painter, or of the more active figure of
the archbishop, his friend and brother in the community,
who was, according to the story which we have just given
preferred to his high office by Angelico's modest recomen-
dation.

Antonino Pierozzo was a Florentine, the son of a notary,

who at the early age of fifteen joined the community of Dominicans, then in the course of formation upon the hillside of Fiesole, in the year 1405. " By the ingenuousness of his appearance and the humble and affectionate manner in which the boy presented himself to them, the monks recognized the precious gift which God made in him to the new congregation." He was sent for his monastic training to Cortona, where he was the companion of the two brothers Giovanni and Benedetto, a very few years older than himself, of whom we have already spoken. Antonino's talents were different from theirs, but, so far as the community was concerned, even more important. He would seem to have been born with the gift of organization and administration, and even before the young monks left Cortona, when he was but thirty, had risen to be their prior, an office which he continued to hold in Fiesole when they were transplanted. there. He was the first prior of San Marco, and if tradition is true as to his advancement to the see of Florence by the interposition of his humble brother the painter, it is but another instance of the curiously accidental and fortuitous way in which real excellence sometimes stumbles into recognition.

" 'There are some who live by truth and some who live by love,' says Padre Marchese, in one of the rare passages of eloquence to which he rises in his valuable but somewhat heavy volume; 'the first, easily forgetful of this lower world, roam through purely ideal regions, and when they find themselves in a true but ignored and unknown corner, they lose themselves in abstraction, taking delight in it; the second, entirely active, are more disposed to do good to others than to conduct arguments; where there is suffering to alleviate, tears to wipe away, necessity to provide for, there they are in their element, and out of such labors they find neither pleasure nor honor. The region of the ideal has neither limits nor boundary, and the more it is sought by many and noble explorers, the more infinitely it widens out ; but in addition to this it has terrible tempests, by which the too bold or unskillful voyagers are shipwrecked and lost. It is not thus in the region of holy charity, where there is perennial calm and sweetness such as human tongue cannot describe. One of the beings of this description, made to live by love, was Sant' Antonino. Not that his intellect was inferior or unable to rise to subtle disquisitions ; but in all his learned researches he always had some purpose truly Christain to render his knowledge useful and profitable to the people. He explains and expounds the laws, human and divine, in which are to be found the occasion and the guarantee of duties and rights. He makes clear and regulates morality by pointing out to men the offices of Christian and civilized life ; and to souls enamored of heaven, uncloses the treasures of that celestial wisdom which speaks to men of a better country, laboring continually, by word and deed, by the example of a most innocent and austere life, to lead the fallen back to the path of virtue ; with such potent charity that never was heart so hard but it softened before so much gentleness, nor intellect so depraved that it did not yield to his reasoning. In this way his example was a continued stimulant and excitation to his brethren in religion, who, uniting with him in that ministry of love, renewed everywhere the religious sentiment which the discords and corruption·of the clergy had attenuated and almost made an end of. These pious works gave him a great place in the love and reverence of the people.' "

Thus Antonino became the Florentine apostle of benevolence and those works of kindness and charity which Christianity has made familar to men. The story of his life and labors and miracles—those prodigies which procured him his canonization, as well as many fully authenticated acts of loving-kindness which might well entitle him to rank among those whom their fellow-men called blessed—are painted under the arches of the cloister of San Marco, not perhaps with supreme skill, or with any lingering grace of Angelico's art, but clear enough to give an additional reality to the history of the man. Among those frescoes, indeed, is one poor picture, which has a historical interest much above its value in point of art—a picture in which the archbishop is represented as entering (barefooted, as it is said he did, in humility and protest against the honor which he could not escape) in solemn procession at the great west door of the cathedral, for his consecration. The façade now a mass of unsightly plaster, as it has been for generations, here appears to us decorated halfway up with the graceful canopy work of Giotto's design, showing at least the beginning which had been made in carrying out that original plan, and its artistic effect. This makes the picture interesting in point of art; but it has still another interest which probably will strike the spectator more than even this reminiscence of the destroyed façade, or the picture of good Sant' Antonino muffled in the gorgeous vestments appropriate to the occasion. In the foreground of the crowd which looks on at the procession, stands a tall figure in the Dominican habit, with the cowl as usual half covering his head, and his marked and powerful, but not handsome features standing out with all the reality of a portrait against the vague background. To be sure it is an anachronism to introduce Savonarola, for Archbishop Antonino was dead long years before his great successor came to Florence : but painters in those days were not limited by vulgar bonds of accuracy in point of date.

The good archbishop, however, was not, so far as the evidence shows, a man of genius like his friend the painter, or like that later prior of San Marco whose name is forever associated with the place. But he possessed that noble inspiration of charity, which perhaps more than any other, makes the name of a churchman dear to the race among which he lives. The sagacious, shrewd, and kindly face which looks at us, still with an almost humorous observation, in the bust which remains in the convent, would scarcely perhaps suggest to the spectator the tender depth of loving-kindness which must have been in the man. In Florence, with its perpetual succession of governments, its continually varying ascend‑ ency, now of one party, now of another, the commu‑

nity was exposed to still greater vicissitudes of fortune than are the inhabitants of our commercial towns, who are exposed to the caprices of trade. Those, who one day had power and office and the ways of making wealth in their hands, were subject on the next to ruinous fines, imprisonments, exile, descent from the highest to the lowest grade. · When Cosimo de' Medici returned from the brief banishment which his rivals had procured, neither his wisdom nor the lessons of adversity sufficed to make more maganimous than his predecessors, or to prevent him from treating those rivals and their party in the ordinary way, degrading many of their adherents from their position as *grandi* or nobles, and spreading havoc among all the opposing faction who held by the Albizzi against the Medici. The result was, as may be easily supposed, a large amount of private misery proudly borne and carefully concealed, that poverty of the gentle and proud which is of all others the most terrible. We have said that probably Antonino was not a man of genius at all; but we revoke the words, for what but the essence of Christian genius, fine instinct, tender penetration, could have first thought of the necessity of ministering to *i poveri vergognosi*, the shame-faced poor. Florence had misery enough of all kinds within her mediæval bosom, but none more dismal than that which lurked unseen within some of those gaunt, great houses, where the gently born and delicately bred starved, yet were ashamed to beg—each house bringing down with it in its fall, through all the various grades of rank which existed in the aristocratic republic, other households who could die but could not ask charity. The kind monk in his cell, separated from the world as we say, and having the miseries of his fellow-creatures in no way forced upon his observation, divined this sacredest want that uttered no groan, and in his wise soul found out the means of aiding it. He sent for twelve of the best men of Florence, men of all classes

—shoemakers among them, woolspinners, members of all the different crafts—and told them the subject of his thoughts. He described to them " to the life," as Padre Marchese tells us, the condition of the fallen families, the danger under which they lay of being turned to suicide or to wickedness by despair, and the necessity of bringing help to their hidden misery. The twelve, touched, to the heart by this picture, offered themselves willingly as his assistants; and thus arose an institution which still exists and flourishes, a charitable society which has outlived many a benevolent scheme, and given the first impulse to many more. Antonino called his charitable band *Providitori de poveri vergognosi ;* but the people, always ready to perceive and appreciate a great work of charity, conferred a popular title more handy and natural, and called those messengers of kindness the *Buonuomini di San Martino—* the little homely church of St. Martin, the church in which Dante was married, and within sight of which he was born, being the headquarters of the new brotherhood. on the outside wall of this humble little place may be seen the box for subscriptions, with its legend, which the Good Men of St. Martin put up at the beginning of their enterprise, a touching token of their long existence. The nearest parallel we know to this work is to be found in the plan which Dr. Chalmers so royally inaugurated in the town of Glasgow, abolishing all the legal relief in his parish, and providing for its wants entirely by voluntary neighborly charity, and the work of Buonuomini, like those of St. Martin—one of the most magnificent experiments made in modern times, but unfortunately, like a song or a poem, ending with the genius which inspired and produced it. It is curious to think that the Scotch minister of the nineteenth century was but repeating the idea of the Dominican monk in the fifteenth. We are in the habit of thinking a great deal of ourselves and our charities, and

of ranking them much more highly than the good works
of other nations; but it is nevertheless a fact, that while

THE BIGALLO.

Dr. Chalmers' splendid essay at Christian legislation died
out in less than a generation, and was totally dependent
upon one man's influence, Prior Antonino's institution has
survived the wear and tear of four hundred years.

There is another institution still existing in Florence to which Prior Antonino's influence was of the greatest importance, and exercised in a manner very unlike our modern Protestant idea of what a monk, and especially a Dominican, would do. Every visitor of Florence must have noticed the beautiful little building, at the corner of the piazza which surrounds the baptistery, which is called the Bigallo. This house was originally the headquarters of an older society specially devoted to the care of orphan children and foundlings, which had been diverted—perverted—into an orthodox band of persecutors for the suppression of the heresy of the Paterini, by another Dominican, St. Peter Martyr, a gory and terrible saint, whose bleeding head appears perpetually in the art records of the order. Antonino was not of the persecuting kind, and perhaps the Paterini, poor souls, had been extirpated and got rid of. However, that may be, the benevolent Prior got the captains of the Bigallo also within the range of his tender inspiration. He sheathed their swords, and calmed down their zeal, and turned them back to their legitimate work; and within the charmed circle which holds the baptistery, the Campanile and the cathedral, standing where Dante must have seen it many a day from the stone bench whence he watched the Duomo, the Bigallo still carries on its work of charity, bringing up orphans and receiving destitute children, with no longer any idea of warring against parties. This change, brought about entirely by the prior of San Marco, has almost more importance as a sign of character and Christian feeling than had it been a new institution established by his means; for indeed the Middle Ages were never grudging in their charities. Some of his rules for his special creation, the " Buonuomini," are very unlike our modern way of organizing charity. The money which was given them for their charitable use was to be spent at once: " He severely prohibited any accumulation, or that the funds should be put to interest or invested in any permanent way. The work inspired by Providence ought to live by Providence, and they were not to traffic in the charity of the faithful. . . . . He also severely prohibited any interference of public authority, whether civil or ecclesiastical, with the institution, to change its laws or regulate the use of its funds; and at the same time forbade the *Providitori* themselves to give an account of their private ministrations to any person whatsoever. New and

BROTHERS OF THE MISERICORDIA CARRYING A PATIENT.

bold idea, which gave to the pious work no other protection than the spotless honesty of the workers and the loving care of Providence!" In the fifteenth century, Padre Marchese assures us, the money dispensed by the society was as much as 14,000 gold florins a year, and in the past century amounted to 10,000 scudi—not perhaps a very large sum actually, but important when we consider the size of the city.

It may not be amiss at the same time to mention here another great charitable society, with which it is true the archbishop's name is not connected, but which is entirely in accord with the institutions he created and cherished, which the Florentines of to-day keep up with mediæval devotion, and which the stranger can scarcely pass through the streets without meeting in the exercise of its charitable functions. This is the brotherhood of the Misericordia, whose appearance in the Italian sunshine, veiled figures, black and mysterious, carrying the spectator back into the days of secret penance and expiation, must have struck every one who has visited Florence. This still active and numerous society was established in the thirteenth century by an honest porter, Pietro Borsi, who had the fine inspiration of at once reforming the vices and employing the idle moments of his brother porters, hanging on waiting for work in the Piazza of San Giovanni, by a most characteristic and appropriate charity. He persuaded them to fine each other for swearing, a mutual tax, half humorous, half pious, which pleased the rough fellows; then induced them to buy litters with the money thus collected, and to give, each in his turn, a cast of his trade to the service of the sick and wounded, carrying the victims of accident or disease to the hospitals, and the dead to their burial. In so warlike a city as Florence, amid all the disturbances of the thirteenth century, no doubt they had occupation enough, and this spontaneous good work, devised by the people for the people, marks one of the finest and most characteristic features of the charity of the Middle Ages. The institution grew, as might be expected, developing into greater formality and more extended operations, but always retaining the same object. There are no longer street frays in Florence to make the charitable succor of the Misericordia a thing of hourly necessity, and the litters are no longer carried by the rough, homely hands of laboring men snatching a moment for charity out of their hard day's labors. It is said that all classes up to the very highest, form part of the society nowadays; called by their bell when their services are wanted, in all the districts of the city, prince and artisan taking their turns alike, and it may be together, but with this modification—and with the one addition to its aims that the brothers often nurse as well as carry the sick—the porter's original undertaking is carried out with a firm faithfulness at once to tradition and to Christian charity. The dress is in reality no sign of mysterious shame and expiation, but merely a precaution against any trafficking on the part of the brethren in the gratitude of their patients, from whom they are allowed to received nothing more than a draught of water, the first and cheapest of necessities.

BALLOT BOX FOR MEMBERS OF THE MISERICORDIA.

In the year 1146, the Prior of San Marco was made archbishop of Florence. The delight with which the news of this choice was received by the people, who, after three strange archbishops, a Roman and two Paduans, at last were gratified by the selection of a countryman of their own, and one already popular and beloved, was not, however, shared by Fra Antonino himself. He first heard the news at Sienna, where he had just arrived in the course of one of his journeys as visitor-general of the reformed convents, and was so overwhelmed by it that his first idea was to take flight across the Maremma to the sea-coast, and there find means of transporting himself to the island of Sardinia, where the frightened monk imagined he might

lie concealed till Pope Eugenius, affronted or tired of waiting should fill up the post with some one else. Fortunately Antonino had a nephew who was not unwilling to
see his uncle archbishop of Florence, and who communicated his intention to Cosimo de' Medici and himself took
steps to prevent it, and led back the unwilling ecclesiastic
to Florence. The authorities of the city, entering eagerly
into the matter, wrote him a letter of lively remonstrance.
They reminded him that he had not come to such honor
by any evil means or by his own seeking, but as offered by
the vicar of Christ, and therefore by God himself, to the
public and universal satisfaction. "And what though a
tranquil and quiet life is more to your mind?" cried the
Gonfaloniere who acted as spokesman, "you ought to remember notwithstanding that we are not born for ourselves
alone, but that our country, our friends, our associates,
and even the whole human race have certain rights over
us." Prior Antonino could not resist such an appeal. He
came and submitted to receive the miter and all the necessary honors; but entered the cathedral for his consecration
barefooted and with tears in his eyes. When he took possession of his palace, a scene which must have been almost
comic in the consternation it caused, was enacted. He
broke up the great household, cut off all the luxury and
fine living that had been the rule, declared that nothing
was his but all belonged to the public, for whom it was his
duty to spend his time, his faculties and his life. He
threw himself into his work with ardor, setting himself to
reform the clergy, to institute schools of theology, and even
to write treatises with his own hand for the less instructed;
but charity was always and at all times his ruling passion.
His table became the larder and patrimony of the poor,
and those who surrounded him had almost to put force
upon him to prevent him from emptying his palace altogether and depriving himself even of necessaries.

A few years after his consecration, in the years 1448 and 1449, one of those great plagues which terrified the mediæval mind, and of which we have so many terrible records, came upon Florence; and what Boccaccio recorded a century before became again visible in the stricken city. Almost all who could leave the town fled from it, and the miserable masses smitten by the pestilence died without hope and almost without help. But we need not add, that the archbishop was not one of the deserters. He gathered round him some "young men of his institution," Padre Marchese tells us, and bravely set himself to the work of charity. He himself went about the miserable streets leading an ass, or mule, laden with everything that charity required—food and wine and medicine, and that sacramental symbol of God which was the best charity of all—*necessariis ad salutem animæ et corporis,* as an ancient writer testifies.

At a later period, when Florence was afflicted with a plague of another kind, the noble old man came to its rescue in a way still more original and unlike his age. The people, ignorant and superstitious as they were, had been deeply terrified by some unusual convulsion of the elements, the appearance of a comet for one thing, which was followed by earthquakes, terrific storms, and many signs and wonders very alarming to the popular mind. Besides these natural terrors, they were excited by foolish addresses, prophecies of the approaching end of the world, and exhortations to fly and hide themselves among the caves and mountains, like the lost in the Apocalypse. The archbishop was not before his age in scientific knowledge ; but he instantly published a little treatise, explaining, as well as he could, the nature of the commotions that frightened the ignorant, "according to the doctrine of Aristotle and the Blessed Albertus Magnus." It was poor science enough, the historian allows, but yet as good as could be had at the time; and the authority of the archbishop calmed the minds of the people. The reader will find, if he wishes, in the legend of Sant' Antonino, and in the pictorial story of his life which may be seen in the lunettes of the cloister of San Marco, a great number of incidents purely miraculous; but his biographer does not enter into

MONEY BOX OF BUONUOMINI DE SAN MARTINO.

these pious fancies, finding enough to vindicate the saint-ship of his archbishop in the honest and undeniable work for God and man which he did in his generation. There is but one incident in this noble and simple record in which the good Antonino was a little hard upon nature. The garden attached to the archbishop's palace was a beautiful and dainty one, in which former prelates had taken great delight, refreshing their dignified leisure in its glades. But an archbishop who takes his exercise in the streets, leading a pannicred mule laden with charities, has less need, perhaps, of trim terraces on which to saunter. Archbishop Antonino had the flowers dug up, and planted roots and vegetables for his poor, in respect to whom he was fanatical. One grudges the innocent flowers ; but the old man, I suppose, had a right to his whim like another, and bishops in that age were addicted sometimes to less virtuous fancies—ravaging the earth for spoil to enrich their families and to buy marbles for their tomb. It was better on the whole to ravage a garden, however beautiful, in order to feed the starving poor.

Antonino died in 1459, gliding peacefully out of the world "as morning whitened on the 2nd of May," when Girolamo Savonarola, coming into it, was just seven years old, a child in Ferrara. The good archbishop ordered that all that was found in his palace when he died should be given to the poor. All that could be found was four ducats, so true had he been to his vows of poverty. And thus the greatest dignitary of San Marco passed away, followed out of the world by the tears and blessings of the poor, and the semi-admiration of all the city. It is not difficult to understand how the perpetual appeals of the people, who knew him so well and had occasion so good to trust in his kindness, living, should have glided with natural ease and fervor into the *Ora pro nobis* of a popular litany, when the good archbishop took his gentle way to heaven, leaving four ducats behind him, on that May morning. The world was a terribly unsatisfactory world in those days, as it is now ; and full of evils more monstrous, more appalling, than are the sins of our softer generation; but at the same time, the gates of heaven were somehow nearer, and those rude eyes, bloodshot with wars and passion, could still see the saints so unlike themselves going in by that dazzling way.

CHAPTER IX.

III.—GIROLAMO SAVONAROLA : HIS PROBATION.

THERE could not well be a more remarkable contrast than between Archbishop Antonino, the good providence and charitable ministering angel of Florence—he, who, in his fervor of benevolence erected a great charitable institution specially for the aid of those whom Cosimo de' Medici had ruined, without, however, quarreling with Cosimo, or showing any horror of the state of public affairs which led to so much calamity—and the next prior of San Marco, the next great churchman visible to us over other men's heads in this crowded city. Though there is no name more closely associated with Florence, Girolamo Savonarola was not a Florentine. He was born in Ferrara, in September, 1452, the grandson of an eminent physican at the court of the duke, and intended by his parents to follow the same profession. He was one of a large family, not over rich, it would appear, and is said to have been the one on whom the hopes of his kindred were chiefly placed. And he was a diligent student, "working day and night"—as we are told by his earliest biographer Burlamacchi, his contemporary and disciple, whose simple and touching narrative has all the charm of nearness and personal affection—and attained great proficiency in the "liberal arts." Learned in the learning of his day, and in that philosophy of the schools which held so high a place in the estimation of the world—studying Aristotle, and afterward, with devotion, St. Thomas Aquinas—he

CRUCIFIXION: FRA ANGELICO, CHAPTER HOUSE, SAN MARCO.

251

had to all appearance a happy career before him, wealth
and honor and local celebrity. But he was not, unfortunately for himself, one of those who take without question
the good the gods provide. He was deeply thoughtful,
looking with eyes of profound and indignant observation
upon all the ways of man, so vain and melancholy. They
were, however, more than vain and melancholy in young
Girolamo's day ; the softer shades of modern evil were exaggerated in those times into such force of contrast as
made the heart of the beholder burn within him. On one
side, unbounded luxury, splendor and power ; on the other
the deepest misery, helplessness, abandonment—the poor
more poor, the rich more brutally indifferent of them than
we can understand ; and every familiar human crime with
which we are acquainted in these latter days set out in
rampant breadth of color and shameless openness. Italy
was the prey of petty tyrants and wicked priests; dukes
and popes vying with each other which could live most
lewdly, most lavishly, most cruelly—their whole existence
an *exploitation* of the helpless people they reigned over, or
still more helpless " flock " of which these wolves, alas,
had got the shepherding. And learning was naught, and
philosophy vain, in those evil days, notwithstanding that
the great Renaissance was already in full force, a period
lauded and celebrated to the echo, and which the historical
student scarcely dares to rate at its just moral value. But
what were grammatical disquisitions, or the subleties of
mediæval logic, or even the discussions of a Platonic society
to a young soul burning for virtue and truth, to a young
heart wrung with ineffable pity for suffering and horror of
wrong? So soon as Savonarola began to judge for himself,
to feel the stirrings of manhood in his youth, this
righteous sorrow took possession of his mind. His only
mode of expression at the time was the rough but
impassioned verse in which youth so often finds relief

for its confusion and multiplicity of thoughts; and some of his early poems show how deeply penetrated he was by indignation and disgust for all the evils he saw around him. "Seeing," he cries, "the world turned upside down :"

> " . . . . in wild confusion tost,
>   The very depth and essence lost
> Of all good ways and every virtue bright ;
>   Nor shines one living light,
> Nor one who of his vices feels the shame.

> " Happy henceforth he who by rapine lives,
>   He who on blood of others swells and feeds,
>   Who widows robs, and from his children's needs
> Takes tribute, and the poor to ruin drives.

> " Those souls shall now be thought most rare and good
>   Who most by fraud and force can gain,
>   Who heaven and Christ disdain,
> Whose thoughts on other's harm forever brood."

This profound appreciation of the evils around him made young Girolamo a sad and silent youth, an *animo sdegnoso* like the great poet who had gone before him. "He talked little and kept himself retired and solitary," says Burlamacchi. "He took pleasure," adds Padre Marchese, "in solitary places, in the open fields or along the green banks of the Po, and there wandering, sometimes singing, sometimes weeping, gave utterance to the strong emotions which boiled in his breast." The city raged or reveled behind him, its streets running blood or running wine—what mattered—according to the turn of fortune ; the doctors babbling in their places, of far-fetched questions, of dead grammatical lore ; and no man thinking of truth, of mercy, of judgment, with which the lad's bosom

was swelling, or of the need of them ; but only how to
get the most wealth, honor, pleasure, fine robes, and pranc-
ing horses, and beautiful things, and power.   Outside the
gates on the river side, the youth wandered solitary, tears
in those great eyes, which were *resplendenti, e di color
celeste*, his rugged features moving, his strong heart beating
with that high and noble indignation which was the only
sign of life amid the national depravity.   In the midst of
these deep musings there came a moment, the historians
say, when the music and the freshness of existence came
back to the boy's soul, and the gates of the earthly paradise
opened to him, and all the evil world was for a moment
veiled with fictitious glamour, by the light which shone out
of the eyes of a young Florentine, the daughter of an exiled
Strozzi.   How long this dream lasted, no one knows ; but
one of his early biographers informs us that it ended with
a scornful rejection of the young Savonarola, on the ground
that his family was not sufficiently exalted to mate with
that of Strozzi, one of the proudest and most powerful
houses in Florence.

After this little episode of happy delusion, when the
magical mist and glamour, which might have blinded him
temporarily at least to the evils around him, dispersed into
thin air, his darker musings came back with renewed
power.   He describes to his father, in the touching letter
which intimates his entrance into the cloister, the motives
which moved him, "in order that you may take comfort
from this explanation, and feel assured that I have not
acted from a juvenile impulse, as some seem to think."
These were: the "great misery of the world, the iniquities
of men, ... so that things have come to such a pass
that no one can be found acting righteously.   Many times
a day I have repeated with tears the verse,

"'Heu fuge crudeles terras, fuge littus avarum!'

I could not endure the enormous wickedness of the blinded people of Italy; and the more so because I saw everywhere virtue despised and vice honored. A greater sorrow I could not have in this world." Alone and solitary among people who did, and who put up with, all these evils, with no one to sympathize with his feelings, perhaps even scoffed at for his exaggerated views, he endured as long as it was possible, and while he was silent his heart burned. Disgusted with the world, disappointed in his personal hopes, weary of the perpetual wrong which he could not remedy, he had decided to adopt the monastic life for some time before his affectionate heart could resolve upon a separation from his family. "So great was my pain and misery," he says in the letter to his father already quoted, "that if I had laid open my breast to you, I verily believe that the very idea that I was going to leave you would have broken my heart." He relieved his burdened mind during this melancholy time by writing a little essay on "Disdain of the World," which he left behind with simple art, "behind the books that lie in the window-sill," to prove hereafter an explanation of his conduct. His mother, divining some resolution in him which he had not expressed, looked at him with such meaning and pitiful eyes, "as if she would penetrate his very heart," that the young man could not support her gaze. One April morning, as he sat by her playing a melancholy air upon his lute, she turned upon him suddenly and said, "My son, that is a sign we are soon to part." Girolamo durst not risk himself to look at her, but, with his head bent, kept fingering the strings with a faltering touch.

Next day was a great festa in Ferrara, the 24th of April, St. George's Day—one of the many holidays which stood instead of freedom and justice to conciliate the people. When all the family had left the house to share in those gay doings, which were brightened and made

sweet by the glorious spring of Italy, the young man stole
out unnoticed, and with a full heart left his father's house
forever. This was in the year 1475, when he was twenty-
three. He went away, lonely, across the sunny plain to
Bologna, where he presented himself at once at the Dominican convent. At this melancholy moment of his life,
sick as he was as well of the learned vanity as of the
louder crime of the world, he had no desire to be either
priest or monk. He asked only in his despair to be a lay
brother, to ease his soul with simple work in the garden,
or even, as Burlamacchi tells us, in making the rude robes
of the monks—rather than to go back all day long to
"vain questions and doctrines of Aristotle," in which
respect he said, there was little difference between the frati
and ordinary men. But presently his mind changed as the
lassitude which succeeds an important step brought down
his very soul into unquestioning obedience. It might indeed seem yet another commentary on the vanity of human wishes that the young monk, so tired of all mundane
things, and sick at heart for truth and contact with
nature, should have found himself thrown back again, as
soon as he had fairly taken refuge in his cloister, upon the
old miserable round of philosophy, as lecturer of his convent. He obeyed readily, we are told, when placed in this
post, a docility which good Burlamacchi takes as a sign of
grace in him—but who can tell with what struggles of the
reluctant heart, and how deep a pang of that disappointment which so often attends the completion of a long
maturing resolve? Soon after he wrote the letter to his
father which I have quoted—a letter full of the tender
sophistry which disobedient yet affectionate children so
constantly employ to blunt the edge of parental disap-
probation, and in which the question of duty is begged
with many a loving artifice, and heart-broken beseechings
brought in instead of argument. "Do you not think that

it is a very high mark of favor to have a son a soldier in
the army of Jesus Christ ?" . . . " If you love me, seeing
that I am composed of two parts, of soul and body, say
which of them you love most, the body or the soul. . . .
If, then, you love the soul most, why not look to the good
of that soul?" Such pleas have been repeated from the
beginning of the world, I suppose, and will be to its end,
whenever a good and loving child obeys a personal impulse
which is contrary to filial duty, but not to filial tenderness.
" Never since I was born did I suffer so great mental
anguish as when I felt that I was about to leave my own
flesh and blood and go among people who were strangers
to me," adds the young man. But the sacrifice had then
been accomplished, and for years thereafter the young
Savonarola, now Fra Girolamo, had to content himself
with "the Aristotle of the cloister instead of the Aristotle
of the world," and to go on with what he felt to be dry
and useless studies, making what attempt he could to
separate from them "all vain questions, and to bring them
back as much as he could to Christian simplicity," while
yet his heart burned within him, and wickedness un-
warned and wrong unredressed were rampant in the
outside world.

Perhaps, indeed, the first effect of this desperate resolution of his, this plunge into the church by way of escaping from the world, was to convince the young man of
the corruption of the church in a way more sharp and
heartfelt than before. No doubt it directed him to look
with eyes more critical and enlightened upon those ecclesiastical powers who were now the officers of his own army,
and more distinctly within his range of vision ; and with a
pope such as Sixtus IV., and many inferior prelates
worthy of their head, it is not to be wondered at if the
bitter wrath and sorrow of the young reformer blazed
higher and clearer still. As he had written in " De Ruina

Mundi " (in the verses which we have already quoted) his
horror of the sins of the world, so in " De Ruina Ecclesia."
which now followed, he laments the sins of the church.
He sees the true church herself in a vision, and hears from
her that her place has been invaded by a shameless creature
—*una fallace superba meretrice.* " With eyes that are
never dry, with head bowed down, and sad soul," the
" ancient mother " complains to him :

> " She took my hand, and thus with weeping, led
> To her poor cave, and said—
> ' When into Rome I saw that proud one pass
> Who mid soft flowers and grass
> Securely moves, I shut me up and here
> Lead my sad life with many a tear.' "

The wondering spectator listens, and sees her bosom torn
with a thousand wounds, and hears enough " to make
stones weep " of the usurpation of the harlot. Then his
whole soul breaks forth in a cry, " Oh God, lady ! that I
could break these great wings !' What utterance was ever
more characteristic of the future purpose of a beginning
life? Though the *antica madre* bids him rather be silent
than weep, the thought of breaking those *grandi ali*, and
striking a blow at the thousand corruptions which disgraced
Christendom, never abandoned the thoughts of the young
Dominican. He had to be silent perforce for years, and to
teach the novices, and lecture upon philosophy, as if there
was no greater evil in the world than a defective syllogism ;
but the great discontent in his mind never ceased to smolder
until the hour of conflagration came.

Even, however, out of these undesired studies, Savonarola's active intelligence—which seems to have been
restored to the steadiness of common life, and to that
necessity of making the best of a lot, now unalterable,
which so often follows a decisive step--appears to have
made something useful and honorable. He wrote a

compendium of philosophy, "an epitome of all the writings, various as they are, of the Stagyrite," a work which, according to Padre Marchese, "might have acted as a stepping-stone to the "Novum Organum." Another treatise of a similar character he had begun upon Plato, the study of whose works had been much promoted in Italy by the learned Greeks who were so highly thought of in many of its intellectual centers, but this Savonarola himself tells us he destroyed. "What good is there in so much wisdom, when now every old woman knows more?" he asks with characteristic simplicity. Such were his occupations during the seven years which he passed in Bologna, a time of quiet, of rest in some respects from the chaos of youthful fancies, and of distasteful but bravely surmounted work. His convent seems to have acted upon the sorrowful young dreamer as sharp contact with actual life so often acts upon visionary youth. It forced him to take up his burden and labor at common things in the long interval of waiting before the real mission of his life came to him. Monastic writers throw a certain ecclesiastical romanticism over this natural result, by distinguishing it as the fruit of monastic obedience, the new soul of the cloister ; but the same thing appears in almost all noble and strong natures when life in its real aspect is accepted, not as a matter of fancy and choice, but of unalterable necessity and duty. There was no particular value in the logic which Fra Girolamo taught the young Dominicans ; but there was efficacy inestimable in that sense of certainty and life established which led him to do the work which lay at his hand, and accept it, though it was not that which pleased him best.

After some years of this obscure work he came to Florence, the scene to which his historical existence belongs. Professor Villari informs us, though without giving any authority, that the young monk came to his

new home with hopeful and happy anticipatious, pleased
with the fair country, the purer language, the higher
civilization of the people, and with the saintly associations
which the blessed Antonino had left so fresh and fragrant.
It is easy indeed to believe that after toiling across the
rugged Apennines, when the Dominican, still young and
full of natural fervor, came suddenly out from among the
folds of the hills upon that glorious landscape ; when he
saw the beautiful vision of Florence, seated in the rich
garden of her valley, with flowers and olive-trees, and
everything that is beautiful in nature, encircling that
proud combination of everthing that is noble in art ;
his heart must have risen at the sight, and some dilation
of the soul, some sense of coming greatness have been
permitted to him, in face of the fate he was to accomplish
there.

The state of Florence at this period was very remarkable.
The most independent and tumultuous of towns was spell-
bound under the sway of Lorenzo de' Medici, the grandson
of the Cosimo who built San Marco; and scarcely seemed
even to recollect its freedom, so absorbed was it in the
present advantages conferred by "a strong government,"
and solaced by shows, entertainments, festivals, pomp, and
display of all kinds. It was the very height of that classic
revival so famous in the later history of the world, and the
higher classes of society, having shaken themselves apart
with graceful contempt from the lower, had begun to frame
their lives according to a pagan model, leaving the other
and much bigger half of the world to pursue *its* super-
stitions undisturbed. Florence was as near a pagan city
as it was possible for its rulers to make it. Its intellectual
existence was entirely given up to the past; its days were
spent in that worship of antiquity which has no power of
discrimination, and deifies not only the wisdom but the
trivialities of its golden epoch. Lorenzo reigned in the

midst of a lettered crowd of classic parasites and flatterers, writing poems which his courtiers found better than Alighieri's, and surrounding himself with those eloquent

LORENZO DE' MEDICI.

slaves who make a prince's name more famous than arms or victories, and who have still left a prejudice in the minds of all literature-loving people in favor of their patron. A man of superb health and physical power, who can give himself up to debauch all night without interfering with his power of working all day, and whose mind is so versatile that he can sack a town one morning and discourse upon the beauties of Plato the next, and weave joyous ballads through both occupations—gives his flatterers reason when they applaud him. The few righteous men in the city, the citizens who still thought of Florence above all, kept apart, overwhelmed by the tide which ran in favor of that leading citizen of Florence who had gained the control of the once high-spirited and freedom-loving people. Society had never been more dissolute, more selfish, or more utterly deprived of any higher aim. Barren scholarship, busy over grammatical questions, and elegant philosophy snipping and piercing its logical systems, formed the top dressing to that half-brutal, half-superstitious ignorance which in such communities is the general portion of the poor. The *dilettante* world dreamed hazily of a restoration of the worship of the pagan gods; Cardinal Bembo bade his friend beware of reading St. Paul's epistles, lest their barbarous style should corrupt his taste; and even such a man as Pico della Mirandola declared the "Divina Commedia" to be inferior to the "Canti Carnascialeschi" of Lorenzo de' Medici. This extraordinary failure of taste itself, in a period which stood upon its fine taste as one of its highest qualities, is curious, but far from being without parallel in the history of the civilized world. Not so very long ago, indeed, among ourselves, in another age of classic revival, sometimes called Augustan, Pope was supposed a much greater poet than Shakespeare, and much inferior names to that of Pope were ranked as equal with, or superior to, our prince of poets. The whole mental firmament must have contracted about the heads of a people among whom such verdicts are possible; but one great distinction of such a time is its own strongly held opinion that nothing has ever been so clever, so great, so elevated as itself.

Thus limited intellectually, the age of Lorenzo was still more hopeless morally, full of debauchery, cruelty and corruption, violating oaths, betraying trusts, believing in nothing but Greek manuscripts, coins, and statues, caring for nothing but pleasure. This was the world in which Savonarola found himself when, waking from his first pleasurable impressions, he looked forth from the narrow windows of San Marco, by the side of which Angelico's angel faces stood watching the thoughts that arose in his mind. Those thoughts were not of a mirthful kind. Fair Florence lying in bonds, or rather dancing in them, with smear of blood upon her garments and loathsome song upon her lips; and the church, yet more fair, groaning under the domination of one evil pope, looking forward to a worse monster still—for the reign of the Borgias, culmination of all wickedness, was approaching—became apparent to him as he gazed; and who can wonder if visions of gloom crossed the brain of the young lecturer in San Marco, howsoever he might try to stupefy and silence them by his daily work and the subtleties of Aristotle and Aquinas? A sense of approaching judgment, terror and punishment, the vengeance of God against a world full of iniquity, darkened the very air around him. He was not then a great preacher; but yet was sent out like the others to preach in the towns and villages about at penitential seasons; and even at this early period could not keep from uttering the burden of prophecy which already filled his soul. Wherever he was allowed to speak, in Brescia, in San Geminiano, the flood poured forth, and in spite of himself he thundered from the pulpit a thousand woes against the wicked with intense and alarming effect. But when he endeavored to speak in lettered Florence herself, no one took any trouble to listen to the Lombard monk, whose accent was harsh, and his periods not daintily formed, and who went against all the unities, so to speak, as Shakespeare once, when England was in a similar state of refinement, was held to do. In San Lorenzo, where Savonarola first preached, there were not twenty-five people, all counted, to hear him; but San Geminiano among the hills, when it heard that same voice amid the glooms of Lent, thought nothing of the Lombard accent, and trembled at the prophetic woe denounced against sin; and in Brescia the hearers grew pale, and paler still years after, when the preacher's words seemed verified. Woe, woe, he preached in these Lent seasons; woe—but also restoration and the blessing of God if men would turn from their sins. Between the utterances of his full heart and glowing soul, Fra Girolamo came back to teach his novices in the dead quiet of San Marco—not preacher enough to please the Florentines, who loved fine periods—and lectured in the cool of the cloister or in some quiet room, as if there had been nothing but syllogisms and the abstractions of metaphysics in the world. It is apparent, however, that Florence had seized upon his affections with all the vehemence of a passion. Though the city gave him no friendly reception, he loved her, as so many have done who were not born her natural children. He relinquished his own city and all the associations of his earlier life, and " clave " to his new dwelling place as a man is bidden in scripture to cleave to the partner of his life. It was natural to his vehement soul, when once it had thus made its choice, to find in the object of that choice the very queen of cities, the center of the world, a kind of Jerusalem, typical and exalted; and such was the light in which the city appeared to Savonarola from the moment in which he cast in his lot with her, and adopted her fate and fortunes as his own.

The crisis in his life occurred when, probably on one of

his preaching tours, he attended the Dominican chapter at
Reggio, and was there seen and heard by a genial, gentle
young courtier, Giovanni Pico della Mirandola, one of
Lorenzo's most affectionate flatterers and friends. This
court butterfly was the most learned creature that ever
fluttered near a prince, but full of amiable sentiments and
tender-heartedness, and the kindly insight of an unspoiled
heart. He saw the frate of San Marco among the other
Dominicans, his remarkable face intent upon the delibera-
tions of the Council; and heard him speak with such
power and force of utterance that the whole audience was
moved. Probably something more than this, some personal contact, some kindly gleam from those resplendent
blue eyes that shone from underneath Fra Girolamo's
cavernous brow, some touch of that *urbanitá*, *humile*,
ornato e grazioso, upon which Burlamacchi insists, went
to the heart of the young Pico, himself a noble young
gentleman amid all his frippery of courtier and virtuoso.
He was so seized upon and captured by the personal attractions of Savonarola, that he gave Lorenzo no peace until he
had caused him to be authoritatively recalled from his
wanderings and brought back permanently to Florence.
Young Pico felt that he could not live without the teacher
whom he had thus suddenly discovered, and Lorenzo,
unwitting, at his friend's request, ordered back into Florence the only man who dared stand face to face with himself, and tell him he had done wrong. Savonarola came
back perhaps not very willingly, and betook himself once
more to his novices and his philosophy. But he had by
this time learned to leaven his philosophy with lessons
more important, and to bring in the teachings of a greater
than Aristotle, taking the Bible which he loved, and
which, it is said, he had learned by heart, more and more
for his text-book; and lanching forth into a wider sea of
remark and discussion as day followed day, and his mind
expanded and his system grew.

We are not told whether Pico, when his beloved friar
came back, made Fra Girolamo's teaching fashionable in
Florence ; but no doubt he had his share in indicating to
the curious the new genius which had risen up in their
midst.   And as the frate lectured to the boy-Dominicans,
discoursing of everything in heaven and earth with full

CORRIDOR IN SAN MARCO.

heart and inspired countenance, there grew gradually
about him a larger audience, gathering behind the young
heads of that handful of convent lads, an ever-widening
circle of weightier listeners—men of Florence, one bringing another to hear a man who spoke with authority, and
had, if not pretty periods to please their ears, something
to tell them—greatest of all attractions to the ever-curious
soul of man.

It was summer, and Fra Girolamo sat in the cloister, in the open square, which was the monks' garden, "*sotto un rosajo di rose damaschine;* a rose-tree of damask roses. Never was there a more touching, tender incongruity than that perfumed canopy of bloom over the dark head covered with its cowl. Beneath the blue sky that hung over Florence, within the white square of the cloister with all its arching pillars, with Angelico's Dominic close by, kneeling at the cross-foot, and listening too—this crowd of Florentines gathered in the grassy inclosure encircling the scholars and their master. A painter could not desire a more striking scene. The roses waving softly in the summer air above, and the lads in their white convent gowns, with earnest faces lifted to the speaker—what a tender central light do they give, soft heart of flowers and youth, to the grave scene! For grave as life and death were the speaker and the men that stood around and pressed him on every side. Before long he had to consent, which he did with reluctance, to leave this quiet cloister and return to the pulpit where once his Lombard accent had brought him nothing but contempt and failure. Thus the first chapter of Fra Girolamo's history ends, under the damask rose-tree in the warm July weather, within those white cloisters of San Marco. In the full eye of day, in the pulpit and the public places of Florence, as prophet, spiritual ruler, apostle among men, was the next period of his life to be passed. Here his probation ends.

CHAPTER X.

IV.—GIROLAMO SAVONAROLA—THE PREACHER.

It was in compliance with the entreaties of the laymen who crowded his cloister, almost displacing his novices, that Fra Girolamo consented to preach in the convent church, a larger place, where greater numbers might find room. After some delay, "smiling" upon his petitioners "with a cheerful countenance," he told them that on the next Sunday he would read in the church, lecture and preach; adding, Burlamacchi tells us, "And I shall preach for eight years;" which afterward came true.

It was on the 1st of August, 1489, that this event took place. The church was so crowded, the same authority tells us, "that there scarcely remained any room for the frati, who, in their eager desire to hear, were obliged to find places on the wall of the choir, and were so determined not to lose the lecture, that scarcely any remained in the offices of the community, and door and sacristy were alike deserted. Of the laymen present, most stood all the time, and some, laying hold of the iron railings, hung from them as well as they could, in their great desire to hear." He preached upon a passage in the Revelation. "Three things he suggested to the people. That the church of God required renewal, and that immediately ; second that all Italy should be chastised ; third, that this should come to pass soon." This was the very beginning of his prophetic utterances in Florence, and immense though his popularity was, " great contradictions," as Burlamacchi says, at once

arose in respect to him, some thinking him thoroughly
sincere and true, some that though learned and good he
was crafty, and some, that he gave himself up to foolish
visions; for in this first sermon, amid much that was drawn
from the Scriptures, he mixed up the particular revelations
which he firmly believed were made to himself—a circumstance not so astonishing in the fifteenth century as it
would be now, but yet exciting the contempt of many in
that lettered and elegant age. The excitement thus
produced was very great. The Florentines were totally
unused to the fervent natural eloquence of a preacher who
rejected all traditions of oratory, and, careless of fine style
or graceful diction, poured forth what was in him in floods
of fiery words, carried away by his own earnestness and
warmth of feeling. To see a man thus inspired by his
subject, possessed by what he has to say, too much in
earnest to choose his phrases or think of anything—taste,
literature, style, or reputation—except that truth which he
is bound to tell his auditors, and which to them and to him
is a matter of life and death : this is at all times a wonderful and impressive spectacle. No simulation can attain
the same effect : the fervor may be vulgar, it may be
associated with narrow views and a limited mind ; but
wherever it exists, in great or small, in learned or unlearned,
the man possessed by it has a power over his fellow-men
which nothing else can equal. Savonarola was neither
vulgar nor limited in mind, and his whole soul was intensely
practical, concentrated upon the real evils around him,
diverted into no generalities or speculations, not even
diffused abroad upon the world and mankind in general,
but riveted upon Florence in particular, upon the sins,
strifes, frauds, and violences which made the city weak and
put her down from her high estate. She was enslaved, she,
once the freest of the free; and Savonarola was burning
with that almost extravagant love of civic freedom which

distinguished the Italian republics. She was corrupt, and the man who loved her like a mistress could not support the sense of her impurity. It shamed him and wrung his heart, as if indeed this chosen city of his affections had been a woman whom he adored. So intense, so personal, were Savonarola's sentiments that this image is not too strong to express them. He carried the passionate fervor with which a brother, a father, might struggle to reclaim a lost creature very dear to him, into his relations with the city which, now finally awakened to see what manner of man was in her midst, watched him curiously, and by degrees suffered herself to be drawn into ever more eager attention to the frate, whose power and genius she had at length discovered. Burlamacchi informs us, in his simple narrative, that the effect produced upon those who heard him, by his *parlare veloce e infiammativo*, was that of a miracle. "The grace of God appeared," he says, " in the lofty words and profound thoughts which he gave forth with a clear voice and rapid tongue, so that every one understood him. And it was admirable to see his glowing countenance and fervent and reverent aspect when he preached, and his beautiful and appropriate gestures, which rapt the very soul of every one who heard him, so that wonders and amazing appearances were seen by many while he was in the act of preaching." These wonders were such as the devout imagination fondly attaches to all popular apostles. Some believed they saw an angel on each side of him as he preached. Some saw the Madonna in glory, blessing him with fair, uplifted hand, when he blessed the worshipers around. But the real effect of his sermons was great enough to enable his followers to dispense with miraculous adjuncts. It does not appear, nor is it probable that Savonarola preached, as is our English custom, on every Sunday, or regularly from week to week, but according to the wise practice of his church, occasionally,

and in the seasons appropriated to special spiritual exercise.
By the Lent of 1491 San Marco had become too small for
the crowds that came to hear him, and he removed to the
Duomo, where he remained during the rest of the eight

SAVONAROLA: FROM THE (RECENT) BUST IN SAN MARCO.

years which was the limit, as it is said he prophesied it
would be, of his mission to Florence and the world.

Few buildings could be more appropriate to receive a
preacher so impassioned and listeners so intent. The
cathedral of Florence has not the wealth, the splendor,
nor the daylight of the great St. Peter's of which Michael

Angelo said that it should be the sister—"*piu grande, ma non piu bella*"—of Santa Maria del Fiore. It has nothing of the soaring grace and spiritual beauty of our northern Gothic. It is dark, majestic, mystical—a little light coming in through the painted windows, which are gorgeous in their deep color, not silvery, like the old jewel-glass of the north. The vast area is bare and naked in a certain superb poverty, fit to be filled with a silent, somewhat stern Italian crowd, with a mass of characteristic Tuscan faces—vigorous, harsh, seldom beautiful. One can imagine the great voice, *veloce e infiammativo*—lighting up a glow of passionate feeling in all those responsive gleaming eyes—coming out of the dark circle under the dome, and resounding over the heads of the crowd which filled the nave. No scene could suit better the large bare nobleness of the place. Before he came to the cathedral the preacher had so far advanced in boldness, and in the certainty of that burden of woe which he had to deliver, that still greater and greater "contradictions" had risen up against him. "When he thought of this," says Burlamacchi, "he was sometimes afraid, and in his own mind resolved not to preach of such things. But everything else that he read and studied became odious to him." Before Septuagesima Sunday in the first Lenten season in which he preached in the cathedral, he seems to have made a distinct pause of alarm, and a serious effort to change the entire form, style, and argument of his preaching. "God is my witness," says Savonarola himself, "that the whole of Saturday and the succeeding night I lay awake thinking, but could not turn myself, so completely was my path closed to me, and every idea taken away except this. In the morning (being weary with long watching) I heard this said, 'Fool, dost thou not see that it is God's will thou shouldst preach thus?' And so that morning I preached a tremendous sermon." Burlamacchi speaks of this same sermon as *mirabile e stupenda.* The flood which the preacher had attempted thus to restrain broke forth with fiercer force than ever. And even the very tumults that rose against him, the *grandissima contraditione,* no doubt excited and stimulated his hearers. Burlamacchi's description of the crowds who came to hear him sets the strange scene very distinctly before us:

" The people got up in the middle of the night to get places for the sermon, and came to the door of the cathedral, waiting outside till it should be opened, making no account of any inconvenience, neither of the cold, nor the wind, nor of standing in winter with their feet on the marble ; and among them were young and old, women and children of every sort, who came with such jubilee and rejoicing that it was bewildering to hear them, going to the sermon as to a wedding. Then the silence was great in the church, each one going to his place: and he who could read, with a taper in his hand, read the service, and other prayers. And though many thousand people were thus collected together, no sound was to be heard, not even a ' hush,' until the arrival of the children, who sang hymns with so much sweetness that heaven seemed to have opened. Thus they waited three or four hours till the padre entered the pulpit. And the attention of so great a mass of people all with eyes and ears intent upon the preacher, was wonderful : they listened so, that when the sermon reached its end it seemed to them that it had scarcely begun."

In the midst of this crowd were many notable persons, little likely to be led away by the common craze after a popular preacher ; men whose hearts ached to think of the loss of their ancient liberties as Florentines, and who instinctively felt that they had found in this brave frate and his passionate grief over surrounding evils, an ally and spokesman beyond their hopes ; men who, trained in Lorenzo's court to an admiration of intellectual power, could not but perceive its presence in the cowled Dominican; and men voiceless by nature, whose righteous souls were sick and sad at the daily sight of the corruption round

them.   One of these latter was Prospero Pitti, canon of the
cathedral, a wise and pious old man, of whom Burlamacchi
tells us that he too for years had borne his homely testimony
against the evils of the time, prophesying as so many a
humble prophet does in evil days, that the vengeance of
God must soon overtake the crimes and vices that were
visibly rising to a climax before his eyes.   This old canon
was one of those who cherished the beautiful imagination
so long current in those ages, and fondly transmitted from
one generation to another, of the Papa Angelico, the
heavenly-minded pope, true vicar of Christ, who was one
day to come, and revive and renew the Christian world,
convert the infidel, and make the church glorious as when
her Divine Founder planted her on earth.   Among the
wide and general prophecies of vague vengeance for sin
and vindication of the righteous in which this old priest
had relieved his soul was one, more particular, of many
preachers to be sent forth by God to sound trumpets of
warning to the sinful, and especially among them of a
prophet who should arise in the order of the Predicatori,
" who should do great things in Florence, and who after
much labor should die there."   When the old canon suddenly heard a voice rise in his own cathedral, " intoning,"
with prophetic force, *gladius Domini super terram cito et
velociter*, he bent his head between his hands, and after an
interval, turning to his nephew, Carlo Pitti, who was at
his side : " This," said he, " is that holy prophet of whom
I have talked to you for ten years."   Nor was Canon Pitti
the only " devout person " who had note from heaven of
the coming of the preacher.   Another noble citizen of
Florence passing through the Via di Servii in company
with some of his friends, one morning in the year 1487,
before Savonarola had been recalled to Florence, felt himself plucked by the mantle by a stranger absolutely unknown to him, and whom he never saw again, who drew

him within a neighboring church, and there revealed to
him as was done to the woman of Samaria "all things that
ever he did;" finishing with the news that by the intercession of the Virgin a certain Fra Girolamo of Ferrara
was coming to Florence to save the city from the destruction due to her sins. This, and much more, Burlamacchi
relates, with primitive simplicity and faith; and no doubt
such tales flew about the streets, and added to the general
interest in the preacher, and to the excitement with which
his glowing discourses were received.

These discourses were but little philosophical, notwithstanding the fact that Savonarola seems to have been one
of the first, if not the very first, who took in hand to de-
monstrate the reality and power of Christianity by the light
of natural reason, leaving revelation and spiritual authority
aside—a serious undertaking for a man who himself saw
visions and received revelations; but proving—a doctrine
which is strange to the common mind—the compatibility
of a certain noble good sense and philosophical power with
those gifts of enthusiasm and lofty imagination which
carry the inspired soul beyond the limits of the seen and
tangible. Nothing is more real than this conjunction, yet
nothing is more generally wondered at or more frequently
denied. His sermons, moreover, were profoundly practical : the personal appeal of a man full of indignation, sorrow, and love, to the faulty, the cruel, the arrogant and
selfish, who, notwithstanding all these evil qualities, were
still men, capable of repentance, of goodness, blessedness
heaven itself, could but their hearts be moved and their
minds enlightened. Our space forbids us to quote at any
length; and the addresses of an orator, aided by all the power
of sympathetic voice, gesture, and look, can rarely bear
the ordeal of print, much less of translation. But his
denunciations of avarice, usury, and rampant worldliness
are as strenuous and impassioned as his exhortations to

prayer and the study of the Bible are touching and beautiful. Many efforts have been made to prove by his subordination of rites and ceremonies to spiritual truth and
sincerity, by his elevated spiritual appreciation of
the love of Christ, of faith in Him, and of the supreme
authority of Scripture, that Savonarola was an early Luther
an undeveloped reformer, an unconscious Protestant.
But he was a Protestant only so far as every man is who
protests against evil and clings to the good—no other dissent was in his mind. Wherever he saw it he hated evil
with a vigor and passion such as our weakened faculties
seem scarcely capable of ; but Savonarola's Protestantism
ended there, where it began. We cannot refrain from
quoting one beautiful passage on the nature of prayer,
which shows the profound spiritual sensibility and insight
of the man:

" He who prays to God ought to address Him as if He were present;
for He is everywhere, in every place, in every man, and especially in
the souls of the just. Seek Him not therefore on the earth, or in
heaven, or elsewhere—seek for Him in your own hearts; do as did the
prophet who says, 'I will hear what God the Lord will speak.' In
prayer, a man may be attending to the words, and this is a thing of a
wholly material nature; he may be attending to the sense of the
words, and this is rather study than prayer; and, lastly, his whole
thoughts may be directed to God, and this alone is true prayer. It is
unnecessary to be considering either sentences or language—the mind
must be elevated above self, and must be wholly absorbed in the
thought of God. Arrived at this state, the true believer forgets the
world and its wants; he has attained almost a foreshadow of celestial
happiness. To this state of elevation the ignorant may arrive as easily
as the learned. It even frequently happens, that he who repeats a
psalm without understanding its words utters a much more holy
prayer than the learned man who can explain its meaning. Words in
fact are not indispensable to an act of prayer: when a man is truly
rapt in the spirit, an uttered prayer becomes rather an impediment,
and ought to yield to that which is wholly mental. Thus it will be
seen how great a mistake those commit who prescribe a fixed number

of prayers. God does not delight in a multitude of words, but in a
fervent spirit."

These, however, were the gentler breathings of the
apostle. Not such was the "*predica molto spaventosa*" the
"*mirabile e stupenda predica*" with which he opened his
ministrations in the Duomo—announcing the sword of the
Lord which was to smite the earth—to the great emotion
and fear of the people who heard and believed, and to the
raising of ever greater and greater "*contradizioni*" among
those who resisted his influence. There was even, we are
told, talk in the Medicien household in the Palazzo Riccardi
of sending him away from Florence. "We shall do to this
Fra Girolamo as we did to Fra Bernardino," cried the courtiers, referring to a Franciscan of great zeal and worth, who
had been driven out of Florence in consequence of the
warmth of his exhortations against usury, and his endeavors (successfully carried out by Savonarola) to found a
Monte della Pietà, or public institution for giving on the
most merciful terms temporary loans to the poor. A letter
of Savonarola's, written about this time to his dear friend
Fra Domenico of Pescia, who was absent on a preaching
expedition, shows the state of tumult, yet hopefulness, in
which the prophet and his convent were.

"Dearest brother in Christ Jesus, peace and joy in the Holy Spirit.
Our affairs go on well; indeed, God has worked marvelously, so that
to the highest point we suffer great opposition; of which when you
come back you shall have all the details, which it is not necessary to
write. Many have doubted, and still doubt, whether that will not be
done to me which was done to Fra Bernardino. Certainly, as to that
our affairs are not without danger; but I always hope in God, knowing,
as says Scripture, that the heart of kings is in the hand of the Lord,
and that when He pleases He can turn them. I hope in the Lord,
who by our mouth does much; for every day He consoles me, and
when I have little heart, comforts me by the voices of His Spirt,
which often say to me: Fear not, say certainly that with which God
has inspired thee; for the Lord is with thee: the scribes and Pharisees

struggle against thee, but shall not overcome. Be comforted then,
and be joyful; for our work goes on well. Do not be troubled if few
come to the sermon in that other city; it is enough to have said these
things to a few—in a little seed there is virtue hidden. I very often
preach the renovation of the church and the troubles which are to
come, not of myself, but always with a foundation on the Holy Scriptures, so that none can find fault, except those whose will is not to
live righteously. . . . . All are well, especially our angels, who
wish to be remembered to you. Keep well, and pray for me. I wait
your return with great eagerness, that I may tell you the wonderful
things of the Lord. From Florence, the 10th of March, 1490."*

The brother to whom this letter was addressed, in the
midst of commotions, alarm, and hopefulness, was the same
brother Domenico, his faithful companion and follower,
who afterward died with him; and few things could be
more touching than this glimpse into the convent and the
tender mention of *i nostri angioli*, the novices whom the
brethren loved, and in whom their hearts found a natural
escape from the straitness of monastic life. These lads no
doubt, in their white angelical dresses, were Fra Girolamo's
pupils still, notwithstanding the greater labors on which
he had entered. Their cells even now, all open and
empty, stand with pathetic significance under the guardian-
ship of that little chamber in which Savonarola lived and
labored, watching over his "Giovanati," his "Angioli,"
the youths in whom his tender soul found children to
love.

While the work of the prophet thus began, the best days
of Lorenzo were passing but too rapidly. Peace was in
Florence, while all Italy was in commotion, a phenomenon
which is periodically apparent among these mediæval
Italian cities whenever prince or despot was wise enough or
strong enough to hold the balance among his less astute
contemporaries, and secure tranquillity for his own state by

---

* This ought to be 1491, as it was then the custom to date the year
not from January as we do, but from the 25th of March.

judicious manipulation of the others. Lorenzo had secured entire control over the community which still called itself a republic, and before this time had settled into that superb indifference to all that might come after him which was the very soul of his philosophy as it was the inspiration of his verse.

"The Magnifico," says Padre Marchese, who is no lover of the Medici, "called to him, from every part of Italy, men of genius, writers and artists of reputation, in order by their works to distract all strong and noble intelligences from thoughts of the country. So had Pericles done, and Augustus. . . . Poets of every kind, gentle and simple, with golden cithern and with rustic lute, came from every quarter, to animate the suppers of the Magnifico; whosoever sang of arms, of love of saints, of fools, was welcome, or he who drinking and joking kept the company amused. First among them were Politanio Luigi, and Luca Pulci, Bienivieni, Matteo Franco, and the gay genius of Burchiello. This troop of parasites went and came, now at the villa ot Careggi, now at Poggia Cajano, now at Fiesole, now at Cafaggiolio. Lorenzo, ready for everything, now discussed with Argiropolo, the doctrines ot Aristotle, now with Ficino discoursed upon Platonic love, or read the poem of the "Altercazione;" with Politian recited some Latin elegy, or the verses of his own "Selva di Amore;" with the brothers Pulci the "Nencia da Barberino;" and when Burchiello arrived, laid aside his gravity, and drinking and singing, recited a chapter of the "Beoni," or of the "Mantellaccio," or some of his own Carnival songs. Sometimes a select band of painters and sculptors collected in his garden near San Marco, or under the loggia of the palace in the Via Larga designing, modeling, painting, copying the Greek statutes, and the *torsi* and busts found in Rome, ot elsewhere in Italy. . . . . And in order that the Florentine people might not be excluded from this new beatitude (a thing which was important to the Magnifico), he composed and set in order many mythological representations, triumphal cars, dances, and every kind of festal celebration, to solace and delight them; and thus he succeeded in banishing from their souls any recollection of their ancient greatness, in making them insensible to the ills of the country, in disfranchising and debasing them by means of temporal ease and intoxication of the senses. . . . . Of all these feasts and masquerades Lorenzo was the inventor and master; his great wealth aiding him in his undertakings. In the darkening of twilight it was his custom to issue forth into the city to amuse himself, with incredible pomp, and a great retinue on horse and on foot, more than five hundred in number, with concerts of musical instruments, singing in many voices, all sorts of canzones, madrigals, and popular songs. . . . . When the night fell, four hundred servants with lighted torches followed, and lighted this baccahanalian procession. . . . . In the midst of these orgies a handful of foolish youths were educated and grew up, who made open profession of infidelity and lewdness, and laying aside all shame, gave themselves up to every kind of wickedness, emulating each other in the depths of naughtiness to which they could attain. The people, with their usual sense of what is appropriate, called them the Compagnacci."

This was the aspect of Florence in the days when Savonarola began his reform. False culture, false gayety, filled the city; art flourished, being encouraged and patronized on every hand: and from the Magnifico, whose power was so great and whose life was so splendid, but all at the mercy of Fate, and ready to perish in a day, down to the humblest of his retainers, every one addressed himself to the day's pleasure with that wild pagan jollity which is half despair, and which knows it has nothing to calculate upon beyond the moment. *"Di doman non ci e contezza,"* they sang. Whosoever can be glad, let him be glad to-day, for no man knows what will be to-morrow. Such were the songs that echoed through the streets. It is not to be supposed that Lorenzo, or any other living man, was ever consciously wicked enough to desire to debauch the mind of a people by this often renewed sentiment, but it was doubtless the expression of his own feelings, as it is the superficial sentiment, at least, of that pagan system which he tried hard to bring back. But Lorenzo, amid all the gayety which was natural to him, was a wise potentate; and it is evident that the preacher of San Marco very soon caught his attention and awakened his interest. When his courtiers talked of driving the Lombard monk out of the city, as they had driven Fra Bernardino, Lorenzo does not appear to have taken any share in the threatening

which were no doubt intended to please him, but kept his
eye upon the bold Dominican with curiosity and interest,
and not, it would almost seem, without a sense that here
was a man of the regnant class, like himself—one of his
own kingly kind, though so unlike him—a man worth
knowing, worth making a friend of, if that might be possible. The intercourse between them, in so far as it can
be called intercourse, forms such a striking episode as is
rarely to be met with in history.

In July of the same year, 1491,* the Dominicans of San
Marco elected Fra Girolamo to be their prior, with the intention, Padre Marchese thinks, of doing all in their power
to support and protect him, but very probably because
they were proud of the great preacher and his fame, and
believed him capable of every success. But the good
brethren soon found that they had no easy or persuadable
ruler in their new prior. It was the habit of the time
that each newly-elected superior should go to pay his
respects to Lorenzo—to thank him for his protection, and
recommend the convent to his good graces. The elders of
the community, prudent men and politic, waited discreetly
to see Prior Girolamo do his duty in this particular, but
when they found him obstinately shut up in his cell, and
showing no inclination to budge, fear seized their minds.
They rushed to the prior's cell and demanded why he did
not fulfill his duty. "Who elected me to be prior—God
or Lorenzo?" he said. What could the *primi padri* answer?
Their hearts quaking, they replied, that of course it was
God. "Then," said the prior, "I will thank my Lord
God, not mortal man." Poor *primi padri!* it is easy to

---

* Professor Villari, the latest and most careful of Savonarola's
biographers, seems, I do not know on what ground, to reject the
circumstantial narrative of Burlamacchi and other contemporaries, and
to place this election later in Fra Girolamo's life after the death of
Lorenzo.

understand the trouble they must have been in at such
a marked neglect of the authority which protected the

SAVONAROLA'S CELL.

convent. No doubt there were still some old men there
who had been at San Marco in Cosimo's day, when the
Pater Patriæ came and lived among them and made them

proud. Lorenzo, however, when he came to hear of this, did not take it in anger, as they evidently expected him to do. It is indeed impossible not to feel that the real sentiments of this great prince and able statesman were very different from those of his sycophants. I am disposed to think that the Magnifico had genius enough to understand Savonarola, and to feel an almost wistful desire for his friendship and the approval, had that been possible—or at least the sympathy—of one so high-minded. There would seem, too, a lingering sense of humor in the remark he is reported to have made when he heard of the new prior's neglect of him—a half-amused complaint—"A stranger has come to live in my house," he said, "and does not think it worth his while to come and see me!" But it is evident that Savonarola's reticence stimulated the desire of the other to know this one man who never bowed before him. Lorenzo was more generous than Haman—no evil purpose was in his heart toward the stranger in the gate who took no notice of his greeting. He began to haunt San Marco with a curiosity and interest which melts the heart of the looker-on. He would go to hear mass in the church; then stray into the garden to walk there, almost like a lover who haunts the precincts of his lady's house in hope of a chance meeting. It had been the custom in the convent when such a noble visitor appeared that the elders of the community should hasten to accompany him, to entertain him with conversation, and make themselves agreeable to the gracious potentate. Accordingly, when Lorenzo was seen in the garden walks, off rushed the friars again, those same *primi padri*, deeply conscious of the Magnifico's power. "Padre Prior," they cried, "Lorenzo is in the garden!" "Has he asked for me?" said the prior, calmly intent upon his studies. The troubled monks were obliged to say "No." "Then let him take his walk in peace," said Prior Girolamo. Burlamacchi tells us that Lorenzo was "stupefied" by this continual resistance. But still he was not wroth. He sent presents to the convent ; he dropped gold pieces in the box—evidently a very unusual liberality —when he came to San Marco ; but Savonarola resisted still. When the box was opened and the golden scudos seen, the prior carefully laid them aside, and sent them to the *Buonuomini di San Martino* to be distributed to the poor, to the intense disappointment of certain good frati, who had already in their minds destined this unlooked-for wealth to the repairs and larger needs of the convent. "The silver and copper are enough for us," said Savonarola ; "we do not want so much money." Lorenzo's disappointment and mortification at this most marked rejection of his overtures were naturally great. He had taken so much trouble, and shown so great an eagerness to conciliate Savonarola, that one feels disposed to think that the prior was somewhat churlish, and to be sorry for the magnate thus constantly repulsed in his efforts.

The next step which Lorenzo took seems singularly simple, if he had any real hope of still winning over the preacher, and was directed rather to the task of influencing his public work than of gaining his private friendship. He sent five noble citizens of Florence, all men of note and weight, directing them to make pretense of having gone of their own accord, out of regard to the peace of the city and the good of the convent, to beg Savonarola to moderate the tone of his sermons, and to cease his denunciation of the general corruption. These men were Domenico Bonsio (afterward the envoy of the signoria to the pope), Guid' Antonio Vespucci, Paolo Soderini, Francesco Valori (a citizen of the greatest influence in Florence), and Bernardo Rucellai, the cousin of Lorenzo. How these magnificent mediæval figures, in their scarlet mantles, must have crowded the little cell with its one chair and commodious desk, in which the prior lived ! or perhaps he received so important a party in the chapter-house, underneath Angelico's great fresco. When they had stated their errand, which they did with much confusion and embarrassment, abashed in spirit by the nature of the commission, the Dominican looked at them with his penetrating eyes, and read their secret. "You tell me that you have come to me of your own accord for the good of the city, and for the love you bear this convent," he said, "but I tell you it is not so. Lorenzo de' Medici has sent you here ; therefore, tell him from me, that though he is a Florentine, and the greatest in the city, and I am a stranger, yet it is he who must leave Florence, and I who must remain. He shall go away, but I shall stay." The shamed and discomfited ambassadors, themselves deeply impressed by Savonarola, went hastily away with this message, which they received as a prophecy, and the uncompromising prior told the whole story soon after from the pulpit, in the presence of some of the envoys. After this the disappointed Magnifico, repulsed in all his attempts, turned to a much less worthy expedient, quite beneath the idea of him which his former actions induce us to form. As he could not conciliate, he endeavored to crush this rebellious friar. A certain Fra Mariano, whose eloquent style and well-turned sentences had been the delight of all polite church-goers before Savonarola rose upon the firmament, had retired to a convent built for him by Lorenzo outside the Porta San Gallo. From this seclusion the Magnifico drew him in the hope of recalling the allegiance of the Florentines to the courtly orator, whose trained eloquence and elocution were far beyond anything the Dominican could boast. Fra Mariano came from his convent, and preached in the church of San Gallo, after vespers, on Ascension Day, 1491 ; but as he came with no good meaning, out of hostility to Savonarola, and desire to please his patron, his appearance was an entire and painful failure. His text was the verse, "Of the times and seasons knoweth no man;" and his effort was to prove the futility of the prior's preaching; but he lost his head and his temper in the hot polemical discourse to which his zeal moved him, and did himself and his cause much more harm than he did to Savonarola. This was the last episode but one in the curious conflict which went on, without any personal meeting, between the prior and the Magnifico. One memorable scene, however, was yet to come.

When Savonarola sent that prophetic message to Lorenzo, "He shall go away, but I shall stay," there was no doubt a mysterious menace involved; and this was extended in private conversation with a Franciscan friar who had heard Lorenzo's courtiers express their determination to drive the prior of San Marco from the city. Burlamacchi informs us that, to this Franciscan, Savonarola foretold exactly the death of Lorenzo within the year, and also of the Pope Innocent VIII., both of which took place within the time indicated. Lorenzo fell ill in the early spring of the year 1492, and then occurred a scene which has been often told and retold, but which is one of the most striking and remarkable of that or any time. Lorenzo was still in the full vigor of his life and of his great powers, Florence at his feet, flatterers on every side, and everything going well with him when his summons came. *Di doman non ci è contezza.* So he had said and sung : Let us eat and drink, for to-morrow we die ; words often lightly said and gayly, though they embody the very soul and essence of despair. When that to-morrow comes, however, few of the believers in this so-called gay philosophy find much comfort in the eating and drinking, the revelry and enjoyment, of the past; and when it was Lorenzo's turn suddenly out of his sunshine to enter this gloom, conscience awoke within him. He thought upon certain things he had done, which no charitable interpre-

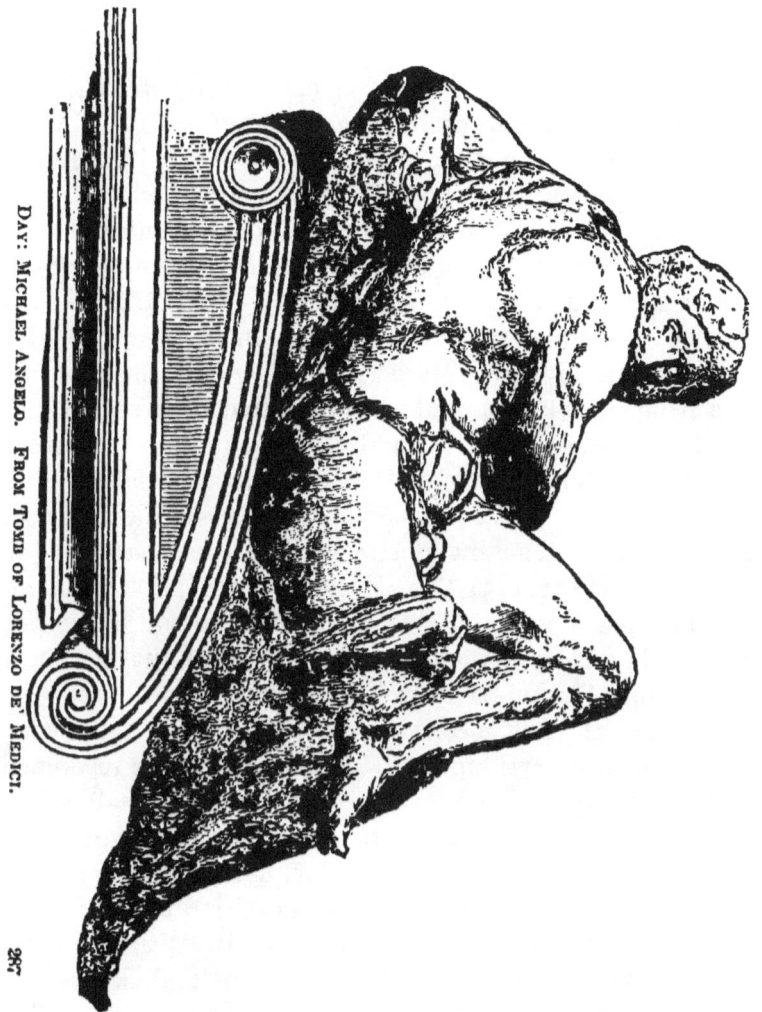

DAY: MICHAEL ANGELO. FROM TOMB OF LORENZO DE' MEDICI.

265

tation could explain away, or cheerful sophistry account
for, and an agony of desire to get himself pardoned arose
in his mind.   He was too able and clear-sighted not to see
through his own priestly parasites, the Fra Marianos, who
flattered and humored him as much as his secular friends
did.   Only one man could the dying Magnifico think of,
whose absolution would be sufficiently real and true to
carry comfort with it, and that one man was the friar who
had repulsed him, the Mordecai in his gates, the Dominican stranger, who no doubt had appeared an arrogant and
intolerant priest, notwithstanding his genius, to the genial
prince who, for the sake of that genius, had condescended
to seek him.   That this should have been the case is a
singular and touching testimony to the character of
Lorenzo.   He sent to San Marco for the prior when he
felt his state desperate.   "I am not the person he wants;
we should not agree : and it is not expedient that I should
go to him," said Savonarola.   Lorenzo sent back his
messenger at once, declaring his readiness to agree with
the prior in everything, and to do whatever his reverence
bade ; and upon this promise the prophet was induced to
obey the summons.   It was in the villa of Careggi, amid
the olive gardens, that Lorenzo lay, dying, among all the
beautiful things he loved.   As the prior took his way
through the Porta San Gallo up the hill, with the companion whose duty it was to follow him, he told this monk,
"Gregorio vecchio," that Lorenzo was about to die.   This
was, no doubt, a very simple anticipation, but everything
the prophet said was looked upon by his half-adoring
followers as prophecy.   When the two monks reached the
beautiful house from which so often the magnificent
Lorenzo had looked out upon his glorious Florence, and in
which his life of luxury, learned and gay, had culminated,
the prior was led to the chamber in which the owner of all
these riches lay, hopeless and helpless, in what ought to

have been the prime of his days, with visions of sacked cities and robbed orphans distracting his dying mind, and no aid to be got from either beauty or learning. " Father," said Lorenzo, " there are three things which drag me back, and throw me into despair, and I know not if God will ever pardon me for them." These were the sack of Volterra, the robbery of the Monte delle Fanciulle, and the massacre of the Pazzi. To this Savonarola answered by reminding his penitent of the mercy of God. The dramatic climax of this scene, it is necessary to add, is omitted from the account given of Lorenzo's death-bed by Politian ; but we think it well to quote it in full from the detailed and simple narrative of Burlamacchi, who seems to us at least as satisfactory a witness.

" ' Lorenzo,' he said, ' be not so despairing, for God is merciful, and will be merciful to you, if you will do three things I will tell you.' Then said Lorenzo, ' What are these three things ?' The padre answered, ' The first is that you should have a great and living faith that God can and will pardon you.' To which Lorenzo answered, "This is a great thing, and I do believe it.' The padre added, ' It is also necessary that everything wrongfully acquired should be given back by you, in so far as you can do this, and still leave to your children as much as will maintain them as private citizens.' These words drove Lorenzo nearly out of himself ; but afterwards he said, 'This also will I do.' The padre then went on to the third thing, and said, 'Lastly, it is necessary that freedom, and her popular government according to republican usage, should be restored to Florence.' At this speech Lorenzo turned his back upon him, nor ever said another word. Upon which the padre left him and went away without other confession."

We do not know where to find a more remarkable scene. Never before, so far as we can ascertain, had these two notable beings looked at each other face to face, or interchanged words. They met at the supreme moment of the life of one, to confer there upon the edge of eternity, and part—but not in a petty quarrel ; each great in his way,

the prince turning his face to the wall in the bitterness
of his soul, the friar drawing his cowl over his head,
solemn, unblessing but not unpitiful—they separated after
their one interview. "Talking of Lorenzo afterward, the
padre would say that he had never known a man so well
endowed by God with all natural graces; and that he
grieved greatly not to have been sooner called to him, because he trusted in the grace of God that Lorenzo might
then have found salvation." Curious revenge of one great
soul upon another : the prince had sought the unwilling
preacher in vain, when all was well with Lorenzo ; but the
preacher "grieved greatly " not to have been sooner called,
when at last they met ; and Savonarola recognized in the
great Medici a man worth struggling for, a fellow and
peer of his own.

Thus Lorenzo died at forty-four, in the height of his
days, with those distracting visions in his dying eyes,
"*Che quasi mi pongono in disperazione*"—the sacked
city, the murdered innocents of Pazzi blood, the poor
maidens robbed in their orphanage :

> "In the lost battle, borne down by the flying,
> Where mingles war's rattle with groans of the dying ! "

He had been victorious and splendid all his days, but
the battle was lost at last, and the prophet by the side of
his princely bed intimated to Lorenzo, in that last demand
to which he would make no answer, the subversion of all
his work, the downfall of his family, the escape of Florence from the skillful hands which had held her so long.
The spectator looking on at this strange and lofty conflict
of the two most notable figures of their time feels almost
as much sympathy for Lorenzo, proud and sad, refusing
to consent to that ruin which was inevitable, as with the
patriotic monk, lover of freedom as of truth, who could

no more absolve a despot at his end than he could play a
courtier's part during his life. As that cowled figure traversed the sunny marbles of the loggia, in the glow of the
April morning, leaving death and bitterness behind, what
thoughts must have been in both hearts! The one, sovereign still in Florence, reigning for himself and his own
will and pleasure, proudly and sadly turned his face to the
wall, holding fast his scepter, though his moments
were numbered. The other, not less sadly, a sovereign
too, to whom that scepter was to fall, and who should reign
for God and goodness, went forth into the spring sunshine, life blossoming all about him, and the City of
Flowers lying before him, white campanile and red dome
glistening in the early light. Life with the one, death
with the other ; but nature calm and fair, and this long-
lived everlasting earth, to which men great and small are
things of a moment, encircling both. Careggi still stands
smiling on the wealthy slope, looking from its many windows and its painted loggia upon Florence, proving that
its great master was wrong when he sang *" Di doman non
ci é contezza ; "* for this far-distant to-morrow has more
knowledge of that death-bed scene of his than of all the
festas and all the singing that has happened there since
his time.

Lorenzo de' Medici died, leaving, as such men do, the
deluge after him, and a foolish and feeble heir to contend
with Florence roused and turbulent, and all the troubles
and stormy chances of Italian politics ; while the prior of
San Marco returned to his cell and his pulpit—from which
for a few years thereafter he was to rule over his city and
the spirits of men—a reign more wonderful than any that
Florence ever saw.

CHAPTER XI.

V.—SAVONAROLA AS A POLITICIAN.

THE first great event which followed in the public life
of Florence and at the same time in the history of Savonarola, after the death of Lorenzo de' Medici, was the very
curious and picturesque episode of the visit of Charles of
Anjou—Charles VIII. of France—to the city of Florence.
A more remarkable and exciting incident has seldom found
a place in any record of the risks to which small states are
liable.   There was no quarrel between Italy, so far as such
a general title could be given to the Italy of that day, and
France.   Certainly there was no quarrel between Florence
and France.   But there has scarcely ever been a time when
the many divisions, the contending cities, republics and
princedoms of Italy have not been a temptation to her bigger neighbors on every side of her.   A country so rich and
splendid could scarcely fail to awaken covetings; and nothing could give more opportunity to the invader than the
condition of this warring family, every member of which
clung with desperation to its own precarious independence,
though quite indifferent to the enslaving of its brethren.
The immediate cause of the French invasion was the usurpation of Ludovic the Moor, Ludovico Sforza, who had
dethroned his own nephew, the rightful duke of Milan, and
reigned (like one of Shakespeare's dukes), keeping this
nephew in confinement.   The wife of the imprisoned
prince, however, was the daughter of the king of Naples,
who threatened Ludovico continually, and disturbed him in

the possession of his usurped and ill-gotten power. To put an effectual stop to this disturbance, Ludovico invited France, in the person of her young and romantically disposed monarch, to invade Italy and take Naples, a jewel worthy of even an imperial crown. France, history tells us—or at least all wise Frenchmen—resisted and disliked the enterprise; but, strangely enough, Italy, the country threatened with invasion, invited it, and, theoretically at least, rejoiced in the prospect; and even eyes so penetrating as those of Savonarola saw a deliverer divinely sent in the uncouth figure of Charles of Anjou, the least comely of all knights-errant. Nothing could more clearly show the despairing disgust of the people with their princes and their governments than even a momentary sentiment of welcome toward the foreign invader, who could scarcely fail to be the enemy of the commonweal. But it is apparent that this unnatural pleasure yielded to the excitement of terror when the invader really set out: for many things seem desirable enough at a distance which are appalling on a nearer approach.

Lorenzo de' Medici had been dead about a year and a half, during which time his son Piero held a tottering sway in Florence, when the French army crossed the Alps. The first news of their setting out, exaggerated by all those popular tales of gigantic strength and barbarian ferocity which attach generally to all invaders, and which in those distant ages rumor gave full voice to, was received in Florence on one of the days when Savonarola preached in the Duomo; and thither the excited populace rushed to hear what he had to say about this terrible event. He had already warned them of One who should come, like a new Cyrus, over the hills to punish the wicked and purge Italy of her sins. As it happened, his series of discourses upon the building of Noah's ark—that spiritual shelter in which he had entreated his hearers to take refuge—had come to an appropriate and striking point which chimed in strangely with the event of which all his great congregation had just heard with excitement, agitation, and terror. "Behold, I, even I, do bring a flood of waters on the earth," were the words of his text. He gave it forth " with a terrible voice " over the heads of the hushed and awe-stricken multitude in the gloom of the great cathedral; his voice sounded like sudden thunder, and a shudder of painful interest and emotion rose through the vast assembly, moving the preacher as much as the hearers. He had prophesied the death of the tyrant, and Lorenzo was dead; he had prophesied the coming of this Cyrus, and for a long time had held up, so to speak, over the head of the guilty city, that sword of the Lord which was to avenge and destroy. Now the crisis and the very moment had come. The people, we are told, hurried through the streets after his discourse, "more dead than alive," in gloomy silence, not venturing even to confide to each other the alarm that filled their souls. They had indeed almost wished for, almost invited, the new Cyrus, feeling that indefinable hope in his coming which, when human circumstances are desperate, every great change brings with it—but the stranger became appalling as he drew near. And soon other news arrived, which added to the terrible uncertainty of the districts which lay in the invader's way, whether they were to regard him as the scourge of God or the great deliverer, as both of which he had been promised by the prophet. At the very beginning of the campaign the French dispersed the Neapolitan fleet, and taking a small sea-side town, in which they had left a garrison, sacked and destroyed the unhappy little place—a terrible example and warning to all others. This happened when Charles was making his way across the flats of Lombardy; and Florence was the next stage in his progress. The town was rich, splendid, tempting in every way to the northern invader. The fighting men who had so often defended it were out of fashion ; the Magnifico was no longer a firm and wise Lorenzo, but wavering and foolish ; and the town itself watched its ruler like the unwilling captive it was, on the strain to catch the moment when it might twitch the chain by which he held it out of his unwary hand. This moment came very soon. Piero, in his fright, went out to meet his fate. When he heard of Charles' approach, he hurried to meet him, and, with signal folly, by way of propitiating the invader, put the only defenses the intermediate country possessed into his hands, thus opening to Charles the way to the city without securing any conditions of compensation or guarantees of peace.

When the news of this base surrender reached Florence the whole city was in an uproar. Terror and indignation and passionate patriotism all united to make the populace half frantic with excitement. That fear which even the bravest may be permitted to feel for the fate of a great city full of helpless and unwarlike persons in the hands of a conqueror mingling with the exasperation of a proud people betrayed, brought on one of those paroxysms of popular frenzy in which the mob is capable of almost anything— of heroic and sublime self-defense, or of mad license, carnage, and anarchy, according to the touch which sways it. Mutterings against the rich citizens who had made their wealth by oppression—against the partisans of the Medici party, the betrayers of the state—and against all rulers and authority—along with a feverish anxiety for the the safety of Florence, rose among the crowds like the gathering of a tempest. But, leaderless, counselless, as they were, one impulse swayed the people. They knew of one man at least, whose voice was to be trusted, who would speak to them boldly and freely, without fear or favor—a

man so deep in the counsels of heaven that he had seen all
along this trouble coming. With one accord they rushed
to the cathedral. " Such a dense mass of people had never
been seen in it ; they were so closely packed that no one
could stir." The man in the pulpit to whom they all
looked, might no doubt have led that dark moving mass—
Italian crowd of men, always remarkable to behold, thronging there in all the dim corners, scarcely visible except by
the thrill of breath and motion, the gleam of dark eyes and
stern faces—to meet the invader, and perhaps by miraculous momentary passion to turn him back ; or might,
with a spirit more congenial to the time and place, have
given just the stimulus that was wanted to make the
injured people avenge itself terribly upon its tyrants. He
did neither. Stretching out his arms over the crowd, with
the emotion of one who shared their every tremor and
pang, he called out to them to repent and pray. The
scourge had come, the blow had descended ; but yet
Florence was in the hand of a God never slow to pardon.
" Repent," he cried, " for the kingdom of heaven is at
hand ; " and again, "Pardon, oh Lord, pardon those Florentines who desire to be thine." This was how Savonarola
took the tide at its flood. He might have made himself
autocrat—dictator—and so, indeed, for a time he was—
and taken whatever revenge he pleased upon his enemies ;
but the only revenge he bade his fellow-sufferers take was
upon themselves, whose sins had caused this chastisement;
and the remedy was reformation, not of the state only,
but of every individual. The excited mass calmed down
under this wonderful appeal. Their vows of vengeance
against their betrayers died on their lips. In gravity and
humility they dispersed to await the event, whatever it
might be, with something like national dignity. The best
men of the city, so long kept under, came to the front in
this moment of general agitation ; and the sense of tremen-

dous danger—danger unspeakable, yet not unmixed with hope—fortunately subdued all dissensions among the different sections of officials who still had a remnant of power in their hands, and could do something yet for the salvation of the city. While the signory and their counselors consulted, Savonarola held the populace as in a leash. He kept calm within the walls, whatever might be without, absolutely preventing, not only domestic tumult and anarchy, but those sudden and wild experiments of revolutionary government which are as dangerous. The first excitement having been thus mastered, the city appointed another solemn deputation to go to Charles, and do all that was possible to be done to mend matters. One of these ambassadors, and the most important, was Savonarola. Before setting out he delivered another great sermon. " The Lord has heard your prayers, and caused a great revolution to end peaceably," he said. " If you would have the Lord continue His mercy to you be merciful to your brethren, your friends—even your enemies. The Lord has said to you, ' I will have mercy.' Woe to them that disobey Him." When he had left this solemn charge upon his great flock, the prophet turned, with a precaution in which there seems a certain humorous kindness, to the smaller immediate band of his followers, which had its special dangers too. He called the brethren of San Marco together in chapter, and warned them not to go about boasting that their prior was the ambassador of Florence to the king, but rather to keep within their convent walls, and help him with their prayers.

Thus he set out on his mission. The reader need not be told Burlamacchi's simple tale of the miraculous draught of fishes brought into the net of the unwilling fisher at Librafratta, who was sent out in a storm to catch fish for the padre's dinner—a miracle quite unnecessary, by the way, since the simple historian himself adds that Savona-

rola ate nothing but an egg. He traveled on foot, with a
few companions chosen from among his own monks, his
noble colleagues in the mission having gone on before.
These men, among whom was Piero Capponi, one of the
most noble of living Florentines, had already had their
interview with the king before the monks arrived. But
the chief result they seem to have obtained was to scare
Piero de' Medici, who still lingered, after his ignoble
bargain, among the hangers-on of Charles, and whom the
arrival of a new Florentine embassy, elected independently
of himself, and coming to protest against his shameful
doings, woke up at once to the desperation of his own
cause. At sight of them he hurried off back to Florence,
where he was refused admission to the palace of the signoria, except as a private individual, and finally driven out
of the city, not without tumults, and some bloodshed.
Capponi and the rest, however, made little of Charles, who
would promise nothing, and postponed all negotiations until he should be in Florence. With this most unsatisfactory
decision they returned, full of fear and trouble, to the
agitated city, which had begun to sack a few palaces, and
fall upon a few Medici by way of expending that overplus
of excitement which now there was no preacher in the
Duomo to still by his voice.

It was then that Savonarola reached the camp. Perhaps
he thought his mission would be more successful were it
unmingled with the arguments and negotiations of the
statesmen, with which, indeed, it had nothing to do. He
saluted Charles, when introduced to his presence, as the
"great servant of Divine Justice." As such the preacher
had always regarded this king, who in himself was not
great. And Charles was full of curiosity to see the man
who had given him so elevated a mission, who had described
him as the new Cyrus, the scourge of the wicked, the

deliverer of the righteous.* There was not, however, much food for vanity to Savonarola's address. He told the king, indeed, that, years before, this visitation had been revealed to him, and bade him enter boldly, gladly, into Florence as the avenger of Him who triumphed on the Cross.

" Nevertheless, most Christian king, listen to my words," said the prophet. " God's unworthy servant, to whom this has been revealed, warns and admonishes thee, by God's authority, that according to His example thou shouldst show mercy everywhere, and especially in Florence where (though there are many sinners) He has many servants and handmaidens, both in the world and in the cloister, for whose sake it is thy duty to spare the city. . . . . In God's name I exhort and admonish thee to help and defend the innocents, the widows and orphans, and poor, and above all modesty and purity. . . . . In God's name I admonish thee to pardon the offenses of the Florentines and other people who may have offended thee. . . . . Remember thy Saviour, who, hanging on the Cross, pardoned His murderers. Which things if thou doest, oh king, God will increase thy kingdom, and give the victory. . . . . But if thou dost forget the work for which the Lord sends thee, He will then choose another to fulfill it, and will let the hand of His wrath fall upon thee, and will punish thee with terrible scourges. All this I say to thee in the name of the Lord."

So spake the prophets to the ancient kings, who were, perhaps, scarcely more appropriate executors of the Divine will than Charles of Anjou. The king and his generals were moved by this remarkable address, and though no promises were made to Savonarola any more than to his colleagues, he returned with better hopes, and brought a

---

* Padre Marchese here pauses to remark how strange to the ears of the Frenchmen it must have been to hear that this manifestly unjust invasion had been predicted by Savonarola, and was recognized by him as divine mission. This, however, is a complication of the matter which had nothing to do with the straightforward contemplation of the event, from one side only, which was natural to Savonarola.

little comfort with him to the gloomy and agitated city, in which his very presence was of itself a strength. He returned at once to his congenial work, restraining the people as he only could, speaking to them of mercy and judgment, of peace and brotherhood, while war and all its tumults were so near, and when any unguarded blaze of popular wrath might at any moment have destroyed the city, and given to history a sack of Florence with all its inevitable horrors.

Meanwhile Capponi and his colleagues made all the hasty preparations they could for a desperate resistance, should the worst come to the worst. In this condition of affairs, Florence had to do what many an individual has to do in the exigencies of private life : to decorate her streets and throw wide her gates, and prepare pageants of welcome for the insolent visitor, whose very smile was an offense, but who, if offended, had strength enough to crush her under his heel, and make her streets run with blood. A more exciting moment could not be imagined. All the available troops the republic could collect lay unseen in peaceful cloisters and in the depths of the great old palaces, ready for instant action if need were, when the great bell should ring; the houses were filled with ammunition and provisions, even with materials for barricades (the idea of which, we are told, was first picked up by the French in this strange visit); and over all these grim preparations waved the flags, the tapestries on the balconies, the awnings over the streets. It was November, probably one of those grim, gray days which the city of Florence has her share of, and with which her grave and stern splendor is not uncongenial—for it rained when the *cortége* marched in at the gate of San Frediano, and across the turbid river to the Medicean palace in the Via Larga, where everything had been prepared with due magnificence for the king's lodgings, and where all the costly and beautiful art collections made by the great Lorenzo and his wealthy predecessors were. The visit lasted for ten days, and during that time it may well be supposed how hard the struggle was to keep the people in subjection, to prevent all feuds among themselves, and all needless irritation of the triumphant and probably insolent strangers, who though they professed to be friendly visitors, yet felt themselves conquerors, and would have liked nothing better than to have been let loose upon the magnificent city. Once, indeed, during their stay an incident occurred which showed the Frenchmen that all the strength was not on their side, nor the danger upon that of the Florentines. "Whether by accident or design," says Professor Villari, in his valuable narrative, "a report was spread through the town that Piero de' Medici had appeared at one of the gates: the great bell tolled continuously, the streets were all in motion, the people in a state of furious excitement, the very earth seemed to bring forth armed men, all hastening to the piazza: the gates of the palaces were closed, the towers were armed, and barricades prepared in the streets. . . . . It was soon found that the report was false, and the tumult subsided as rapidly as it had arisen. But a deep impression was made on the minds of the foreigners."

This the reader will easily believe who has ever beheld a scene of popular excitement, even in a much less warlike age and less dangerous occasion in the lofty and narrow streets of an Italian city. The great bell clanging from the old tower, the cow lowing, as the Florentines said in familiar fondness—was a sound known all over the city; and it is one which would rouse Florence now as well as then. The aspect of the same streets on the morning of a much less difficult revolution, that of 1859, when, in comparative silence, without bell to rouse them, or visible token for their gathering, the tramp of men suddenly filled

the streets, and crowds emerged into the piazza—crowds so
unlike the crowds of other places, no flutter of women or
children about, a dark moving throng of men—was a sight
not to be easily forgotten. Even the crowd of a market-
day, when there is nothing more alarming than a mass of
loud-talking, gesticulating contadini and townsmen mingled
together in the great noble square, is sufficient of itself to
give an idea of what the scene was when, by all the narrow
ways, the citizens were pouring into that general center,
and every straight street looked liked the gate of a castle, at
which three could defy a thousand. Perhaps, it is a relic
of those stormy times which keeps the feminine element
so much out of the Florentine crowd, even in its most
peaceful aspect, and thus confers upon the most harmless
throng an air of dark force and purpose, of something
about to be done, which helps the modern spectator
better than anything else to realize the passionate scenes
of former times.

Charles VIII. was hard to get rid of. Not only the
ordinary motives which tempted the invader of these
fighting days, cupidity and thirst for conquest, but also the
fact that Piero de' Medici was praying for his help on one
side, while the republic, firmly holding by its newly regained liberty, faced him on the other, kept the French
negotiators in a dubious mood. Their own position was
not without its dangers. The escape of some prisoners
whom the French were leading bound through the streets
—an incident which has been used with much effect in the
noble fiction of " Romola "—roused the inhabitants of the
Borgo Ognissanti to such a pitch of indignation that, in a
sudden fury of assault from windows and doors, and a
hundred points of vantage, they fell on the redoubtable
Swiss, then " the finest infantry in the world," and drove
these mountaineers so sharply to their defenses, that even
the brave Swiss trembled at the thought of " a city which

the sound of a bell could convert into an armed castle,"
and where it might chance that they should find themselves shut up, with every window and every street-corner
pouring forth a fiery hail upon them. This impression
made upon the minds of his soldiers helped Charles to see
more clearly; but yet at the very last moment his pride
and obstinacy came uppermost, and the king, turning
furiously away when his *ultimatum* was rejected by the
Florentines, broke up the negotiations by exclaiming,
"Then we shall sound our trumpets." "And we our
bells!" cried brave Piero Capponi, snatching the insulting
treaty, which he had just in the name of Florence rejected,
from the secretary's hand, and tearing it in pieces. This
outburst of patriotic impatience driven desperate brought
the Frenchmen to their senses.

> " Lo strepito dell' armi e de' cavalli
> Non potè far che non fossi sentita
> La voce d'un Cappon fra cento Galli."

(The din of arms could not prevent our Cappon's voice
from sounding high above a hundred (*Galli*) cocks.)

This is the account of the historians. Burlamacchi
gives a somewhat different view of the transaction. According to him, Capponi's bold speech so roused the rage
of the king, that he at once decided to sack the city; and
Savonarola, almost forcing his way into the palace, had to
be brought upon the scene to frighten and subdue Charles
before this cruel purpose was abandoned. The narrative
is wonderfully picturesque, and no doubt refers to an actual interview which took place a little later, when Savonarola was sent to expedite by all the arguments in his power
the king's departure from the city.

'When he saw the servant of God," says Burlamacchi, "accord
ing to the custom of the king of France, he rose to show him respect
But the servant of God took out a little leaden crucifix which he car

ried always about him, and holding it up to the king, said, 'This is He who made heaven and earth. Honor not me, but honor Him who is King of kings, Lord of lords, and who makes the world to tremble, and gives victory to princes according to His will and justice. He punishes and destroys impious and unjust kings ; and he will destroy thee with all thy army, if thou dost not give up thy cruel purpose, and annul the plan thou hast formed against this city. . . . . Knowest thou not that it matters little to the Lord whether He gets the victory with few or with many? Have you forgotten what He did to Sennacherib, the proud king of the Assyrians? or how, when Moses prayed, Joshua and the people overcame their enemies? So shall it be done to thee. . . . . Thus spoke the padre to the king, filling him with terror, and threatening him, in the name of God, always with the crucifix in his hand. And he spoke with so much power and effect, that all who were present were struck with dismay and terror, and the king and his ministers were moved to tears. Then the padre took the king by the hand, and said to him, 'Sacred majesty, know that it is God's will that thou shouldst leave the city without making any other change, otherwise thou and thy army will here lay down your lives.' "

Thus Burlamacchi describes the last scene, before Charles unwillingly passed on his way. On the 26th of November, the city got rid of its troublesome and dangerous visitor, without any more serious cost than that of the Medicean art-treasures, and all the beautiful things with which the palace had been decked for the king's reception. The French "looted"—to use a modern word—the princely house in which they had been lodged, plundering it from hall to garret, valets, and barons, and the king himself taking share in the spoil. But this was a small fine to pay for the comfort of getting free of so great a danger and embarrassment. And when the tramp of the departing army had died on the air—when Florence breathed freely, and the agitated people could pause and reckon their gains and losses—it then appeared that the scourge of God, which had only been waved innoxiously, as it were, over their heads, had brought benefit and blessing unawares, as their prophet had ever promised. When the danger was over, and the excitement began to subside, Florence opened her eyes to find that a great revolution had happened in her history. The Medici were gone—their power, built up so gradually and so wisely, had vanished in a moment. Piero might bluster or threaten outsides the gates, but within he had no power. Once more, after the lapse of years, the Florentines were free.

The old machinery of government, however, which was the most cumbrous of all the systems in Italy, and afforded more scope for the tyranny or a faction than for the wide freedom at which theoretically it aimed, had fallen rusty and out of gear : and the first thing to be done was to decide upon some possible way by which the vessel of state might again be got under pilotage. In former times, the first step to be taken in such an emergency was to call a parlamento—a vague mob who assembled in the piazza without check upon its pretensions, or even guarantee of citizenship—a mob which it was very easy to leaven with noisy men here and there, good for leading the voices of the rest, and suggesting the hasty decisions in which every mob delights. Such a vague, foolish, popular assembly had invariably committed the sovereign power into the hands that were most clever in managing it, the dominant party, whatever that might be ; and with its facile vote and ready confidence, had fallen into a mere farce and laughable parody of a popular institution, the masquerade under which despotism disported itself. What other way than this farce of popular election with its *Balìa*, its cheerful giving over of the freedom of Florence to the strongest, the loudest-voiced and most specious claimant, and all its fictitious appearance of spontaneity—could be found !—what was to be put in its place ! This the city began to ask itself with one mind, great and small discussing the point, and a great deal of agitation accompanying the discussion. Italy was at this period the only country in the world in which politics, as we understand the word, can be said to have existed at all. No other race was as yet sufficiently advanced in civilization, or secure of intervals of peace, to have time for the consideration of constitutional questions or theories of government. But the land of Machiavelli was already an adept in such theories; and Machiavelli himself, if not already a notable personage, was at that moment, with all his wisdom un-developed in his young head, moving about the streets of this very Florence, and waiting for his time to strike in, and take his part in all the debates and curious questions which possessed the popular mind. Professor Villari furnishes us with a glimpse of Italian feeling on this subject, which is fortunately brief enough to quote :

" There existed in the breasts of the Florentines such an innate love of liberty, that when unable to enter freely into discussions in the councils, they retired to their closets to reason on affairs of state, and to create political science. In consulting their works, we always find that they begin by laying down this doctrine—that the greatest felicity which man can hope to find on earth, is to have a share in the govern-ment of his country. . . . Starting from the one idea, that to govern is the greatest happiness, that which man most desires—it naturally follows that all would aspire to it, that all would be desirous to hold the reins of government in their native land, and that every man would strive to attain this, however it might injure other men. Such principles must naturally give rise to the danger of relapsing into tyranny, as happened in almost all the governments of Italy. To the question, What is a perfect government? the whole school of Italian politicians had but one answer—That in which no tyranny can exist. And what is the form of government in which tyranny cannot exist? That which shall be so regulated as to satisfy at one and the same time all the passions of all orders of the citizens. In every city, they said, there will be a few who will try to rule over all; the *ottimati* (patricians) will strive for honors, the people for liberty. Hence they desired to have a mixed government, uniting in itself the various interests of monarchy, aristocracy and democracy, so as to satisfy the ambitious, the *ottimati*, and the people, and by such means they hoped that secure liberty would be established."

When the Florentines, full of these sentiments, found themselves at last relieved from all intruders, and from the one supreme family which, in spite of their struggles, had ruled them for the last sixty years, they immediately rushed with eager enjoyment into the preliminaries of reconstruction, debating among themselves (as unfortunately we have more than once seen done in later days) the ideal constitution which should make all men, or at least all Florentines, happy. But the delight of thus reforming the constitution of a state is a dangerous one, and it is evident that all ordinary affairs stood still in Florence while the signoris and their counselors, the most important citizens, endeavored to come to a decision, and to make up their minds whether the new constitution should resemble that of Venice, or should be merely a reconstruction of the ancient system. During the earlier part of these discussions Savonarola did not interfere with the statesmen whose business it was, but went on with his usual occupations, exercising all his influence and power over the mind of Florence to make the populace tranquil, to encourage the people in that way of well-doing which he believed had been the means of their preservation from the invader, and to relieve the poverty and distress which abounded in the city. For the latter object he entreated the rich to make personal sacrifices—to give up their pomp and pleasures—to apply to the service of the poor the money which they would have spent upon education at the university of Pisa, then temporarily closed, Pisa being still in rebellion and revolution—and, going further still, with a liberality and good sense such as is conventionally supposed to be unusual in churchmen, he entreated that the building of costly churches and convents might be discontinued, and that the very plate and decorations of the churches might be sacrificed to relieve the general distress. "But, above all," he added, "let some settlement be

come to by which the shops can be re-opened and work
found for the people." As the days passed on, however,
and no decision was made, the smoldering energy within
him took fire. Though it was not his business, he could
not stand by any longer and see the comfort and power
of the city endangered by delay. Suddenly, on the 12th
of December, a fortnight after the departure of the
French, he introduced the subject in his sermon, and with
great force and earnestness pressed upon his hearers the
example of Venice, and recommended the formation of a
great council on the Venetian model as the best thing for
Florence. "Your reform must begin with things spiritual,
which are superior to all that is material, which constitute
the rule of life, and are life itself," he said; and he quoted
with admirable effect the saying of Cosimo de' Medici,
that "States are not governed by Paternosters," to show
that this sentiment was the sentiment of tyrants, enemies
of the commonweal, and not of loyal citizens. "If you
wish to have a good government," he added, "it must be
derived from God;" and with this preface he threw the
full weight of his support into the proposal of the popular
party.

This, it is evident, at once decided the question. The
discussions which had been going on fruitlessly for all
these wintry days, in the midst of a bewildered and anxious
community, which scarcely knew what side it ought to
take, suddenly cleared up and came to a conclusion. The
people, delighted to have the question settled, shouted
through the streets for the Great Council after that fashion
of the Venetians. A crowded "meeting," as we should
now call it (and the word has by this time got transplanted into all languages), of men—women and children
being excluded—was held soon after in the cathedral.
With evident agitation and emotion the great preacher
went into the pulpit. He told his immense and eager

audience that the time had come which he had predicted,
that all had happened which he had announced to them,
and that now it remained for themselves to decide what
their future fate should be. " There now begins," he said
" a new era for your city. In your hands lies your own
fate. Your future will be what you choose it to be—great,
noble, strong, well-cemented, envied ; or weak, torn
asunder, abject, unhappy, under the impression of a worse
servitude. By this time you have learned to know by
what arts freedom is repressed, and those by which it is
regained and preserved, and that corruption, pleasures,
and pastimes have often reduced the city to misery.
Exercise, then, your judgment, gather the fruit of experience out of misfortune, and so use your power that
freedom henceforward may not be the privilege of the few
for the oppression of many, but a universal benefit, the
patrimony of all citizens whose age and worth entitle them
to possess it." These noble and dignified words add a
consecration of highest and wisest patriotism to the sacred
associations of that dim, splendid Duomo of Florence, from
which many a day the preacher had sent his hearers
pierced to the heart by pricks of conscience, by deep repentance and tender piety ; where he had brought about a
spiritual revolution, and restrained by spiritual means
alone a most turbulent people ; and from whence now he
sent his fellow-citizens in a glow of patriotic excitement,
bent on securing their freedom and guarding it forever.
Alas, that eternity is brief which hangs upon the sentiments of any multitude, but not less noble on that account
is the impulse, not less great the hand that gave it.
Savonarola had not attempted to intrude himself into the
political world, or to leave his own range of subjects, his
own still nobler cares and occupations, at his own will. He
had kept within the modest shade of his cloister, except
when the call of his countrymen brought him forth, spend-

ing his life between that seclusion and the publicity of the
pulpit, where he did what an army could scarcely have
done—preserved peace, and swayed the soul of Florence
from wrath and civil strife to judgment and mercy, the
only real foundations, as he taught, of national prosperity
and calm. But as he had gone to the invader at the call
of the people to bid him come, and to bid him go—so now
he stepped forth, when necessity was, to cut the knot of
opinion and give the powerful aid of his advocacy to what
he held to be the best of political systems. The Medicean
party—still secretly existing, though cowed, and not daring to make themselves known—the ambitious, the lovers
of the old *régime,* and those bigoted conservatives who love
no change, even when it is for the better, had maintained
a kind of struggle up to this moment ; but against Savonarola they could not keep up any struggle. The effect of
his recommendation was so great and so instantaneous that
without further difficulty the thing was done. His first
sermon on the subject was preached on the 12th of
December, and by the 23rd of the same month this
settlement of political affairs was finally agreed to by all
parties ; the Consiglio Maggiore, the Great Council after
the manner of the Venetians, was instituted ; and after all
these contentions and arguments there ensued a moment
of peace.

It is scarcely consistent with my purpose to enter here
into any detailed description of the elaborate system of
government in Florence. So elaborate was it, and so
curiously contrived to make opportunities for despotism
in the midst of every appearance of democratic freedom,
that the complicated structure is most difficult to understand. The new system was less elaborate, but so many of
the old names and old offices were retained, that it is still
somewhat difficult to follow and fathom it. The Great
Council, however, instituted by Savonarola, and consisting

nominally of all the citizens of Florence, in reality em-
braced but a small number of them. It was not, as in
Venice, confined to persons of noble birth, but to the class
of citizens entitled *benefiziati*. These *benefiziati* were, as
their name implies, a class already distinguished among
their neighbors. To become one of them it was necessary
to have been elected to some civil office, great or small ;
the privilege descended to sons and grandsons only, so that
the entire body consisted of the *seduti* or those who had
actually *sat* in some chair of magistracy, and the *reduti*,
those who without acting had been *seen*, or elected to
similar office—and their immediate descendants.* Thus
it will be seen that the large democratic conception of a
council of all the people dwindles at once into reasonable-
ness and practicability, and that in reality it was to the
judgment of select and experienced men, already aware, in
their own persons, or in those of their fathers, of the risks
and conditions of rule, that power was given. In a population of 90,000 there were but 3,200 *benefiziati*, still a very
large parliament certainly; but this body was again *sterzato*,
or divided into three sections, each division holding office
for six months in turn; and no man under twenty-nine was
eligible for the Great Council. Another smaller body,
composed of citizens of not less than forty years of age,
called the *Ottanta*, or eighty, were appointed at the same
time to form a kind of Second Chamber, Senate, or House
of Peers, and the old Executive, the signoria, who bore
office but two months at a time, were still retained as the
apex of all. The rules of this hierarchy are strange enough
to modern eyes, and embody a complete reversal of our
parliamentary customs. In Florence, under the new *régime*,

---

* In order to afford entrance to the ambitious into this privileged
class it had been usual in many cases to draw two names for each
vacant appointment, one of which was *seduto*, or actually drawn for
the office, the other complimentarily *reduto*, seen or made visible.

the signoria proposed, the Ottanta discussed, the Great
Council, or House of Commons, voted only, in silence.
The last was the final tribunal in all questions of government, but its members were only permitted to speak by a
special call from the signoria, and never against a measure
proposed; notwithstanding that it was their all-powerful
vote which decided everything—a very strange and apparently cumbrous arrangement.

Still more strange, however, was the mode in which all
the laws passed by these three states of the realm were
really introduced. It was Savonarola from his pulpit in
the Duomo, or in the church of San Marco, who first laid
them before the eager city. Without abandoning his own
sacred subjects, without for a moment giving up his high
position as a prophet and messenger of God, this extraordinary man set forth his scheme of taxation, his proposal
for a general amnesty, and, perhaps most important of all,
his plan for a final court of judicial appeal against the
sentences of the Otto, the Florentine bench, so to speak,
who were the supreme judges of all cases, both political
and criminal, banishing, imprisoning, and confiscating at
their pleasure, without any check upon their proceedings.
It is scarcely possible to imagine a more curious state of
affairs. The preacher propounded these laws with all the
consciousness in him and about him of a divine inspiration;
the people listened—the great mass of them, I suppose, as
thoroughly convinced that God had spoken by His servant,
as was that humble yet bold servant himself—while the
judicious no doubt pondered, and the statesmen criticised.
Had Lorenzo been alive, and a really great and patriotic
prince, I cannot imagine a more splendid kind of depotism
than these two men might have made between them—the
preacher thus proposing, expounding, giving out his great
new projects of government to the people; and the wary
prince behind, noting everything, watching the effect pro-

duced and how the current of opinion turned, taking advantage at once of the enthusiasm of the mass and the comments of the wiser minority, himself committed to no definite action till all had been weighed and pondered. For a little while this was really how government went on in Florence; the original impulse in everything came from Savonarola. It is scarcely possible to believe that he was not in his turn, at least to some degree, advised and prompted by the statesmen who were at the same time his followers. But nothing of this appears, if it existed ; and there is nothing in the wonderful story to contradict the impression which no doubt possessed the mind of the prior of San Marco—that he spoke as a kind of prime minister of God, expounding the mind of the unseen and omnipotent Monarch whom Florence, scorning all baser sovereignty, had taken for her king. He stood up in his place—and where so fit a place as the Duomo for God's interpreter?— and proposed those laws which he felt came to him direct from Heaven; and after a little while, in the full plentitude of democratic freedom, the signoria, the ottanta, and the consiglio maggiore carried them into practical force, pass- ing them by elaborate voting as if originated by them- selves.

I do not believe that it ever could have occurred to Savonarola that this extraordinary and unprecedented prophetical rule was as completely a depotism as the gov- ernment of Florence had been in Lorenzo's or in Cosimo's time. To him it was the reign of God, whose will was conveyed to His people through his own unworthy lips; and at the same time the reign of the people, whose hearts God turned to accept that will of His, in which lay their salvation. Noble, generous, and great—and, what is more wonderful, often wise—were the laws thus made for Florence, dictated by the purest patriotism, and by a mind utterly elevated above all thoughts of aggrandizement, either personal or ecclesiastical. Savonarola employed his power for no end but the benefit of the people—to enrich or advance his order, his church, or his special convent would never seem to have entered his mind; his enemies say that he loved power, and to those minds which are unable to comprehend his strong conviction that God spoke by him, this is a welcome explanation of a character otherwise incomprehensible. But it scarcely seems to me possible that any spectator of a more sympathetic understanding could thus misjudge Savonarola. He ruled like the ideal tyrant of the poetic imagination—his heart full of God and the people, without a corner in it for himself, or any time to waste upon that atom of humanity. But this sway, though more noble perhaps than any other mission which the mind can conceive, was impossible. Nature, always cognizant of the meaner possibilities with which she is more familiar, prohibits it, except by moments when the great soul takes her by surprise, and the whole world is momentarily subdued. This was the case in Florence for two years. One of the greatest and most wonderful of reigns; but an impossibility, a thing out of nature, which could not last. "After the revolution of 1494," says Villari, "we at once recognize in almost every word of the *Provisioni* the impress of the democratic friar. Latin becomes Italian; a new form, a new style are apparent, a new spirit animating them; they speak almost with the voice of Savonarola, and very frequently are nothing more than extracts from the sermons in which he had recommended the adoption of the law." Such a heroic episode in history can be but brief. Its dangers are as great as is the generous splendor of its power; for who can ensure that a mere man will not lose his head on such an elevation, or that such simple things as genius and goodness can hold head against the intoxications of power? If they could do so even, no one would believe it, and therefore from the beginning the doom of such a leader among men is sealed. But it is something when it lasts long enough to show even for a single year what it is to be so ruled from Heaven ; and when the man, sure of so much misjudging, can leave behind him that evidence of his work and his meaning to put—when at last, in the long course of time, the world becomes impartial—his adversaries to the blush.

Even the moment of Savonarola's triumph, however, was disturbed by some opposition. The appeal which he insisted upon in political cases against the decisions of the *Otto* (the *Sei Fave,* as it was called, judgment being given by a ballot, and two-thirds of the eight being necessary to make the majority) was given, in spite of him, not to a limited and select court, as he wished, but to the consiglio maggiore in full—much too large and popular an assembly to be trusted in such cases. This disappointment of his hopes seems to have been the first sign that his day began to be over, though it was some time later before his general influence failed ; and indeed, as often happens, his popular power seemed for a time all the greater and more evident, after the heart of it had been touched by decay. The picturesque popular demonstrations which keep hold of the imagination longer than laws or practical reforms all took place when the real power of the great preacher was on its wane.

The carnival of 1496 found him silent, in obedience to a brief from Rome ; but I will not in this chapter, which is devoted to his climax of power and influence, enter upon that darker portion of his story. He was silenced, but his active spirit was still untouched, and his courage little broken. The carnival had been in the days of the Medici a very Saturnalia of license ; and of all the wild Florentine revelers in that season abandoned to folly, none were more wildly riotous than the children—those city children,

sharp-witted and precocious, who are everywhere the
amusement and the despair of the more serious community.
In such a center of municipal life as Florence, with a civic
limitation so much more intense, so much more strict than
anything which exists among us, it can scarcely be
supposed that the lads of the town yielded in boldness or
acuteness to the London street boy or Parisian *gamin*, both
of whom are troublesome enough to manage. These young
Florentines had been used to be rampant in carnival time,
and they had various privileges scarcely consistent with
the comfort of their fellow-citizens. These Burlamacchi
describes as the stones, the stiles, and the *capannucci*.
"The stiles were long pieces of wood which were placed
across the street, and no one, especially no women, were
allowed to pass until they had paid something which was
afterward spent in a supper. The *capannucci* were great
trees raised in the squares or wide streets, round which
were placed a quantity of faggots and broken wood to
burn in the evening, over which there were great fights
with stones and other arms, not without the sacrifice of
some lives on each occasion." Savonarola, always tender
of the young, to whom the lads of his convent were *i nostri
angioli*, had his attention directed to this lawless youth of
the city, the most difficult class perhaps to deal with.
All other kinds of authority had been tried in vain to curb
their frolic, especially the dangerous war with stones. Set
aside from his greater and graver work, the prior of San
Marco took this enterprise in hand. We are not informed
how he first got hold of so shifty and tumultuous a band,
but he did get hold of them in some way. Fra Domenico,
his most faithful and devoted follower, became his chief
instrument, most likely because he shared his chief's love
for the children ; the reader may recollect that it was to
him that the message about *nostri angioli* was sent. The
Florentine urchins were organized according to their

quartieri, like their fathers; they were made to choose captains for themselves, one for each district, and counselors for the captains. No doubt this skillful perception of the dawning political impulses of those citizens in bud, pleased the lads, and gave them a new sense of importance. Then, without interfering with their cherished amusements, Savonarola turned them to better uses. He set up little altars in the streets instead of the *stili*, where the children still begged, but for the poor (one hopes they had some kind of social supper all the same; and no doubt Fra Girolamo saw to that, being hard only upon himself). He gave them other songs to sing, not the evil rhymes of the old days—and sent them about the city in procession, in long angelical lines, white-robed and carrying crosses, and finally he indulged them with a *capannucci* greater than any they had ever seen—the big Bonfire of Vanities, for which they had themselves collected the materials. What were the exact component parts of this bonfire can never be known; and doubtless as long as there is any one sufficiently interested to discuss the subject, Savonarola's enemies will reproach him with having destroyed precious works of art in this carnival offering, while his apologists attempt to prove the impossibility of any such sacrifice. I think there can be little doubt that the latter have the stronger case. For not only was the preacher a man of perfect good sense and moderation, but he was himself a poet, the friend of poets and of painters, with a school of art existing under his very wing, to keep him from committing himself. Professor Villari thinks it most likely that the dresses, and masks, and wigs, prepared for the carnival itself, formed the bulk of the bonfire; and a pretty heap might soon have been made of these follies, did they at all correspond in 1496 with what they were in later days. And if a volume of Boccaccio or a few copies of the "Canti Carnascialesch"—or even some of Botticelli's or

Bartolommeo's academical studies—got into the mass
here and there, I do not suppose any great harm was
done.

George Eliot has given so admirable and so humorous a
description of the preparations for this great bonfire, in
"Romola," that the writer would be bold indeed who would
attempt to repeat the sketch. Those who have seen Fra
Bartolommeo's portrait of Savonarola, and marked the
sweetness and benignity, not untouched by humor, of the
homely face there presented, will scarcely refuse to believe
that, in the midst of his great and tragic labors, some
consciousness of the comic side of this demonstration may
have been in the mind of the great preacher, as he watched
the children in their white dresses marching round the
great piazza, clustered all over the loggia of Orcagna, and
filling up, a merry crowd, the solemn *ringhiera*, under the
gray walls of the palace, where he himself was so soon to
be condemned. While the clear young voices sang their
hymns, the glare of the burning lighted up the fresh faces,
the picturesque white groups, the darker Tuscan crowd
around them, and the dark strong Tuscan walls, built for
the use of centuries, behind all. Benvenuto's delicate
Perseus was not there in those days, nor yet the huge
David of a greater artist; but the Judith and Holofernes
just erected, marked, or was meant to mark, the triumph
of freedom and the republic over tyranny. No doubt by
this time the heart was going out of Savonarola's power,
but popular enthusiasm still remained; and in the piazza
the blaze of the burning vanities flickered red upon steadfast walls and flower-like faces—faces bearing the look of
angels—instead of the small demoniac crowd which usually
discharged their missiles at each other round the blazing
bonfire. Once more, the vanities were to flame there
within sight of a devout rejoicing throng; and then
another burning was to follow, more solemn, more terrible,
not of vanities. Was he aware of this in his half-inspired

soul, to which the idea of martydom had already become familiar? Anyhow, without attributing to him such distinct foreknowledge, one can understand with what a smile, and with what a sigh, as the white lines moved on, their songs dying in the distance, Savonarola with his cowl over his head, must have turned away.

One more pretty scene, and work of mercy accomplished, and all the brighter part of his great life was over. It was on Palm Sunday, Burlamacchi tells us, that a procession of these same children, in their white robes, with garlands on their heads, set forth from San Marco on a progress round the city to open the *Monti della Pietà*, which at last Savonarola had been able to institute. They were like beautiful angels out of heaven, Burlamacchi says; sometimes they shouted " Viva Gesù Cristo !" their king; sometimes, " Viva Firenze !" the next and dearest object of every patriot's heart. After them went many ladies, and even " many grave and noble men, full of ability and prudence," all with the palms which the prior had blessed, and the little red cross which was his token. The long line of the procession went round the city, winding through all the narrow streets, a multitude following under the fresh sunshine of the spring—and defiled into the austere gloom of San Giovanni, lighting up that solemn place, and into the cathedral, singing with lovely youthful voices. As they passed, the lookers-on wept and smiled upon the children, and threw alms to them for the new institution. "And so much joy was there in all hearts that the glory of paradise seemed to have descended on earth and many tears of tenderness and devotion were shed. They went to all the four *quartieri*, establishing a *Monte* in each, and securing for them a little endowment to begin with from the alms they collected. *E cos ogni no poi se ne ritornò a casa motto edificato*," says simple Burlamacchi. It was almost the last gleam of gladness in Savonarola's life.

CHAPTER XII.

THE SPERIMENTO.

IT DOES not seem within the reach of human possibility that any man who ventures to put all his being and happiness on the cast, in the hope of regenerating, be it his country, be it his class, be it—greater and more desperate enterprise still—the world and the human race, should come to any but a tragical ending. Even in the softened manners of these later ages, when violent persecution has gone out of fashion, the reformer has rare fortune indeed whose heart and hope has not died in him before life does, and whose period of triumph is anything but brief. Savonarola's reign of genius and spiritual purity was short, but it was for some time almost absolute, a heavenly despotism, perfect in its motives, grand in all its aims ; yet, as we have already said, impossible, a thing contradicted by every principle of ordinary humanity, and too exceptional even to be safe, though higher in all its intentions and most of its results than those governments which are practicable. So long as it lasted, immorality and luxury were out of fashion in Florence, the vileness which calls itself pleasure was paralyzed, and immodesty and impurity scared into corners out of sight. Nor were the more violent sins of the time less discountenanced. Savonarola in his own person was the national guard, the police, the civic protector of the place. For the first time in history the revolution which changed the government of Florence was unattended by massacre or, in any but one instance, by

confiscation. The streets were safe, the populance quiet,
notwithstanding the high strain of excitement in which,
with so many dangers threatening, they must have lived.
Instead of indulging that excitement in the much more
usual and congenial task of sacking a palace, the men of
Florence hurried to the Duomo, where the fervid and
splendid eloquence of the friar gave that stimulus to mind
and heart which has always to be supplied somehow, and
which, in most cases, the crowd finds for itself in less
satisfactory ways. His words were their wine, his eloquence their theater. He communicated to them that
high and fine intoxication of enthusiasm and feeling which,
when it does take hold of the crowd, drives lower and
grosser excitements out of court. Unfortunately it is the
excitement itself, not the noble objects of it, that lays
strongest hold upon the crowd; and it is at all times
easier to be a Piagnone, a Puritan. a member of a party,
than it is to love God and deny one's self. And as every
one of these exciting and magnificent addresses insisted
upon justice, peace, charity, and purity, the millennium
itself must have arrived in Florence in the end of the
fifteenth century, had that great voice continued dominant,
as it was for a time.

This, however, could not be. Savonarola had his close
and devoted circle of true followers, men of like nature
with himself, the religious minds and pure hearts which
happily exist in greater or smaller number at all times.
He had beyond these the large mass of his party, people
religiously affected by his preaching, and so far moved by
intense faith in him as to make many personal sacrifices
under his influence, and range themselves wholly on his
side. A larger circle still, so large at one time as to
embrace all that was noble and patriotic in Florence, held
by him politically, feeling his great influence, always
nobly exerted, to be the salvation of the city. This vast

outer circle—too multitudinous to be ever made into a
religious party, often caring nothing for religion, and made
up of persons who, but for their strong sense of the necessities of Florence, and the use of the friar to keep order,
and sway the masses in the right direction, would have
been naturally the opponents of the great religious reformer—was the cause at once of his absolute triumph and
of his ruin.   They used him, for purposes not ignoble,
and willingly made of him their bulwark against Piero
de' Medici, their old tyrant, against the new tyrants whom
a *parlemento* might have saddled them with, and against
anarchy and internal tumult.   But his prophetical threat-
enings were folly to them, his purity distasteful, his piety
superstition.   When he said, "Be free," they cheered him
to the echo; when he said "Be pure," the effect was very
different.   Now here, now there, at that point and at
this, these supporters fell off from him, joined the ranks
of his enemies, among whom, but for patriotism, they
would alway have found a more congenial place; and
gradually—the tide ebbing ever more and more as the
momentary impulse toward a reformation of manners, by
which the whole city had been superficially affected, died
away—left the prophet, who had once felt himself almost
the prime minister of a theocracy, in the shrunken position of the leader of a religious party.   It had been premature, alas! though a heavenly delusion, that great shout
which all the noble Tuscan walls had seemed to echo,
Viva Gesù Cristo nostro Re! Jesus Christ was not yet to
be King of Florence, any more than of other fleshly king-
doms; and Savonarola, after he had accomplished his
divine and unrewarded drudgery, and freed Florence and
tamed her, for the use of all these magnificent signori,
dropped back into the prior of San Marco, the head of
the Piagnoni, the religious leader against whom the world,
the flesh, and the devil, silenced and crushed for a moment, had now once more risen up in free fight.

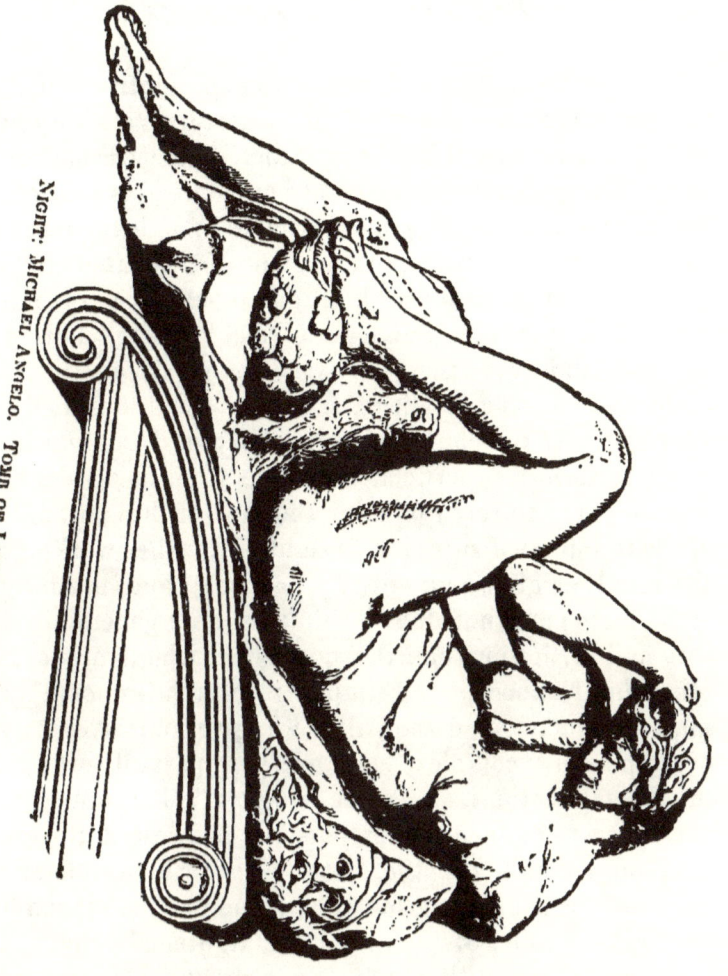

NIGHT. MICHAEL ANGELO. TOMB OF LORENZO DE' MEDICI.

It is the fashion nowadays to make speculative studies of
the unrevealed sensations of men whose lives are long over,
and to decide how they thought and felt, with authority,
as if distance lent not enchantment, but distinctness to
the mental vision. We pique ourselves upon being more impartial than the contemporaries, who either hated the man
and abused him, or loved him, and could see no evil in
him. It is our high privilege to be able to see how good
he was, and yet that he was not good, at the same
moment ; but this privilege, like all others, has its disad-
vantages. If the contemporary sees too close, and is too
ready to form a superficial judgment from facts alone, we
are too ready to rely upon our theories of human nature,
and our supposed superior insight into the workings of
the mind, as giving an entirely new color and meaning to
these facts ; and nothing, I think, is more general in history and criticism, than the confusion which arises from
our refusal to accept the simpler interpretation of a great
man's character, and the pains we give ourselves to find
every person "complex," and every important event full
of "complications." To be single-minded, once one of
the highest commendations possible, has ceased to appear
sublime enough for the imagination, which demands a
labyrinth of conflicting motives, through which it can have
the satisfaction of picking its enlightened way. The
meaner pleasure with which the ordinary observer often
exerts himself to lessen a heroic figure, and show how a
great purpose may be brought down by dilutions of
small motives, is perhaps more general still ; but this latter is not a sentiment upon which it is agreeable to dwell.
The later historians—who, without any such miserable intention, but rather with the desire, we may suppose, of
explaining to themselves a character so singularly swayed
and guided by faith in the unseen, have taken up the idea
that Savonarola was largely moved by love of power, and

that a determination to be himself the greatest influence
in Florence was more strong within him than even his desire to save Florence, though that was great—do but
repeat what all his contemporary accusers, by every diabolical means in their power, attempted to prove, but without
much success. By delirious words wrung from the lips of
a sufferer in torture, and by falsified records, forged pro-
cesses, and signatures fraudulently obtained, the Florentine
signoria, in the end of the fifteenth century, tried very
hard to make out that the prophet, who had swayed all
Florence for years, was not only a false prophet, but one
who had pretended to possess prophetic gifts, for his own
selfish advancement perhaps, or at least for "pride and
vain glory." Savonarola's modern accusers do not go so
far, neither do they use such discreditable means; but
the forgone conclusion that it is impossible for any man
to have believed as he did, and to have acted simply and
vehemently (as his nature was) on that belief, lies behind
all their endeavor to introduce some strain of lesser motive into his impassioned soul.

It is not my business to explain how such a man, in the
full plenitude of his genius, should be able to believe
devoutly and with whole soul in miracles, in spiritual
communications to himself or others, in visible inter-
positions of divine power, and a perpetual supernatural
intervention in the affairs of the world. All the influences
of his age favored his belief, and the greater part of his
contemporaries fully shared it; yet these facts are not
necessary, it seems to me, to make that faith fully credible,
however incomprehensible. Five hundred years later, in
the nineteenth century, Edward Irving, a man of kindred
mind, believed as fervently, as undoubtingly, as Savonarola,
looked for miracles as he did, and received with full faith
various miraculous occurrences which (he thought) proved
the justice of his expectations. Irving has been explained

like Savonarola, and even in a less worthy way. We have been told that mere vanity, and a mad desire for popular favor, moved the one, just as we are told that love of power actuated the other. These lower qualities are supposed to supply the interpretation of their characters, the *fin mot* of the enigma, the solution of all that is mysterious and unlike other men in them ; while at the same time they provide that "complexity" in which the modern imagination delights. For my part, I cannot but think that the simpler view is not only much truer, but far more helpful to us in our endeavors to understand such men. The moment we can believe and realize that all they said was to themselves absolutely true, that their faith was what they describe it to be, that their hopes, expectations, and motives, were such as they constantly and unvaryingly profess—their complexity of character may indeed suffer, but they themselves become infinitely more comprehensible. The number of such men is few, and their fate is seldom encouraging to any who should, of set purpose, take up the mantle as it falls from their shoulders. Such a one as Francis of Assisi, simpler soul in a simpler age, might indeed receive his tokens of God's supreme love in some mysterious way, which words cannot explain, and die of the glory and of the joy of it, happier than his successors, leaving a wondering confused crowd to give what account they could of the miracle. But not such is the lot of later prophets. Girolamo Savonarola in 1498, and Edward Irving in 1832, both died disappointed, looking vainly, straining wistful eyes to the last, for a miracle which never came. Are they shamed in their pathetic trust because they are disappointed ? Surely no. The rash charlatan who casts off his God altogether, and all the bonds of belief when his expected miracle fails him, may invite the imputation of low motives and self-love at the bottom of his preceding enthusiasm. But those great servants of

God, who do their work for naught : who, looking for miraculous acknowledgment get none, yet stand fast and faithful though humiliated : who are dumb, opening not their mouths, because He has done it, yet in the depths of their hearts cannot tell why : seem to me in their defeat and downfall to have as deep a claim upon human sympathy as ever was put forth by fallen hero or discrowned conqueror. On the contrary, instead of comprehending the profound and tragic pathos of their disappointment, history half exults over it, as a fitting recompense for their unfounded pretensions, and setting down of their spiritual pride. Ungenerous and ignoble judgment ! More wonderful than Savonarola himself is the human sentiment which can sigh over a potter's frantic attempts to get from nature a glaze for his hideous lizards, yet stand unmoved at the sight of the prophet's struggle and agony to have his higher work acknowledged by his Master, and of that sublime disappointment which never at its deepest falls one step from faith.

At the same time we lay claim to no unnatural perfection for Savonarola. He had no doubt many of the prejudices of his time, and was colored by it as all men are. Besides the vague insinuations as to love of power, etc., which are freely hazarded against him, one act of his life has been cited as a proof of his inferiority to his own high standard, and determination to clear rivals out of his path. This one event is the execution of Bernardo del Nero and his four companions, found guilty of scheming for the restoration of Piero de' Medici—an event which Savonarola is not represented even by his enemies, as having endeavored to bring about, but simply as not interfering to prevent. According to all the various histories this execution was demanded by the people with absolute fury. Bernardo del Nero was an old man, and of high character, but he had been a partisan of the Medici all his life, and after their expulsion, while holding the highest public office in a republic frantically afraid of, and opposed to, the Medici, he allowed himself to be drawn into a conspiracy for bringing them back. Such an attempt (when unsuccessful) can be considered as nothing but high treason, and has everywhere and in all circumstances ensured the severest punishment. Savonarola had been the constant and persevering opponent of the Medici since his first appearance in Florence. He had resisted the blandishments, the threats, and even the last appeal of the great Lorenzo; and no toleration for the race had ever subdued his vehement, almost violent, condemnation of their usurped position in Florence. It was the fear that anarchy and misgovernment might bring them back with their *parlamentos* and disguised tyranny that drove him to take the part he did in politics. So early as October, 1495, about the time when the government of Florence was resettled after the expulsion of the Medici, he himself from the pulpit denounced all who should endeavor to re-establish despotism in the city as worthy of death, and recommended that the same punishment should be accorded to them as the Romans gave to those who desired to bring back Tarquin. It seems hard to see, after this, why he should have interfered to deliver Bernardo del Nero and his companions. At the time of their condemnation he was no longer the powerful leader he had been. He had shrunk, as I have said, from the spiritual ruler of Florence to be the head of the Piagnoni, and it would have required an exertion of personal influence much greater than that word from the pulpit, which a few years before had swayed the city, to do anything effectual for the help of the condemned ; indeed he had retired from the pulpit altogether, and was shut up in San Marco, silent and excommunicated. These, however, are secondary points in consideration with the fact that we have no right to suppose Savonarola wished to interfere on their behalf. Except on the vague general principle of humanity—a principle unknown to his age and of very doubtful advantage to the world at any period—I cannot see why he should have interfered. The men were enemies to all he thought best for Florence; emissaries of her tyrant, plotters for her enslavement. His sole reason for pleading for them must have been that they were his personal enemies. This reason of course is what may be called the sentimentally Christian one—evangelical to the letter. But I cannot see why Savonarola should have done anything which he believed injurious to his adopted country for the selfish and personal reason that these men were his enemies, any more than he would have been justified in saving an enemy of Florence because he was his friend. Friend or enemy had little to do with the question. They were universally condemned by Florence; their existence was a danger to Florence; and there is not the slightest evidence anywhere that Savonarola's opinion was different from that of the city, or that he wished to interfere.

This event took place in 1497. He had reached the climax of his greatness in 1495, when the consiglio maggiore was appointed by his advice, and the entire fate of the city seemed to hang upon his will. For the moment Florence was unanimous, and the first sketch of her new laws and free institutions came from the pulpit in the Duomo, where wooden galleries were raised from the floor to the roof, and every inch of the solemn area was filled up with eager listeners. In the same year the pope wrote to him with specious protestations of regard, inviting him to Rome in order to derive instruction from his prophetical teaching; and a cardinal's hat was offered to the preacher whose name and fame had already spread over Italy. Burlamacchi tells the following characteristic story of the manner in which the pope's attention was drawn to Savonarola:

" He had preached a very terrible and alarming sermon, which
being written down verbally was sent to the pope. And he, indignant, called a bishop of the same order, a very learned man, and said
to him—' Answer this sermon, for I wish you to maintain the contest
against this friar.' The bishop answered, ' Holy father I will do so ;
but I must have the means of answering him in order to overcome
him.' ' What means ?' said the pope. The bishop replied, ' This
friar says that we ought not to have concubines or to encourage
simony. And he says the truth. What am I to answer to that ?'
Then the pope replied, ' What has he to do with it ?' The bishop
answered, ' Reward him and make a friend of him ; honor him with
the red hat, that he may give up prophesying and retract what he
has said.' This advice pleased the pope, and after he had conferred
with the protector of the order, he determined to follow it, and sent
to Florence Messer Ludovico da Finara, an excellent man, master of
the sacred palace, with orders first to dispute with the friar, and if he
could not overcome him to offer him, from the pope, the position of
cardinal if he would give up his prophesying. And so it was done :
for the priest aforesaid came secretly to Florence, and went to the
preaching, when it pleased God that he was discovered and recognized by a Florentine merchant who had confessed to him in Rome.
This merchant immediately informed Fra Girolamo, who sent for the
priest and received him in the convent with great kindness, arguing
with him for three days As Messer Ludovico, however, found that
he could not overcome, he at last said to him, ' His Holiness has
heard of your goodness and wisdom, and wishes to give you the
dignity of a cardinal, provided you will go no further in predicting
things to come.' To which the padre answered, ' God forbid ! God
forbid ! that I should refuse the mission and embassy of my Lord ;
but come to the preaching to-morrow and I will give you your
answer.' And on the following morning he ascended the pulpit with
great impetuosity of spirit, and confirming everything he had before
prophesied, said, ' I want no other red hat but that of martyrdom,
reddened by my own blood.' Which things Messer Ludovico hearing, carried to the pope · and he, awe-stricken, declared that this
could not but be a great servant of God, marveling much, and struck
dumb by his constancy and firmness, and adding, ' Let no one speak
of him to me more, either for good or evil.' "

The pope, however, was not a man to remain "*spaven-
toso*" or struck dumb by awe and wonder. He was that

Roderigo Borgia, father of Cæsar Borgia and Lucretia, the highest impersonation of mediæval crime and corruption, whose name outweighs that of many innocent or worthy popes, and is a perpetual reproach to the church and hierarchy bought and polluted by him. During the years that followed he made repeated attempts to get this preacher—whose very existence shamed him, and who from the first day of his work till now had ever ceased to denounce the sins of the clergy—into his hands. The conflict between them continued with many vicissitudes for three years—years so full of tumult and of labor, and so rife with great events, that it is almost incredible that they should have been so few. When the constantly changing signoria of Florence was of Savonarola's party, their ambassador at Rome fought fiercely in his favor, laboring to modify the angry letters and hinder the excommunication which was about to be lanched against him. When the signoria were of the party called Arrabbiati, they did all they could, on the contrary, with the concurrence of the pope, to silence the great voice, now broken with sickness, weariness, and disappointment, which once had been omnipotent in Florence—until now and then the tumult of factions became too much for them, and they too were compelled to resort to his help to calm the city. In June, 1497, the excommunication long threatened was at last lanched against him, and formally published in the cathedral. Savonarola obeyed it for a time ; he retired into his convent, closed his eloquent lips, and withdrew himself as much as such a man could from the outer world, occupying himself with his writings, which seemed for the moment his only way of communicating with the great flock outside of San Marco which he once led like a shepherd. This was the moment in which, had he been a Luther, his Protestantism would have developed ; but such was not the turn of his mind. It did not occur to him to

doubt the institutions of his church, or to question her
authority. The question that arose within him, taking
form and force as time went on, was of a different yet very
natural kind—a question not of the church's power, but of
the legality of the pope's election. Alexander VI. was a
monster of iniquity. He had purchased the popedom by
gold as much as any merchant ever bought wool or silk ;
was he therefore true pope at all? or rather a monstrous
usurper and pretended pope, having no real authority over
the consciences of the faithful? I do not pretend to decide
whether mere difference of race is enough to explain why
this partial and limited view of the question was the one
which struck the Italian. In all races, I suppose, there
will be some who, loyal to the theory of absolute obedience,
will gladly take refuge in an accidental circumstance
which excuses their rebellion ; and it cannot be said that
Savonarola was not justified by every law both of nations
and the church, in objecting to the foul Borgia who had
purchased his office. No doubt it cast a gleam of somber
hope upon his confinement to think that it still might be
possible to get free of this contaminated sway without any
outward insubordination against constituted authority, or
anything like that rending of the beautiful robe of the
church which to so many in all ages has been the sorest of
misfortunes as well as the darkest of sins. Whether
Savonarola was wrong in this, according to the strictest
rule of the Catholic Church, I doubt much—but he certainly was right in reason. He was not in any way prepared to discuss the question whether there should or
should not be a pope at all ; but surely the most loyal
believer in the popedom may object to a bad pope, a
simoniacally appointed pope, upon whose claims to the
office there could not be two opinions. With the modern
historian who exultingly condemns him on the ground at
present so much debated, that obedience to the pope means

something absolute, quite irrespective of the nature of the commands given : and the anxious monastic biographer who reluctantly condemns him as exceeding the limits of lawful resistance, I have equally little sympathy. The better Catholic he was, the more he was justified in all and any endeavor to cleanse Christendom of the intruder, the false shepherd in the fold, who lived only to ravage and rob and devour.

There would seem to be little doubt that this conviction grew upon Savonarola's mind during the six months of silence to which he submitted in obedience to the sentence of excommunication—and that gradually, as this weary time of silence passed over his head, the tedium worked upon him, making every argument on this point more telling, and deepening a hundredfold his sense of the incapacity of the unworthy pope to judge him. On Christmas day, '98. he could refrain no longer, and in his own convent he opened his lips once more, addressing "a vast multitude of people" after the celebration of a solemn mass. Encouraged by this first step, and stimulated by the growing disorder and anarchy in Florence — which many still believed Savonarola could put down, as he had put them down before—his friends re-erected the wooden galleries in the Duomo, and so influenced the signoria that they themselves requested him to preach ; which he did accordingly. The sermons which he preached at this time, however, though not less splendid in their eloquence than of old, have changed their character. They are occupied chiefly with this question of the excommunication, examining it with much skill and subtilty indeed, but with that less elevated strain which seems inevitable when a man descends from the great things of God to questions which concern himself. To prove that his own condemnation was invalid the friar went further than that ground of the wrongly appointed and unworthy pope, on which he was

safe enough, and following out his subject, declared that
an act so evidently contrary to charity could not be
right, and that the potentate, prince, or pope, who acted
contrary to Christian teaching, was consequently without
Christ and therefore without authority; and vaguely
threatened to "turn a key"—to bring down summary
vengeance upon a corrupt church. It seems somewhat
doubtful to make out what he meant by this; whether he
expected some external miracle to justify him among all
his enemies, and prove God's will beyond dispute—to him,
no doubt as to his age, a not unreasonable expectation; or
whether the active effort which we find him some time after
engaged in, to have a general council of the church called
together, was in his mind. These sermons, however,
though wonderful in their force and impassioned eloquence,
may well be less attractive to the modern reader than
his former preaching. The sense of wrong is in them, the
personal strain of attack and defense, the vehemence
natural to a man who felt for the first time his own position
assailable, and was compelled to think of himself. Perhaps a certain fainting of heart and the melancholy
irritability and impatience of weariness and discouragement
contributed to give this harsher and shriller tone to all he
says. No doubt his great and generous soul was impatient
to be thus forced out of his high work and mission into
those meaner arts of self-defense.

The rest of Savonarola's life might almost be told in a
few great pictures. He preached but once in the cathedral
at the request of the signoria, on Septuagesima Sunday;
but perceiving that, as Burlamacchi tells us, "every day
raised some new sedition against him, it appeared to him
better to give way to wrath; and therefore he retired to
San Marco, where he preached only to men, sending away
the women, on account of the small size of the church, but
reserving Saturday for them, that they might not be

altogether discontented." At the end of one of his sermons
he announced that on the first day of the carnival he
would, if any of his adversaries would dare the experiment
along with him, appear in some public place, holding the
Sacrament in his hand, and appeal to God by solemn
prayer to send fire from heaven and burn up him—whether
himself or his antagonist—who was in the false way. This
ordeal seems simple enough to have called forth a champion
on the other side; but no one answered the appeal. Savonarola, however, kept his word. On the first day of the
carnival, according to Burlamacchi (Villari says the last),
after a solemn mass in San Marco, he came out of the
church in his priest's robes, carrying the Sacrament, and
ascended the pulpit, which had been raised in the square
outside. The Piazza of San Marco is a very ordinary
square nowadays, planted with a few commonplace bushes
and modest bit of turf· but how strange must have been its
aspect on that spring morning, "filled with many thousands of men," through whom came the procession of
monks, surrounding their prophet. For half an hour the
whole vast multitude was still, praying for the reply from
Heaven. Savonarola made them no eloquent address—the
day of his great preaching was over—and one cannot but
feel that something like despair in his heart must have
been the cause of this pathetic endeavor to call forth an
answer from God. All that he said was simple enough.
"If I have said anything to you, citizens of Florence, in
the name of God, which was not true ; if the apostolical
censure pronounced against me is valid; if I have deceived
any one—pray to God that he will send fire from heaven
upon me and consume me in presence of the people; and I
pray our Lord God, Three in one, whose body I hold in
this blessed Sacrament, to send death to me in this place if
I have not preached the truth." Then for half an hour
there was silence, except from the rustle of the multitude

which knelt around. It is scarcely possible to imagine a more striking scene. The people prayed and waited, filling the square to its furthest corner; the monks round the pulpit, upon the steps of their church, with deeper anxiety or more certain triumph, knelt in the same solemn appeal. Above them all, raised so that every one could see him, stood the prophet, his rugged and homely but inspired countenance raised to heaven, his pyx in his hands. And no fire came from the blue Italian sky, shining over them, in that serene calm of nature which stupefies with its tranquillity the eager restless soul, looking in vain for an answering and visible God.* When the solemn half hour was done the prophet and his monks went back, chanting a *Te Deum*, to their cloisters. Was he satisfied with that success, which was simply a negation? Who can tell? We have no right to form imaginations of our own on such a subject; yet it is hard not to suppose that the very fire from heaven, which he invoked, would have been a relief to the terrible tension of mind with which such a man strains his soul upward, gazing and longing for that word of acknowledgment, that touch of comfort which never comes. But faith was more strenuous and robust in those days, and perhaps Savonarola was as triumphant as the simpler souls about him, who threw all their excitement into their *Te Deum*, and had no troublous thoughts behind.

This incident must have happened in the end of February or beginning of March, and we are told that Savonarola invited his adversaries, especially the Franciscans, to an-

---

* The reader will remember the beautiful description of this scene in "Romola," to which fine picture the present narrative of necessity approaches so near as to provoke a dangerous comparison. The incident of the sudden sunbeam, which George Eliot introduces with so much effect, is not noted by Burlamacchi, from whom chiefly this account is taken.

other very curious ordeal. He proposed that they should go with him to a cemetery, and there attempt to raise one of the dead. The young Pico della Mirandola, who afterward wrote the life of Fra Girolamo, and was one of his devoted disciples, even went so far as to propose that his uncle Giovanni, who had been buried not long before in San Marco, should be the object of the experiment; which, indeed chimes in with the suggestion of certain recent scientific writers in a remarkable way. Savonarola's faith was strong enough, it is evident, to have invited all the safeguards of scientific scrutiny which would satisfy even Professors Huxley and Tyndall. This challenge, too, remained unanswered; but it is scarcely wonderful that it should have called forth another challenge, made in anything but good faith, a short time after, when the famous ordeal by fire was proposed, and eagerly taken up by the party which, in any public tumult which might arise, hoped to find means of putting the dangerous frate out of their way. In this case it was the Franciscans who were the challengers. Whether it was from a perception of the bad faith of his adversaries—who, as the event proved, had no intention whatever of jeopardizing themselves in the more fatal trial they proposed, but only to deliver over their Dominican rivals to the fury of a disappointed mob —or for some less satisfactory reason, the fact is apparent that Savonarola set his face resolutely against this "Sperimento." It was not himself, but his devoted brother and retainer, Fra Domenico, who was originally challenged, and no bridegroom on his marriage morning was ever more ready than was Domenico—one of those simple heroes whose faith knows no faltering, and whose nerves and courage are as manly and steadfast as their conviction is beyond the reach of doubt. When, however, the Franciscan, Fra Francisco di Puglia, found his challange accepted with delighted eagerness by Domenico, he attempted to transfer it to Fra Girolamo himself, and declared that he would only risk the ordeal from which he had no hope of escaping alive in company with the prophet, willing to accept martyrdom as the price of uncloaking the false pretensions of the excommunicated priest, but not for any lesser end.

I am at a loss to understand why Savonarola refused this ordeal. Nothing could be more natural than that his good sense should have seen its vanity ; but yet, as he had already suggested other miraculous experiments, it is almost impossible to believe that this was his sole reason. Perhaps he considered the question already settled by that appeal to God in the Piazza of San Marco ; perhaps he perceived the falseness of the proposal altogether ; but in any case his repugnance to the ordeal is remarkable. Everything he himself says on the subject, and everything his biographer says, is perfectly reasonable. When he tells us that he has too many great works in hand to lose his time in such miserable contests ; when he bids his enemies first answer his arguments in respect to the excommunication, and that then it will be time enough to prove its justice by fire ; we agree with every word, and feel something of the indignant impatience which might very naturally move him. But all that he says in respect to the Franciscan challenge applies equally well to his own ; and the difference between entering the fire with one of his adversaries, and waiting in the Piazza under the sky in hopes that God would strike the false preacher with fire from heaven, is very slight. Perhaps Savonarola himself only saw the utter weakness and foolishness of the proposed test when it was repeated and cast back to him by his adversaries ; perhaps he saw that only a popular tumult and his own murder was intended ; and that with a signoria who hated him in office, and his enemies growing stronger every day, no kind of justice or equal trial could be expected. But however that may be, I cannot wonder that his enemies, one and all, should fix upon this seeming inconsistency. Burlamacchi tells us that he declared himself quite ready to enter the fire, "but with this condition—that the ambassadors of all the Christian princes, and the pope's legate, should be present, and that they should promise and bind themselves, if he came out unhurt, to proceed immediately with the help of God to a universal reform of the church." For no lesser reason would he subject himself to the experiment, and such a condition was out of the question. It must, however, be added, that he had just undertaken the greatest and most disastrous enterprise of his life, and with the conjunction of various devoted friends, had written letters to all the great Christian monarchs, begging them to call together a general council. This he had gradually come to believe was the sole hope remaining for the church ; and it may easily be supposed that having made this last appeal and effort for a great reformation, the petty strife in the Piazza becomes a weariness to him, and the ordeal showed itself in its true colors. His mind had already gone beyond the smaller personal question, to the great one of a universal reformation. "Why," he himself says, "should we enter the fire to prove the excommunication invalid ? We have no occasion to have recourse to supernatural ordeals, since we have already with effective reasoning proved the excommunication to be null, to which reasoning no one either in Rome or Florence or elsewhere has attempted to reply. Miracles are not necessary when there is room for natural reason. Therefore to make this trial would be to tempt God. And if our adversaries," he continues, "say that our reasonings are sophistical, yet make no answer to them, and therefore seek miracles, we reply that, these being the great things of prophecy, we constrain no one to believe more than they will, but encourage them rather to live godly and as Christians.

And I say that this is the greatest of miracles—to make them believe those things which we preach, and every other truth which proceeds from God. And though I have proposed to manifest and prove great things under the name of the key, with supernatural signs, I have not therefore promised to do such things in order to annul the excommunication, but for other reasons, when the time shall be come."

I do not pretend to say that Savonarola's reasoning here satisfies my mind. What is distinctly evident is that he did not choose to accept the ordeal thus forced upon him, in which he was wise—for nothing but treachery was intended—but not consistent. Fra Domenico, however, his loyal henchman, never faltered. He was one of those stout men-at-arms to whom in their perfect and simple manhood is given that part which our great poet allots to women—"He for God only, she for God in him." Domenico was for God in and through Savonarola. His belief in his master was absolute. Cheerfully as a man goes to a feast would he have walked into any fire, or dared any danger, confident not to be harmed indeed, yet ready to endure all that earth and hell could do against him, as he did endure manfully, and without flinching, the tortures of the rack. Savonarola, we are told, did all in his power to hold his eager brother back, but in vain. And no sooner was the challenge proclaimed, than not only the monks of San Marco, but the entire multitude of the Piagnoni party declared themselves ready to enter the fire in his defense—the latter interrupting him in his sermons with cries of entreaty to have this privilege granted to them. Burlamacchi tells us a pretty story, how when the padre was walking one evening in the convent garden with Fra Placido (fit name for a companion in that meditative stroll through the retired garden of a monastic quiet!), a beautiful boy, of noble

family, came to him with a paper, on which he had
written his childish pledge of devotion, offering himself for
the ordeal ; " but doubting that the writing was not
sufficient for such a step, fell at his feet, and entreated
him earnestly (*cordialmente*) to be allowed to enter the
fire ; and the padre answered, ' Rise, my son, thy good
will is pleasing to God.' And he gave him the liscense."
As he put his name to the boy's harmless vow, according
to a formula in which Savonarola had pledged himself to
produce one, two, or even ten champions on his side,
according to the number produced on the other, he turned
to Fra Placido, looking on, "Many such papers have been
brought to me," he said, "but by none have I had such
consolation as by this child, for whom God be praised."
It does not require much imagination to fancy the
moisture that must have come into those kind blue eyes
which look out at us still from Bartolommeo's picture, as
the prophet blessed the willing little would-be martyr.
But this soft garden scene, with the cool, sweet evening
atmosphere around, the noble little enthusiast, and the
gentle Brother Placid, is about the last in which we see
the doomed man breathe freely. Doomed for wishing well
to Florence and to mankind—for working night and day
through laborious years, seeking naught but his people's
freedom, purity, truth, and godliness, his cause was
already hopeless. Even at that moment his letter to the
king of France about the council had fallen into the
hands of the duke of Milan, and had been forwarded to
the pope ; and henceforward there was neither hope nor
help for him.

On the 7th of April, the Friday before Palm Sunday,
with immense preparation and eagerness of the people,
the great ordeal by fire was appointed to take place.
The Piazza has seen very strange sights, but none more
extraordinary. In the center a great pile was erected,

covered with all kinds of imflammable substances, and with a path through it wide enough for the passage of the two champions. The square was lined with troops ; five hundred soldiers of the republic were stationed by the Loggia dei Signori, the platform in front of the palazzo Vecchio, generally called the *ringhiera*. These were supposed to be impartial, to keep order among the vast multitude who thronged the Piazza. Directly opposite, in front of the old house called the Tetto dei Pisani, which fifteen years ago was still standing, and used as a post office, but which has now entirely disappeared, were ranged a second band of five hundred men, the bitterest enemies of San Marco, the well-known Compagnacci, or wicked companions, under their leader, Dolfo Spini. The Loggia dei Lanzi, or dell' Orcagna, so well known to all visitors of Florence, which forms the left side of the square, was divided in two, and allotted to the rival con-vents, San Marco having one side, the furthest from the palace, and the Franciscans the other ; and in front of the place allotted to San Marco were three hundred armed Piagnoni, under the leadership of Marcuccio Salviati, pledged to protect their leader against his enemies. Savonarola had given up by this time his opposition to the mad contest, not as a man of this century would have done it, in sheer despair at the folly, but with the solemn faith of his age in God's personal intervention.

San Marco was early astir on that eventful morning—crowded with excited yet awe-stricken throngs of people, kneeling in long strain of ceaseless prayer. Savonarola celebrated mass, and the crowd approached the altar and communicated, returning one by one to their prayers. "So much gladness was in their hearts," says Burlamacchi, "that the face of all things smiled out of the certainty of victory." The Padre Fra Girolamo, very fervent, and full of the spirit, went into the pulpit in his priest's robes, with great solemnity, and, in a short sermon, exhorted the faithful to love Christ, encouraging them to be steadfast in the faith, and adding these words: "So far as has been revealed to me, if the ordeal takes place, the victory is ours, and Fra Domenico will come out of it unhurt; if however it will take place or not, this the Lord has not revealed to me. But if you ask me what I think, I say, as a mere man, that after so many preparations, I would rather it took place than not." He then reminded his brethren that when Fra Domenico went into the fire, they were to continue in prayer until the moment when he came out; and then he gave them the benediction. At this moment the mace-bearers of the signoria came to call the monks to the ordeal, and they set out in solemn procession, Fra Domenico, in a red cope, preceded by all the brethren, and followed by Savonarola and two others, in priestly vestments, carrying the sacrament. This procession wound through the streets, followed by crowds of eager Florentines, over whose heads rang the psalm, "*Exurgat Deus, et dissipentur inimici ejus,*" to which many of the crowd responded, chanting as Savonarola had taught them, the first verses of the psalm as a chorus. "And as there was in that crowd many thousand persons, so great was the sound that the earth underfoot appeared to tremble, and great fear and terror filled the hearts of the enemies." All Florence was astir, pouring into the Piazza, every entrance of which was guarded as in the time of *parlamentos;* and, except devout women who had watched the monks go forth to this extreme test, and whom Savonarola had charged to remain in the deserted church, praying for the champion and the cause, we hear of no one who was not in the great square, looking on breathless at the contest. The streets of busy Florence were deserted, except in that one great heart of the city, throbbing high with fierce excitement, with wild hope and

tremor of expectation, where the eager Florentines waited
for a miracle, a new thing never seen before in the experience of man.

So far everything seemed in favor of the Dominicans.
Savonarola was there facing the crowd, calm and commanding, in the vestments of his office; and there was
Domenico, strong as his dauntless soul and joyful heart
could make him, more than ready, eager for the trial. But
the champions on the other side, the monk who had given
the challenge, and the other who was to represent him in
the flames were both invisible, hid in the palace, where
every means that could be used was being tried to warm
up the valor which had chilled at sight of these terrible
preparations. The other Franciscans were moving about
full of agitation, consulting among themselves and with
their partisans, and doing all that could be done to gain
time. They found fault with Domenico's cope, which he
took off instantly; and then with his Dominican habit,
which they suggested might have been enchanted against
the fire, and which he immediately changed, taking the
dress of young Alexander Strozzi instead, who, thinking it
was to be his proud lot to share the sacrifice, went to Savonarola eagerly for his blessing, with the *Te Deum* bursting from his youthful lips. The day went on in this endless and vain struggle. Who does not know the weariness
of the hours thus passed by a crowd worked up to fever-
point of excitement, but from which the event for which
it waits is kept back. If it is only the passing of a royal
pageant, the momentary view of a public visitor, how
much anger mixes with the disappointment of the throng
when it is balked of the sight it waited for! All these
comings and goings—the agitated consultations of the
Franciscans, their fault-finding with one thing after another, the hurrying to and fro of the commissaries appointed to guide each party, and their many references to

the palace where the signoria sat unseen—tantalized and wearied the crowd, which could not tell how the delay was occasioned, and weary and fasting began to lose patience. From half-past twelve to the hour of vespers, this tragi-comedy went on. The signoria remained unseen in the palace, the Franciscan champion kept out of sight, and Savonarola and his brethren waited—they too suffering somewhat, can it be doubted? from the long strain of excitement and delayed expectation. A thunderstorm swept across the Piazza, then a tumult arose ; but neither storm nor tumult was enough to disperse the crowd or make a natural end to the situation. At last, as the day waned, the signoria finding it impossible to screw up their champions to the sticking-point, put a stop to the ordeal altogether, and sent word to Savonarola to depart with his brethren. He remonstrated, declaring his party on their side to be ready, but with no effect, and the mace-bearers were sent to dismiss him from the Piazza. But he who had come with no better escort than these same mace-bearers could not go back in the same simple way, "Then it was clearly seen," says Burlamacchi, "that his enemies sought no other miracle than the death of Fra Girolamo." The signoria, however, in mere shame, could not refuse him the protection of their troops, and it was all that the five hundred soldiers of the republic, along with the band of armed Piagnoni, led by Salviati, could do, to convey the unoffending Dominicans, whose share in the disap-pointment of the people had been quite involuntary, back to their convent. The two captains arranged their men "*come una luna,*" says Burlamacchi—in the form of a crescent—and putting Fra Girolamo and his followers in the center, struggled back to San Marco, along the same streets which they had traversed in the morning in peace-ful procession intoning their psalm. The Compagnacci, wild with the thought of having lost their opportunity, and

the baser populace, maddened by the loss of the expected
miracle, surged round the returning band like an angry
sea. " Worst of men !" " Put down the Sacrament,"
they cried, " now is the time ;" and, with every kind of
contumely and vain attempt at violence, this hoarse and
frantic multitude accompanied the strange procession.
Even Fra Girolamo's former friends joined the cry. Why
had not he at that supreme moment proved his cause and
glorified their belief in him forever and ever by himself
going through the fire, which had all been wasted, and
now could burn nobody? The very Piagnoni who loved
him must have felt the chill of disappointment strike to
their hearts ; and a great revulsion of feeling, unreasonable, but not unnatural, moved Florence. Who can doubt
that the very monks, who were but common men, like
others, felt it as they streamed back crestfallen to the
church in which the women still knelt, trembling to hear
the hoarse insults of the advancing crowd? Savonarola
had enough spirit left to make his way to the pulpit, where
he told briefly the story of this sad and tedious day, ending, as he always did, by exhorting his hearers " to pray and
to live a good life." Then he retired to the little cell in
the corner, the four humble walls, without even one of
Angelico's angels to glorify them, to which since then
many a pilgrimage has been made. His life had been in
danger often enough before, but never had the voice of the
people swelled the cries of his enemies. He uttered no
complaint to mortal man, but the prophet had fallen, fallen
from his high estate! He who had once been king and
more than king, in Florence, had been hooted through the
streets, and preserved with difficulty from the rage of the
disappointed mob. God whom he had invoked had not
arisen nor had his enemies been scattered. He had given
the best years of his life to the city—his heart's love and
restless labors ; night and day, in health and sickness, he

had been at her call ; he had been ready to supply her even
with the wonder, the miraculous exhibition for which she
craved ; and for all this service she paid him with scorn,
abuse, and insults. Perhaps—who can tell?—there mingled in this bitter disappointment an aching wonder
whether it would have been better for him, the higher soul,
to have taken upon him robust Domenico's part, and proved
his faith by devoting himself all alone to the fire? When
the more exalted way does not touch the common heart,
sometimes the vulgar wonder does. Ought he, in spite of
all the higher uses for him, in spite of the possible council on which his heart was set, and that reformation of the
church which had been before his eyes since first he entered the cloister, to have stepped aside from the loftier
path, and taken upon himself that yeoman's service? Who
could tell? Shut up alone in his little chamber, with the
darkness falling round him, and chill discouragement and
the disappointment of love in his heart, no doubt Savonarola on that night tasted all the bitterness of death.

CHAPTER XIII.

THE PROPHET'S END.

WHY THE failure of the ordeal by fire should have brought such ruin upon the party of San Marco it is hard to say. The failure was in no sense their fault; their champion was ready, and more than ready, anxious for the trial—while his challenger skulked invisible. They had not provoked the strife, yet they came forth in the sight of all Florence to maintain it. The tedium and weariness and disappointment of the day had borne not less but more heavily upon them than upon the enraged and baffled spectators. Yet Florence unanimously laid upon their shoulders the guilt of her *spectacle manqué*. And not only mediæval Florence in the cinque-cento, but many an enlightened modern commentator, has echoed the enraged disappointment of the crowd. Why did not Savonarola take this upon himself? they cry. Why neglect these easy means of proving the divinity of his mission, or at least the divinity of his belief in it? Had he done so he would have been denounced as a madman and fanatic—a man whose wisdom in word and counsel was neutralized by the tragical grotesque folly of his ending. He lived liked a prophet but died like a mountebank, we should all have said; and instead of the spectacle it would have been the man who was a failure. I do not doubt that only the noble good sense, which is in most cases a component of genius, fortified Savonarola himself from that impulse of heroic weakness which was the strength of Fra Domenico ; and that afterward, in the melancholy self-questionings of conscious ruin, he must have asked himself many a time whether it would have been better for his mission and God's truth if he had left his higher ministrations and taken that meaner desperate office upon him ? Gods knows what were the real thoughts in the forlorn heart of the fallen ruler. Everything was against him within the city and without—and God himself, out of those clear, unanswering skies, vouchsafed no sign, such as so many fainting souls have looked for. To serve unacknowledged, so serve for nothing, to receive as wages anguish and tribulation and tears, is not this the pay we have been told of, since the first soldier of Christ took service ? Was not this the recompense in our lower world of the Master himself? He saved others, therefore Himself he could not save—most splendid of all reproaches that ever mortal tongue has spoken. But with every new claimant who receives this payment of agony, there is a struggle, before the sufferer can realize that once more it is to be so, that good has not yet overcome evil, nor heaven begun to reign on earth. Savonarola, like his brethren, had believed that a new Jerusalem was to be revealed in Florence, with streets better than those paved with gold of the Apocalyptic vision, full of honor and truth. He had held to this hope strenuously, desperately, as long as a man might. Now he knew that it was to be with him as with the others that had gone before him. He must have learned this final lesson on the night of that disastrous Friday when he withdrew all alone and silent to his solitary cell.

He had not long to wait. The following Sunday was Palm Sunday, the day which commemorates one of the most touching events of the gospel, and which has always in it a certain pathos yet hopefulness, so near the crisis of the Saviour's woes, so near the moment of His victory.

Two years before, on that same day, Fra Girolamo, in all
the glory and joy of an apparent public reformation, had
trodden the stony streets following the long procession
of white-robed children who marched from quarter to
quarter of the old city, "like beautiful angels just come
out of paradise," establishing the *Monti* in each district
of Florence. The streets which had resounded then with
the hymns chanted by all those fresh, sweet, childish
voices, were alive now with dark groups full of menace
and wrath. Florence, preternaturally tranquilized for
a moment by one great influence, had returned to her
old use and wont, and felt herself at ease in it, breathing
flames and slaughter more easily than blessings, and
longing for a victim. Savonarola preached sadly in the
morning, bidding a kind of farewell to the people. In
the evening a brother of San Marco, Fra Mariano, who
was one of those who had offered himself for the fire, was
to preach in the cathedral. This the authorities of the
Duomo, moved by the Compagnacci, determined to prevent. The enemies of San Marco gathered in crowds
about the doors and corners of the streets on the way to
the cathedral, and assailed with gibes and insults, sometimes with showers of stones, sometimes with blows, the
faithful followers who, in spite of everything, took their
way to the evening sermon. Fra Mariano was finally
assailed and driven away as he was in the act of ascending
the pulpit; and this first open breaking out of the incipient
riot set the population on fire. Shouting "a San Marco !
a San Marco !" ("*Assamarcho! assamarcho col fuocho!*"
writes one literal chronicler), they precipitated themselves
upon the convent. The monks were singing vespers in
the calm of the April evening. All the chief members of
the party were in and about the church, full of fears and
foreboding. Outside, while the mad multitude hurried on
with shouts and clamor, little bands of the Compagnacci

took possession of the corners of the narrow streets, preventing the Piagnoni from any sudden rally. Some of
the incidents of this terrible evening carry us back to
similar accounts of mad revolt against religion in our own
country. A young man of the noble family of the Pecori
was going quietly along, not even to San Marco, to hear
vespers at the Annunziata, saying over to himself some
pious prayers or couplets. "Oh, villain, still psalm-
singing?" some one cried, and the frantic crowd, making
a rush at the helpless lad, hustled him from hand to hand,
till struck through with a lance, he died on the steps of
the Innocenti, the great orphan hospital which still stands
in the Piazza of the Annunziata. At another point in the
way, a spectacle-maker, a good man, came rushing out
from his door, his slippers in his hand, to remonstrate
with the rioters and endeavor to restrain them, but a
blow on the head with a sword soon made a conclusion of
his appeal. When the mob reached the church, vespers
were over, and the worshipers, sad and alarmed, were
kneeling to say their final prayers before leaving this
beloved center of their faith, not knowing what might
happen ere to-morrow. Many were surprised at their
devotions by the tumult outside in the Piazza and by
a sudden shower of stones, before which the women and
helpless persons took to flight.

Then the peaceful church with its few lights, the
kneeling silent worshipers, the still monks flitting here
and there, all at once gave way to the sudden excitement
of a castle besieged. As the congregation fled, the doors
of the church and convent were hurriedly shut upon the
infuriated crowd, and the few laymen within took hasty
counsel and prepared for defense. Savonarola does not
seem to have been in the church at the moment, but as
soon as he was aware of what had happened, he hastily
put on his priest's robes, took a crucifix in his hand, and

crossing the cloisters, directed his steps toward the door. Here, however, his adherents threw themselves in his way, and held him back, entreating him not to expose himself and them to instant death. Among these men was the impetuous old Francesco Valori (killed that night in the streets in a vain attempt to bring help), and other noble and trusty soldiers. While these warlike citizens restrained his first impulse to yield, Fra Benedetto, one of the brethren, a skillful and delicate illuminator of manuscripts, came up under the dim arches hastily armed and full of warlike zeal. Even with the roar of the crowd outside the wall ringing in his ears, Fri Girolamo bade his faithful brother put down the unseemly weapons. Then he called the monks together, and led them singing through the cloisters, which were darkening into night, and into the dim partially lighted church with its deserted area and closed doors ; there he placed the Sacrament on the altar, and kneeling with his black-cloaked and white-robed brethren round him, awaited the issue. When Valori and the rest (there were but thirty of them with a few old halberds, cross-bows, and guns) entreated permission to defend the convent, he said, No : but probably already engrossed by a consciousness of the end which had visibly begun, does not seem to have paid any further attention. Fra Domenico, stout soul, who no doubt would have liked but too well to join them, bade them, on the contrary, defend themselves, before he joined his master at the altar.

And then there ensued a scene as striking as it was tragical. Through the dust and smoke and tumult of the brave but hopeless defense, a few rude heroic figures gleam, coming and going, apart from, yet belonging to, the still kneeling group around the altar. The young friars, men like others, and Florentines, with warm blood in their veins, could not keep up the passive attitude to which their

superiors called them. One by one they began to defend
their sacred citadel, fighting with lighted torches, with
crosses, whatever they could lay hands on. Young Fra
Marco Gondi, a novice, broke a great wooden cross on the
heads of the assailants of the choir, meeting dauntlessly,
with that weapon only, the naked swords of his enemies.
Another novice, Giovanni Maria Petrucci, "of great soul
and robust frame, dressed like an angel (in the white robe
of the Dominican novice) and of beautiful countenance,"
broke the lances with his strong young hands "like
matches" (*solfanelli*), says the simple narrator ; and the
German, Henrico, with his fair locks, appears half angelic,
half demoniac in the smoke and din, armed with an old
arquebus, and shouting "Save thy people, oh God!" the
refrain of the psalm the peaceful brethren had been
chanting, at every shot he fired. This Henrico was *cosi
animoso*, so dauntless in youthful valor, that he rushed
through the crowd of assailants who now filled the church
to get his arquebus, and fought his way back again to the
choir, which he defended like a young Saint Michael,
flaming in generous wrath at the doors of the sanctuary.
The gates of the church had been fired to admit the crowd,
and the place was full of smoke, of fierce cries and tumult.
Inside the choir, for which these brave novices fought in
their angel robes, another noble lad, one of the Panciatici,
lay dying on the altar steps, receiving the last Sacrament
from Fra Domenico, and breathing out his soul joyfully
with the light of enthusiasm on his face. "I have never
been so happy as now," he cried with his last breath. This
valiant defense daunted the multitude, and there was
evidently a pause, during which some dried figs and wine
were brought to the exhausted monks. Savonarola took
advantage of the pause to send his brethren out of the
church in decorous procession as before into the dormitory.
At this moment there arrived a commission from the

signoria, begging Fra Girolamo, Fra Domenico, and Fra Silvestro to go at once to the Palazzo, and thus save the convent from further attack. While Savonarolo considered this proposal, another embassy arrived hastily with more imperative orders to bring the three friars at once, but with a written promise, says Burlamacchi, that they should be brought back in safety when the tumult was quelled.

"When he heard this he said he would obey, but first withdrew with his brethren into the great library, where he made them a beautiful address in Latin, exhorting them to continue in the way of God with faith, patience, and prayer, telling them that the way to heaven was by tribulation, and that none ought to deceive himself on this point; and quoting many ancient examples of the ingratitude of Florence for benefits received from their order. . . . . and that it was no wonder if he too, after so many labors and troubles, should be paid in the same money, but that he was ready to accept all with satisfaction and gladness for the love of his Lord, knowing that the Christian life consists in nothing else than to live godly and endure evil. And thus, while all around him wept, he finished his sermon. When he went out of the library he said to the laymen who waited for him outside, 'I expected this, but not so soon or so suddenly,' and comforted them, bidding them lead a good life, and be fervent in prayer."

Nothing can be more touching than the sad calm of this leave-taking, after the din and tumult with which the air was still echoing. Withdrawing into the first library, Savonarola confessed to Fra Domenico, and received the Sacrament; then ate something, the weeping monks again crowding round him, and kissed them one by one, answering with gentle words their endeavors to detain him, their prayers to go with him. Benedetto, the miniaturist, he who had armed himself at the first sound of warfare, yet shamefaced, had put away his weapons, at the word of the prophet, would scarcely be restrained, and pushing aside the officers, struggled to accompany his master. It was nine o'clock of the April night when this sad scene was

over, and out of the convent, leaving all this love and
sorrow, the two devoted brothers went forth into the raging
sea of mad enemies, breathing fire and murder, which had
been beating for all these hours against the walls of San
Marco. They were immediately swallowed up in the
hoarse roar of the furious crowd, which pressed so closely
round them that their conductors could scarcely save them
from its violence. The officers joined their weapons over
the heads of the prisoners, making a " roof of arms " over
them to keep them from murder at least; but were incapable
of defending them from the insults shouted in their ears,
the stones thrown at them, even the blows of the crowd.
Thus Savonarola, his hands tied behind him, and every
insult that vulgar cruelty could devise heaped upon him,
made his last progress through these Florentine streets. It
is also his last authentic and certain appearance in this
life, until, when falsehood and torture had done their
worst, he emerged once more six weeks after into the May
sunshine in the great Piazza, and died there, like his master, for the love of those who murdered him.

I have said nothing of the third monk who was associated
with these two nobler and greater men. Fra Silvestro
Maruffi was one of those weaker beings, by whom, chiefly,
the mystical visions and raptures which form a distinct
class of phenomena by themselves, and which no reasonable
person can regard without interest—come. He represents
the clairvoyant, the " medium " of modern life, the nature
sensitively alive to occult influences, which in all ages has
been the wonder of the sane and thoughtful, yet has rarely
failed of a certain influence upon high-toned and imaginative
minds. All dreamers of dreams and seers of visions are
not of this type, as witness Girolamo Savonarola himself
and Saint Theresa, a man and a woman of the greatest
mold possible to humanity. I do not attempt to explain
these noble persons, or to follow them through the mysteries

which to some critics seem mere aberrations of mind;
neither indeed can I explain the much lower and more
common character of Fra Silvestro, and trace out how
his weaker visions and ecstasies at once filled out and
stimulated those of Savonarola. He was a good man,
as became apparent at the last, but his nerves were in a
pre-eminently excited and hysterical condition, and his
organization of a very peculiar kind. His inspirations were
not those great ones which Savonarola believed to be
communicated to himself, those intimations of evil to come
and of reformation to be accomplished, which were as true
as the daylight; but revelations much more practical and
matter of fact. It was Silvestro, for instance, who directed
how Domenico was to enter the fire, carrying the Sacrament,
and laid down all the conditions of that act of faith, as if
they, and not the faith itself, gave safety. Such detail of
prophecy is always impressive to the crowd; and Savonarola
himself had received undoubtingly, and had given credibility
by his own faith in them, to those minute prophetical
indications of what was to come. It was for this reason
that a being so much inferior to the others had the honor
of sharing in the condemnation of his master and the
faithful Domenico. Fra Silvestro, timid and nervous, hid
himself while the siege of San Marco was going on; he
had not the courage to take his place in the choir with his
brethren, a mark for the stones and arrows of the assailants.
But when the morning came after that awful night, and
stealing from his hiding-place he found the monks weeping
over their lost leader and desolated sanctuary, the better
soul awoke in poor Silvestro. So at least Burlamacchi
says, according to whose narrative the repentant brother
set out at once for the palazzo and gave himself up. There
is unfortunately, however, another account of the occur-
rence, which would seem to show that he was carried there
by force, his hiding-place having been betrayed. In any

case he was a poor companion for the two nobler and greater men who had preceded him there.

I have said that this night's progress through the crowd was Savonarola's last authentic appearance till the moment of his execution. He disappears here out of the common daylight, and from the eyes of honest onlookers, to the torture-chamber and prison where his fiercest enemies were about him, and worse than enemies, a professional liar, Ser Ceccone, the notary, found a place at his side as his sole historian, bribed to furnish a record which should justify the murder upon which all were bent. The signoria, no longer restrained, even by a shadow of that public opinion to which Savonarola had given form and power, appointed on their own responsibility a council of seventeen citizens to try him, among whom were his most implacable enemies, that Delfo Spini, captain of the Compagnacci, from whose sword he had been again and again rescued with difficulty, among the others. But not even this furiously prejudiced and unjust tribunal; not even the tortures to which his quivering frame was subjected, are so great a stigma upon the government of Florence as the willful falsification of the records—into which public crime by universal consent, they are acknowledged to have fallen. The miserable chronicle of lies was printed, then with the precipitation of shame withdrawn from circulation; but various copies exist in various stages of elaboration, some ungrammatical, incoherent, and betraying in every line the gaps left and the additions made, some pared and shaped into an appearance of unity. The reader who is interested in this dismal chapter of history will find a careful examination of the whole in Professor Villari's book, which our space does not permit us to follow. On the whole it would seem to be allowed that Savonarola's fortitude at some moments yielded to the torture, and that in the delirium of pain he now and then rejected his own pretensions to prophetical insight,

and confessed himself to have founded his predictions, not
upon direct divine revelation, but "upon his own opinion,
founded upon the doctrines and study of the Holy Scriptures." Apparently this was the only distinct "confession,"
so called, which even the rack could bring from his tortured
lips. But the trial altogether is so involved in doubt that it
is impossible to put faith in any part of it, except, perhaps,
in those portions which are wholly in Savonarola's favor,
and in which with a melancholy pride he defends himself,
his purity, and honesty, against his adversaries—for this it
is evident could not have come from their hostile hands.

These tortures of mind and body continued for eleven
days, through all those memorial days of a still more divine
passion which he could have commemorated more fitly in
the services of his church, had he been at liberty. He
was entirely separated from his companions, being imprisoned by himself in the Alberghettino, a small chamber
in the tower of the Palazzo Vecchio, that proud "Rocca"
which hangs suspended over Florence. There for about
six weeks, in the "little lodging" which Cosimo de'
Medici had once occupied before him, the great prophet
lay, sometimes crushed and bleeding, sometimes perhaps
with miserable self-reproaches in his mind, not knowing
what words the torture might have wrung from him, a
severer torment than the rack itself. But his confessions,
if he made any, must have been meager enough, since the
signoria were compelled to write to the pope in the following words:

"We have had to deal with a man of the most extraordinary
patience of body and wisdom of soul, who hardened himself against
all torture, involving the truth in all kinds of obscurity, with the intention either of establishing for himself by pretended holiness an
eternal name among men, or to brave imprisonment and death. Notwithstanding a long and most careful interrogatory, and with all the
help of torture, we could scarcely extract anything out of him which

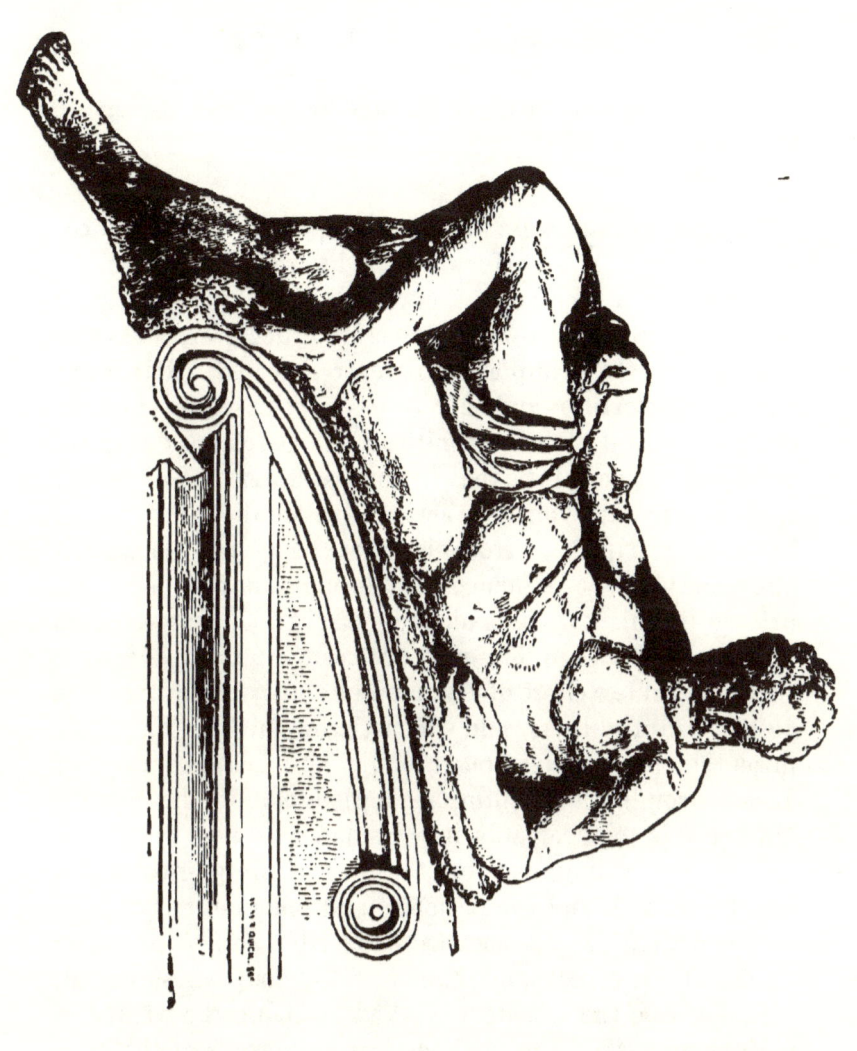

he wished to conceal from us, although we laid open the inmost recesses of his mind."

The other friars were dealt with separately. Domenico, as brave and straightforward as he was devoted, never wavered for a moment. They told him that his master had recanted and owned himself a deceiver, but the courage of this simple hero never wavered. His body wrung by torture and his heart by this more terrible sting, he still declared his faith in Fra Girolamo's inspiration, and his certainty that it was the work of God which they had undertaken together. Silvestro did what might have been expected from his weakness; he succumbed altogether to the influence of the rope and the boot, and uttered in his torments all the blasphemies suggested to him, although even his evidence seems to have added to the irresistible weight of testimony in favor of Savonarola's absolute uprightness and honesty of faith. Thus the miserable process went on through those last dark days of Lent, through the triumphant gladness of the Easter. On one side torture, suffering, human weakness sometimes failing, yet brightened by the heroic simplicity which could not fail, and the patience and magnanimity which regained their sway as soon as the terrible pangs were over; on the other, cruelty, oppression, falsehood, basest of all; while outside the vile story worked, exciting the wicked to blasphemous rejoicing, and torturing the souls of the good and pious with many a doubt and fear. Even Benedetto, true brother, who had struggled so hard to go with that company of martyrs to the death that awaited them, was so overcome with shame and miserable doubts, that he describes himself as "like a thrush that had been struck to the ground." Sore and sick at heart this faithful soul shrank away, hiding his face, to Viterbo; where in the stillness his courage and faith came back to him, and his conviction that the master whom he knew so well could have been no deceiver. And it is to this conviction and his unwearying search into all the facts connected with the false record, that we owe a great part of our knowledge of the truth. The monks in San Marco as a body were less noble; wholly noble and faithful in such a dire emergency no body of over two hundred men, I suppose, ever was. They made their submission to the pope, abjuring Savonarola in the first sting of his supposed retractation, and were received back into the paternal favor of Alexander. Thus the poison worked at once, the minds of the bystanders being too much bewildered by the terrible tragedy going on in their midst to be able for the moment to separate falsehood from truth.

Savonarola, after his first "examination," had nearly a month of quiet in the little prison, which, after all, was not less spacious or comfortable than his cell. This was owing to the negotiations between the pope and the signoria, the latter being anxious to exact a price for their services, a tax upon clerical property ; and Borgia, on the other side, being desirous to have his prey in his own hands at as cheap a rate as possible. This resting time the victim employed in a manner befitting his character and life. He wrote two meditations, one upon the *Miserere* (51st Psalm), and the other on the 31st Psalm in which he poured out his whole heart in communion with God. With the right hand which had been spared to him in diabolical mercy that he might be able to sign the false papers which were intended to cover him with ignominy, he still had it in his power to leave a record of that intercourse with his heavenly Master in which his stricken soul found strength and comfort. Between the miserable lies of the notary Ceccone, over which those Florentine nobles in the palace— magnificent signoria not skillful in such lies, to do them justice—were wrangling ; and the stillness of the little

prison hung high in air over their heads, where a great
soul in noble trust yet sadness approached its Maker, what
a difference! Lover and friends had forsaken him, honor
and credit were gone from him, his very brothers had
lifted up their heel against him, and God had not owned,
as once he had hoped, his devoted service. But yet God
was true, though all men were liars ; God was true though
He hid His face. The soldier of Christ had been over-
borne in the fight, broken and cast down ; but not less
did he trust in his leader and his cause, which one day
should overcome.

This quiet lasted till the pope's commissioners arrived,
who were at last to give a good deliverance, on Florentine
soil, to the three prisoners. They came into Florence on
the 19th of May—Romolino, a bishop after Alexander's
own heart, and Torriano, the general of the Dominicans—
boasting that they had the sentence ready, and were about
to make a famous blaze (*un bel fuoco*). Notwithstanding
this foregone conclusion, as his enemies still hankered after
something to justify themselves, Savonarola was again
"examined" before them, and all the tortures which he
had already gone through were repeated, the answers given
by him in this case being entirely falsified, and bearing no
trace or show of reality. The minutes of this latest
examination were not even signed or acknowledged by any
one, being too bad to obtain even a pretense of belief. On
the 22nd of May the sentence of death was published, and
that same evening was communicated to the condemned.
It was their last night on earth. Domenico received the
news as if it were an invitation to a feast ; poor Silvestro
was full of agitation ; but Savonarola took it with perfect
calm, expressing neither pleasure nor reluctance. No
doubt the three days' torture which had intervened had
deadened every bodily feeling in him. The record of this
last night is very full. One of the penitents of the order

of the Temple, by name Jacopo Nicolini, came to Fra
Girolamo's cell, according to the vow of that brotherhood,
to comfort the doomed man during his last hours—a veiled
figure, like one of those merciful brethren of the Misericordia who are still to be seen about the streets of Florence, covered from head to foot in a black robe and hood
which conceals the face. To this man Savonarola appealed to procure him a last interview with his brethren
—a request which was with some difficulty granted.
Strangely enough this meeting was appointed to take
place in the great hall of the consiglio maggiore, the hall
built under Savonarola's influence for the council which
had been established by his advice, and which a few years
before the admiring populace had declared must have
been built by the angels so quickly did it rise. His own
work ! And here it was, in the darkness of the great hall,
in the soft May night, that the three tortured prisoners,
their limbs contorted out of shape, their hearts transfixed
with many an arrow, met again. Savonarola's companions
had been both made aware of his supposed confession, but
no word of reproach, no question or explanation seems to
have passed between them. If they had ever believed
these slanders, the sight of their master's worn countenance was enough to give them clearer insight. At once
he took his old place, their father, their ruler. Domenico
he chid gently for his desire to be burned alive, bidding
him remember that to choose the way of death was not
for them, but to endure it firmly ; and Silvestro he warned
against his intention of speaking to the people from the
scaffold, reminding him that our Lord made no vindication of His innocence on the cross ; then on their knees
they received his blessing. After this, Burlamacchi tells us,
they were separated from each other in different corners
of the hall ; and Savonarola, weary and worn out, begged
of his benevolent attendant, Nicolini, to sit down and

make a pillow of his knee, where he might rest his head.
Lying down apparently on the floor, with this support, he fell
asleep, and in his sleep spoke and smiled, his kind supporter
looking on awe-stricken and reverential, while the night
dispersed slowly out of all the dim corners, and the blue
morning stole upon the world, and the great barred windows grew light; strangest midnight watch surely that
ever that good brother held.   On the marble overhead
were the warning verses which Savonarola himself had
written :

> " If this great council and sure government,
>   O people, of thy city never cease
>   To be by thee preserved as by God sent,
>   In freedom shalt thou ever stand, and peace."

The dawn that slowly made these lines legible, lit the
worn face of him who wrote them—of him who had made
this stately chamber rise and that "sure government"
stand fast—a face now worn and scarred with torture,
though smiling in the soft ease of momentary childlike
sleep; while outside in the piazza the pile was rising, the
cross being erected on which this very morning he was to
die.   If art should ever rise again in Florence, such a
picture as this might well stir the old heart in the city for
which Savonarola died.

When the sleeper woke, he thanked warmly and
cordially the good man whose knee had served him for a
pillow : and, Burlamacchi tells, to reward him for this good
office, warned him that all the distresses prophesied as
coming upon Florence should come in the days of a pope
called Clement—a prophecy which was noted down. Then,
the sun being now risen and their last day begun, the
three friars once more drew together and celebrated their
last sacrament.   Here Savonarola made a final confession
of his faith :

"Having then in his hands his Lord, with much gladness and fervor of spirit he broke forth in these words: 'My Lord, I know that Thou art that Trinity, perfect, invisible, distinct in three persons, Father, Son, and Holy Spirit. I know that Thou art that Eternal Word who didst descend into the womb of the Virgin Mary, and didst rise upon the cross to shed Thy most precious blood for us miserable sinners. I pray Thee, my Lord, I pray for my salvation. I entreat Thee, Consoler, that this precious blood may not have been shed for me in vain, but may be for the remission of my sins, of which I ask Thee pardon, from the day when I received the waters of holy baptism till now ; and I confess to Thee, Lord, my sins. And I ask Thee pardon for everything, spiritual or temporal in which I may have offended this city and all this people, and for every offense of which I am unaware.''

The three companions said these words together, then received the holy communion; and so went out to the piazza, where the messengers of death were waiting for them. Here a change came over the weak brother Silvestro such as happened to the feeble-minds and ready-to-halts of the old Puritan fable. All at once his weak frame erected itself, his timid countenance lighted up. He went down the stairs with this new light in his eyes, saying that now was the time to be strong, to meet death with gladness. And so the three went out into the open daylight after their long confinement, into the fresh air of the May morning. I will not describe over again that well-known scene; how the bishop who unfrocked Savonarola, trembling and confused by his office, declared him to be separated from the church militant and triumphant ; but was corrected by the calm victim who said, one cannot but think half in pity for the error and the agitation, '' From the church militant, yes ; but from the church triumphant, no ; that is not yours to do ;'' how thus disrobed the three brothers passed on to the seat of the pope's commissioners who gave them absolution ; and then to the tribunal of the civil power ; by whom they were given up to the

executioner; and how, one after another they died;
Domenico, forbidden to speak aloud, chanting under his
breath a *Te Deum*, while Savonarola himself repeated the
Creed as he went slowly along toward his death.   He
raised his eyes when he had ascended the ladder and paus-

MARTYRDOM OF SAVONAROLA (From an old picture).

ing for a moment, looked the multitude in the face.
Many among them still expected him to speak to them, to
vindicate himself, to crush his enemies by a miracle; but
by this time miracles and self-vindications were far from
his mind.   He looked at them, with what thoughts God
knows—most likely with but a vague consciousness of
their presence, his soul being already hid with Christ in
God, and all unworthy passions and thoughts gone out of

him. Christ did not vindicate Himself upon the cross, or
make any plea of innocence—why should Christ's servant
have done so ! His boat of life had already jarred upon the
soft shores of the eternal land : what was it now to him—
that tumultuous ocean of faces, as tumultuous as fickle,
and as uncertain as any sea !

So died the great preacher of Florence, the great prior
of San Marco, the most powerful politician, the most disinterested reformer of his time. Florence learned after he
was gone that her only chance for freedom lay in taking up
again and tardily following the system he had instituted;
but did it, one is almost glad to know, too late; and so fell
under the hated sway of the Medici, and out of one tyranny
into another, till recent events have given her back a
better existence. And Rome and Christendom found out
what it was to have crushed the good genius within the
church when the ruder German revolt burst forth, and
tore the Christian world asunder. The faithful in Florence
kept up a secret memory of the martyrs as long as there
remained a Piagnone in the city, and strewed flowers in the
stony square where he died, and burned lamps before his
picture in their houses. Fra Benedetto, after that momentary pause of miserable doubt and dismay which we have
recorded, threw aside his palette and his brushes, and gave
himself up to the examination of all the false documents
ot the trial, and to the clearing of his master's fame. So
did Burlamacchi, from whom we have quoted, also a
Dominican brother, of a noble family of Lucca; and others
of Savonarola's followers, for whom henceforward the great
object of existence was to vindicate his memory. Even in
the city of Dante, no greater figure has its dwelling. The
shadow of him lies still across those sunny squares and the
streets through which in triumph and in agony he went
upon his lofty way; and consecrates alike the little cell in
San Marco and the little prison in the tower, and the

great hall built for his great council, which in a beautiful poetical justice received the first Italian parliament, a greater council still. Thus, only four hundred years too late, his noble patriotism had its reward. Too late! though they do not count the golden years in that land where God's great servants wait to see the fruit of their labors—and have it, sooner or later, as the centuries come and go.

CHAPTER XIV.

THE PIAGNONI PAINTERS.

THE history of the convent of San Marco, which occupies so important a place in the records of Florence in the latter part of the fifteenth century, ends as it began, with art. The period of fame and activity which Fra Angelico began, Fra Bartolommeo brought to a conclusion. With more advanced knowledge and growing culture, but not with higher intentions or a diviner touch of genius, the two frati, who rank among the most distinguished of Florentine painters—second in influence and power only to the great Michael Angelo himself, the heroic Jupiter of that Olympus—stand fitly side by side notwithstanding the difference between them. Bartolommeo has more of the human, less of the celestial, than his angelical brother, but is not less religious, less noble, or less pure. The first is saintly, a cloistered soul, incapable of evil, and knowing nothing of it except as a hideous abstraction. The second is a man who has lived among men—Baccio della Porta, a painter-student, and journeyman in a famous *bottega* before he assumed the Dominican cowl as Brother Bartholomew; but his manly and noble pictures are as free from soil or worldly sentiment as the holy visions of his predecessor, and their convent might well take a unique glory from the possession of such a pair, even had no greater and more tragic fame come to it from another quarter. No other monastic institution has had such a double crown, and it is curious to find the home and center of the great mission

of Savonarola—he who was the burner of vanities, and the
enemy, as his enemies say, of the beautiful—thus nobly
distinguished by art.

Before, however, we enter upon the story of the last
great painter of San Marco, it may be well to indicate the
two others, of great note in their day, and one at least of
whom has come, as it were, into fashion in our own, who
belonged both to the Piagnoni party, and whose adhesion
should be a sufficient reply to all blasphemers who assail
Savonarola on this point. Sandro Botticelli, who was no
pietist by nature, nor likely to be subject to fanatical impulses, and Lorenzo di Credi, one of the exactest and most
careful of workmen, were not the kind of men to have
sacrificed their labor and deprived themselves of useful
studies in obedience to any mistaken notion even of their
religious leader. It is quite possible indeed that these great
artists may have availed themselves with professional delight of the opportunity of getting rid of the bad drawings
in their respective *bottegas*, the weak efforts of 'prentice
hands in the Bonfire of Vanities, but we decline to believe
that they could have allowed anything really beautiful or
precious to perish ; for painters, above all men, who know
the toil and pain of making, are least likely to destroy or
agree without protest to the destruction of good and true
work. The names of Botticelli, Lorenzo, and Fra Bartolommeo are sufficiently great to support the reputation, so
far as the arts are concerned, of a religious party most
tragically in earnest, and which all but revolutionized
Florence. Michael Angelo was not of the party of the
preacher, indeed he was linked by many ties of kindness
and gratitude to that of the Medici ; but we are told that
to the end of his life he spoke of Savonarola with interest
and regard such as few others inspired him with—a tolerable
collateral evidence that the reformer had sinned less in
respect to art than he is supposed to have done. Such a

body of tacit testimony in his favor ought to overbalance a great deal of vague accusation.

The name of Sandro Botticelli has come into sudden increase of fame in these latter days among writers and critics at least, and has been recalled to the general public by the recent exhibitions of the old masters, in which there have been some fine examples of his powers. Several of his best-known works agree so completely with the name of Piagnone, that without further examination the superficial observer might well accept it, as explaining and giving meaning to the beautiful sadness and melancholy contemplative aspect of many of his pictures. So much is this the case that we confess it was with a certain shock and reluctance that we accepted the unquestionable evidence of dates which proved that there could be no connection between the painter's love of the Florentine prophet and adherence to the " weeping " party that clung to him—and that sad *tondo* of the Uffizi, which is perhaps of all Botticelli's works the one which most readily occurs to the minds of those lovers of pictures who are not deeply learned in art ; that Mary, rapt in a strange transport of anticipated sorrow, putting forth a tremulous hand to write her *Magnificat*, though already in her heart feeling herself the *Mater Dolorosa ;* and all those wistful angels, hushed by the same overwhelming consciousness, exchanging looks of tender pity touched with awe. Where else could the young painter have found the secret of these wonderful pensive faces? But somewhere else he must have got it, not in the cloisters of San Marco, but in Fra Lippo Lippi's cheerful *bottega,* where the robust young Tuscan, as homely and genial as Giotto himself, and as fond of a joke, learned his trade. Botticelli's character and reputation, all that is known of him, and his antecedents, are utterly unlike a Piagnone ; and he was middle-aged, and had reached a time of life when the style is

formed and new influences tell but little upon it, by the
time that Savonarola's great reputation began. Yet all
the vehement impassioned sadness of the great soul which
foresaw judgment and terror and pain to come in the very
levity and thoughtless delights of a corrupt society, shows
through that eloquent canvas, at once oppressing and
touching the beholder; for the woe in it is generous,
heavenly, not vulgar or personal. Like Fra Angelico,
who could not paint a crucifix without tears, the sharpness
of the anguish which he represented piercing his tender
soul as he worked out its details, it seems impossible to
doubt that Botticelli too realized, with such a pang of
sympathy as leaves the heart sore, that agony to come
which rose vague and terrible before the eyes of the
mother as she magnified the Lord for her grand distinction
and honor among women—and the pitying knowledge of
the angels, appalled at the thought of what that soft
infant, round-limbed and innocent, had to bear. The
painter is himself as one appalled, struck by a sudden
sense of all it means, this mystery of Godhead in the flesh,
which so lightly, all day long, so many painter-youths
about were working at. And though in his life there is
but little trace of the solemnity which broods over his
canvas, it is to be seen in his pictures of all subjects, even
in his Venus—a cloud somewhere shadowing the sun, a
perception, dim and terrible, of griefs that must come,
howsoever they may be disguised, or how distant soever
they may be for the moment. This is the very soul and
sentiment of his work, his highest inspiration in art; and
to ourselves the picture of the Uffizi is the very emblem
and celestial standard of the Piagnoni, though it came
into being before the very name of them was invented, or
their leader was more than a nameless novice in his convent. This cannot be the highest level of art; but though
too sorrowful and bowed down, too full of pathetic mean-

ing for that eminence, there is a depth of melancholy suggestiveness in it which is infinitely touching, and which
gives by times a means of relief and expression to the
oppressed and burdened soul which Raphael on his
heavenly heights of calm cannot supply.

To say how unlike the sentiment of the painter's life
was to this which breathes from all his work is scarcely
possible. The one is the antipodes of the other, for a
personage more jovial and *insouciant* could scarcely be
found in history. Sandro, who was the son of Mariano
Filipepi, was one of the perverse lads whose abundant
energy will never work in the legitimate channels, and
who rend the souls of all belonging to them before they
find any congenial method of employing themselves. He
was educated, or at least an unsuccessful attempt was made
to educate him, "in all," Vasari tells us, "which it is
usual to teach to children before they are old enough for
the shop;" but Sandro loved neither reading nor writing,
and had a head *si stravagante* that his father at last,
giving up his own plans, whatever they were, yielded to
the boy in desperation, and apprenticed him to a goldsmith called Botticello, from whom, according to the
fantastic custom of the time, he has taken his surname.
The goldsmiths of those days were artists, some of them,
like Francia, painters in their own person, and Sandro
speedily developed an inclination for the higher art. He
was then placed in the school or shop of Fra Lippo Lippi,
where he worked so well as soon to rival his master. The
picture of which we have spoken was painted while he was
still a young man and under these early influences, and his
reputation soon spread so widely that he was called by the
pope to work in the Sistine Chapel. Here, Vasari tells us
he earned a great deal of money, but living hand to mouth,
as was his custom, brought none of it back with him.
"With one hand he received his gains and with the other

profusely threw them away," says Baldinucci, who has a
way of amplifying Vasari's statements which makes the
reader suppose he has gained some further information on
the subject. As soon as Sandro had finished the portion
of the wall allotted to him, he hurried home penniless to
that beloved Florence which none of her children liked to
leave. Here another fancy seized him. Being a "sophistical person," according to Vasari, and having apparently
got tired of his natural trade for the moment, he set himself to expound Dante by a capricious impulse, though
himself uninstructed, *senza lettere*, a freak which his
biographers condemn roundly as withdrawing him from
the application necessary for his art. At the same time he
illustrated the "Inferno" by woodcuts, which were failures,
being badly cut ; the best of his productions in this kind,
the same authority tells us, was a composition entitled the
" Triumph of Fra Girolamo," which was better done. All
this irregular occupation wasted the painter's time, and
was the occasion of "infinite disorder in his affairs,"
which never apparently were very flourishing. Vasari
attributes to Savonarola the sin of thus distracting the
painter from his legitimate craft, but there does not seem
the slightest foundation for this reproach. As Botticello
grew older, however, we are told that he fell into *disordine
grandissimo*, giving up his work altogether, and dropping
into miserable depths of poverty. Perhaps it was the
paralyzing effect of that great shock of Savonarola's death,
which shook the very existence of his followers, to which
the misfortunes of the painter may be attributed ; but this
is merely a peradventure. A small pension allotted to him
by the Medici, and the help of his friends, kept the old
man from actual want. But though his life was thus unsatisfactory, wasteful and poor, he was a merry man and
loved a jest, diversifying his grave pursuits by practical
jokes and simple-minded *burle*, as Giotto did, though with-

out Giotto's deeper meaning. Vasari reports some of the examples of this homely and boisterous wit with simple enjoyment ; how he mystified the workmen in the *bottega*, how he got the better of the neighbor who made the wall tremble with the vibration of his loom, and other similar stories of the most artless description. One of these shows a curious combination of kindness and rough mockery. A certain Biagio, one of the workmen artists of his shop, had painted a *tondo*, or round picture, no doubt a copy of one of Botticelli's own, which the *maestro* exerted himself to find a purchaser for, instructing the delighted painter to hang it in a good light, and in the morning bring the customer to see it. When, however, Biagio came, accompanied by his patron, he found his picture so transmogrified by the hoods of red paper which Botticelli with the assistance of a mischievous apprentice had fixed with wax upon the figures, that " he saw his Madonna seated, not in the midst of eight angels, but in the midst of the signoria of Florence." This story shows with what simplicity of invention a successful *burla* could be made, to the delight of the shop. Strange to think that the author of this rough though not ill-natured fun should be the same man who painted the Mary of the *Magnificat* with her sad surrounding angels.

On another occasion the jesting painter had accused one of his friends of heresy, of being an Epicurean and believing the soul to perish with the body, whereupon to carry out the jest, the friend summoned him before the Giudice. " It is true that I hold that opinion, in respect to this fellow's soul, for he is an animal " (*una bestia*), said Botticello's friend. " And it is he who is a heretic, who, though he has no education and can scarcely read, ventures to expound Dante and takes his name in vain." Thus the jokers laughed, with more mirth than wit. But the end of the careless painter was sad enough. He died poor, dependent, and decrepit, at the age of seventy-eight, his great works ended long before, and his life concluding with a postscriptal chapter of misery—"Fallen old and useless, and walking with two crutches because he could not hold himself upright," says Vasari ; and they are pathetic words. "He loved beyond measure all who were studious in art, and he earned much ; but all went wrong through bad management and carelessness." Thus ended the laughter and the fun, and those fine tender inspirations full of the profoundest feeling, which are so strangely unlike the fun and laughter.

Lorenzo di Credi was almost in every respect the opposite of this careless and unthrifty man of genius. He was as orderly and regular as the other was negligent, precise rather than reckless, and in all his habits sober-minded and diligent. He was "very partial to the sect of Fra Girolamo, and lived always an honest and good life, full of loving courtesy to all those who gave him an opportunity of showing it." In his art he was so fastidious and careful as to push his virtues almost to the length of faults. "He did but few great works because he took so much pains over each, giving himself incredible trouble . . . . when he was working he would not permit any movement which might cause dust. This extreme diligence," says Vasari moralizing, "is perhaps scarcely more laudable than extreme negligence, for in everything it is well to hold a middle course and keep free from extremes, which are generally odious." Leonardo da Vinci and Perugino were both fellow-students of Lorenzo in the workshop of Andrea Verocchio, and there is through most of his pictures a suggestion of Leonardo and his influence, or perhaps it would be more true to say a gleam from the direct inspiration of the master himself, which Leonardo carried high and far by strength of his great genius, making Lorenzo's less powerful work, guided by the same principles

and founded on the same correct teaching and " true eye "
(*ver-occhio*) of their mutual instructor, look like a study
from his own. He seems to have been Verocchio's favorite
pupil, and ever faithful and loyal to his master, as in all
conditions and relationships of life, a good man ; working

SANTA MARIA NOVELLA.

with the most conscientious elaboration at his grave and
sweet Madonnas who yet have in their matron-beauty a
gleam, a suspicion, of that sidelong look, half sweet, half
sinister, and the long oval face, which distinguish Leonardo.
All that might be sinister, however, in the expression,
melts away under his pure touch, and the tenderness and
sweetness of the well-known subject come out under his
hand with a gentle regularity and composed grace which

is all his own. He filled an important public position
in the town, and was consulted as to every great act of
art enterprise or public works; a good citizen of weight
and consideration, more respectable though perhaps less
interesting than his contemporary, who enjoyed no such
fragrance of good fame.

If, however, these two very different men, members of
the then great and flourishing brotherhood of Florentine
painters, were both more or less influenced by the great
reformer of San Marco, his own special disciple and
brother shows the power of that influence more distinctly
still. Fra Bartolommeo's story has a touching duality
which gives it double interest. Though he was a monk
and lonely man, yet it is the story of two lives which presents itself before us when we reach the name of "Il
Frate," specially so distinguished in the tale of Italian
art; one, pure, gentle, and austere; the other, erratic,
uncertain, doubtful in aim, doubtful in morals, yet no less
distinguished in the annals of faithful friendship than in
those of art. When the young Baccio came from the
country, from little Savignano, near Prato, to study in the
workshop of Cosimo Rossellino, another young student,
not so studious or so devoted to art as himself, by name
Mariotto Albertinelli, was already in the *bottega*, working
carelessly enough we may suppose, doing his day's labor
without much thought what his subject was. The lad
from Savignano found a humble lodging near the Porta
San Pietro, with some peasant relations of his own who
were established there and all the *vicinato*, which saw
him daily coming and going to his work, and which ignored
surnames with the custom of the time, distinguished him
with its usual readiness, among all the other Bartholomews,
as Baccio della Porta, and watched his modest ways, and
took him into kindly favor, as a neighborhood, however
gossiping or disagreeable, is always willing to do to the

young and gentle. "He was loved in Florence for his virtue, for he was very diligent at his work, quiet and good-natured, fearing God, loving a tranquil life, flying all vicious practices, and taking great pleasure in preaching and the society of worthy and sober persons." The neighborhood loved the young painter in his friendly gentleness, but what it thought of Mariotto, the young roisterer and gallant, who by some unaccountable fascination had linked himself to Baccio by closet ties of affection, is not in the record. It was, however, a love like that of David and Jonathan, of Orestes and Pylades, a relationship close and faithful beyond question, and which these two very different and unresembling men kept up through all intolerances of youth unbroken, the quieter student moving the less serious one to spurts of study among the *anticagli* of the Medici garden, and gradually transmitting to him by sheer contagion of love his own happy skill in color and form, through at all times Mariotto was "less well-grounded in the art of design" than his friend. When Baccia left the studio of his master to set up a *bottega* of his own, Mariotto went with him to St. Peter's gate, half principal workman, half dearest friend, often working upon the same picture with him, and so completely adopting his style that the two seemed one. They were as one soul, Vasari tells us, living and toiling together in tenderest brotherhood. After awhile Mariotto, who was not so diligent a student as his friend, found a situation for himself, "taking service" with Donna Alfonsina, the wife of Piero de' Medici. What kind of appointment the painter could hold in the great lady's suite it seems difficult to tell. "Because Mariotto was careful to make himself of use she gave him every assistance," and he painted several pictures for her, her own portrait among others, and the usual sacred subjects, which she sent as presents to her relations the Orsini. This lasted till Piero de' Medici was sent

about his business in 1494, when Mariotto went back to
his friend; where "he worked hard to make clay models,
and studied industriously from nature and to imitate the
works of Baccio, so that in a few years he made himself a
diligent and practiced painter; and he took great heart,
seeing his affairs succeed so well, and because, as he worked
in the same manner and imitated the style of his companion, the hand of Mariotto was often taken for that of
the frate." This would seem to have been the most
orderly moment of Mariotto's life; and the conjunction of
the two—the gentle, diligent, orderly young painter, with
his head full of Fra Girolamo's sermons, coming and going
to the convent as to his home, and the much less well-
regulated friend, whom his pure influence kept straight
and kept busy, and improved in art as in life—makes a
very touching and delightful picture. Gay Mariotto,
handsome and idle, kept hard at work, after his fashion,
as long as mild Baccio, ever busy, was there to charm and
still, and no doubt smile at, the vagaries which made no
breach between them; and their union made the _bottega_ at
the gate a cheerful and pleasant place.

This brotherly life, however, was interrupted by the
tragic and terrible event which moved Florence more
deeply than all her revolutions, the martyrdom of Savonarola. Gentle Baccio, not aware perhaps how little physical
power he had, and full of the enthusiasm of love, was one
of those warmest adherents of the prophet who were collected in the convent at the time of its siege. Then the
young painter found out, if he had never discovered it before, that he was not brave. He was _di poco animo_, Vasari
tells us, with that contempt for physical cowardice which
is almost universal, "and too timid, feeling himself little
able to fight for the convent, to wound or kill any one."
But there is a certain bravery in the resolution which
makes a timid man maintain his allegiance to his leader at

a dangerous moment, in which he knows he will not have the heart to distinguish himself. Such a trembling adherent may be more heroic even, in his way, than those devoted novices, brave and strong, of whom we have lately read, and to whom the excitement of the fight was as wine. Baccio shrank from the tumult, the cries and blood and terror that surrounded him, and in his panic made a vow that if he escaped he would dedicate himself to God in the order of St. Dominic. We may be sure that no one was thinking of the quiet painter of the gate in that infuriated crowd, and no doubt after Savonarola was led off, the heart-stricken remnants of his party were fain enough to steal away too, and hide themselves mournfully in the quiet of their houses. The Piagnoni were left in that terrible moment in a condition which might almost be compared to that of the first disciples when a greater Sufferer was taken away from them, all their confused hopes notwithstanding, allowing Himself to be bound and scourged without even the gleam of a wing of one of those " twelve legions of angels " whom, in their ignorance, Peter and John would have called forth without pause or doubt. " We thought it had been he who should have redeemed Israel," the Florentines too might have said, who, with wonder and miserable doubt, saw their prophet fall into the hands of his enemies. The party, it is evident, was struck prostrate, and all the more so when the vile and false so-called recantations of Savonarola were made public, to the confusion and anguish of all who loved him. No doubt this painful interval completed the dejection and utter breakdown of the sorrowful Baccio, combined with his own miserable consciousness of having been unable to strike a blow for his master. As soon as the tragedy was over he went mournfully to Prato for his novitiate, perhaps to see his rustic relations too, once more, and bid farewell to everything. Even his painting he put aside in the deep discouragement of his soul, making a sacrifice of that beloved art as no doubt he felt in the force of overstrained feeling, to the memory of him who had not even a grave upon which such sad funeral-wreaths and trophies could be laid. This was not the way to overcome the depression that had seized him, and yet it would be hard to blame the tender-hearted painter even for such a mistaken triumph of grief and love.

This event excited, as may be believed, both sorrow and anger among his friends, who "grieved infinitely to have lost him, and still more to hear that he had made up his mind to give up painting," though he had left many works unfinished. No one, however, felt it so deeply as poor Mariotto, thus deserted by his good angel, and probably with a consciousness in his mind that, so far as his power went, he had helped to bring about the tragedy which thus fell back in *contre-coup* upon himself. Almost ne would have made himself a monk too, but that he hated the monks. "Mariotto was confounded and almost out of himself at the loss of his friend; and so strange did the news appear to him that he could take pleasure in nothing, and if he had not constantly avoided all intercourse with the frati, of whom he continually spoke ill, being of the faction who were against Padre Girolamo, the love of Baccio worked so strongly in him that he himself would have been capable of taking the cowl along with his companion." He took, however, what was more to the purpose, the charge of Baccio's uncompleted works, and seems to have labored at them with despairing fervor, holding fast by the better traditions of life so long as there was something to be done for his friend. "He concluded the works with so much diligence and love that many were unaware of his share in it, believing that one hand had done all, which brought great credit on art." But after this labor of love was over, poor Mariotto's *desperazione* overcame all

better counsels. He was a " *persona inquietissima*," by
nature, according to Vasari, " *e carnale nelle cose di amor
e di buon tempo sulle cose delle rivere* "—loving the table and
other forbidden pleasures. And after this grief and sudden
rupture in his life, all the gentle bonds that held him to
work and goodness were broken. He was suddenly seized
with disgust for " all the sophistries and refinements of the
art of painting, and having been often bitten by the tongues
of painters, as is their hereditary custom, he resolved to
give himself up to the lowest, idlest, and gayest occupation,
and opened a fine tavern outside the Porta San Gallo, and
another at the Porta Vecchia, which he kept for many
months, declaring that he had now found an art without
muscle, flesh, or perspective, and what was of still more
importance, without criticism. and which was exactly the
contrary of the art he had left—an art which imitated flesh
and blood; whereas his present trade made flesh and blood;
and that in this every one who knew he had good wine
praised him, whereas in the other every one blamed him."
Miss Horner, in her " Walks in Florence," informs us that
the mad painter afterward changed the locality of his tavern and established himself in no less sacred a place than
the house where Dante was born, and where, up to a very
recent period, traces of arches were still visible on the walls,
which showed where the *loggia* or balcony had been in
which Mariotto entertained his guests. " Albertinelli's
tavern became the resort of all the men of genius or talent
in Florence," she adds, " and here might daily be seen
Michael Angelo, Benvenuto Cellini, and other artists of
renown." This throws a little air of social romance over
the painter's degradation, but it is, we fear, of doubtful
authority. There is nothing in Vasari about such fine
company, and Benvenuto was the friend of Michael Angelo's
later days, not of his youth. Poor Mariotto's foolish enterprise was in the very beginning of the sixteenth century,

when Buonarotti was under thirty, and lasted but a very short time, being rather a bravado of despair, the wild expedient of a man who felt himself shipwrecked and rudderless on the angry sea of life, than a serious undertaking. " When this too failed (*venutogli anco questa a noja*—when it came to grief, as we should say), with remorse for the meanness of the calling, he returned to painting." The reader we believe will scarcely like Mariotto, poor soul, the less for the entire confusion of life and thought which drove him to so wild an expedient. The mingling of shame and pain and harsh laughter with which he speaks of it shows the state of his mind plainly enough.

Meanwhile Baccio, now Fra Bartolommeo, was not, we fear, much more happy in his cloister. The mild and gentle painter took a long time to get over the impression of that night of siege and of his friend's long agony and martyrdom; nor do dates sufficiently help us here to make us sure how soon the researches of Savonarola's friends set him right with his humbled and suffering disciples as to the falsified record of his so-called confessions. Bartolommeo became a monk after his probation at Prato, in the year 1500, two years after Savonarola's death, and for at least two years more he remained, sad and silent, in his cell, " paying attention to nothing but the offices of divine service and the severities of the rule." But about this time, fortunately, a certain Bernardo del Bianco had built a chapel in the old Badia of Florence, adorned with all that art could do to make it beautiful, with groups of *terra cotta invetriata*, after the manner of the Della Robbias, and much fine and varied decorative work—to whom there suddenly came the happy fancy that nobody but Baccio della Porta could paint for him the picture of St. Bernardo, his patron, with which he meant to crown his chapel. On this distinct suggestion his friends roused themselves, and the new prior of San Marco with the brethren, and all to

whom Brother Bartholomew was dear, set to work to persuade him, for the good of the chapel and its founder, and
for the honor of San Marco, and for the advantage of his
art, to take brush in hand once more. What arguments
they used we are not told, but they were at length success-

"DEVIL" IN MERCATO VECCHIO.

ful, and Fra Bartolommeo took up again, but languidly, his
accustomed tools. The result was the great picture of the
vision of St. Bernard, which Vasari describes with enthusiasm. St. Bernardo writing looking up sees a vision "of
our Lady, with her child, borne in the arms of angels," and
gazes upon this vision with rapt countenance, "contemplating it so that well may be seen in him I know not what

of celestial influence which shines through the picture to
those who look at it with attention." But it required still
a greater event to rouse the gentle monk back again into
enthusiasm and delight in his work. At this time, about
the year 1405, the young Raphael, fresh from the studio of
Perugino, and in the very beginning of his own beautiful
career, came to Florence, and whether as seeing something
akin to his own pure mind and art in the pictures of Il
Frate, or, according to an unpleasant suggestion, finding
Michael Angelo too busy and too great to notice him, sought
the acquaintance of the cloistered painter. Raphael was
but twenty-three at the time, in all the freshness of his
unsullied youth, and Fra Bartolommeo, still young enough
to learn and to sympathize, had reached the *mezzo di cam-
min di nostra vita.* It adds an association the more to San
Marco, which has so many memories, when we realize these
visits made by the young Umbrian painter, from whom
already men began to expect great things, to the famous
Florentine, whom sorrow and love had taken the strength
from, and in whose heart life and art and the renovating
influences of nature were but beginning to stir after the
great blow which had almost paralyzed his being. How
the monk must have roused himself to lead his young companion about through the cells of the brothers, where
Angelico's visions of beauty still shone bright and fresh
from the walls! And with what animated admiration and
criticism must the two have stood, almost caressing with
soft gestures—indicating here and there a lovelier touch
than usual, as painters have the tender trick of doing—
those celestial emanations from a spirit akin to their own!
Who can wonder that Bartolommeo's lagging energies came
back to him in a rush of new life under the soft, glowing
eyes of Raphael, and amid all the eager talk, the fresh suggestions, and still more soothing praises of the beautiful
youth, a visitor half as heavenly as Gabriel himself, and

almost as unlike the ordinary visitors of the cloister. They taught each other: the elder some tradition or combination of color which the younger was glad to learn, while the Umbrian in his turn communicated to the Florentine the rules of perspective; or so at least formally the chroniclers say. Perhaps it was only mutual enthusiasm for the art which was so dear to both which communicated itself between the two, and those most agreeable and effectual lessons which come by sight alone, the unconscious benefit conveyed by a sketch more noble, a tint more sweet, than any which the charmed beholder has yet been able to produce for himself. And who can doubt that all that great story of prophetic passion and martyrdom with which, despite all the disloyalty of the trembling community, every stone of San Marco must still have vibrated, was poured into the young listener's ears, relieving the speaker's heavy-laden soul? That was an era to count from in the mild existence of the monk. He began to breathe again, and to paint with heart and good-will, no doubt pleased and excited by the eagerness of his accomplished scholar to see how he mixed his colors and produced his loveliest effects.

The most busy and remarkable period of Fra Bartolommeo's life comes after this re-awakening. Raphael is said to have spent some portion of the four succeeding years in Florence coming and going to other places: and here he painted some of his most lovely pictures—the Madonna del Cardellino for one, and that so inappropriately named La Belle Jardinière for another—taking new strength and energy from the great things he had seen, among others, the cartoons of Leonardo and Michael Angelo, which were intended for the decoration of that grand chamber of the consiglio maggiore of which we have already spoken. These great designs, though never executed, seem at least to have served a noble purpose in stimulating the tender genius of the younger painter, less severe and perhaps less splendid in individual force than these giants, who took his lesson from the frate too, ready to see and acknowledge the excellence of all that was lovely. *"Raffaelo, ch'era la gentilezza stessa,"* says Vasari; his coming roused the mild Baccio of old out of the sadness of the cloister, and brought his dejected spirit back to the manifold gladnesses of art.

Bartolommeo perhaps had scarcely had fair play for his genius up to this time. He had but begun to work independently when his sympathetic soul became involved in that great prophetical work of Savonarola, which in its impassioned reality of meaning was so apt to sweep all lesser things away as secondary; and though he had evidently made a vigorous attempt to shake off from his mind the burden of his master's downfall and death, yet he had not succeeded in doing so, and had passed some of the best years of his life under the weight of that discouragement. Now at last he was free and felt his strength. He was no more than thirty-six, in the hey-day of his powers, and for the first time stimulated by manly ambition, emulation, and sympathy to fullest exercise of them. Perhaps even that wild freak of the erratic Mariotto had done something for his friend in proving to him at least the necessity of his own influence to set and keep that doubtful personage right; and perhaps too the vivifying touch of his new friendship called back again the smoldering warmth of the old, which the great catastrophe of his life had dulled and dropped for the time. Life altogether indeed revived in his soul. In 1508 he made an expedition to Venice, to the widening of his horizon and increase of his vigor, and came back bringing various commissions with him and a mind full of active purpose. The first thing he did on his return was to set the *bottega* at San Marco in order, adding to it a new element of an original kind—a lay partner, no

less, in the person of that wild and willful Mariotto, whom
returning life had restored, notwithstanding all his foolish
vagaries, to his true brother's heart. They entered into a
curious business settlement even, of an unique kind. The
monk naturally had nothing to do with the profits of
his noble and now flourishing trade. They went to the
convent and were managed entirely by its authorities, and
the new arrangement was—a bargain which shows the
professional value of Mariotto's services when under the
regulating influence of his friend—that the newcomer
should receive half of what was earned after the necessary
deductions for expenses. Bartolommeo's share was simply
nothing—he had his cell and his fame; and in consideration of the religious and worthy work in which he was
engaged, he was exempted from the monastic routine of
service in the choir—but no more. It was in 1509 that
the partnership began, and it went on for three fruitful
and splendid years in the same harmony which had
characterized the beginning of the two young painters in
the shop at the Porta San Pietro, both of them working at
the same picture, a dual artist, in such harmony that it is
hard to tell which hand is which, or indeed that there were
two hands at work. But this union lasted only till 1512,
when it was dissolved, probably, the critics think, by the
interposition of a new prior, or rather the return of an old
one, Santa Pagnini, to San Marco, shortly after whose
arrival the bond, so touching and full of interest, was
broken. We are not told for what reason or by what
means this was done, nor how the mild soul of the monk
was moved in such a disruption. Probably the very
amiability and softness of his character made it affect him
less than the impetuous Mariotto, whose heart was rent
once more by a mingled passion of rage and wounded
feeling. Padre Marchese believes that it was now at this
later period, that he took to tavern-keeping in his despite

and misery; but there seem no clear indications of the date of that curious episode, though there is no doubt as to its reality. Mariotto did not very long survive this renewed breach. He died in 1515, leaving behind him much work which was not perfect, and one great picture, more distinct in its solitary greatness than one production often is in the life's work of a notable painter. Perhaps it tells the more for being thus solitary. It is the well-known Visitation, which we remember filling with its lovely, majestic presence, one small room in the Pitti, many years ago. Mary and Elizabeth, meeting in the way, stand in the foreground of the canvas, in front of a great Roman archway against the blue sky; the elder woman steps forth eagerly to greet the mother of her Lord, who, with modest eyes cast down and an ineffable, sweet consciousness in her face and attitude, receives the mysterious welcome. I have heard of a woman, sadly lonely in a strange country, and little aware of the merits of the picture, poor soul! who would go and linger in the room "for company," wistfully wishing that the kind, penetrating, sympathetic look of that old, tender Elizabeth could but fall on herself. Here too is a mystery—where our poor Mariotto, undisciplined and perverse spirit, willful and impatient and even *carnale* as Vasari is obliged to allow, could have got the meaning of that tender womanly communion, last secret of the hearts of mothers. Genius has strange gifts in it, comprehensions incomprehensible, knowledge nohow conveyable by teaching of man; and this we suppose made the wild fellow in his unruliness capable of sounding that coy depth of human feeling and putting it on his canvas, to the consolation of strangers centuries after; though probably he himself was never aware how great a thing he had done.

Poor Mariotto! he was not nearly so good nor so great a man as Fra Bartolommeo, or even as the gentle and diligent

Baccio whom he loved so dearly before his cloister days; but we trust the reader will like, as we do, to linger upon all that is known of this faulty, tender-hearted, foolish fellow. He seems to have risked his life, according to Vasari, in some foolish feats of arms, to gain credit with some equally foolish "light o' love"—*alcuni amori*, the old biographer says, as if there were more than one of them. "And as he was neither very young nor very skillful in such undertakings," the rash gallant had the worst of it, and took to his bed in consequence. He was carried to Florence afterward from La Quercia, where the air was too sharp for him; but though he was only forty-five he had no strength to rally, and died there in November, 1515, after a few days' suffering, in the arms of his truest lover of all, comforted in his last moments by that beloved Baccio from whom he could not live or thrive apart. Such a union between two painters is not unparalleled in the history of art, and whenever it occurs it carries with it the heart of the spectator, especially in such a case as this, where the two men, so persistently faithful to each other from boyhood to the grave, were so curiously unlike in nature. The wayward Mariotto throws a gleam of affectionate interest all through upon the much more orderly path of the frate, whose higher powers and purer character kept him always on a loftier level, but who yet owes something to his troublesome partner. Probably in his lifetime he was little more than an anxiety and a charge to the pious monk; but the figure of Fra Bartolommeo, so timid in life, so bold in art, would be much more abstract and less lovable without Mariotto the perverse companion, to whom existence was impossible without him, whom he inspired and reclaimed and never gave up till death separated the pair. And even death did not separate them long. Two years more the frate lived and painted, with skill and cunning undiminished, for he was still in the full

vigor of life.   And it is evident that love for his art grew
upon him with years.   After his separation from Mariotto
he had an illness, and was sent into the country to a
dependency of San Marco, the convent of Santa Maddalena
in the valley of Mugnone.   Here in the leisure of his con-
valescence he was permitted to work '' for his diversion and
recreation '' upon the walls, leaving a Madonna here and
there, in the chapel, in the refectory, traces of his hand
wherever he had passed.   Then he went to Rome to see
the great works which Raphael and Michael Angelo were
doing in the Vatican and Sistine Chapel, and it is said
began a picture here with the intention of showing his
gratitude to the convent which lodged him, but, unfavora-
bly affected in his health by the Roman air, had to leave it
unfinished.   The rest of his life was spent between work
and illness.   When he was sick his brothers sent him to
the country, where still he worked, and some of his grand-
est and most ambitious productions date from these last
broken and melancholy years.   On some of his pictures the
legend *Orate pro pictore* is touchingly inscribed.   He died
in October, 1517, at the age, Vasari says, of forty-eight,
perhaps a little younger, scarcely two years after the ending of his friend.   According to the same authority, he
was partially paralyzed on one side, ''in consequence of
continuous labor under a window, the light from which
struck on his back,'' and was on this account sent to the
baths of San Filippo.   The only heirs whom he left behind
him were the young monks he had trained, specially Fra
Paolo of Pistoia, a painter of no great eminence, to whom
fell the brushes and materials, which were all the property
of which the monk-painter died possessed.   But the
inheritance which he left to the world was greater than
that which any mortal successor could inherit, and remains
to us of these distant centuries a great and perpetual possession.

The portrait of Savonarola which we prefer, and which forms the frontispiece of this volume, is said to be one of Bartolommeo's earliest works, while still he was only young Baccio of the gate, an enthusiastic youthful follower of the great frate. It may be inferior in point of art to the more idealized portrait in the semblance of Peter Martyr which he painted at a later date, but it is to us infinitely more attractive. No other portrait of Fra Girolamo possesses, we think, the homely reality and character of this. It is not the conventional prophet nor the preacher conscious of his mission, whom the painter at a later date felt it necessary to set forth, in character as it were, with dilated eyes and inspired front ; but it is the benign leader of *i nostri angioli*, the father for whom those white-robed novices fought at the doors of the choir, the man who threw himself, with the natural fervor of love and fellow-feeling, into the hearts and lives of other men, and ruled Florence by the great affection he bore her. The little picture hangs now in Savonarola's cell at San Marco, an unaffected and genuine portrait worth all the prophetic idealizations in the world.

Fra Bartolommeo was the inventor of the lay figure, so universally used by painters since his day, the first example of which is mentioned as a valuable possession in the memorandum of the dissolution of partnership between himself and Mariotto in January, 1512. It was to remain in possession of the monk till his death and then to pass to his friend, who, as the reader is aware, did not survive to have it. Probably it helped Fra Paolino in his feeble work. It is said to be preserved still in the guardaroba of the Florentine academy.

Thus the last echo of the glory of San Marco died out of Florence. The convent *bottega* produced no new genius to preserve its reputation ; and the community which had so deeply moved and influenced Florence dropped back into the natural obscurity of a humble brotherhood. For a hundred years it had been foremost in goodness and genius. Angelico, Antonino, Savonarola, Bartolommeo, a fair succession, had made it famous in art and good works, and placed its friars at the head of such a revolution and reformation as Italy has never seen. Now the greatness and the fame effaced themselves, tragic shadows of an undeserved disgrace having followed the crowning glory. The gentle image of Fra Bartelommeo, however, wiped out those harsher evils, and consigned the home of so many great spirits to a natural, soft, and beautiful decay.

And Florence, to which such springs of new life and freedom had come, inspired by that Dominican whom she slaughtered in her public square, fell into a decay of all her noble qualities which was not beautiful. One effort still the better soul of the great city made before it succumbed to tyranny and servitude. And of that last effort we will now try, so far as our space permits, to make an imperfect record, that the story of which we have attempted to trace the beginning may have at least an indication of what was its end—though not the real ending of the great perpetual city built for the future as well as for the past.

DAWN: MICHAEL ANGELO. FROM TOMB OF GIULIANO DE' MEDICI.   393

CHAPTER XV.

MICHAEL ANGELO.

WE DO well to pause, even after the notable personages
who have passed in shadow before us, ere we approach
the figure of the greatest Florentine master, he who stands
alone among the crowd, exceeding all, as his gigantic
statue towers over all other works, alone at once in greatness and in individuality; more universal in his genius,
more notable in his person, than any contemporary artist,
unless indeed it be the kindred but much less well-known
figure of Leonardo, whose prodigious powers we all take to
a great extent on trust, impressed still, at the distance of
centuries, by the extraordinary impression which he made
upon his time. But Buonarotti stands in no mysterious
glory, vaguely disclosed among the mists of ruin and the
still more vague vapors of praise, like Leonardo. His
steps are all clearly traced for us across the far distance,
his actions, his works, even his thoughts, preserved in distinctest certainty; and himself, even in his characteristic
features, in his ways of speaking as in his ways of working,
in the infirmities of his temper and the greatness of his
soul, is as well known to us, nay, better, than if he lived
to-day. There was a third as great as the others we have
named living at the same time in Italy; but to compare
Raphael with either of these veterans would be almost as
strange as to measure the angel of the Annunciation with
the men who gaze at him in the pictures. Raphael's very
youth cuts him off from the comparison, and the manner

of his mind, in which the characteristic peculiarities of the others find no place. He is not one who appeals to the intellect and the judgment as they do. He does but take our heart, smiling, leaving us scarcely aware whether it is the mightiness of his genius, or the sweetness of human sympathy which subdues us to him. But the others are not unconscious. From the first to the last Michael Angelo is aware of himself. He knows his power and that he is not as other men ; with no generous confidence of sympathy but with a certain conscious despotism, he rules, nay, domineers, over us, pleased if we tremble somewhat as well as applaud, and feel his superior greatness to the - bottom of our hearts. He stands like his own David, looking down upon the smaller figures around him, with no kind delusion in his mind as to the difference between them. And as he has thus held his place, supreme in Florence from his youth, almost from his childhood, not without a certain brag of his strength, half humorous, half angry, so he does still ; reigning imperiously, not careless of his sway nor indifferent to the homage which he will force out of us rather than go without it. In the picture galleries and on the hillside, confronting us in the public piazza at the very doors of the old palace, and in the deepest gloom of the dark cathedral behind the altar, surprising us even in the dimness with his princely presence, he is everywhere, throwing vivid words at us when there is nothing else to be done, and even by means of the great works of others leaving a certain trace of proud magnificence to show where he has passed by. More people, we believe, think, when they look at the great gates of San Giovanni, of him who said they were fit to be the gates of heaven than of him who made them ; and when we pass by Donatello's San Giorgio, the critic who for all comment gave that noble figure the word command and bade him "March !" is almost more present with us than

the older sculptor. And from his early youth, when he
called the splendid church of Santa Maria Novella, all
sweet and shining in those frescoed glories which his own
boyish hand helped to dress her in, his bride—to that
moment in which he chose his resting-place in Santa Croce,
at the exact spot where, when the great doors were open,
he could see the cathedral from his grave, and watch the
glorious dome, through all the centuries, rising steadfast
against the Italian sky, his very sayings usurp the sovereignty of the city, putting him before us wherever we
turn, and whether we will or not, first and foremost before
any other man.

The story of Michael Angelo's long life has been so often
told that, so far as information goes, it may be thought a
work of supererogation to give it over again ; but it is
impossible even to think of Florence and leave out the
man who, of all the despots of Florence, is the most
potent, and the only one whom all Florentines accept
heartily with no jealousy of his power.   He is altogether
different from the homelier type of Tuscan character, the
pâte which produced such men as Giotto, Donatello, and
Botticelli—a race joyous and robust and simple, children
of the soil and of the sunshine ; but he is still more
characteristically Florentine in his masterful force and
haughty personality, manifestly of the same blood as him
who made the great journey through hell and heaven.
Men of this class are always remarkable whatever may be
the landscape that incloses them.   They are like mountains,
austere and solitary, in a grandeur of nature which no
effort can bring others up to, or amiable inclination bow
down.   Such men have always a certain gloom about them,
a habit of imperiousness, an impatience almost pitiless of
the smaller crowd around, to which, on the other hand,
they can be as gentle as angels when the meaner mass
perceives its own inferiority.   Perhaps the half solemn, half

contemptuous, bravado which we find in Michael·Angelo, the pleasure he evidently had in making it apparent how easily he could excel and overpass other men, was peculiar to himself; but the consciousness of an elevation above their kind is common to this type of greatness, a quality not so attaching or attractive as the brotherliness of the sweeter nature, but perhaps more impressive to the common imagination, which always in its soul believes more in self-assertion than in natural humility. The great artist was but a boy-apprentice in the workshop of Domenico Ghir-landajo when he drew round one of his master's designs, in the hands of a fellow pupil, the correct outline of the figure which the head of the *bottega* had drawn badly or carelessly, a boyish feat which is much more important as an evidence of character than even as a proof of the super-lative genius which taught him more than his master could —for the incident shows his contemptuous indifference to the feelings of others as well as his wonderful power. Subordination does not seem to have been one of the virtues possible to Michael Angelo. Then and after he brooked no control or reproof, and having no doubt of his own right to be first, took his place, always·with an arrogance which, whether we like it or not, we are forced to accept as an integral part of his character. The same mixture of scorn does not appear in the more solemn arrogance of Dante. When the poet said, "If I go who will stay? and if I stay who will go?" the utter serious-ness of the question veiled the prodigious self-estimation in it; but the painter's attitude is one of proud carelessness, like that of a being so much above all others that even they themselves could have no doubt on the subject. So intense a sense of personal value and importance is not amiable, but it is as we have said, deeply impressive to the common mind, and entirely characteristic of these memorable men.

Like Dante, too, Michael Angelo was of noble birth, a
fact which perhaps accounts in some degree for the marked
difference between him and the lowlier class of artists
already indicated. It was but a *petite noblesse* after all;
neither the poet nor painter came from any lofty house, or
was born in the purple; but yet no emperor was more unlike a mediæval peasant or craftsman than the artist who
boasted a surname and belonged to the Buonarotti was unlike those who were of the soil, the son of John or Peter,
the apprentices of a Brunellesco, or a Botticello, picking
up a name in this quaint way. Cimabue, as we have
already remarked, is almost the only other in the long succession of Florentine painters who shares this distinction.
Scarcely one of them besides bears his father's name.
Giotto, Donatello, and the rest have nothing but those
given to them at their baptism to make glorious. Domenico of the Garlandmaker and Andrea of the Tailor are still
more homely in their means of identification, and many
more wear a changed version of their master's name, like
those quoted above (Brunelleschi from Brunellesco, Botticelli from Botticello), instead of the non-existing patro-
nymic; while others are distinguished by locality, as Baccio
of the Gate, Pietro of Perugia, Paola of Verona. Michael
Angelo, however, was separated from the common herd by a
good round, mouth-filling set of syllables, and a legendary
descent from the counts of Canossa, a legend which the
great family was delighted to give its sanction to, when
the distant kinsman became a great man, courted by popes
and princes. It would be vain to say that he took any importance from this fact. The much nearer and more important fact that he was himself Michael Angelo moved him
a great deal too much to leave room for any smaller pride
about the counts of Canossa; but such was his actual condition, and it is not without importance in his life and
character. He had hot knightly blood in his veins, little

disposed to turn off a foolish piece of condescension, as
Giotto did, for example, with the laugh and shrug of peasant humor, maintaining its independence with a sharp but
good-humored gibe, as peasants do everywhere—a mode of
treatment, let us allow, by which the artist gets the better
of his silken adversary more effectually than were he ever
so indignant. But the son of the Buonarotti, like the son
of the Alighieri, was at all times an *animo sdegnoso*, too
indignant when not too contemptuous, of pretenses of superiority, to put up with them lightly or turn them off as
a jest.

Michael Angelo was born in March of the year 1474, according to the old reckoning, '75 according to ours, so that

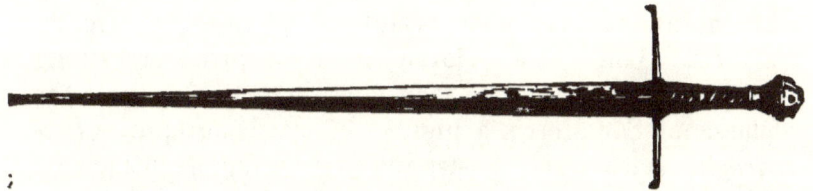

M. ANGELO'S SWORD.

the spring of the year 1875 saw the fourth centenary of his
birth. His father held an honorable office as podesta or
chief magistrate in the little town of Caprese, and the child
was sent to the hills near Arezzo, according to the custom
of his time, a custom which prevails in many parts of the
world to this day, to be nursed by the wife of a mason,
from whom, he declared afterward, he derived his love of
the chisel. His father, Ludovico, had so many children
and so little money, that he was fain to get his sons disposed of in "the arts of wool and silk," but seems to have
been somewhat disinclined to allow that one of them from
whom he expected most, to engage in the art of design ;
though one would have thought the arts were sufficiently
honored in Florence to prevent the struggle which so often

attends the selection by a promising youth of one of those three crafts of genius which are so universally marked as vagabond and unreliable in the opinion of the sober-minded of all countries and generations. He was scolded and sometimes beaten by his father and his elder brothers, "thinking perhaps," says Vasari, "that this faculty of his, uncomprehended by them, was something mean and unworthy of the ancient house." Finally, however (and there was not much time lost, for he was but fourteen after all), the boy was apprenticed to Domenico Ghirlandajo, and began the formal study of art. It was the moment when the greatest of the Medici was at his highest point of power, and the encounter between the great Lorenzo in his mature manhood and the young Buonarotti at the very beginning of his career, is full of picturesque circumstances. Lorenzo, who loved art as he loved everything that was beautiful, had collected in a garden near the piazza of San Marco, a number of classic antiquities (*anticagli*), statues and busts, and every scrap of antique art which could be scraped together by diligent collectors, agents everywhere for the princely Florentine. It was the very height of the Renaissance, and Lorenzo and his favorite society were deeply classical, prizing nothing that was not Greek, and very eager to introduce as many classic customs as possible, and to found a school of art which should rival that of Athens. In his garden, with perhaps a side gleam from the example of Plato changed to suit the circumstances, where all his wealth of *anticagli* was arranged, Lorenzo placed the old sculptor Butoldo, who had been a pupil of Donatello, and sending round to the art *bottegas* in the city, desired that any of the youths who were inclined toward sculpture should come and study there. Among those who were sent by Ghirlandajo was Michael Angelo, who took to the clay and marble with an eagerness and rapid comprehension that astonished everybody. "After a few days," Vasari tells us, the lad was so advanced as to attempt to copy a faun's head in marble; and though he had never before touched either marble or chisel, his attempt was so successful that the magnifico was startled. So pleased was he that he began to banter the boy, reminding him that his faun was old, and that old people lose their teeth, and that it was very unlikely that the mouth of his model would have been in such perfect condition. "It seemed to Michael Angelo, in his simplicity, loving and fearing the master as he did, that he meant what he said," Vasari tells us, and his is the most agreeable version of the story, though there are others who represent the youthful Buonarotti as doing that for policy which Vasari says he did out of his simplicity, a more natural explanation at so early an age. But whether simpleness, or cunning, so it was that the boy took the magnifico's hint, broke out the tooth of his faun, worked at the jaw to make it appear that the tooth had dropped out, and putting the completed work in Lorenzo's way, waited, no doubt with a beating heart, to see what he would say next time. The great man was delighted with the effect his joke had produced. It became one of his favorite stories, which he told to his friends and laughed at with kindly enjoyment; and he lost no time in showing his goodwill, taking the youth into his house, where he ate at his own table and was treated like Lorenzo's own children, and at the same time bestowing a place on his father. This good fortune lasted for four years, till the time of Lorenzo's death; and during this time the boy-sculptor must have had many opportunities of self-improvement, and especially that of intercourse with the most cultivated men of his time, the wits and philosophers and connoisseurs who collected round Lorenzo's table. When the magnifico died, his unworthy son and successor, Piero, continued his father's patronage to the young artist, but not in Lorenzo's princely way. Instead of great subjects, sacred and classic, in marble, Piero set the sculptor to make a statue of snow, which, however, considering that the artist was scarcely twenty, probably did not disturb him so much as it has disturbed his worshipers since, as a slight to his great powers.

When the Medici family was expelled from Florence, Michael Angelo seems to have been seized with a temporary panic, lest perhaps he, almost a member of Lorenzo's family, should share the disgrace and ruin which no doubt the party expected must follow the downfall of their head, as had always happened heretofore ; an unnecessary panic, as it happened, for Savonarola's influence kept all the demons of party retaliation in check. No doubt, however, the fright was good for the youth, enlarging his horizon by the sight of Venice and Bologna, in which last place he found a warm welcome. Shortly afterward he was taken to Rome, where his fame had gone before him by means of a Cupid sold to Cardinal Riario as a genuine antique. Here, before he had reached the age of twenty-five, he executed the great Pietà in St. Peter's, still known as one of his most perfect works, and, it is evident, by that and other productions had got himself so great a reputation that even his own city recognized his greatness and showed its recognition in a curious practical way. There was in Florence a certain mass of marble which had been badly *abbozzato* a hundred years before by Maestro Simone da Fiesole, whose intention had been to make a giant out of the huge marble nine braccia high, but who had only gone far enough to spoil it, and leave a shapeless wreck upon the hands of the operai of the cathedral, the commissioners of works. There had been talk of handing over this piece of valuable material to Leonardo and various other sculptors ; but either Michael Angelo himself, seeing possiblities in the stone, claimed the refusal of it, or the operai, who felt it was not for their credit to give it to a stranger without first offering it to one of their country-men, took the initiative, as another story says. Anyhow the permission was given to him to try his powers upon it, after he had shown to the authorities a model of the great figure which he already saw within the shapeless irregular-ities of old Simone's spoiled work. "Michael Angelo made a model in wax," says Vasari, "of a young David with a sling, intended for the front of the Palazzo, to show that, as David had defended his people and governed them with justice, so whosoever governed that city should boldly defend it and justly govern it ; and he began this statue in the works of Santa Maria del Fiore, where he made a tower with wood and stone round the marble, and worked it out there without being seen by any one." Huge, though the mass of marble was, it was so awkwardly shaped by the mistake of the old artist who had spoiled it, that it was a matter of no small labor as well as genius to evolve out of it the splendidly-proportioned and gigantic youth whom the young sculptor, all his energies stirred by the difficulty of the undertaking, saw in the stone. The failure of the material to afford full expansion to this heroic figure is apparent, we are told, in one of the shoulders of the David, "which ought to advance a little further and to be more fully rounded, but which is flat in consequence of the imperfection of the marble, in which still appear the strokes of the chisel by which it was first so unskillfully begun." "Certainly Michael Angelo per-formed a miracle," cries Vasari, "in thus resuscitating one who was dead." The great work was begun in 1501 and erected in the place which it held till very recently, before the door of the Palazzo Vecchio, in 1504, a proof, says one of the commentators, of the "terrible genius, with which Divine Providence had endowed" the sculptor. There is a description of Michael Angelo's work, given years after this, when he was an old man, which recurs forcibly to the mind when we endeavor to realize the singular and striking scene which Vasari thus indicates— "I have seen Michael Angelo at the age of sixty. . . . make more chips of marble fly about in a quarter of an hour than three of the strongest young sculptors would do in an hour—a thing almost incredible to him who has not seen it. He went to work with such impetuosity and fury of manner that I feared almost every moment to see the block split in pieces. It would seem as if, inflamed by the great idea which inspired him, this great man attacked with a species of fury the marble in which his statue lay concealed." What then must have been the eager energy of the work, when the young artist of twenty-five, shut up in the solitude of his huge shed with that contorted mass of whiteness, *storpiato* and *guastato* by his predecessor, out of which his David was struggling, getting limb and sinew gradually free as blow after blow resounded on the stone, worked in a fury and passion of inventing, day after day, till the long throes were over and the imprisoned had got free?

With all this we are obliged to confess that the great David—the pride of the Florentines, standing white and great as we have seen it against the stern Tuscan walls of the Palazzo Vecchio, gigantic in its roundness and force of youth—touches our heart individually in nowise, and is absolutely indifferent to us. We do not attempt to defend ourselves from the well-merited stigma of want of taste and artistic appreciation, but freely acknowledge a personal defect which happily is not general. But this dullness in respect to the work need not diminish the interest with which we regard its creation, the conflict of the sculptor with the spoiled marble, out of which he forced the perfection of this imaged manhood against all hope or precedent.

as picturesque and interesting an incident as any in the annals of art.

After this great effort in sculpture, the most remarkable that had been made since the awakening and revival of art, Michael Angelo seems to have turned off at once, by some caprice of nature or sport of circumstance, to the other branch of his great craft, so different in its requirements from the grandeur and stillness of sculpture. Circumstances no doubt had to do with the composition of the great cartoon intended for the decoration of that hall of the Consiglio Maggiore, which Savonarola had built, and in which he spent the last night of his life ; but it must have been sheer caprice that led him to paint the picture now in the tribune of the Uffizi, about which Angelo Doni, for whom it was painted, endeavored to bargain with such disastrous effect, the haughty painter doubling his price like the Sibyl, for every reduction attempted to be made. The power of this picture is so thrust upon the spectator by the uncomfortable attitude of the Virgin, that the subject loses in sweetness and grace more than can possibly be gained by any exhibition of the artist's mastery over strained muscles and colossal form. The Cartoon of Pisa, as it is called, was produced at the request of the signoria, in competition with another cartoon, which has also perished (or at least survives only in a fragment copied by Rubens), by Leonardo. Michael Angelo's cartoon represents soldiers bathing, and suddenly disturbed by the appearance of the enemy, a subject entirely after his own heart. Scraps of it only have come down to posterity, the cartoon having been torn in pieces, according to Vasari, by the envious hands of the sculptor Baccio Bandinelli, whom it would be absurd to speak of now as a rival of Buonarotti, though he considered himself as such in his day. The most perfect idea of what it was is to be had from an old copy in the possession of the Earl of Leicester, which has been engraved, and of which Mr. Black gives a photograph in his beautiful book.* These pictures make but an episode in the life of the great artist. It pleased him to put away one tool and take up another, transferring to the canvas the grand forms and muscular development of sculpture and, curiously enough, revenging himself for the stillness of the one in the vehement action of the other. Neither Leonardo's picture nor his was ever executed.

Immediately after this interval of painting occurred that encounter of two of the most notable men of their time, which has given a striking and humorous page to the history of art. Julius II., probably some years after his accession to the papacy, sent for the great sculptor, whose temper and character were not unlike his own, in order that he might glorify himself with a tomb worthy his own estimate of his glory—a most wise precaution for all who share this impulse of posthumous vanity. The pope and the artist were a fit pair to meet in that great old Rome, so full of memories, and the warlike narrative of their friendship and quarrels, hot on both sides, yet on neither without a dormant personal liking, is amusing and full of interest. With all the hopes of a splendid work before him, not less honorable to himself than to Pope Julius, Michael Angelo had first to betake himself for eight dreary probationary months to the marble-country of Carrara, to choose the blocks for his statues, and to get them painfully conveyed to the sea, to be sent off to Rome. In this exile, during which it is easy to imagine the eager anticipations of the great sculptor, held as it were in the leash and unable to get to work, though with such wealth of virgin material round him, he had hard ado, Vasari tells us, to keep himself from striking out with those fiery, vehement strokes of his, some huge *abbozzo* in the white rocks

---

* "Michael Angelo Buonarotti, Sculptor, Painter, Architect." By Charles C. Black. Macmillan: 1875.

of a cave, as a memorial of himself, "as the ancients had done, grand statues invited by these masses." What pilgrimages we should all have made to that powdery waste had he left some such vast mysterious image as the uncom-

M. ANGELO'S STUDY, FLORENCE.

plete Day, of San Lorenzo, to keep the world in mind of the long days he passed there among the rough marble-cutters of those precious caverns! The blocks which he sent to Rome half filled the piazza of St. Pietro, and the artist set to work *con grande animo.* Such was the eager-

ness of both architect and patron, that a communication
—"a bridge," as Vasari calls it—was made between the
stanze of the Vatican and the shed in the Piazza, which
had been erected over the sculptor and the marble which
he attacked in a sacred fury of creation. It is not difficult
to understand that the perpetual intrusion of such a visitor as the fiery old pope, with the license of age added to
that of absolute power, inquiring, criticising, praising,
blaming with more zeal than knowledge, must have gone
far to drive the equally fiery young sculptor half-frantic
by times, when he had to suspend his chisel and subdue
his *furia* and listen to all his holiness might choose to say,
who had it in his power to steal upon him at any moment,
however critical. Perhaps an impatient word burst from
him at some especially unpropitious visit which nettled
Julius; but at all events when a new arrival of marble from
Carrara made it necessary for the sculptor to get money
from the pope for payment of the conveyance, his holiness
was busy and could not see him. This was repeated two
or three times, at first to the surprise and afterward to
the furious indignation of Michael Angelo, who felt himself
as great and independent as either prince or pope. "You
don't know who it is to whom you refuse admittance," a
wondering bystander had said in his hearing to the lackey
who shut him out. "I know him very well, but I am here
to obey my orders," said the man. Michael Angelo turned
away, breathing fire and flame, and bidding the lackey tell
the pope that if he wanted him he must send for him,
went off to his house, where he gave his servants orders to
sell everything, and left Rome instantly, riding all through
the night at all risks, and never drawing bridle till he
reached Tuscan soil. As it proved, he had taken the only
wise course, for he had scarcely reached Poggibonsi, on the
Florentine frontier, when no less than five couriers arrived
one after another, with letters from Julius recalling him.

But the sculptor was no less proud than the pope. All that the messengers could get from him was a brief note of reply, proudly informing his holiness that it was impossible for him who had been *cacciato via come un tristo* to go back again ; after which he made his way to Florence, settling down, it would seem, into the haughty sadness of an injured man. Notwithstanding this tremendous breach between them, however, a certain hankering after each other is visible between the two who were so fitly mated. Michael Angelo betook himself to the completion of his cartoon, and perhaps began the execution of it in the great hall— so at least one legend says. He was three months at Florence in the proud self-absorption of this quarrel, during which time the pope wrote thrice to the signoria, demanding that his artist should be sent back. At the end of this time Julius came to Bologna, and here the odd quarrel came to a characteristic conclusion. Persuaded by Soderini, the Gonfaloniere, who had already shown himself much his friend, and moved by the patriotic fear of involving his country in the dispute, Michael Angelo was induced to go to Bologna and present himself before his great adversary. Evidently this time the *entree* was not refused to him. When he reached the presence-chamber the artist knelt down apparently not venturing to speak. His holiness cast a sidelong look at him, lowering and stormy. "Instead of coming to us, thou hast waited till we came to thee," he said gloomily. Then Michael Angelo took heart of grace to ask pardon, no doubt a hard thing to bend his mind to; and the two proud men, neither willing to make a step too far, yet both longing to be friends, were silent for an angry and anxious moment ; when happily one of those conciliating courtiers who are always to be found where princes are, ready to smoothe away every difficulty, interposed with ingratiating folly. " Forgive him," said this Polonius, bishop or monsignor or simple retainer, it does not matter which; "your holiness knows that these kind of men are poor ignorant creatures, and good for nothing except in their art." Quick as lightning the pope turned upon the foolish mediator. "It is thou who art ignorant!" he cried, delighted no doubt to have some third person to relieve his mind upon ; and turning the meddler out of the room, gave Michael Angelo his blessing, and received him gladly back into full favor.

Thus ended the quarrel, with a humorous transference of guilt which no doubt filled the old pope with glee. As a pledge of their renewed union, the sculptor made a statue of his patron in bronze for the town, which is described by all who saw it as of most admirable force and likeness. Julius himself, with the same half-amused perception of the difficulties of the case, is said to have asked, when he saw this representation of himself, and especially the proud and spirited action of the right hand which was elevated, whether he was supposed to be blessing or cursing. Michael Angelo, with unusual courtiership, replied that his holiness was warning the people of Bologna to be upon their good behavior, and asked whether he should place a book in the left hand. "No," said Julius, in high good-humor, "not a book, but a sword, for I am no man of letters." Thus it is apparent that the breach had but united two minds so original and vigorous, more closely than before. There is another story, less pleasant, of this statue, which did not long survive, being injured in a riot, and finally re-cast into a cannon called from it La Giulia. Francia, it is said, who was of Bologna, where still his pictures are the inheritance of the city, was brought to see it, as no doubt the whole population was, one way or other; and whether by inadvertence or by jealousy, praised it as " *un bellissimo getto* "—a very fine cast, as if, says Vasari, he praised the bronze more than the art. Michael Angelo was not the man to accept such poor commendation. He answered hotly, that he was no more obliged to Pope Julius for the material than Francia himself was to the chemist who sold him his colors. "You and Cossa are two solemn blockheads," the enraged artist added, in the presence of several *gentiluomini*, to the confusion of Francia. Even this does not seemed to have satisfied his wrath. Shortly after, he saw a son of Francia's, a very handsome youth, to whom he exclaimed, with as much bad taste as injustice, "Thy father can make better faces in flesh and blood than in paint." We are disposed to hope that Francia was not jealous, but only confused by the greatness of the presence in which he found himself, and that Michael Angelo, when his passion was over, recognized the cruel brutality of his speech.

Meanwhile, if the historian may be trusted, mischief was brewing against the sculptor in Rome. According to Vasari, the architect Bramante, who was Raphael's relation and Michael Angelo's enemy, had ere now interposed to arrest the progress he was making—by persuading Pope Julius that it was unlucky for a man to build his own sepulcher in his lifetime ; and secondly, that the then existing Cathedral of St. Peter's was too small to receive fitly the great groups already partially executed, for the completion of which all those blocks of purest marble of Carrara encumbered the Piazza. The San Pietro of that day was not the great temple with which we are all acquainted, and which from all the adjacent heights shows its great dome, the only distinctly visible object upon the vast level of the Campagna, the one thing which is Rome. The older church was an ancient Roman basilica founded by Constantine, rich and splendid with antique marbles, but not raising itself in imposing height, the genius of the city, like the present edifice. We speak of our own age as careless of the monuments of the past, and with still warmer zeal we rave against that eighteenth century

which the *fanaticoes* of the present day are beginning to
rehabilitate.   But even the eighteenth century white-
washing and scraping, covering up and pulling down, did
nothing which can be compared to the daring of the
sixteenth, the Renaissance age, which, without a pause or
a compunction, pulled to pieces the old basilica of Constantine, the earliest cradle of the faith, in order to place
on its site a brand-new cathedral, with its new dome.   Pope
Julius and his advisers did this in *gaieté de cœur*, without a
single pause of consideration or alarm ; and it was natural
that with this tremendous enterprise on his hands, Julius
should cease to be anxious about his sepulcher, especially
as for the moment there was no place to put it, had it been
even more near completion.   Bramante, however, did not
stop here.   He had got the matter of the new cathedral in
his own hands, and had torn the other to pieces, destroying
many of the beautiful marble columns, a fact which it is
said Michael Angelo pointed out to the pope, no doubt
adding to Bramante's inclination to harm him if he could ;
and Vasari attributes to the architect the too cunning
notion that the Florentine artist should be invited to
change his trade, to put aside the chisel, with which
already he had done such wonders, and to take to painting
instead ; thus securing a downfall for the pride of the man
who had shown himself unrivaled and above all competitors in marble.   With this intention he is said to have
suggested to the pope the idea of filling the Sistine Chapel,
the private chapel of the Papacy, with frescoes in remembrance of Pope Sixtus, the uncle of Julius, and of confiding
the execution of them to Michael Angelo.   This too subtle
attempt to ruin an artist by forcing him into the work
which has become almost his highest distinction, is too
fine surely even for a keen Italian brain of the sixteenth
century inspired by profound envy and hostility ; and good
Vasari, who is so often assailed by his critics, may, it is to

be hoped, be as wrong in this as he is often in the more innocent particular of dates. Anyhow, whatever the cause might be, it is certain that Pope Julius, leaving the marbles of his sepulcher for the time, and indeed throwing off all thought of sepulcher altogether in the delight and splendor of these new undertakings, which surely must have had power enough to keep an old man alive if anything could, ordained with imperious yet flattering tyranny, that his Florentine and no other—not Raphael, though Raphael too was a favourite—should paint his uncle's chapel, the place which he used for his own devotions, such as they were. Michael Angelo was profoundly disappointed by this change of plan. He had made his design for the tomb, a design by no means remarkable for its beauty, in the classic taste of the time, and his whole heart was in his marble, which he had chosen so carefully, quarried, and made roads for, and superintended in every stage of its progress, and out of which he had already got four finished figures and eight more which were *abbozzati*, just in that stage of suggestiveness which delights a true artist's soul. But nothing that could be said would turn the old pope from his determination, and probably after their recent breach Michael Angelo had no desire to break with the kind old despot again. He submitted therefore, with one fling in passing at Bramante, who could not fix the scaffolding necessary for him without making holes in the roof, till the sculptor, delighted with the passing triumph, invented on the spot the necessary means and humbled his rival, on the eve of the undertaking, into which he no doubt believed that rival had helped to force him—a characteristic pleasure.

To tell the story of the Sistine frescoes would be too long, though it is full of the same quaint humor which distinguishes all Michael Angelo's intercourse with Pope Julius. They quarrelled perpetually over it; the painter

refusing to uncover his work, the pope insisting on seeing
it, making perpetual invasions even into the dangerous
territory of those scaffoldings from which once in a fit of
passion he threatened to throw the great workman down.
More than once it hung on the balance of a chance whether
the artist would rush off, as he had done before, and leave
his hasty patron to have the works finished as he could.
But, as all the world knows, they were completed to the
admiration of all Christendom and the great content and
glory of Pope Julius, whose perpetual interruptions and
aggravations must on the whole, one would imagine, have
kept the painter amused through his long and exciting
labor, and which add a spark of kindly nature and
character to the grave record. " Oh truly happy age of
ours !" cries Vasari ; " oh blessed workmen, who in your
own time have been able to enlighten the dimness of your
eyes at the fountain of so much light, and to see growing
softly before you by degrees all that was difficult in this
marvelous and singular work !" If Bramante moved
the pope to it out of a malicious intent to ruin Michael
Angelo, no scheme could have failed more signally. The
frescoes of the Sistine left him as unique in painting as
he had been in marble, and filled all Italy with admiration
and pride.

Not even now, however, could the abandoned work over
which he had spent so much thought, the tomb of Julius,
get accomplished. When the pope died, which was only a
few months after the completion of these pictures, he left
to two of his nephews, both cardinals, the charge of
completing, but *con minor desegno*, this memorial, to which
Michael Angelo was but too anxious to devote himself, for
love of the work and for love of the pope who had scolded
and thwarted and loved him. The new pope, Leo X., a
Medici—one of the family to which Michael Angelo owed
his beginning in art, and a great deal of generous friend-

ship and patronage, stopped the execution even of this "minor design," and sent him back to Florence to take in hand the magnificent new works of embellishment and completion by which the church of San Lorenzo there was to be turned into a shrine for the Medici and celebration of their greatness, now raised into loftier elevation than ever by the accession of the new pope. These Medici had been banished from Florence with scorn and hatred eighteen years before; they had been kept at bay ever since by the struggling republic, who feared them as her worst enemies, with a just appreciation of the persistent purpose of the race to make themselves reigning princes of the city, which Cosimo and Lorenzo had ruled astutely by means of all the old forms of constitutional liberty. Slowly and surely, however, while the republic labored on with its cumbrous hierarchy of rulers, the fallen house began to right itself, as rising dynasties have a way of doing, and aided by Pope Julius, whom Florence had thwarted and offended, again got footing in the city in the disastrous year 1512, the same year in which the Sistine frescoes were finished. The dangerous race were admitted "as private citizens only," a transparent fiction in which nobody believed, and were surrounded by mercenary troops who cowed the city, which, with her best men banished and her moment of fate arrived, fell helpless into their hands. The first thing the Medici did was to dissolve the Consiglio Maggiore, instituted by Savonarola, and which perhaps had not proved so successful as was hoped; and to establish a servile government by means of the old farce of a public *Parlamento,* which was the ancient way of flattering the foolish masses into apparent support of despotism. When, however, on the death of Julius, the Cardinal Medici was made pope, Florence, dazzled by the elevation of the first Florentine who had ever occupied the Holy See, almost for very pride forgave the Medici. It was at this moment that Michael

Angelo was suddenly sent away from the work in Rome, to which he felt himself bound both in honor and gratitude. Leo was a man of a very different caliber from his imperious,

HOLY FAMILY, BY M. ANGELO, IN THE BARGELLO. (*Unfinished.*)

eager, and warlike predecessor. Though he has got much false fame as the most cultivated and elegant of popes, there was in him no such *naïve* magnificence, no such impatient curiosity and love for rare and splendid things, as had thrust Pope Julius into all manner of noble under-

takings. Family pride, and a politic intention to please
and amuse the Florentines till their chains should be safely
riveted on their shoulders, would seem to have moved him
more than any such real love of the beautiful and admiring enthusiasm for the perpetual novelty and variety of
genius, which prompted the old pope to hold his sculptor
fast, and to like him all the better for his resistance and
the outbursts of a temper as imperious as his own. Leo's
commission was of little advantage or pleasure to Michael
Angelo, whose submission and obedience to the new pope's
orders, so unlike his proud rebellion against Julius, betrays
at once the melancholy failure of that free Florence which
no longer had the power to protect her sons, and the
heaviness of those bonds of ancient gratitude and friendship which the generous spirit cannot shake off, however
unworthy may be the heirs of an unforgotten benefactor.
Once more the great artist had to take his weary way to
Carrara, or worse still to Serravezza, in the Florentine
territory, where marble had been found, a withdrawal of
custom from the lord of Carrara which brought the enmity
of that potentate upon the sculptor; and to make roads for
the conveyance of the marble, and banish himself to the
savage wildness of those hills in the very height of his
glory and power. The only distinct memorial of this
wretched interval, in which he was kept coming and going
between Florence and these quarries, chafing at the thous-
and delays and longing to get back to real work, is the
finestre inginocchiate of the Florentine palaces, the ironwork
formed like a kneeling figure, which every visitor of Florence must have remarked a picturesque feature of the
streets, and which the great sculptor invented at some stray
moment as he passed, throwing his great imagination into
the humblest as into the highest art.

Leo's pontificate lasted nine years, and remains like a
great desert in Michael Angelo's life, dividing its grander

activities—a curious evidence of that pontiff's patronage of art. And after Leo came the short and unhappy reign of poor Pope Adrian, a good, pious, humble-minded Teuton, as much out of place in that corrupt and splendid court as it is possible to conceive. During this short interval of quiet the artist returned, it is said, to those marbles of the Julian tomb which lay so heavy on his mind and conscience, and which he seemed fated never to complete. The second Medici pope, Clement VII., was elected in 1523 on Adrian's death, and it is to him apparently that the world owes what is perhaps Michael Angelo's most wonderful work, the tombs of the Medici in San Lorenzo, with those marvelous allegorical figures which, if they have ever been equaled, have never been surpassed either in ancient or in modern art. But before we reach this magnificent and melancholy climax of the sculptor's powers, there intervenes an episode at once in his personal history, and in that of his country, without which it is less easy to understand their meaning and to give to his character its full development. Clement VII. was unfortunate. He had not the wisdom of combination which distinguished his great kinsman Lorenzo, and the times were not favorable. Twice over he was driven into the castle of St. Angelo for safety, once by personal enemies, the second time by the German army, which sacked Rome and shocked the world by its atrocities. Florence, which had been sleeping under the re-established rule of his family, seized the moment of the pope's downfall to make one desperate effort for emancipation. The young representatives of the Medici were sent out of Florence, the great council was re-formed, the popular government reconstituted, and for a moment it seemed possible that Florence might again triumph and her old liberties be restored to the city. Then burst forth once more, after the long interval of thirty years, the strenuous religious impulse which Savonarola

had given, and which, sternly suppressed and held down
both by the Republicans of the other party who had killed
the prophet, and by the depraved and despotic Medici, had
endured throughout all persecutions in the Piagnoni party,
the Puritans of the time. Niccolo Capponi—of the same
family as that bold Piero Capponi who defied Charles in
Savonarola's day—the Gonfaloniere appointed, apparently
as Soderini, the last official of this rank, had been, as the
permanent head of the government, belonged to the
Piagnoni party ; and when it began to be apparent that
the Medici were once more gaining strength, and that a
bitter struggle was before the republic, he electrified the
great popular assembly of citizens by suddenly throwing
himself back upon the traditions of that most glorious
moment of recent Florentine history, and proposing to the
astonished but deeply moved council that they should elect
Jesus Christ as King of Florence ! The consiglio maggiore
was Savonarola's special institution, and the memory of a
man so great had sunk deeply into the heart of the people.
All the enthusiasm of old surged up to answer this appeal.
With a quaint regularity such as contrasts strangely with
the fervor of popular passion which moved them, they
put the proposal to the vote, and out of eleven hundred
citizens only eighteen dropped the white bean of dissent
and rejected the heavenly monarch. A memorial of the
election was still, until very recent times, engraved over
the doorway of the Palazzo Vecchio, the monogram of
Christ, sign of the only kingship which Florence would
allow ; and once more " *Viva Gesu Cristo, nostro Re!*" was
shouted about the streets as in the days of the prophet.
This singular echo of the one only strenuous attempt ever
made, entirely independent of party, to establish on a
sound basis the freedom of Florence, has a ring of despair
in it as echoes so often have ; but it animated the town to
its last great struggle as perhaps nothing else could have

done. The name of Savonarola was still a word to conjure withal, for no Florentine whose judgment was worth having, not the most hostile to him, not Machiavelli even, nor Guiccardini, could depise the prophet or think of him as a vulgar fanatic. His genius, his high honor and enthusiastic love of freedom, were as undeniable as his power.

So long as there was war and trouble in Rome, the Florentine revolution was successful, and the patriotic party had everything their own way; but after the emperor's forces had sacked Rome and done their worst, there was a grand peace-making and union among the great belligerents, a union which filled Florence with fear and horror. Florence had made alliance with France, according to her traditionary policy, and had thus rendered herself doubly objectionable to Pope Clement, both as pope and as Medici; and for some time the city hoped that this alliance would help her; but by and by France too made peace, and the alarmed republic found herself standing out against a world of foes, the pope threatening fire and flame, and all the relations and hangers-on of the Medici getting ready to return in double force. Perhaps the fact that they had already sinned beyond reach of forgiveness against Clement and his kinsfolk helped the Florentines to maintain a steadfast face in a moment of great danger. Their lives or their possessions, or both, were forfeit anyhow. In any case exile and social destruction were the best they could expect, and in the very determination which organizes a desperate resistance there is always more or less of hope. At least, for the moment, they were free from the hated presence of the Medici, and to defend their city was the sole possibility that remained to them. The foundation of the alliance between the pope and the emperor was a contract for the marriage of Alessandro, the illegitimate representative of the Medici, with Margaret, the illegitimate

daughter of the emperor; the two to be sovereigns of
Florence, no longer under any pretense of republican
liberty, but openly and simply as the duke and duchess of
a conquered principality. Such prospects as these were
enough to make the most timid burghers fight. The
Florentines sprang to arms with universal consent. They
called their best men to counsel, collected all possible
means of defense, and prepared to do grim battle for their
liberties. The most available way to the city was over the
leafy hill of San Miniato, which even at that distant period
was gay with smiling villas, the country houses of the
wealthy citizens, and here accordingly the first thought of
the defenders turned. From San Miniato even the feeble
artillery of the time must soon have made an end of the
beautiful town below, and the fortifying of this weak point
was the first step. Michael Angelo was almost idle in
Florence at the time, designing *fenestre inginocchiate*, working languidly at Pope Julius's tomb. It would be a strange
idea now to select the greatest artist of the age to fortify
a city threatened with a siege, but there was nothing
strange in it then. He was appointed commissary-general
of the fortifications, and immediately set to work upon
them without either hesitation or doubt of his own powers.
It is true he had been a retainer of the Medici, cherished
and nurtured by them; but all the descendants of his
patron, Lorenzo, had died out, and any loyalty he may
have still felt toward that great name was claimed by no
worthy representative. The young Medici were bastards,
the pontiffs of the name had wasted his time for him and
spoiled his exertions; and his duty to his native city was
infinitely beyond any shred of grateful attachment to
them, or rather to their relations, which might have de-
terred the artist, had they treated him better, from working
against them; but fortunately for Florence and for himself,
the two popes had done nothing to perpetuate the hereditary

friendship. From the broad and peaceful sweep of road
which rounds the base of San Miniato, the traveler may
still see traces of dark masonry stretching upward, over-
grown by the facile vegetation of Italy, which are the last
remains of the walls which the great sculptor built. He
posted cannon upon the top of the tower which now looks
so serenely over Florence, peacefully guarding the dead
who lie there wreathed and covered with *immortelles*,
and distinguished by those fond inscriptions to which the
Italian tongue lends a certain grace. The sun blazes upon
those stony graves all gay with uncongenial ornament,
and shows us nothing nowadays but pretty villas peeping
out from clouds of soft foliage, the olive gardens and
wealthy orchards of the *Colli*, the suburban slopes which
Florence loves. She loved them even then, in that moment
of trouble three hundred and fifty years ago, and had covered them with pleasant houses and peaceful monasteries,
with gardens and fountains and greenness. But in the
spring of 1529, when everything was at its sweetest, bands
of young men with hatchet and axe were set to work on
the smiling hillside, to cut down their own homes, their
own trees, everything which stood in the way of the defense.
It is touching to find that when they had half-pulled to
pieces the convent of San Salvi on the roadside, that convent at the door of which Corso Donati fell dead about
two centuries before, they paused at sight of the fresco
painted there quite recently by Andrea del Sarto, and
spared the half-ruined walls for the sake of the picture,
like true art-loving Florentines. But they did not spare
those villas which were as the apple of his eye to each good
burgher who possessed one. Michael Angelo was sent off
in the midst of these heart-rending clearings to Ferrara, to
study the fortifications there as an aid to his work, and
was received with great courtesy by Duke Alfonso, who
playfully called him his prisoner, proposing, with flattering

grace, the ransom of a picture to be painted when time permitted.   He came back at peril of his life, Vasari tells us, *vinto dallo amore*, and returned to his work on San

HOLY FAMILY, BY M. ANGELO.

Miniato, where he made a kind of armor of bales of wool for the tower on which he placed his cannon, with an artist's care for the old mediæval monument, and so saved it from all hazards. He must have led a strange life at this exciting time. From his engineer work on the hill, among the demolished villas and downtrodden gardens, when he could escape from trench and battlement, he hurried down to his studio and solaced himself with an hour's work at one of the Julian statues, or diverted his thoughts from the troubles of the time by that allegorical Leda which he had begun to paint for the duke of Ferrara; and when such escape was possible, on the very heights themselves, amid his workmen digging and building round him, the great artist employed his impatient powers in a bas-relief of a winged Victory, giving his orders, chisel in hand, and turning back to his own diviner labor when he had measured a trench or watched the strengthening of an earthwork. Had victory been with the Florentine arms, what noble place had that *abbozzo* been worthy of, carved in the free air within the wall that was for the defense, not only of Florence, but of all hope and freedom for the Tuscan race. As it was, this Victory, poor image of the true, perished somewhere in the tumult of defeat, and exists no more.

For Florence was conquered, as everybody knows, by famine and treachery more than by arms—fit agents of the Medici; and her long and glorious career came to a close, never to revive again, under the ignoble sway of an illegitimate duke, not even a lawful Medici, though wearing in their right the first crown of princely authority which had been permitted in the free city. The Medici slew, confiscated and imprisoned, as was their nature, as soon as the power was in their hands, and Michael Angelo was one of those who had to keep in hiding, it is said, in the tower of San Niccoló oltr' Arno, for some time after. But at length it came to the recollection of Pope Clement that San Lorenzo was still uncompleted and that there was but one Buonarotti in the world. Accordingly he sent his emissaries to find the sculptor, with orders to say nothing to him except that his usual allowance was waiting for him, and that he ought to attend to his work. What Michael Angelo replied to the man who first told him this we cannot tell; but hiding breaks the spirit even of the strongest, and he returned to his work, as he was told to do, in silence, working with a somber *furia* at the great figures in the sacristy, by means of which, as no other man in the city was capable of doing, he could write in majestic despair the tragedy of Florence ; how hope had departed, how life had become a desert, and how it was hard to struggle with waking consciousness, but good to sleep and forget—nay, best of all, to be stone, and feel no more.

This is the burden of the famous figures which all the world has thronged to look at since, and which few, we imagine, have parted from lightly or without a profound impression. Of the men to whom so sublime a monument has been raised who knows anything, or cares to know ? The monument is not to an inconsiderable Giulio or Lorenzo, but to the great city which had struggled and erred so long, which had gone astray and repented and suffered and erred again, but always mightily, with full tide of life in her veins and consciousness in her heart, until now the time had come when she was dead and past, chained down by icy oppression in a living grave. Michael Angelo saw that hope was ended in Florence : no more eager conspiracies, no more fortunate revolutions, no other bold burgher or inspired prophet to break her chains ; but the lethargy of death, the chill of the tomb, the very stupidity of unconsciousness, was to be her fate. "How doth the city sit solitary that was full of people !" he might have cried as Dante did when the death of Beatrice darkened heaven and earth to the poet ; yet with a deeper reason. But Baonarotti said nothing. He took the marble which he had quarried out at Serravezza, weary yet

not despairing, and with the fire of grief in his eyes put
forth his somber strength upon it and rent out of its
white depths the symbols of his despair.   Not the still
beauty of the Greeks, the passionless godhead of pure line
and form, the material poetry of a stony perfection.   The
four great figures of Day and Night, Twilight and Dawn,
are instinct with the sentiment of modern thought, that
profound struggle of feeling which ancient art eschews.
As we look at them, suggestions, not one but many, pour
into our minds, indications of mortal conflict and anguish
and hopelessness, of a fatigue and despair of the soul which
goes infinitely beyond the most intolerable weariness of the
body ; yet of the inevitable waking, the acceptance of its
burden and penalty which nature and Providence alike
impose upon men.   Night sleeps, but it is the sleep of a
sublime despair ; not rest but oblivion of ill is what the
great slumberer has desired, yet Sorrow unforgotten hovers
upon the very stillness of her exhaustion ; and with what
pain upon her beautiful brow that sad Aurora wakes, not
the rosy-fingered Aurora of the classics, but a heavy
mortal queen, rousing herself reluctantly, painfully, to
meet the Care who is awake before her !   What anguish,
what mortal conflict, what forced assent to the cruel
laws of nature, submission yet resistance, a duty compul-
sory and terrible yet not to be cast off, and which the
sufferer accepts though he loathes it, too strong in honor
and right to shirk the needful act whatever it may be.
All this, and more than this, is in these gigantic yet
beautiful figures ; and again a something additional in the
great Day, bursting herculean from his stony prison, half
heroic, nothing known of him but the great brow and
resolute eyes, and those vast limbs which are not yet free
from the cohesion of the marble, though alive with such
strain of action.   Here is the great poem of the age, self-
utterance and revelation of a mighty intellect overpowered

by mortal sadness, yet incapable, how painful soever the
exertion, of failing to the claims of life and nature. The
spectator who remembers what was the fate of Florence
and of Buonarotti—compelled, both man and city, to come
back after the defeat of all their hopes to the perpetually
recurring task, to hear the burden which every day brought
with it—will gaze with reverence and an ennobling pang
of feeling at this great setting forth before heaven and
earth of the burden of humanity; not like those mysterious and awful pangs of the Divine Sufferer with which
that age was familiar, and which it saw imaged forth
wherever it turned, in highest and in rudest art; but
something almost more bitter as being less holy, involuntary and aimless anguish, bearing no fruit or recompense
either to God or man. He who can stand unmoved in
presence of these wonderful creations, or leave them without a sense of something learnt and felt beyond the usual
lessons and emotions of ordinary life, passes our comprehension. They mark the climax of Michael Angelo's genius,
the height of power and of expression beyond which no
mortal hand could reach.

Lest we may be supposed to impute too much meaning,
as it is so easy to do, to the great artist in this his most
impressive work, we quote his own interpretation of the
sentiment of his *Notte*, addressed to an anonymous poet
who had in true Italian fashion, in an elegant couplet,
bidden the spectator who doubted the real existence of the
wonderful sleeper, awake her and be answered. Here is,
in the person of his great conception, the sculptor's
reply :

> 'Grateful is sleep, and still more sweet, while woe
> And shame endure, 'tis to be stone like me,
> And highest fortune nor to feel nor see,
> Therefore awake me not ; speak low, speak low." *

---

* " Grato m'è 'l sonno, e piu l'esser di sasso,

The statues which Michael Angelo has placed above the sarcophagi which support his emblematic figures are professedly of two quite unimportant personages—Lorenzo, dead not long before, the father of Catherine de' Medici, portentous infant, then in Florence; and Giulio, his brother who died without even so much distinction as lies in that fact. And which is which no one can now say. We are told that "when remonstrated with as to the features not being correct, Buonarotti replied, with haughty carelessness, that he did not suppose people a hundred years later would care much how the dukes looked"—an unquestionable truth. And yet one at least of these statues is remarkable and interesting in the highest degree, the figure called the *Penseroso*, long supposed to be Lorenzo, now supposed to be Giulio, very likely neither, but a noble representation of thought and intellect in opposition to the insignificant and commonplace good looks of the classical young warrior opposite, embodiments of the reflective and superficial life more striking, as being more natural, than the conventional types represented elsewhere of Rachel and Leah. Perhaps this was the intention of the artist; or perhaps he made the helmeted thinker so impressive and grand because he could not help it, and had exhausted all the capabilities of commonplace in him by the creation of the light-minded and small-brained individual who sits in serene insignificance above the mighty spirits of the Night and Day.

It is almost a relief from the strained feeling which accompanies this greatest of modern works, to find the old fiery humor of the artist breaking out again in presence of a fine gentleman and courtier who came from Ferrara to fetch the picture which Alfonso had asked for, and who,

Mentre che 'l danno e la vergogna dura,
Non veder, non sentir, m'è gran ventura :
Però non mi destar, deh ! parla basso."

finding it so many square feet or inches less than he approved, declared it to be *poca cosa*, a small affair ; which foolish sentiment cost courteous Alfonso his picture, as the wrathful painter sent the emissary packing, and would have no more of him. He gave it afterward in careless generosity to Antonio Micci, his pupil, to portion his sister, not displeased perhaps to show the dainty Ferrarese and all the world how little store he set by the commission of which they had thought so much.

Shortly after the execution of the great group of San Lorenzo, in the year 1534 or '35, when he was approaching sixty, Michael Angelo left Florence. There was nothing to keep him there any longer. He had finished all the work he cared to do, and Alessandro, the new duke, was no friend of the proud artist who had done his best to keep him, and all depotism, at bay. He went to Rome, where he had now the great cartoons of his "Judgment," in the Sistine, to think of, as well as that still unfinished tomb of Pope Julius, which, however, after a long interval he got clear of by the erection of the great " Moses " over his early patron's tomb in San Pietro in Vinculis, though in a setting and with accompaniments very different from those originally proposed, and not very appropriate. And though he had, we think, attained his highest point of achievement, there was still great work before him, the Last Judgment in one class of art, and in another the great dome of St. Peter's, which had yet to be " hung " on Bramante's vast temple. In this latter undertaking, as well as in the cupola of San Lorenzo in Florence, he refused to depart from Brunelleschi's models, which he had already said might be varied but not improved (*Si può la variare, ma migliorare, no*). With the same obstinate loyalty to the great Florentine model, he declared that the dome he was about to make should be the sister of Santa Maria del Fiore —*piu grande, ma non piu bella.* These works were under-

taken under the pontificate of Paul III., the successor of
Clement, who displayed much of the eagerness of Julius to
secure Buonarotti's services and keep him employed. There
is a curious mixture of tyranny and flattery in the words
with which the new pope imperiously took, whether he
would or not, the great sculptor into his service. "I have
wanted you for the last thirty years," said Paul, "and now
that I am pope I will not be disappointed." And Michael
Angelo was no longer the hot-headed young Florentine
of the Julian days, when he treated the pope almost on
equal terms. He had lost courage for such daring deeds,
and had learned the necessities of submission. But though
he was more self-controlled in his intercourse with the
authorities, the old half-savage wrath, mingled with grim
humor, would sometimes break forth now and then, as
when he took dire revenge on Biagio di Cesena, an im-
pertinent courtier, who ventured to criticise the Last
Judgment. Michael Angelo turned the Minos of his great
fresco into a likeness of his audacious critic, with swift
stroke of rage which is like Dante in its grotesque vindic-
tiveness, though no doubt amusement mingled with wrath
before the revenge was half accomplished. "Where has he
placed you?" asked Pope Paul, when the aggrieved official
made his complaint. "In hell," said Biagio. "I am sorry
to hear it," the pope said gravely; "if it had been in
purgatory something might have been done, but in hell I
have no jurisdiction." And there Biagio stands in eternal
expiation of his ill-advised remarks till this day.

Michael Angelo never again returned to Florence. His
exile was voluntary, not forced like Dante's; and while
the one made frantic efforts to return, the other refused
all invitations to go back to the desecrated and subjugated
place. But in both these great and kindred souls a bitterness as profound as their love seems to have risen against
the home of their affections, the peerless city which both

held up to the world with a kind of adoring hatred. Dante
pouring upon Florence the fiery torrents of his wrath, yet
moving heaven and earth to get back to her; and Michael
Angelo fondly copying, though it was against all the habits
of his imperious individuality to copy anything, the beloved
dome of Santa Maria del Fiore, yet refusing so much as to
enter the town upon which at last, after all her struggles
and anguish, the chains of petty despotism had been riveted
are but different manifestations of the same intense
patriotic passion. But in Dante's day there was hope for
the vigorous and turbulent race which had yet so much
fighting and so many revolutions to get through, and every
reason why the *fuor-usciti* should get back if that was
possible; while hope was over for the fallen city upon
which the great Buonarotti turned his back, his heart
heavy with shame and sorrow, with nothing to desire but
that he might be able to forget her and never see her outraged beauty more.

After this climax of genius and grief, however, he lived
twenty years and more in a sufficiently tranquil old age in
Rome; and here it is perhaps, as the softening shadows of
the evening smoothed away most of his fierceness, that the
great artist comes nearest to our sympathies. He was
more happy and more sad personally in the lingering conclusion of his days than he had ever been in his life before.
Till now no softening of domestic love had ever encircled
him except such lingering ties of nature as bound him to
his old father and the brother Buonaroto, whom he loved
most, and of whom in the early days of his work in Rome,
while still he was quarreling with Pope Julius, he wrote,
hearing he was ill, that " if Buonaroto be in danger I shall
leave everything." At the same youthful period, " your
Michael Angelo, sculptor in Rome," as he signs himself,
desires his father to "think only of your life, and let
everything go rather that inconvenience yourself, for it is

more precious to me to have you alive and poor than all the gold of the world if you were dead." But this tender and filial sentiment is all we see of his private existence; and no woman ever seems to have crossed his path to move him till the fair and noble Vittoria Colonna, in middle age and faithful widowhood, came all at once into his life and charmed the old man into that tender and reverential warmth of friendship more delicate and exquisite than any relation between man and man, which is nevertheless as distinct from love, commonly so called, as night from day. He wrote to her, composed sonnets for her, found in her house while she lived in Rome a happy refuge from the weariness of his declining years and many labors, and the best society of the time—and derived from her altogether a new consolation and brightness. All the more sorely did he feel the want of her when vague accusations of heresy drove her from Rome in 1541, after some five years of close intercourse. He is said to have shown his grief at this separation in a most characteristic way. He had hurt his leg by a fall from some part of the scaffolding on which he had been working at the completion of his Last Judgment, just at the moment when this much more serious calamity befell him; and in his misery the proud old man, falling back no doubt with a sore and bitter heart upon all the habits of his lifelong loneliness, shut himself up in his room, trying to defend himself from real suffering by the old harsh traditions of stoicism and independence of external aid. He was baffled in this unnecessary martyrdom by the determined kindness of a Florentine doctor, Baccio Rontini, who forced his way into the room and defied the sufferer to turn him out. But a profounder affliction still lay before him in the death of the beautiful and gracious woman who had thus opened his heart. She died in 1547 and the old darkness fell back deeper and more solitary than ever in the old man's waning days. And Urbino

: :, his faithful servant, whom he had expected, as he
ws, to be the prop and support, *bastone e riposo*, of his
childless age, but who, "dying, has taught me to die, not
unwillingly but with desire for death." Heavily the
shadows fall over every such lingering conclusion. It is
sad to die young ; but sadder still to outlast all loves, and
drop after instead of before one's time into the grave
which has already swallowed up all life's attractions.
And no man, we suppose, ever gets far enough off from
himself and his work, however long he may live, to
estimate that calamity, or take comfort in the fame that
will live after him. Fame at its best is but a poor compensation for all the ills of existence ; it may be a pleasant
crown of happiness, an ecstatic elixir to stimulate the
energies of the youth; but poorer and poorer as the mind
matures, and emptiness and vanity to the aged soul. Here
are his own solemn reflections in the dim twilight of his
closing day :

> " The course of life has brought my lingering days
>   In fragile ship over a stormy sea
>   To th' common port, when all our counts must be
> Ordered and reckoned, works for blame or praise.
> Here ends love's tender fantasy that made
>   (I know the error of the thought) great art.
>   My idol and my monarch; now my heart
> Perceives how low is each man's longing laid.
> Oh thoughts that tempt us, idle, sweet, and vain,
>   Where are ye when a double death draws near
>   One sure, one threatening an eternal loss?
> Painting and sculpture now are no more gain
>   To still the soul turned to that Godhead dear
>   Stretching great arms out to us from his cross."

How can we better take leave of Michael Angelo in his
sorrow and his greatness than with these sad words of
mortal failing, yet everlasting loyalty and hope ? It is

more sad to part in her decay, with no such solemn illumination of trust upon her head, from the Florence of his love. We read with a pang of sympathy that even when so far gone in the mists of the evening the old sculptor roused himself to offer to Francis of France, among other patriotic bribes held out to him, the premium of a great equestrian statue which should make him immortal, to be completed on the day when he should free Florence from her tyrants. Who could doubt that love and genius would have kept the old man alive to keep his promise had the enterprise ever been taken in hand? But Francis died, and this last effort was not even attempted. And Florence and her freedoms died too, for weary centuries lying motionless with the Twilight and the Dawn, the Night and the Day, watching by her ashes in melancholy splendor; though now we trust she is alive again to take up, with better hopes and more harmonious surroundings, the great, noble, uncompleted story of her life.

POPULAR LITERATURE FOR THE MASSES, COMPRISING CHOICE SELECTIONS FROM THE TREASURES OF THE WORLD'S KNOWLEDGE, ISSUED IN A SUBSTANTIAL AND ATTRACTIVE CLOTH BINDING, AT A POPULAR PRICE

BURT'S HOME LIBRARY is a series which includes the standard works of the world's best literature, bound in uniform cloth binding, gilt tops, embracing chiefly selections from writers of the most notable English, American and Foreign Fiction, together with many important works in the domains of History, Biography, Philosophy, Travel, Poetry and the Essays.

A glance at the following annexed list of titles and authors will endorse the claim that the publishers make for it—that it is the most comprehensive, choice, interesting, and by far the most carefully selected series of standard authors for world-wide reading that has been produced by any publishing house in any country, and that at prices so cheap, and in a style so substantial and pleasing, as to win for it millions of readers and the approval and commendation, not only of the book trade throughout the American continent, but of hundreds of thousands of librarians, clergymen, educators and men of letters interested in the dissemination of instructive, entertaining and thoroughly wholesome reading matter for the masses.

[SEE FOLLOWING PAGES]

Abbe Constantin. By LUDOVIC HALEVY.

Abbott. By SIR WALTER SCOTT.

Adam Bede. By GEORGE ELIOT.

Addison's Essays. EDITED BY JOHN RICHARD GREEN.

Aeneid of Virgil. TRANSLATED BY JOHN CONNINGTON.

Aesop's Fables.

Alexander, the Great, Life of. By JOHN WILLIAMS.

Alfred, the Great, Life of. By THOMAS HUGHES.

Alhambra. By WASHINGTON IRVING.

Alice in Wonderland, and Through the Looking-Glass. By LEWIS CARROLL.

Alice Lorraine. By R. D. BLACKMORE.

All Sorts and Conditions of Men. By WALTER BESANT.

Alton Locke. By CHARLES KINGSLEY.

Amiel's Journal. TRANSLATED BY MRS. HUMPHREY WARD.

Andersen's Fairy Tales.

Anne of Geirstein. By SIR WALTER SCOTT.

Antiquary. By SIR WALTER SCOTT.

Arabian Nights' Entertainments.

Ardath. By MARIE CORELLI.

Arnold, Benedict, Life of. By GEORGE CANNING HILL.

Arnold's Poems. By MATTHEW ARNOLD.

Around the World in the Yacht Sunbeam. By MRS. BRASSEY.

Arundel Motto. By MARY CECIL HAY.

At the Back of the North Wind. By GEORGE MACDONALD.

Attic Philosopher. By EMILE SOUVESTRE.

Auld Licht Idylls. By JAMES M. BARRIE.

Aunt Diana. By ROSA N. CAREY.

Autobiography of Benjamin Franklin.

Autocrat of the Breakfast Table. By O. W. HOLMES.

Averil. By ROSA N. CAREY.

Bacon's Essays. By FRANCIS BACON.

Barbara Heathcote's Trial. By ROSA N. CAREY.

Barnaby Rudge. By CHARLES DICKENS.

Barrack Room Ballads. By RUDYARD KIPLING.

Betrothed. By SIR WALTER SCOTT.

Beulah. By AUGUSTA J. EVANS.

Black Beauty. By ANNA SEWALL.

Black Dwarf. By SIR WALTER SCOTT.

Black Rock. By RALPH CONNOR.

Black Tulip. By ALEXANDRE DUMAS.

Bleak House. By CHARLES DICKENS.

Blithedale Romance. By NATHANIEL HAWTHORNE.

Bondman. By HALL CAINE.

Book of Golden Deeds. By CHARLOTTE M. YONGE.

Boone, Daniel, Life of. By CECIL B. HARTLEY.

Bride of Lammermoor. By SIR WALTER SCOTT.

Bride of the Nile. By GEORGE EBERS.

Browning's Poems. By ELIZABETH BARRETT BROWNING.

Browning's Poems. (SELECTIONS.) By ROBERT BROWNING.

Bryant's Poems. (EARLY.) By WILLIAM CULLEN BRYANT.

Burgomaster's Wife. By GEORGE EBERS.

Burn's Poems. By ROBERT BURNS.

By Order of the King. By VICTOR HUGO.

Byron's Poems. By LORD BYRON.

Caesar, Julius, Life of. By JAMES ANTHONY FROUDE.

Carson, Kit, Life of. By CHARLES BURDETT.

Cary's Poems. By ALICE AND PHOEBE CARY.

Cast Up by the Sea. By SIR SAMUEL BAKER.

Charlemagne (Charles the Great), Life of. By THOMAS HODGKIN, D. C. L.

Charles Auchester. By E. BERGER.

Character. By SAMUEL SMILES.

Charles O'Malley. By CHARLES LEVER.

Chesterfield's Letters. By LORD CHESTERFIELD.

Chevalier de Maison Rouge. By ALEXANDRE DUMAS.

Chicot the Jester. By ALEXANDRE DUMAS.

Children of the Abbey. By REGINA MARIA ROCHE.

Child's History of England. By CHARLES DICKENS.

Christmas Stories. By CHARLES DICKENS.

Cloister and the Hearth. By CHARLES READE.

Coleridge's Poems. By SAMUEL TAYLOR COLERIDGE.

Columbus, Christopher, Life of. By WASHINGTON IRVING.

Companions of Jehu. By ALEXANDRE DUMAS.

Complete Angler. By WALTON AND COTTON.

Conduct of Life. By RALPH WALDO EMERSON.

Confessions of an Opium Eater. By THOMAS DE QUINCEY.

Conquest of Granada. By WASHINGTON IRVING.

Conscript. By ERCKMANN-CHATRIAN.

Conspiracy of Pontiac. By FRANCIS PARKMAN, JR.

Conspirators. By ALEXANDRE DUMAS.

Consuelo. By GEORGE SAND.

Cook's Voyages. By CAPTAIN JAMES COOK.

Corinne. By MADAME DE STAEL.

Countess de Charney. By ALEXANDRE DUMAS.

Countess Gisela. By E. MARLITT.

Countess of Rudolstadt. By George Sand.

Count Robert of Paris. By Sir Walter Scott.

Country Doctor. By Honore de Balzac.

Courtship of Miles Standish. By H. W. Longfellow.

Cousin Maude. By Mary J. Holmes.

Cranford. By Mrs. Gaskell.

Crockett, David, Life of. An Autobiography.

Cromwell, Oliver, Life of. By Edwin Paxton Hood.

Crown of Wild Olive. By John Ruskin.

Crusades. By Geo. W. Cox, M. A.

Daniel Deronda. By George Eliot.

Darkness and Daylight. By Mary J. Holmes.

Data of Ethics. By Herbert Spencer.

Daughter of an Empress, The. By Louisa Muhlbach.

David Copperfield. By Charles Dickens.

Days of Bruce. By Grace Aguilar.

Deemster, The. By Hall Caine.

Deerslayer, The. By James Fenimore Cooper.

Descent of Man. By Charles Darwin.

Discourses of Epictetus. Translated by George Long.

Divine Comedy. (Dante.) Translated by Rev. H. F. Carey.

Dombey & Son. By Charles Dickens.

Donal Grant. By George Macdonald.

Donovan. By Edna Lyall.

Dora Deane. By Mary J. Holmes.

Dove in the Eagle's Nest. By Charlotte M. Yonge.

Dream Life. By Ik Marvel.

Dr. Jekyll and Mr. Hyde. By R. L. Stevenson.

Duty. By Samuel Smiles.

Early Days of Christianity. By F. W. Farrar.

East Lynne. By Mrs. Henry Wood.

Edith Lyle's Secret. By Mary J. Holmes.

Education. By Herbert Spencer.

Egoist. By George Meredith.

Egyptian Princess. By George Ebers.

Eight Hundred Leagues on the Amazon. By Jules Verne.

Eliot's Poems. By George Eliot.

Elizabeth and her German Garden.

Elizabeth (Queen of England), Life of. By Edward Spencer Beesly, M.A.

Elsie Venner. By Oliver Wendell Holmes.

Emerson's Essays. (Complete.) By Ralph Waldo Emerson.

Emerson's Poems. By Ralph Waldo Emerson.

English Orphans. By Mary J. Holmes.

English Traits. By R. W. Emerson.

Essays in Criticism. (First and Second Series.) By Matthew Arnold.

Essays of Elia. By Charles Lamb.

Esther. By Rosa N. Carey.

Ethelyn's Mistake. By Mary J. Holmes.

Evangeline. (With notes.) By H. W. Longfellow.

Evelina. By Frances Burney.

Fair Maid of Perth. By Sir Walter Scott.

Fairy Land of Science. By Arabella B. Buckley.

Faust. (Goethe.) Translated by Anna Swanwick.

Felix Holt. By George Eliot.

Fifteen Decisive Battles of the World. By E. S. Creasy.

File No. 113. By Emile Gaboriau.

Firm of Girdlestone. By A. Conan Doyle.

First Principles. By Herbert Spencer.

First Violin. By Jessie Fothergill.

For Lilias. By Rosa N. Carey.

Fortunes of Nigel. By Sir Walter Scott.

Forty-Five Guardsmen. By Alexandre Dumas.

Foul Play. By Charles Reade.

Fragments of Science. By John Tyndall.

Frederick, the Great, Life of. By Francis Kugler.

Frederick the Great and His Court. By Louisa Muhlbach.

French Revolution. By Thomas Carlyle.

From the Earth to the Moon. By Jules Verne.

Garibaldi, General, Life of. By Theodore Dwight.

Gil Blas, Adventures of. By A. R. Le Sage.

Gold Bug and Other Tales. By Edgar A. Poe.

Gold Elsie. By E. Marlitt.

Golden Treasury. By Francis T. Palgrave.

Goldsmith's Poems. By Oliver Goldsmith.

Grandfather's Chair. By Nathaniel Hawthorne.

Grant, Ulysses S., Life of. By J. T. Headley.

Gray's Poems. By Thomas Gray.

Great Expectations. By Charles Dickens.

Greek Heroes. Fairy Tales for My Children. By Charles Kingsley.

Green Mountain Boys, The. By D. P. Thompson.

Grimm's Household Tales. By The Brothers Grimm.

Grimm's Popular Tales. By The Brothers Grimm.

Gulliver's Travels. By Dean Swift.

Guy Mannering. By Sir Walter Scott.

Hale, Nathan, the Martyr Spy. By CHARLOTTE MOLYNEUX HOLLOWAY.

Handy Andy. By SAMUEL LOVER.

Hans of Iceland. By VICTOR HUGO.

Hannibal, the Carthaginian, Life of. By THOMAS ARNOLD, M. A.

Hardy Norseman, A. By EDNA LYALL.

Harold. By BULWER-LYTTON.

Harry Lorrequer. By CHARLES LEVER.

Heart of Midlothian. By SIR WALTER SCOTT.

Heir of Redclyffe. By CHARLETTE M. YONGE.

Hemans' Poems. By MRS. FELICIA HEMANS.

Henry Esmond. By WM. M. THACKERAY.

Henry, Patrick, Life of. By WILLIAM WIRT.

Her Dearest Foe. By MRS. ALEXANDER.

Hereward. By CHARLES KINGSLEY.

Heriot's Choice. By ROSA N. CAREY.

Heroes and Hero-Worship. By THOMAS CARLYLE.

Hiawatha. (WITH NOTES.) By H. W. LONGFELLOW.

Hidden Hand, The. (COMPLETE.) By MRS. E. D. E. N. SOUTHWORTH.

History of a Crime. By VICTOR HUGO.

History of Civilization in Europe. By M. GUIZOT.

Holmes' Poems. (EARLY) By OLIVER WENDELL HOLMES.

Holy Roman Empire. By JAMES BRYCE.

Homestead on the Hillside. By MARY J. HOLMES.

Hood's Poems. By THOMAS HOOD.

House of the Seven Gables. By NATHANIEL HAWTHORNE.

Hunchback of Notre Dame. By VICTOR HUGO.

Hypatia. By CHARLES KINGSLEY.

Hyperion. By HENRY WADSWORTH LONGFELLOW.

Iceland Fisherman, By PIERRE LOTI.

Idle Thoughts of an Idle Fellow. By JEROME K. JEROME.

Iliad, POPE'S TRANSLATION.

Inez. By AUGUSTA J. EVANS.

Ingelow's Poems. By JEAN INGELOW.

Initials. By THE BARONESS TAUT-PHOEUS.

Intellectual Life. By PHILIP G. HAMERTON.

In the Counsellor's House. By E. MARLITT.

In the Golden Days. By EDNA LYALL.

In the Heart of the Storm. By MAXWELL GRAY.

In the Schillingscourt. By E. MARLITT.

Ishmael. (COMPLETE.) By MRS. E. D. E. N. SOUTHWORTH.

It Is Never Too Late to Mend. By CHARLES READE.

Ivanhoe. By SIR WALTER SCOTT.

Jane Eyre. By CHARLOTTE BRONTE.

Jefferson, Thomas, Life of. By SAMUEL M. SCHMUCKER, LL.D.

Joan of Arc, Life of. By JULES MICHELET.

John Halifax, Gentleman. By MISS MULOCK.

Jones, John Paul, Life of. By JAMES OTIS.

Joseph Balsamo. By ALEXANDRE DUMAS.

Josephine, Empress of France, Life of. By FREDERICK A. OBER.

Keats' Poems. By JOHN KEATS.

Kenilworth. By SIR WALTER SCOTT.

Kidnapped. By R. L. STEVENSON.

King Arthur and His Noble Knights. By MARY MACLEOD.

Knickerbocker's History of New York. By WASHINGTON IRVING.

Knight Errant. By EDNA LYALL.

Koran. TRANSLATED BY GEORGE SALE.

Lady of the Lake. (WITH NOTES.) By SIR WALTER SCOTT.

Lady with the Rubies. By E. MARLITT.

Lafayette, Marquis de, Life of. By P. C. HEADLEY.

Lalla Rookh. (WITH NOTES.) By THOMAS MOORE.

Lamplighter. By MARIA S. CUMMINS.

Last Days of Pompeii. By BULWER-LYTTON.

Last of the Barons. By BULWER-LYTTON.

Last of the Mohicans. By JAMES FENIMORE COOPER.

Lay of the Last Minstrel. (WITH NOTES.) By SIR WALTER SCOTT.

Lee, General Robert E., Life of. By G. MERCER ADAM.

Lena Rivers. By MARY J HOLMES.

Life of Christ. By FREDERICK W. FARRAR.

Life of Jesus. By ERNEST RENAN.

Light of Asia. By SIR EDWIN ARNOLD.

Light That Failed. By RUDYARD KIPLING.

Lincoln, Abraham, Life of. By HENRY KETCHAM.

Lincoln's Speeches. SELECTED AND EDITED BY G. MERCER ADAM.

Literature and Dogma. By MATTHEW ARNOLD.

Little Dorrit. By CHARLES DICKENS.

Little Minister. By JAMES M. BARRIE.

Livingstone, David, Life of. By THOMAS HUGHES.

Longfellow's Poems. (EARLY.) By HENRY W. LONGFELLOW.

Lorna Doone. By R. D. BLACKMORE.

Louise de la Valliere. By ALEXANDRE DUMAS.

Love Me Little, Love Me Long. By CHARLES READE.

BURT'S HOME LIBRARY. Cloth. Gilt Tops. Price, $1.00

Lowell's Poems. (EARLY.) BY JAMES RUSSELL LOWELL.

Lucile. BY OWEN MEREDITH.

Macaria. BY AUGUSTA J. EVANS.

Macaulay's Literary Essays. BY T. B. MACAULAY.

Macaulay's Poems. BY THOMAS BABINGTON MACAULAY.

Madame Therese.. BY ERCKMANN-CHATRIAN.

Maggie Miller. BY MARY J. HOLMES.

Magic Skin. BY HONORE DE BALZAC.

Mahomet, Life of. BY WASHINGTON IRVING.

Makers of Florence. BY MRS. OLIPHANT.

Makers of Venice. BY MRS. OLIPHANT.

Man and Wife. BY WILKIE COLLINS.

Man in the Iron Mask. BY ALEXANDRE DUMAS.

Marble Faun. BY NATHANIEL HAWTHORNE.

Marguerite de la Valois. BY ALEXANDRE DUMAS.

Marian Grey. BY MARY J. HOLMES.

Marius, The Epicurian. BY WALTER PATER.

Marmion. (WITH NOTES.) BY SIR WALTER SCOTT.

Marquis of Lossie. BY GEORGE MACDONALD.

Martin Chuzzlewit. BY CHARLES DICKENS.

Mary, Queen of Scots, Life of. BY P. C. HEADLEY.

Mary St. John. BY ROSA N. CAREY.

Master of Ballantrae, The. BY. R. L. STEVENSON.

Masterman Ready. BY CAPTAIN MARRYATT.

Meadow Brook. BY MARY J. HOLMES.

Meditations of Marcus Aurelius. TRANSLATED BY GEORGE LONG.

Memoirs of a Physician. BY ALEXANDRE DUMAS.

Merle's Crusade. BY ROSA N. CAREY.

Micah Clarke. BY A. CONAN DOLYE.

Michael Strogoff. BY JULES VERNE.

Middlemarch. BY GEORGE ELIOT.

Midshipman Easy. BY CAPTAIN MARRYATT

Mildred. BY MARY J. HOLMES.

Millbank. BY MARY J. HOLMES.

Mill on the Floss. BY GEORGE ELIOT.

Milton's Poems. BY JOHN MILTON.

Mine Own People. BY RUDYARD KIPLING.

Minister's Wooing, The. BY HARRIET BEECHER STOWE.

Monastery. BY SIR WALTER SCOTT.

Moonstone. BY WILKIE COLLINS.

Moore's Poems. BY THOMAS MOORE

Mosses from an Old Manse. BY NATHANIEL HAWTHORNE.

Murders in the Rue Morgue. BY EDGAR ALLEN POE.

Mysterious Island. BY JULES VERNE.

Napoleon Bonaparte, Life of. BY P. C. HEADLEY.

Napoleon and His Marshals. BY J. T. HEADLEY.

Natural Law in the Spiritual World. BY HENRY DRUMMOND.

Narrative of Arthur Gordon Pym. BY EDGAR ALLAN POE.

Nature, Addresses and Lectures. BY R. W. EMERSON.

Nellie's Memories. BY ROSA N. CAREY.

Nelson, Admiral Horatio, Life of. BY ROBERT SOUTHEY.

Newcomes. BY WILLIAM M. THACKERAY.

Nicholas Nickleby. BY CHAS. DICKENS.

Ninety-Three. BY VICTOR HUGO.

Not Like Other Girls. BY ROSA N. CAREY.

Odyssey. POPE'S TRANSLATION.

Old Curiosity Shop. BY CHARLES DICKENS.

Old Mam'selle's Secret. BY E. MARLITT.

Old Mortality. BY SIR WALTER SCOTT.

Old Myddleton's Money. BY MARY CECIL HAY.

Oliver Twist. BY CHAS. DICKENS.

Only the Governess. BY ROSA N. CAREY.

On the Heights. BY BERTHOLD AUERBACH.

Oregon Trail. BY FRANCIS PARKMAN.

Origin of Species. BY CHARLES DARWIN.

Other Worlds than Ours. BY RICHARD PROCTOR.

Our Bessie. BY ROSA N. CAREY.

Our Mutual Friend. BY CHARLES DICKENS.

Outre-Mer. BY H. W. LONGFELLOW.

Owl's Nest. BY E. MARLITT.

Page of the Duke of Savoy. BY ALEXANDRE DUMAS.

Pair of Blue Eyes. BY THOMAS HARDY.

Pan Michael. BY HENRYK SIENKIEWICZ.

Past and Present. BY THOS. CARLYLE.

Pathfinder. BY JAMES FENIMORE COOPER.

Paul and Virginia. BY B. DE ST. PIERRE.

Pendennis. History of. BY WM. M. THACKERAY.

Penn, William, Life of. BY W. HEPWORTH DIXON.

Pere Goriot. BY HONORE DE BALZAC.

Peter, the Great, Life of. BY JOHN BARROW.

Peveril of the Peak. BY SIR WALTER SCOTT.

Phantom Rickshaw, The. BY RUDYARD KIPLING.

Philip II. of Spain, Life of. BY MARTIN A. S. HUME.

Picciola. BY X. B. SAINTINE.

Pickwick Papers. By CHARLES DICKENS.
Pilgrim's Progress. By JOHN BUNYAN.
Pillar of Fire. By REV. J. H. INGRAHAM.
Pilot. By JAMES FENIMORE COOPER.
Pioneers. By JAMES FENIMORE COOPER.
Pirate. By SIR WALTER SCOTT.
Plain Tales from the Hills. By RUDYARD KIPLING.
Plato's Dialogues. TRANSLATED BY J. WRIGHT, M. A.
Pleasures of Life. By SIR JOHN LUBBOCK.
Poe's Poems. By EDGAR A. POE.
Pope's Poems. By ALEXANDER POPE.
Prairie. By JAMES F. COOPER.
Pride and Prejudice. By JANE AUSTEN.
Prince of the House of David. By REV. J. H INGRAHAM.
Princess of the Moor. By E. MARLITT.
Princess of Thule. By WILLIAM BLACK.
Procter's Poems. By ADELAIDE PROCTOR.
Professor at the Breakfast Table. By OLIVER WENDELL HOLMES.
Professor. By CHARLOTTE BRONTE.
Prue and I. By GEORGE WILLIAM CURTIS.
Put Yourself in His Place. By CHAS. READE.
Putnam, General Israel, Life of By GEORGE CANNING HILL.
Queen Hortense. By LOUISA MUHLBACH.
Queenie's Whim. By ROSA N. CAREY.
Queen's Necklace. By ALEXANDRE DUMAS.
Quentin Durward. By SIR WALTER SCOTT.
Rasselas, History of. By SAMUEL JOHNSON.
Redgauntlet. By SIR WALTER SCOTT.
Red Rover. By JAMES FENIMORE COOPER.
Regent's Daughter. By ALEXANDRE DUMAS.
Reign of Law. By DUKE OF ARGYLE.
Representative Men. By RALPH WALDO EMERSON.
Republic of Plato. TRANSLATED BY DAVIES AND VAUGHAN.
Return of the Native. By THOMAS HARDY.
Reveries of a Bachelor. By IK MARVEL.
Reynard the Fox. EDITED BY JOSEPH JACOBS.
Rienzi. By BULWER-LYTTON.
Richelieu, Cardinal, Life of. By RICHARD LODGE.
Robinson Crusoe. By DANIEL DEFOE.
Rob Roy. By SIR WALTER SCOTT.
Romance of Natural History. By P. H. GOSSE.
Romance of Two Worlds. By MARIE CORELLI.

Romola. By GEORGE ELIOT.
Rory O'More. By SAMUEL LOVER.
Rose Mather. By MARY J. HOLMES.
Rossetti's Poems. By GABRIEL DANTE ROSSETTI.
Royal Edinburgh. By MRS. OLIPHANT.
Rutledge. By MIRIAN COLES HARRIS.
Saint Michael. By E. WERNER.
Samantha at Saratoga. By JOSIAH ALLER'S WIFE. (MARIETTA HOLLEY.)
Sartor Resartus. By THOMAS CARLYLE.
Scarlet Letter. By NATHANIEL HAWHORNE.
Schonberg-Cotta Family. By MRS. ANDREW CHARLES.
Schopenhauer's Essays. TRANSLATED BY T. B. SAUNDERS.
Scottish Chiefs. By JANE PORTER.
Scott's Poems. By SIR WALTER SCOTT.
Search for Basil Lyndhurst. By ROSA N. CAREY.
Second Wife. By E. MARLITT.
Seekers After God. By F. W. FARRAR.
Self-Help. By SAMUEL SMILES.
Self-Raised. (COMPLETE.) By MRS. E. D. E. N. SOUTHWORTH.
Seneca's Morals.
Sense and Sensibility. By JANE AUSTEN.
Sentimental Journey. By LAWRENCE STERNE.
Sesame and Lilies. By JOHN RUSKIN.
Shakespeare's Heroines. By ANNA JAMESON.
Shelley's Poems. By PERCY BYSSHE SHELLEY.
Shirley. By CHARLOTTE BRONTE.
Sign of the Four. By A. CONAN DOYLE.
Silas Marner. By GEORGE ELIOT.
Silence of Dean Maitland. By MAXWELL GRAY.
Sir Gibbie. By GEORGE MACDONALD
Sketch Book. By WASHINGTON IRVING.
Smith, Captain John, Life of. By W. GILMORE SIMMS.
Socrates, Trial and Death of. TRANSLATED BY F. J. CHURCH, M. A.
Soldiers Three. By RUDYARD KIPLING.
Springhaven. By R. D. BLACKMORE.
Spy. By JAMES FENIMORE COOPER.
Stanley, Henry M., African Explorer, Life of. By A. MONTEFIORE.
Story of an African Farm. By OLIVE SCHREINER.
Story of John G. Paton. TOLD FOR YOUNG FOLKS. By REV. JAS. PATON.
St. Ronan's Well. By SIR WALTER SCOTT.
Study in Scarlet. By A. CONAN DOYLE.

www.ingramcontent.com/pod-product-compliance
Lightning Source LLC
Chambersburg PA
CBHW022024110726
47901CB00006B/1653